CHERUB™

Robert Muchamore
THE RECRUIT
THE GRAPHIC NOVEL

Illustrated by JOHN AGGS
Adapted by IAN EDGINTON

Hodder
Children's
Books

A division of Hachette Children's Books

First published in Great Britain in 2012
by Hodder Children's Books

2

A Catalogue record for this book is available
from the British Library

ISBN: 978 1 444 90318 8

Printed and bound in China.

The paper and board used in this paperback by Hodder Children's Books are natural recyclable products made from wood grown in sustainable forests. The manufacturing processes conform to the environmental regulations of the country of origin.

Hodder Children's Books
a division of Hachette Children's Books
338 Euston Road, London NW1 3BH
An Hachette UK company
www.hachette.co.uk

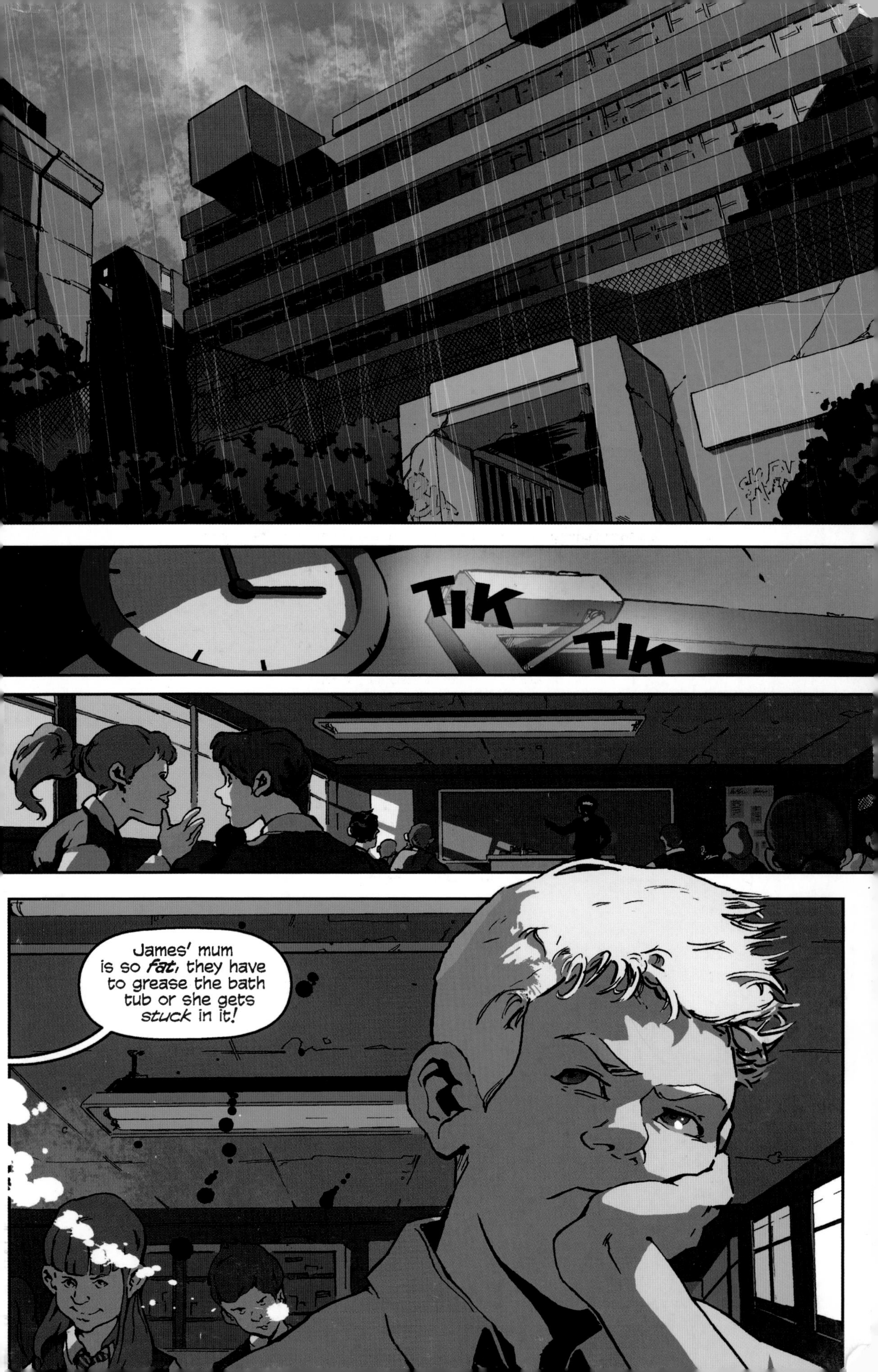
TIK
TIK
James' mum is so *fat*, they have to grease the bath tub or she gets *stuck* in it!

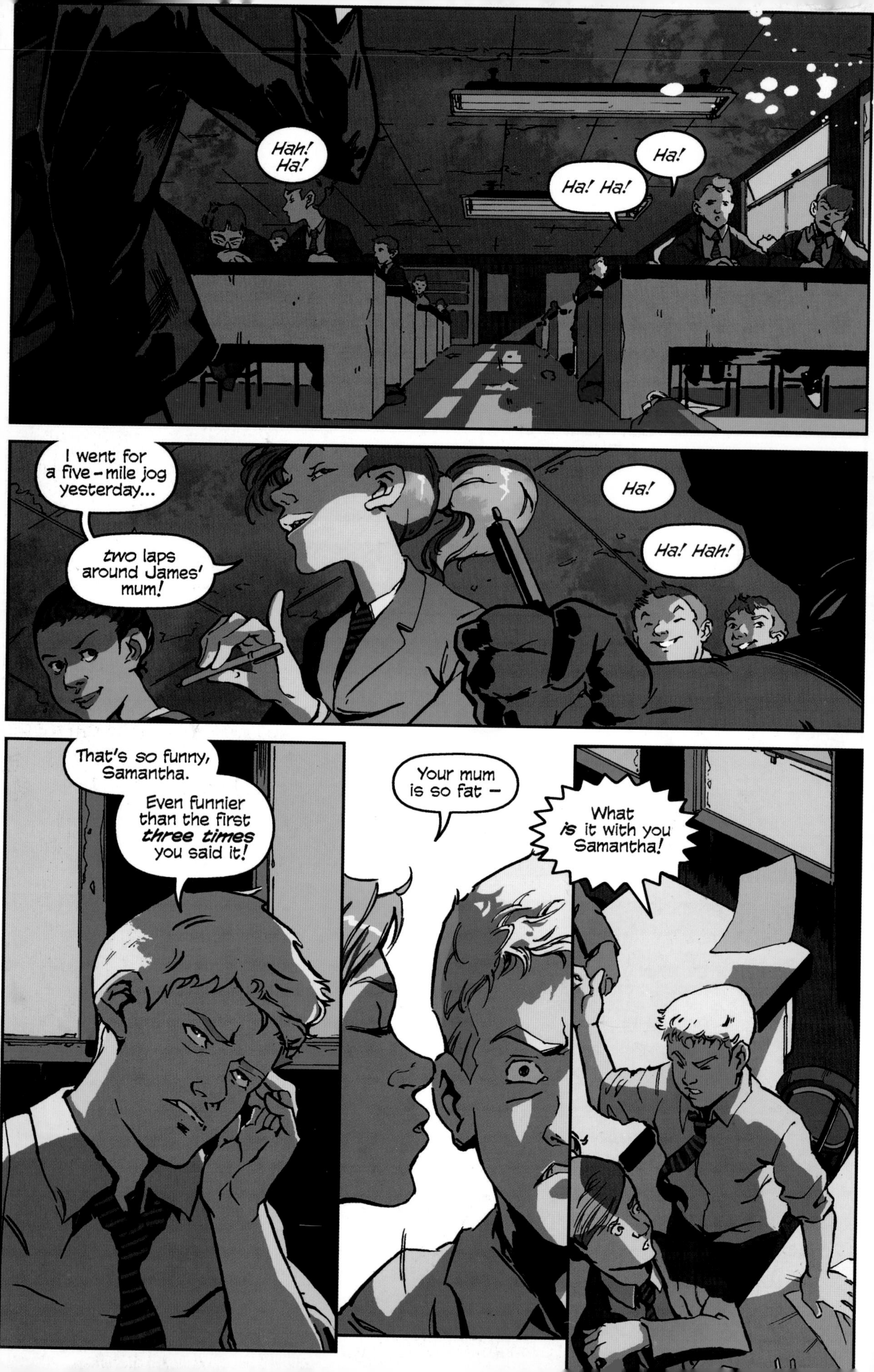
Hah! Ha!
Ha!
Ha! Ha!
I went for a five-mile jog yesterday...
two laps around James' mum!
Ha!
Ha! Hah!
That's so funny, Samantha.
Even funnier than the first three times you said it!
Your mum is so fat –
What is it with you Samantha!

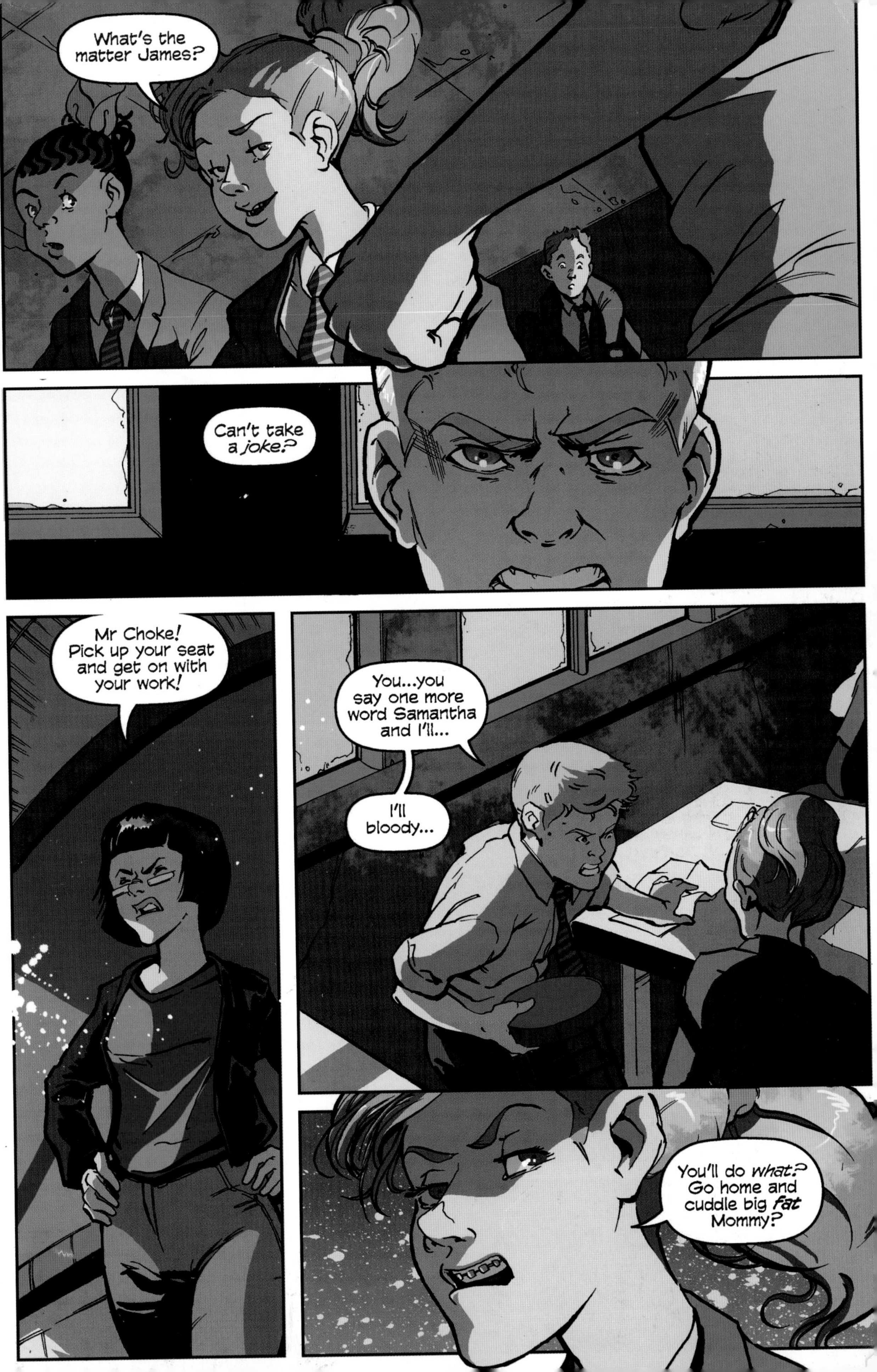
What's the matter James?
Can't take a *joke?*
Mr Choke! Pick up your seat and get on with your work!
You...you say one more word Samantha and I'll...
I'll bloody...
You'll do *what?* Go home and cuddle big *fat* Mommy?

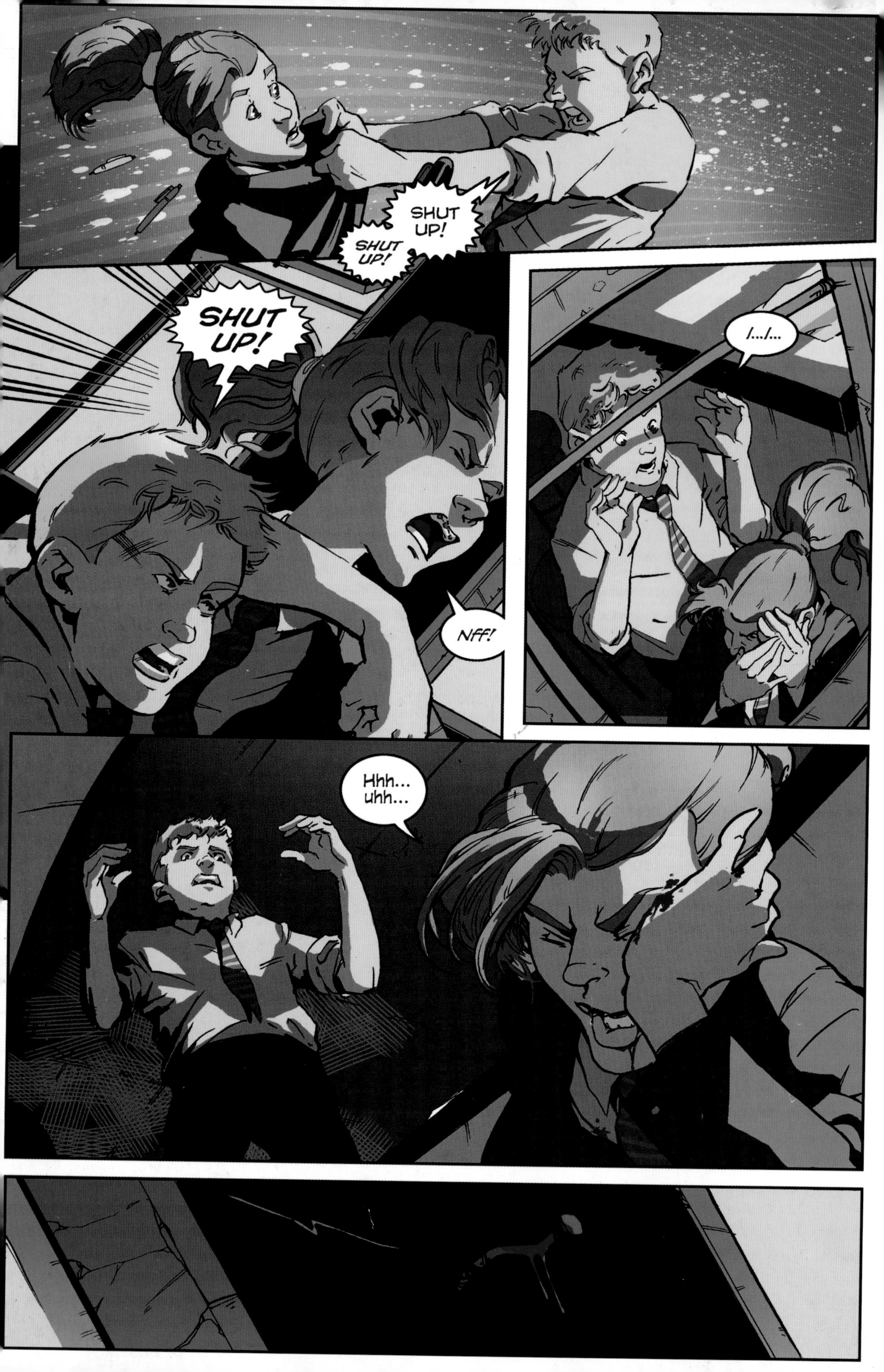
SHUT UP!
SHUT UP!
SHUT UP!
Nff!
/.../...
Hhh... uhh...

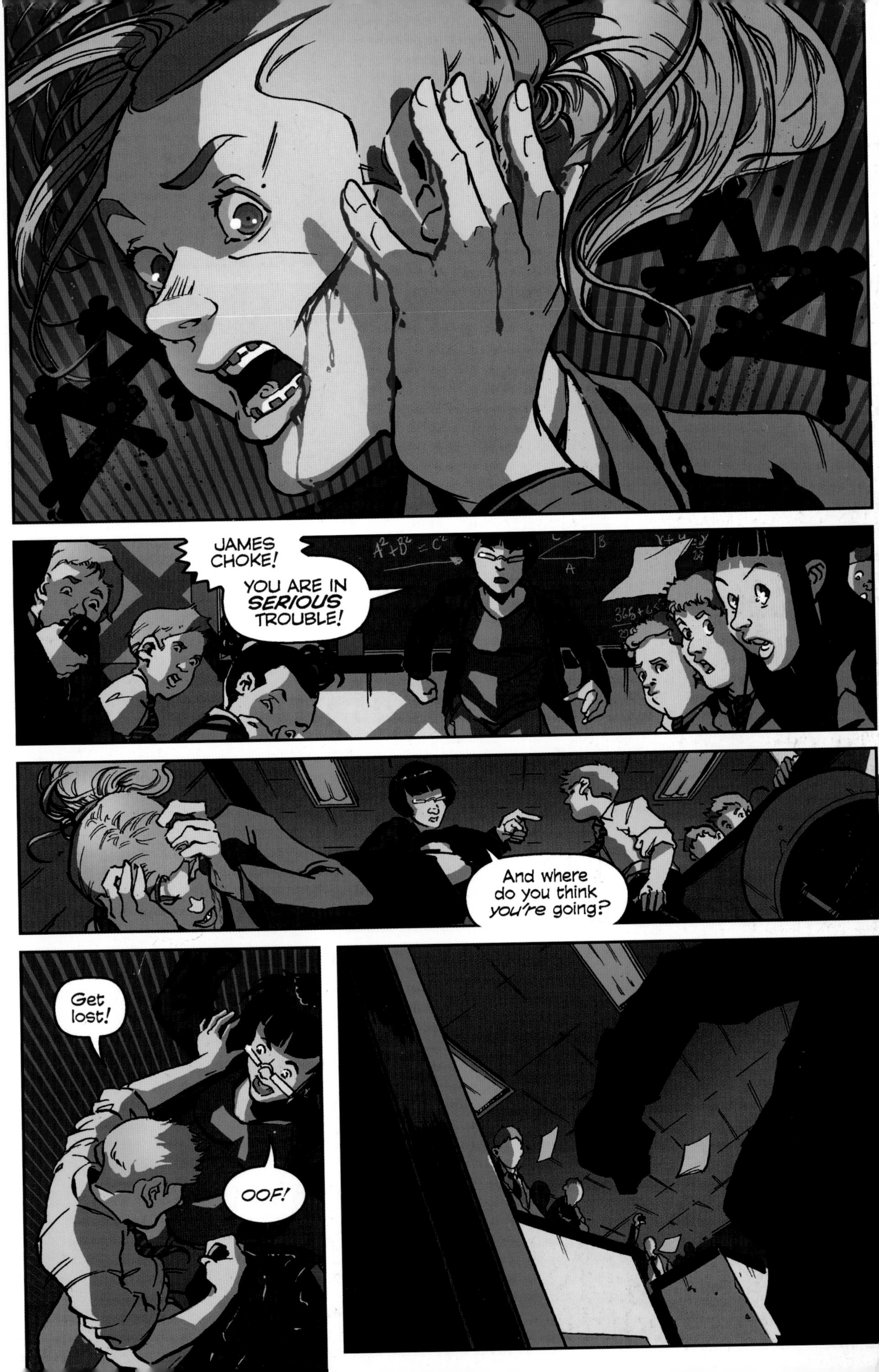

JAMES CHOKE!
YOU ARE IN *SERIOUS* TROUBLE!
And where do you think *you're* going?
Get lost!
OOF!

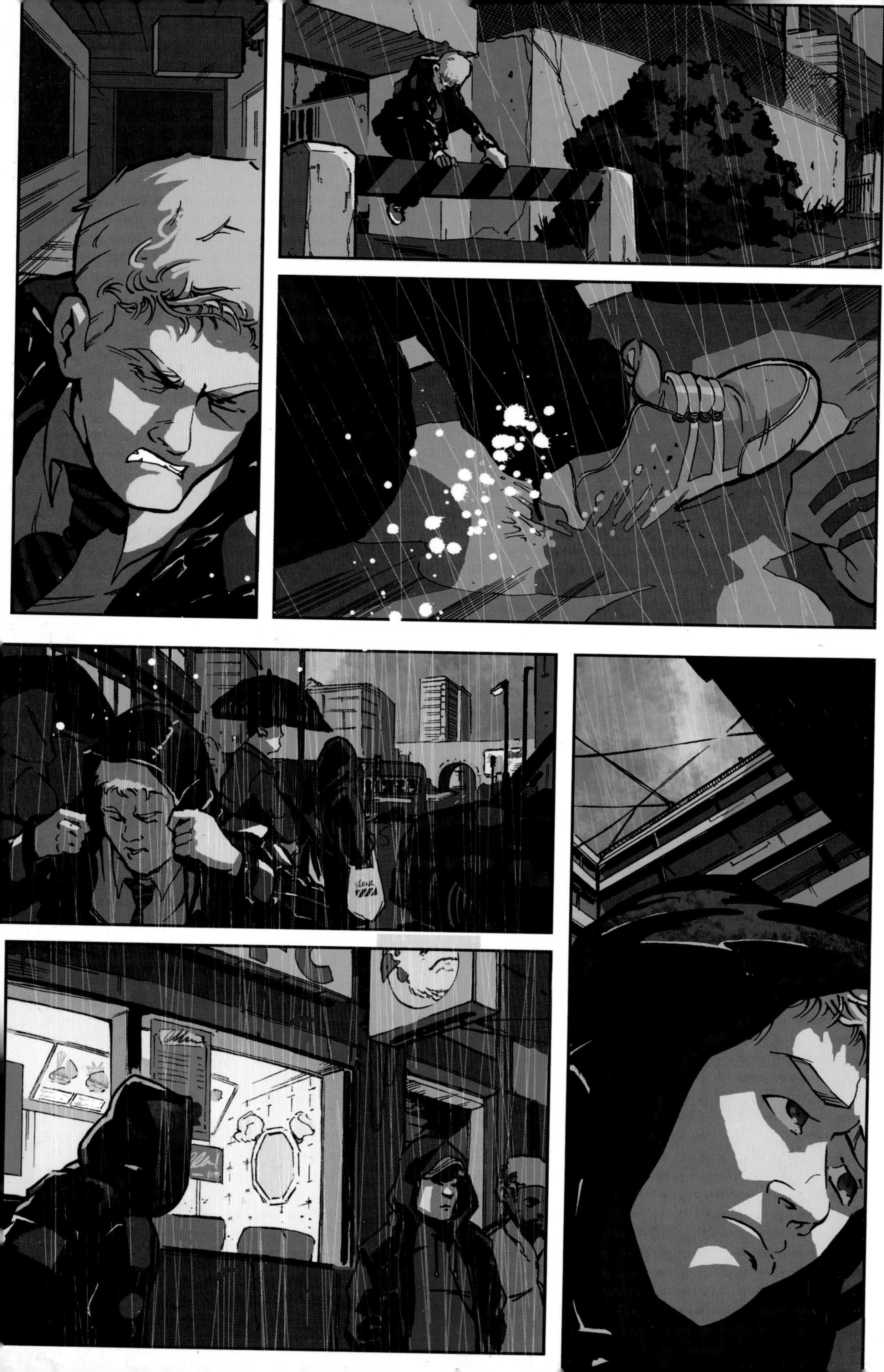

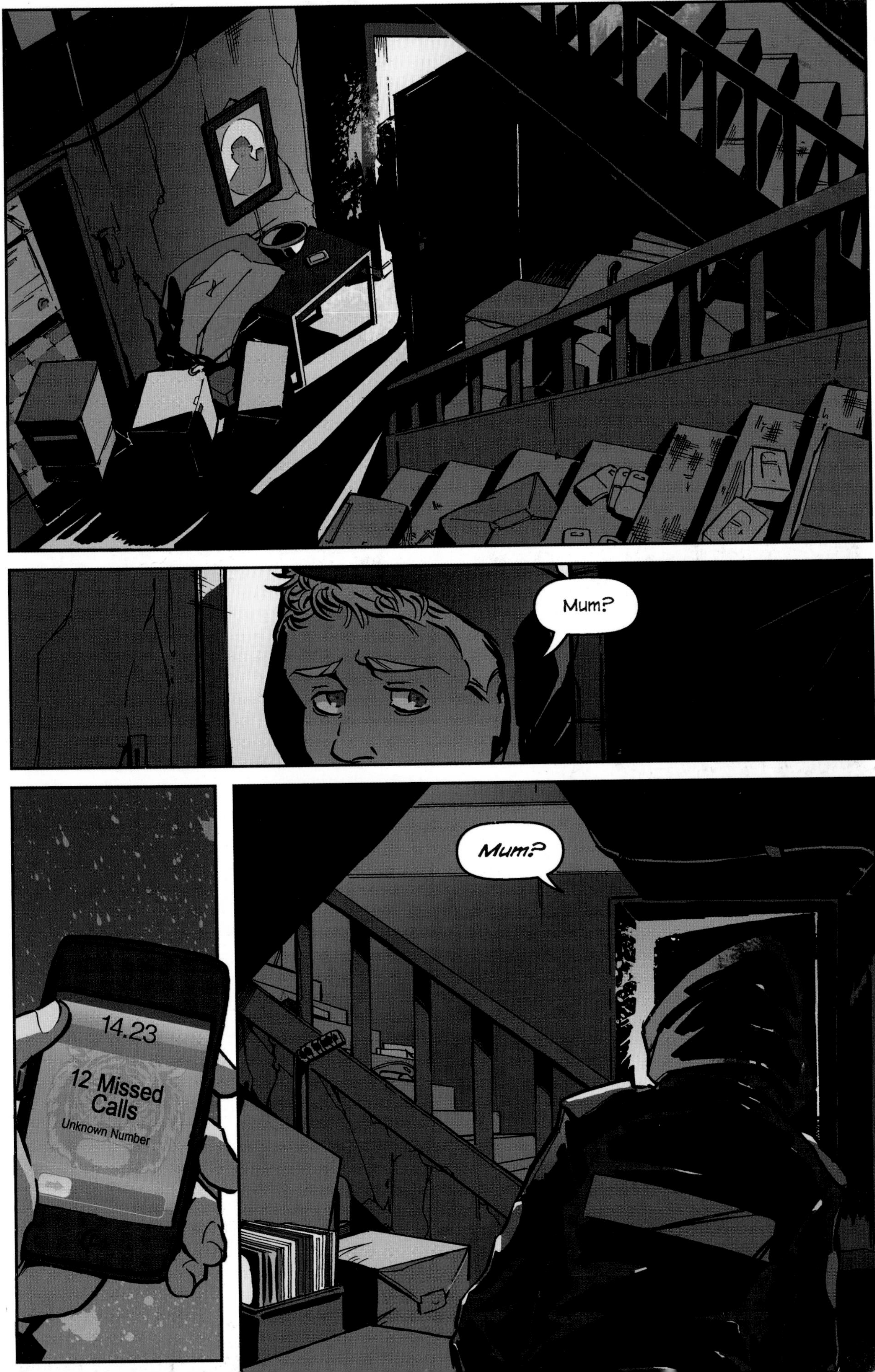

Mum?
14.23
12 Missed Calls
Unknown Number
Mum?

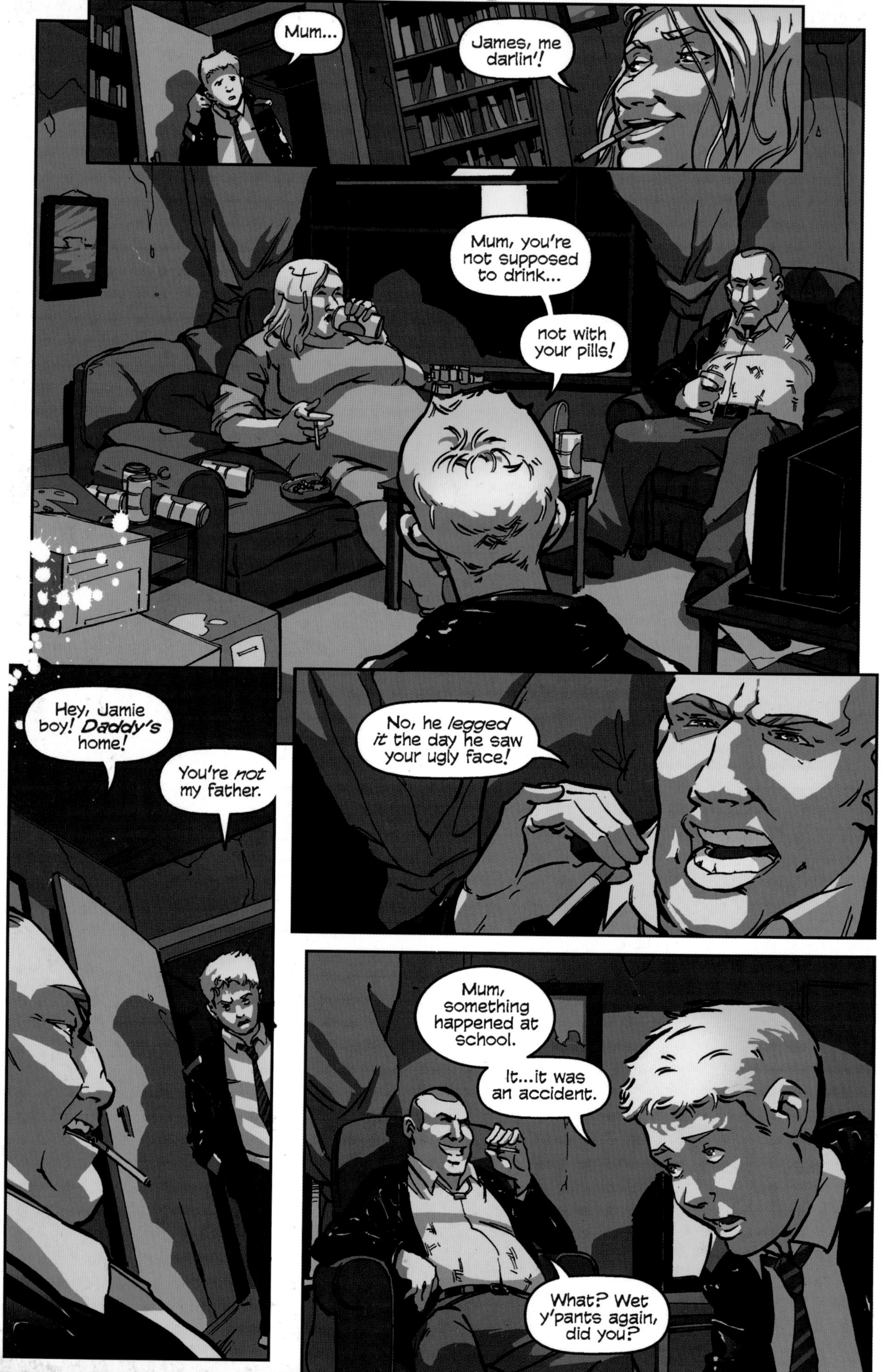
Mum...
James, me darlin'!
Mum, you're not supposed to drink...
not with your pills!
Hey, Jamie boy! *Daddy's* home!
You're *not* my father.
No, he *legged it* the day he saw your ugly face!
Mum, something happened at school.
It...it was an accident.
What? Wet y'pants again, did you?

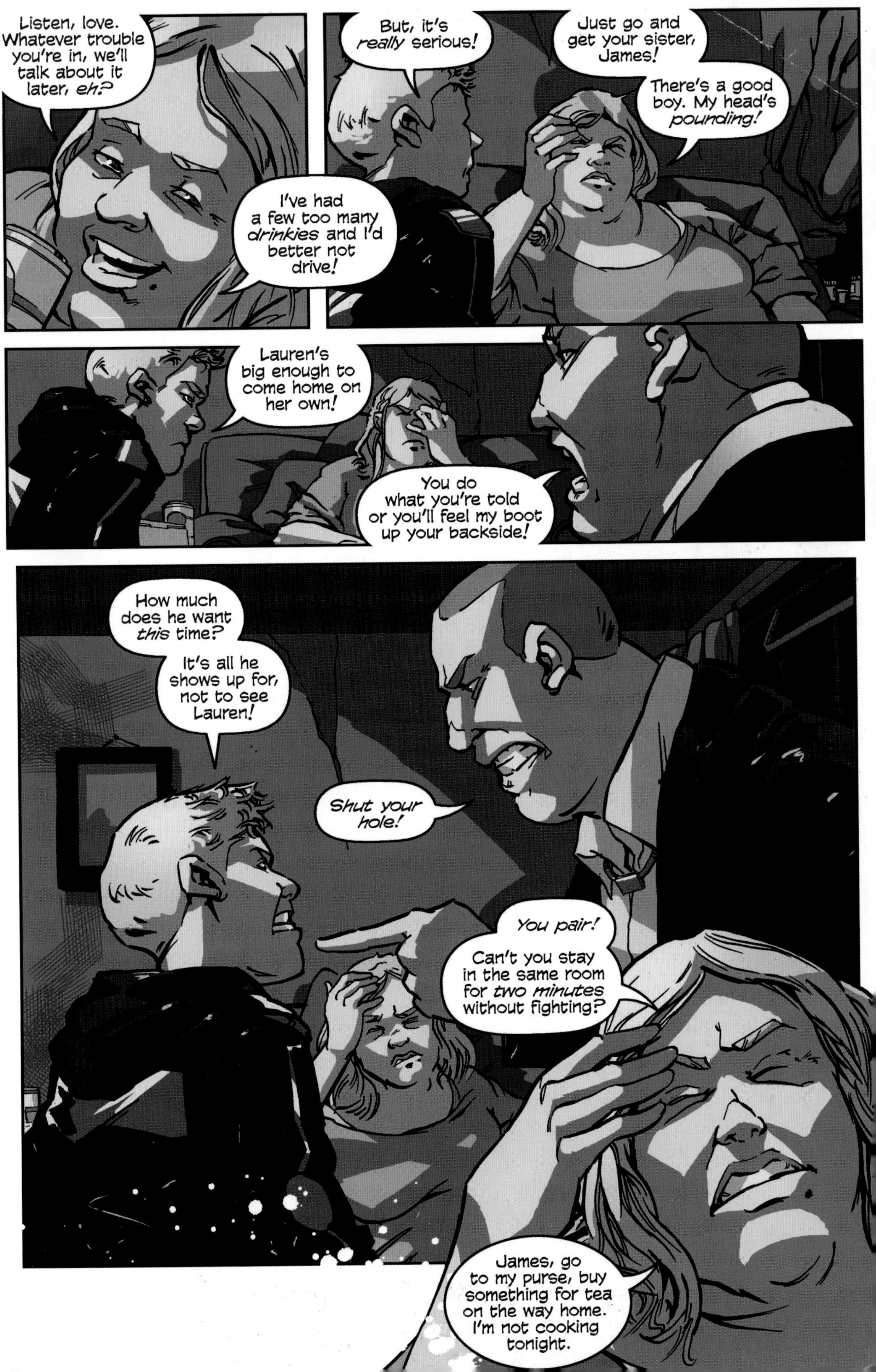
Listen, love. Whatever trouble you're in, we'll talk about it later, *eh?*
I've had a few too many *drinkies* and I'd better not drive!
But, it's *really* serious!
Just go and get your sister, James!
There's a good boy. My head's *pounding!*
Lauren's big enough to come home on her own!
You do what you're told or you'll feel my boot up your backside!
How much does he want *this* time?
It's all he shows up for, not to see Lauren!
Shut your hole!
You pair!
Can't you stay in the same room for *two minutes* without fighting?
James, go to my purse, buy something for tea on the way home. I'm not cooking tonight.

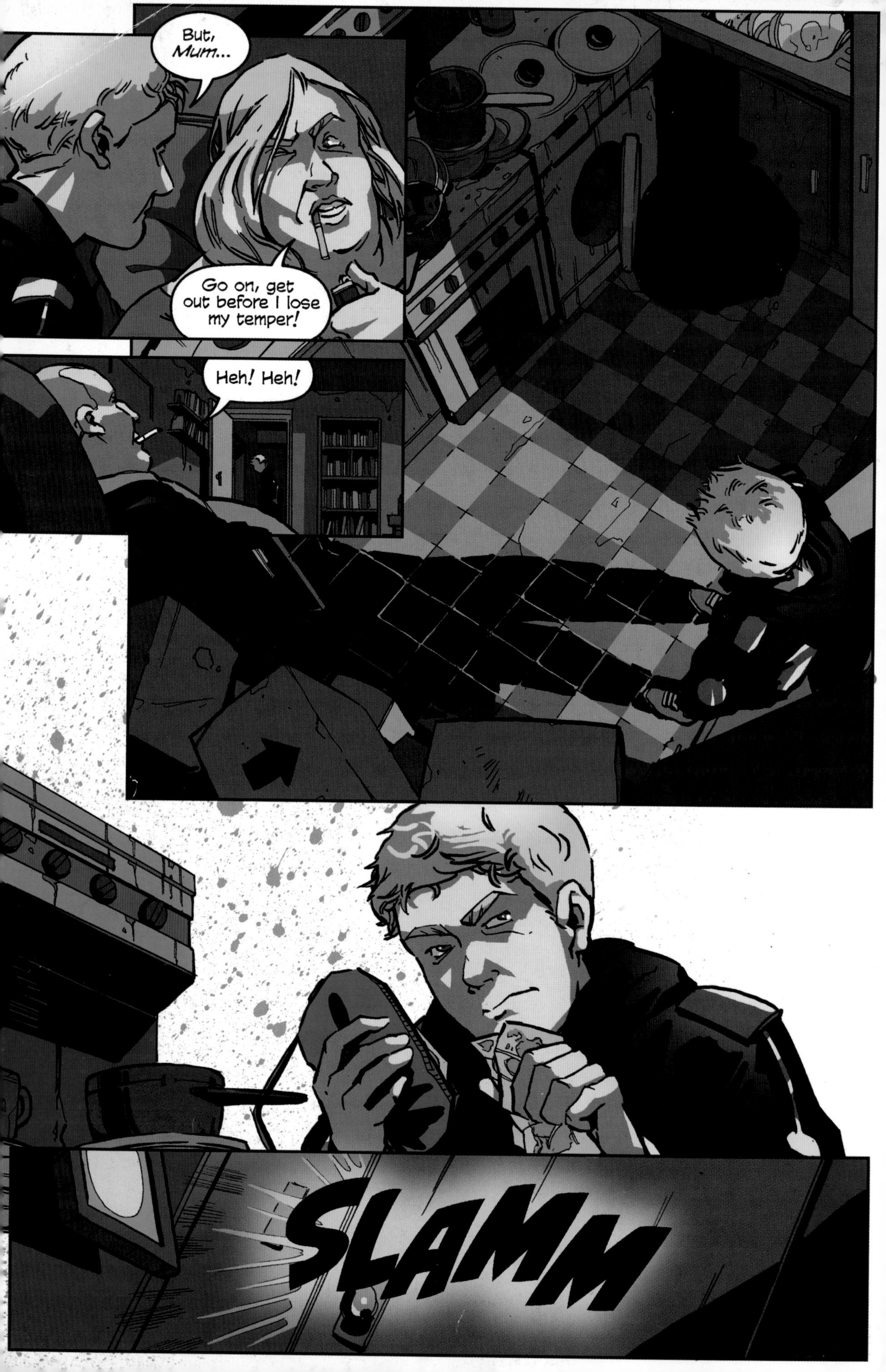
But, Mum...
Go on, get out before I lose my temper!
Heh! Heh!
SLAMM

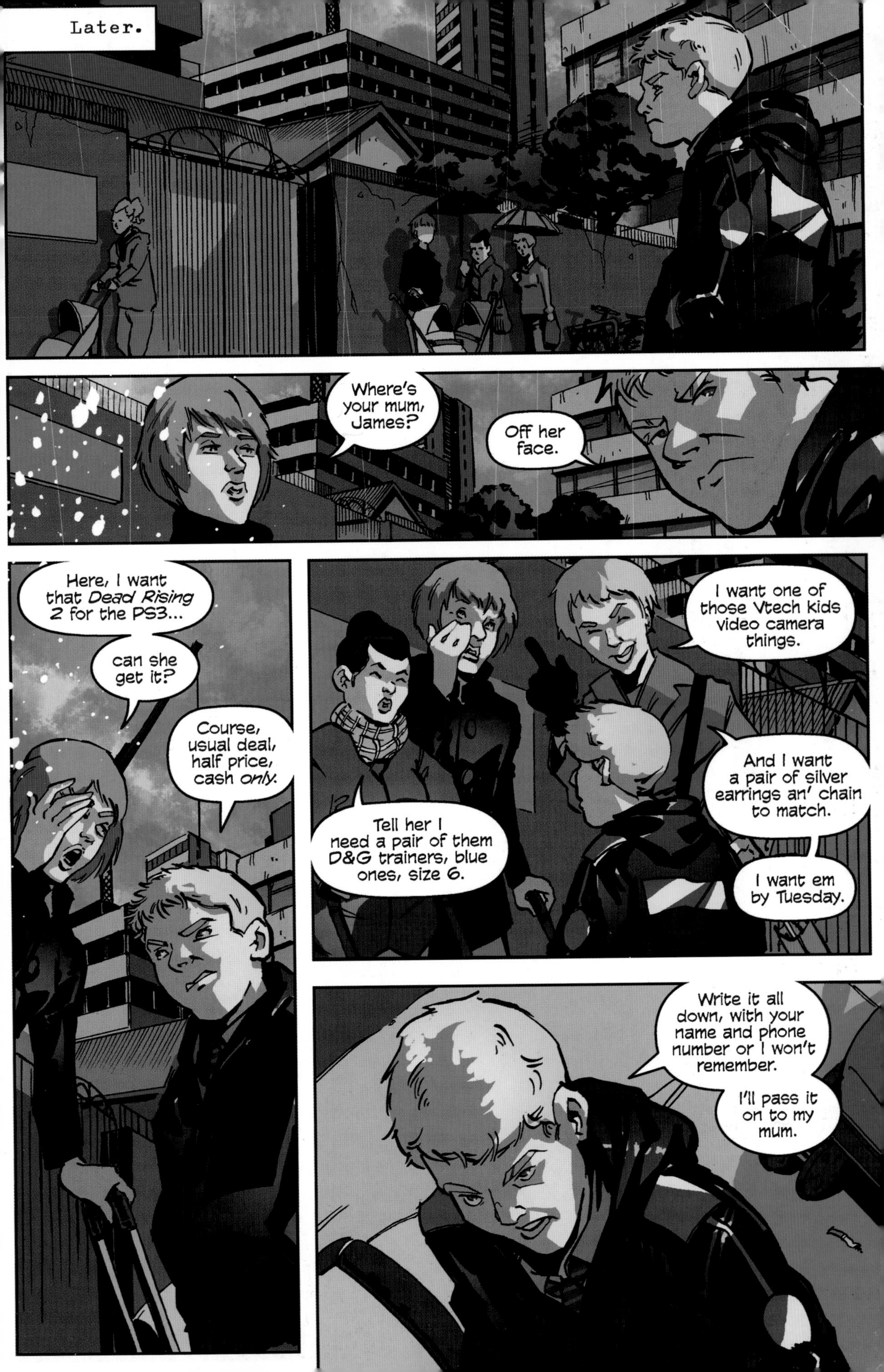
Later.
Where's your mum, James?
Off her face.
Here, I want that *Dead Rising 2* for the PS3...
can she get it?
Course, usual deal, half price, cash *only*.
I want one of those Vtech kids video camera things.
And I want a pair of silver earrings an' chain to match.
Tell her I need a pair of them D&G trainers, blue ones, size 6.
I want em by Tuesday.
Write it all down, with your name and phone number or I won't remember.
I'll pass it on to my mum.

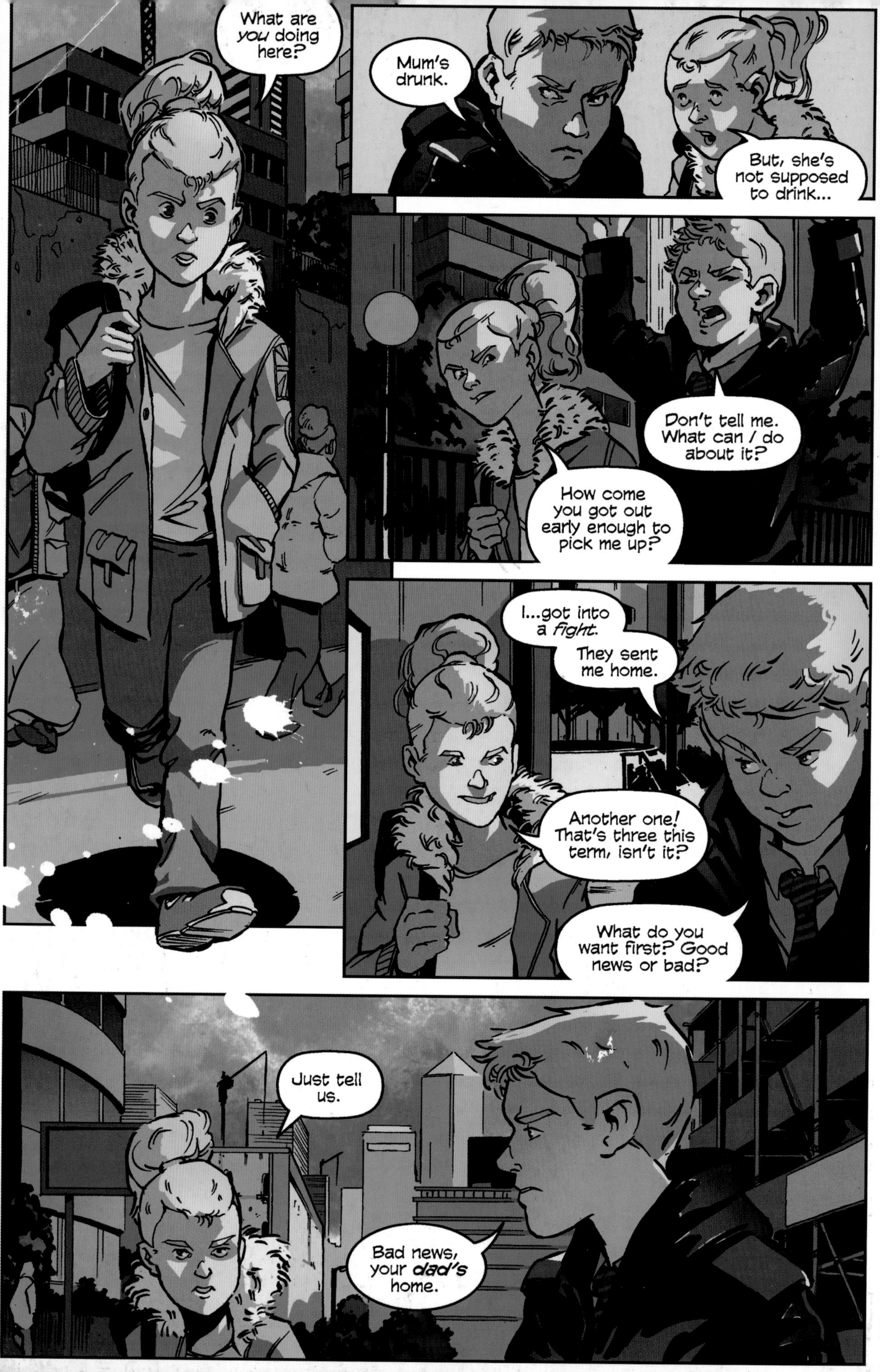
What are *you* doing here?
Mum's drunk.
But, she's not supposed to drink...
Don't tell me. What can *I* do about it?
How come you got out early enough to pick me up?
I...got into a *fight*.
They sent me home.
Another one! That's three this term, isn't it?
What do you want first? Good news or bad?
Just tell us.
Bad news, your ***dad's*** home.

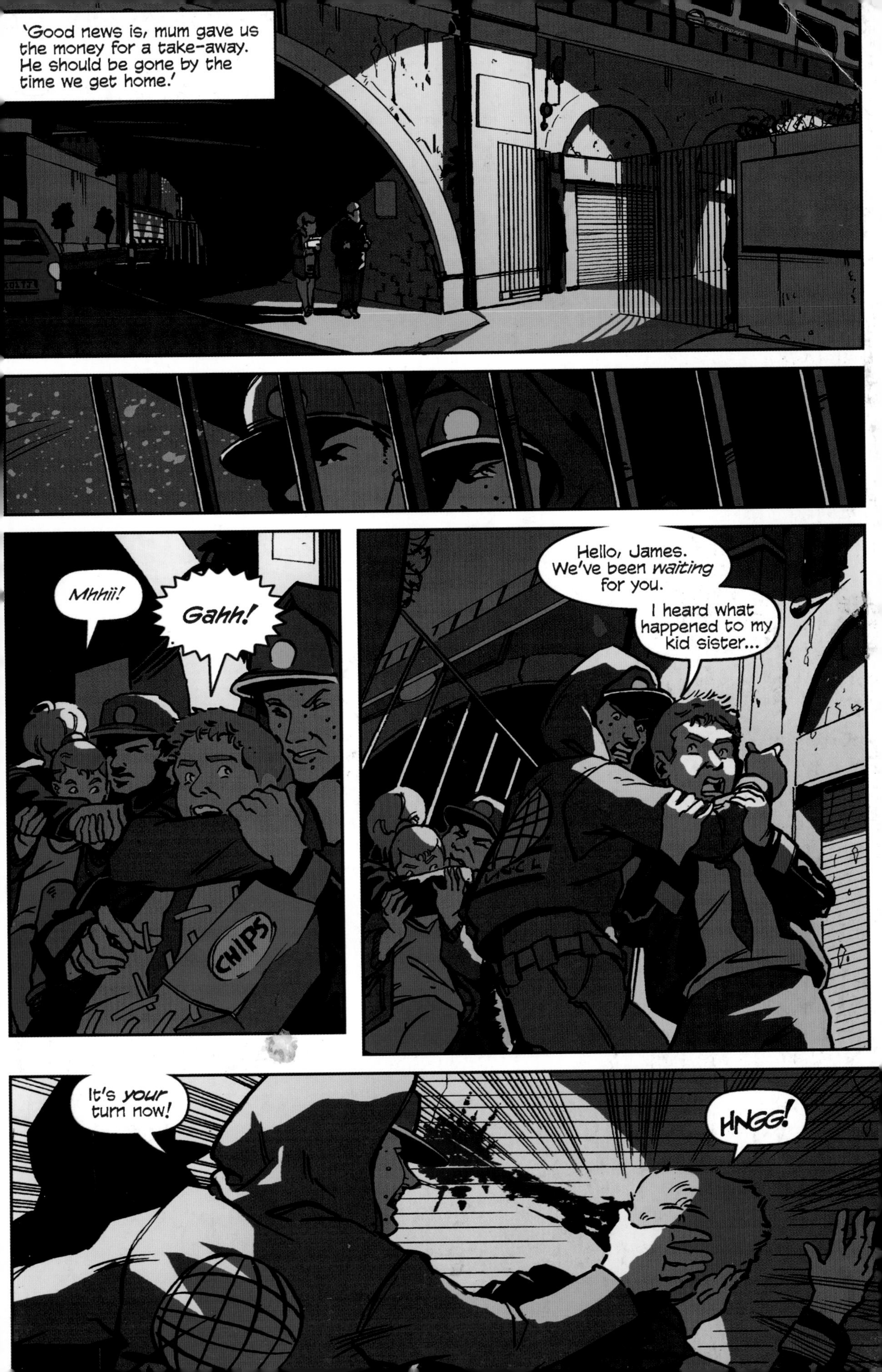
'Good news is, mum gave us the money for a take-away. He should be gone by the time we get home.'
Mhhii!
Gahh!
Hello, James. We've been *waiting* for you.
I heard what happened to my kid sister...
CHIPS
It's *your* turn now!
HNGG!

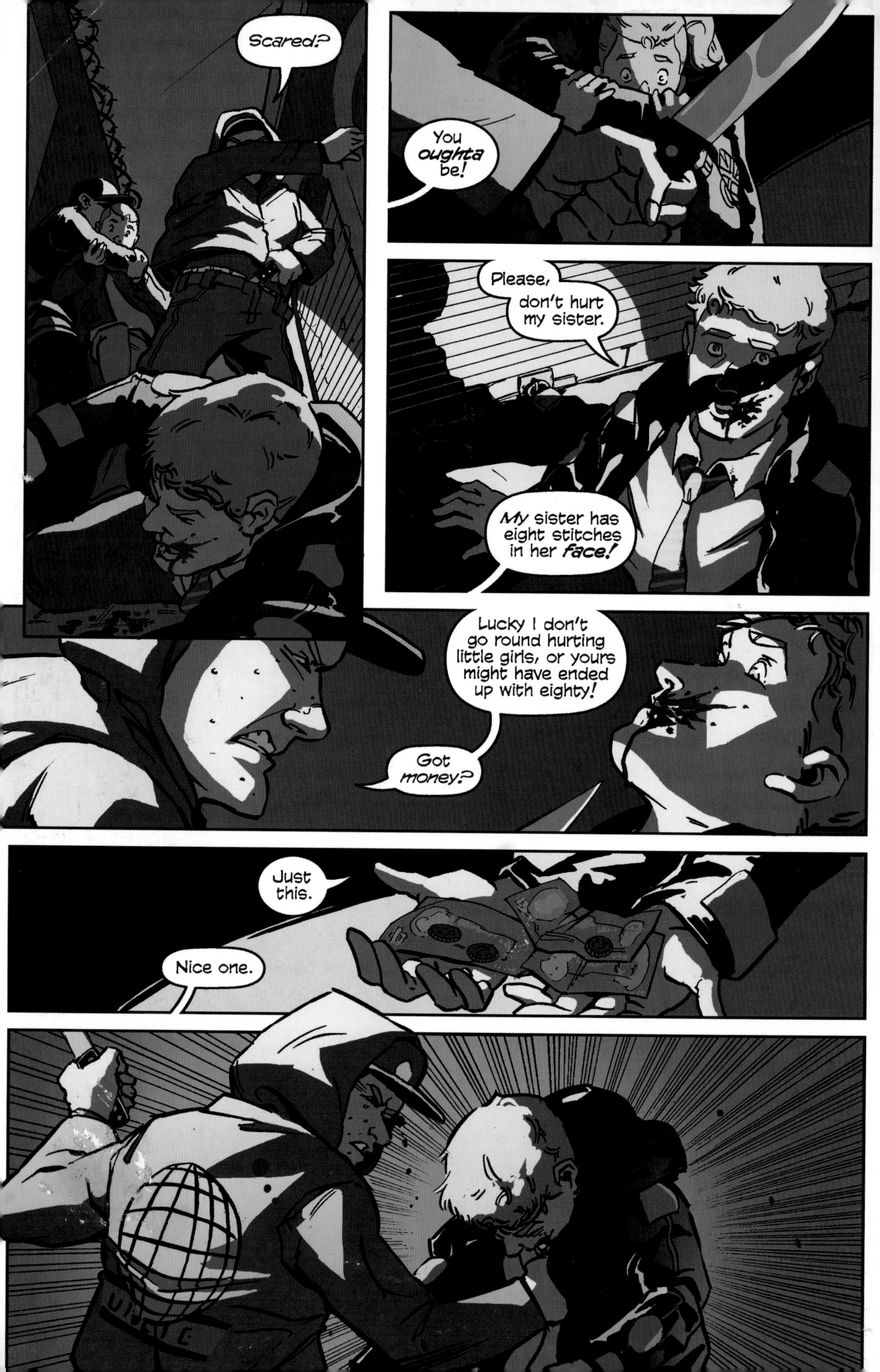
Scared?
You *oughta* be!
Please, don't hurt my sister.
My sister has eight stitches in her *face!*
Lucky I don't go round hurting little girls, or yours might have ended up with eighty!
Got *money?*
Just this.
Nice one.

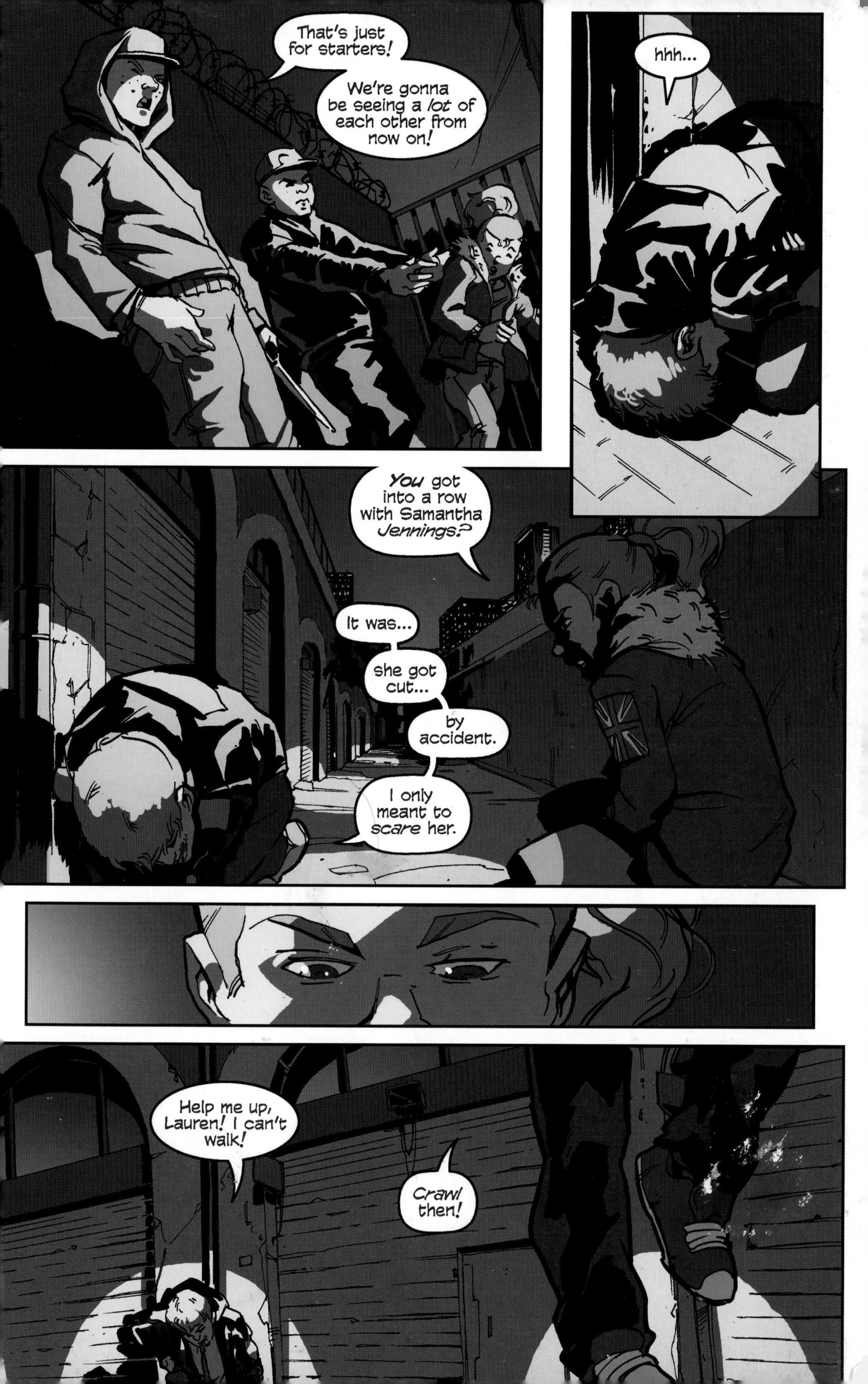
That's just for starters!
We're gonna be seeing a *lot* of each other from now on!
hhh...
You got into a row with Samantha *Jennings?*
It was...
she got cut...
by accident.
I only meant to *scare* her.
Help me up, Lauren! I can't walk!
Crawl then!

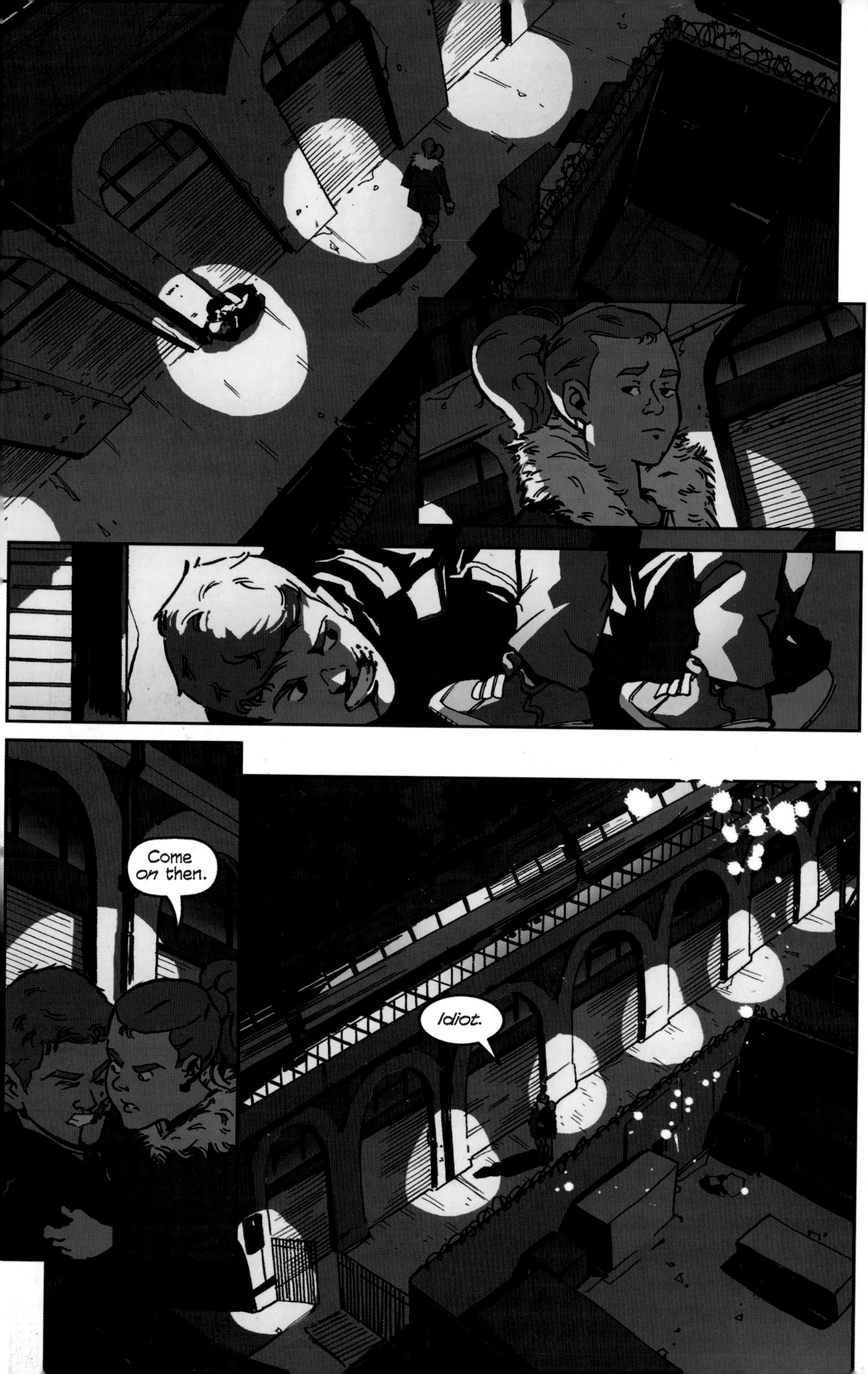
Come on then.
Idiot.

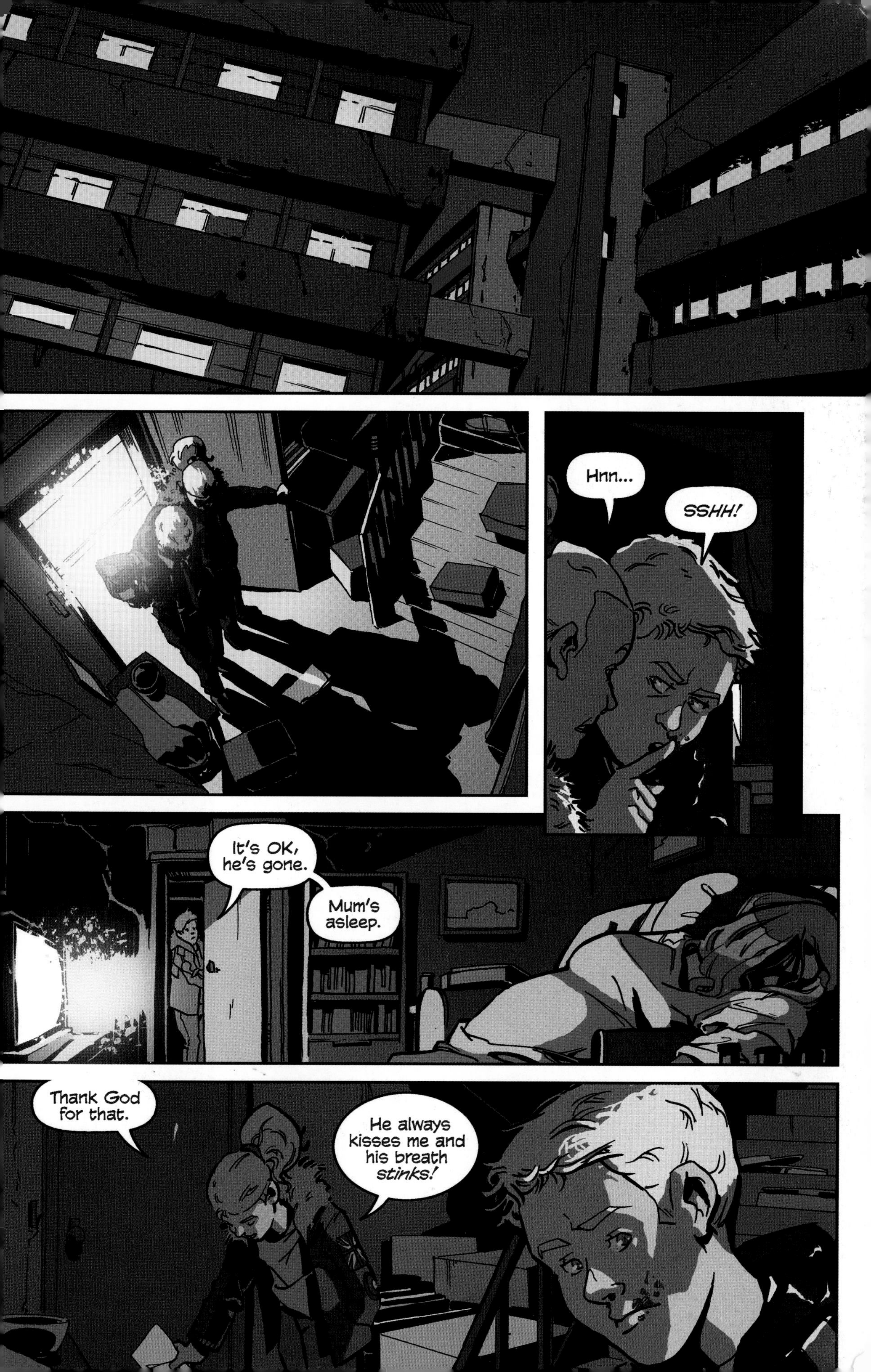
Hnn...
SSHH!
It's OK, he's gone.
Mum's asleep.
Thank God for that.
He always kisses me and his breath *stinks!*

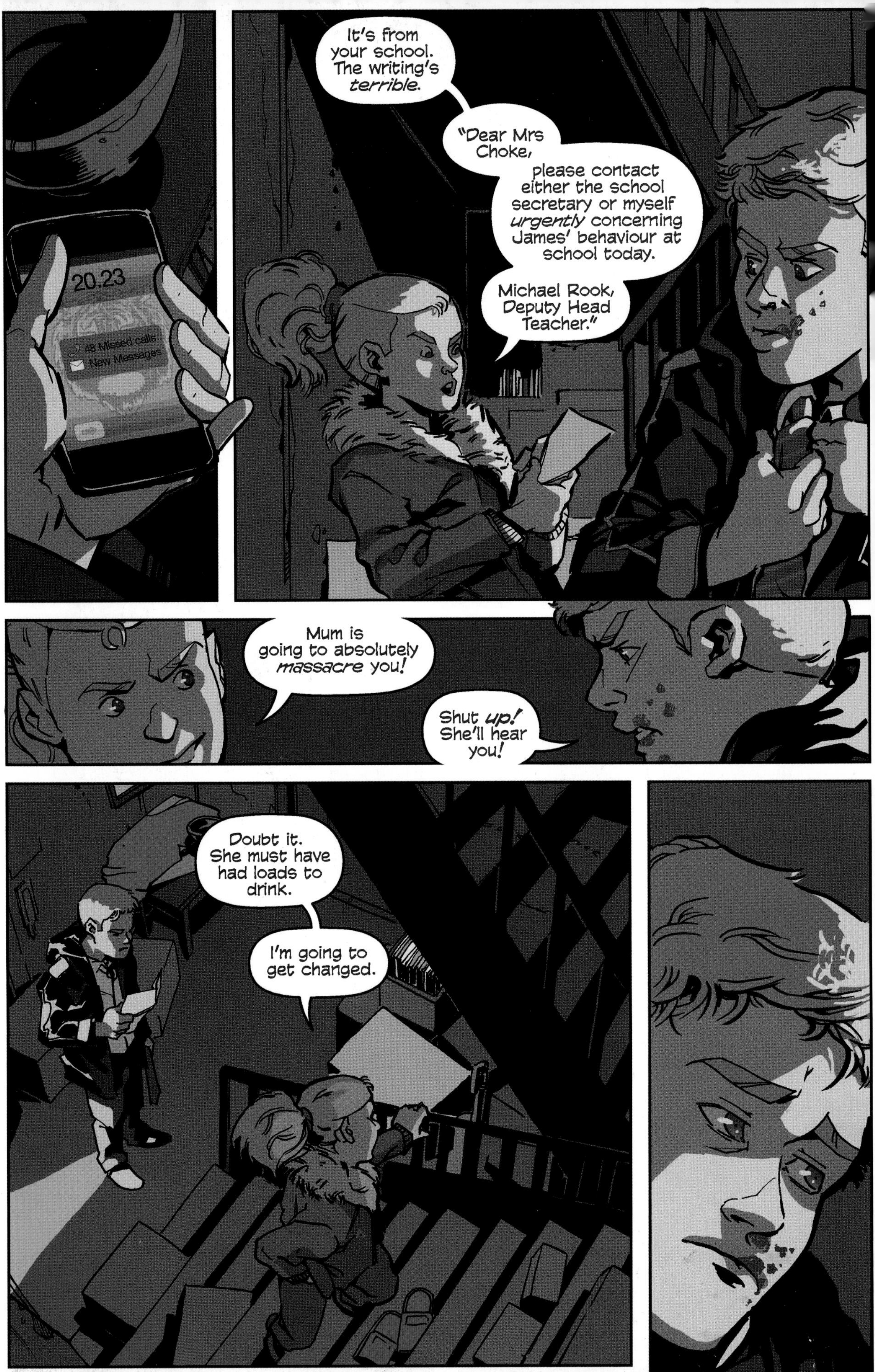
20.23
48 Missed calls
New Messages
It's from your school. The writing's *terrible*.
"Dear Mrs Choke,
please contact either the school secretary or myself *urgently* concerning James' behaviour at school today.
Michael Rook, Deputy Head Teacher."
Mum is going to absolutely *massacre* you!
Shut *up!* She'll hear you!
Doubt it. She must have had loads to drink.
I'm going to get changed.

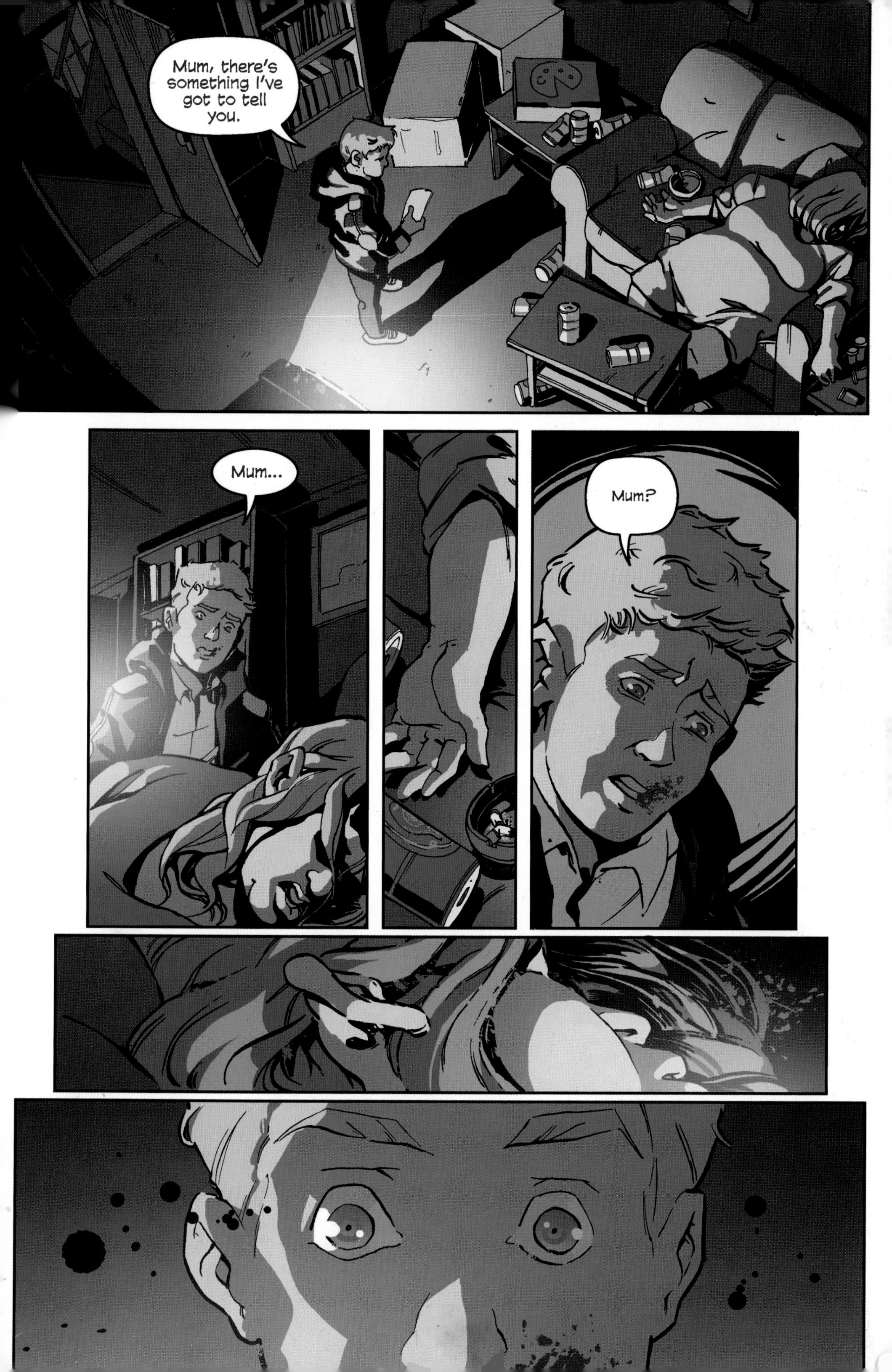
Mum, there's something I've got to tell you.
Mum...
Mum?

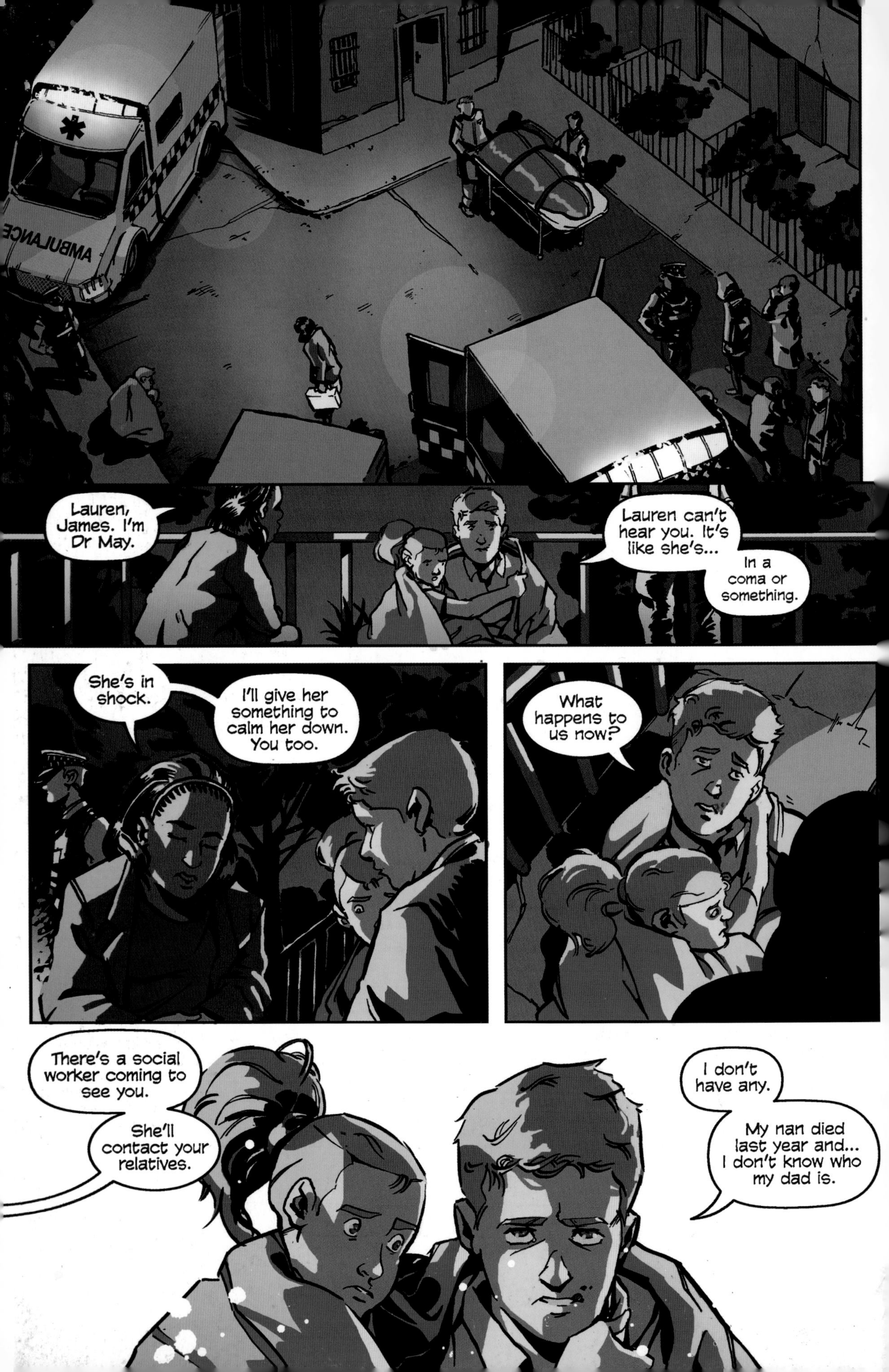
AMBULANCE
AMBULANCE
Lauren, James. I'm Dr May.
Lauren can't hear you. It's like she's...
In a coma or something.
She's in shock.
I'll give her something to calm her down. You too.
What happens to us now?
There's a social worker coming to see you.
She'll contact your relatives.
I don't have any.
My nan died last year and... I don't know who my dad is.

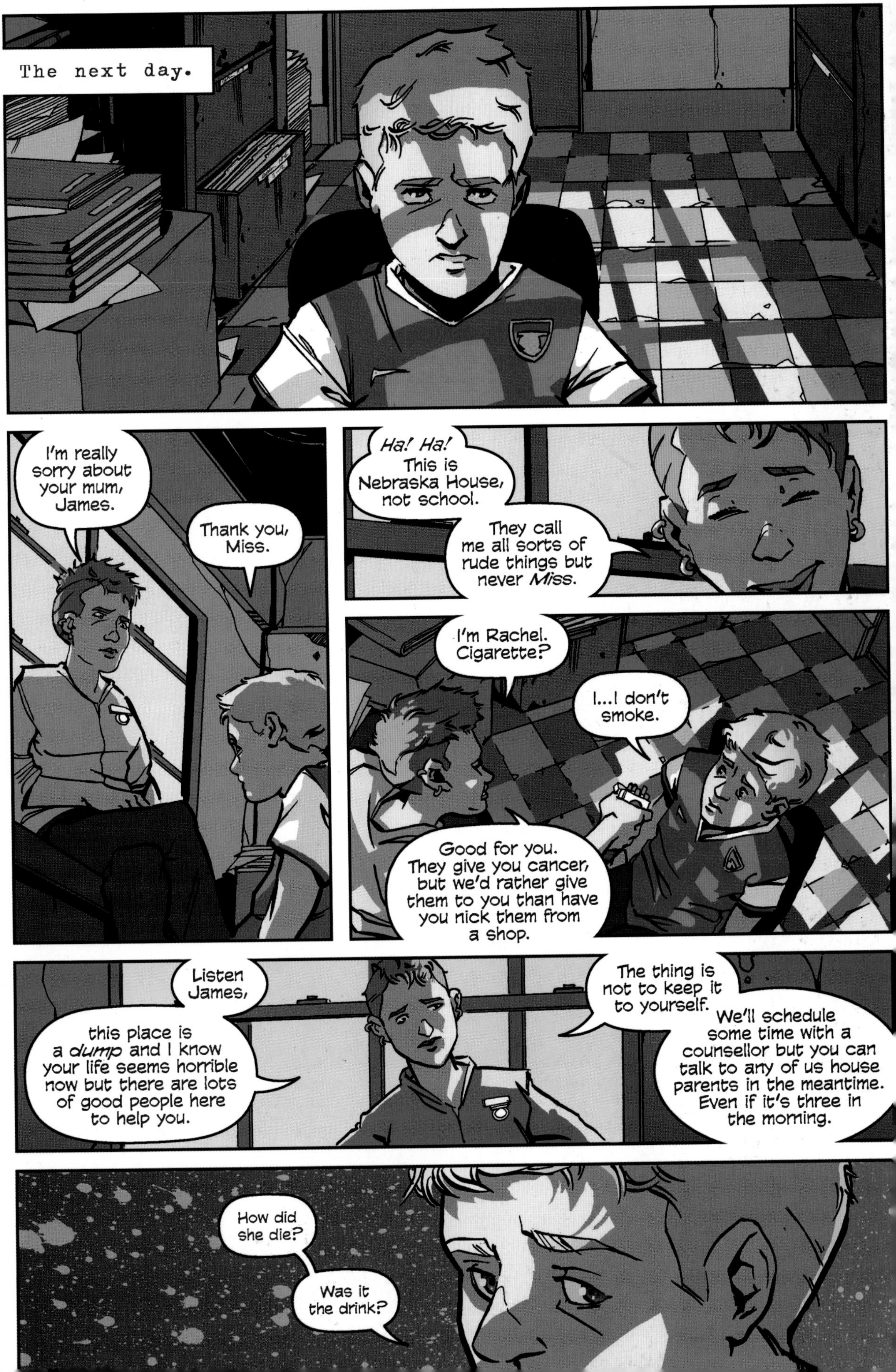
The next day.
I'm really sorry about your mum, James.
Thank you, Miss.
Ha! Ha! This is Nebraska House, not school.
They call me all sorts of rude things but never *Miss*.
I'm Rachel. Cigarette?
I...I don't smoke.
Good for you. They give you cancer, but we'd rather give them to you than have you nick them from a shop.
Listen James,
this place is a *dump* and I know your life seems horrible now but there are lots of good people here to help you.
The thing is not to keep it to yourself.
We'll schedule some time with a counsellor but you can talk to any of us house parents in the meantime. Even if it's three in the morning.
How did she die?
Was it the drink?

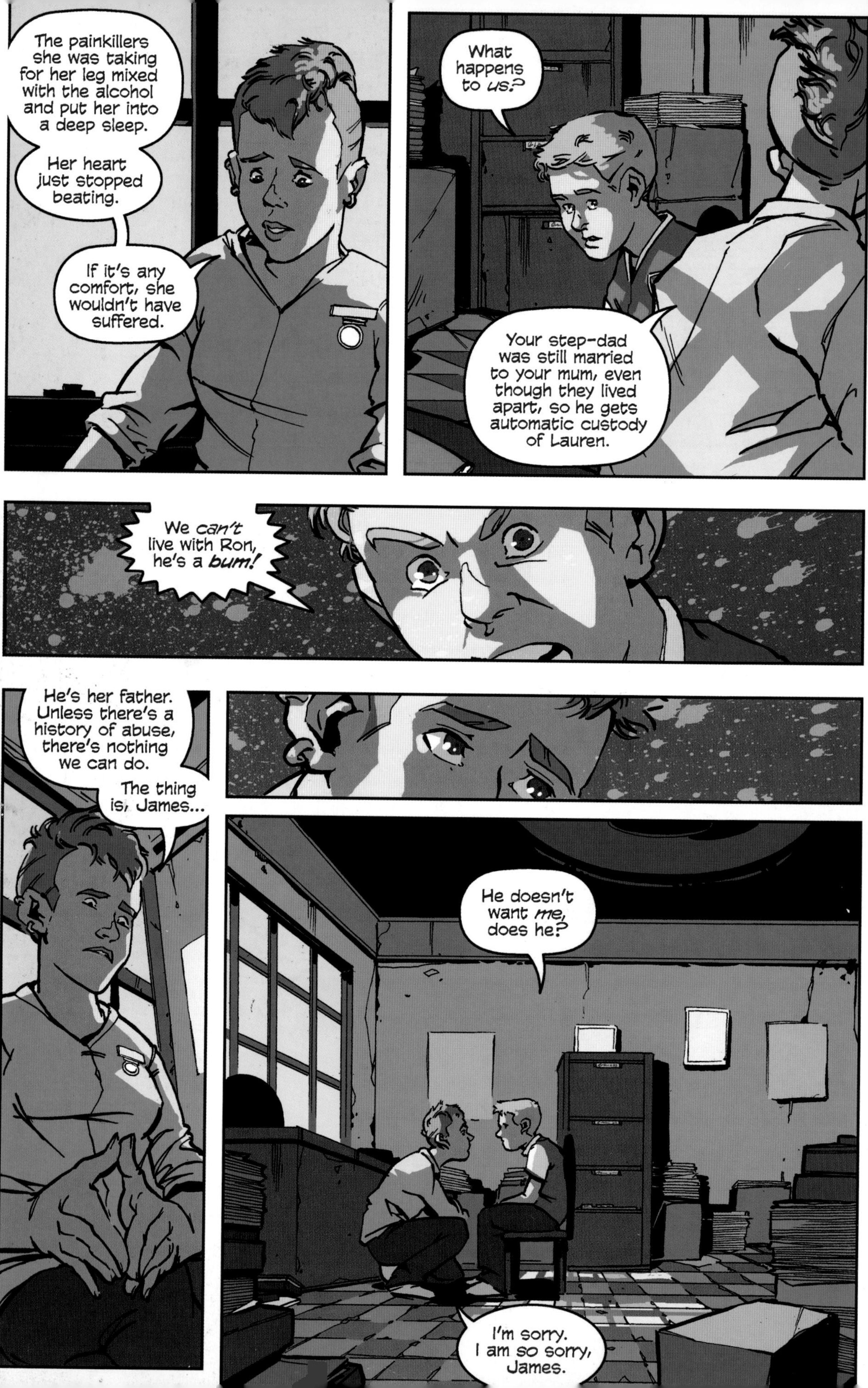
The painkillers she was taking for her leg mixed with the alcohol and put her into a deep sleep.
Her heart just stopped beating.
If it's any comfort, she wouldn't have suffered.
What happens to *us*?
Your step-dad was still married to your mum, even though they lived apart, so he gets automatic custody of Lauren.
We *can't* live with Ron, he's a *bum!*
He's her father. Unless there's a history of abuse, there's nothing we can do.
The thing is, James...
He doesn't want *me*, does he?
I'm sorry. I am so sorry, James.

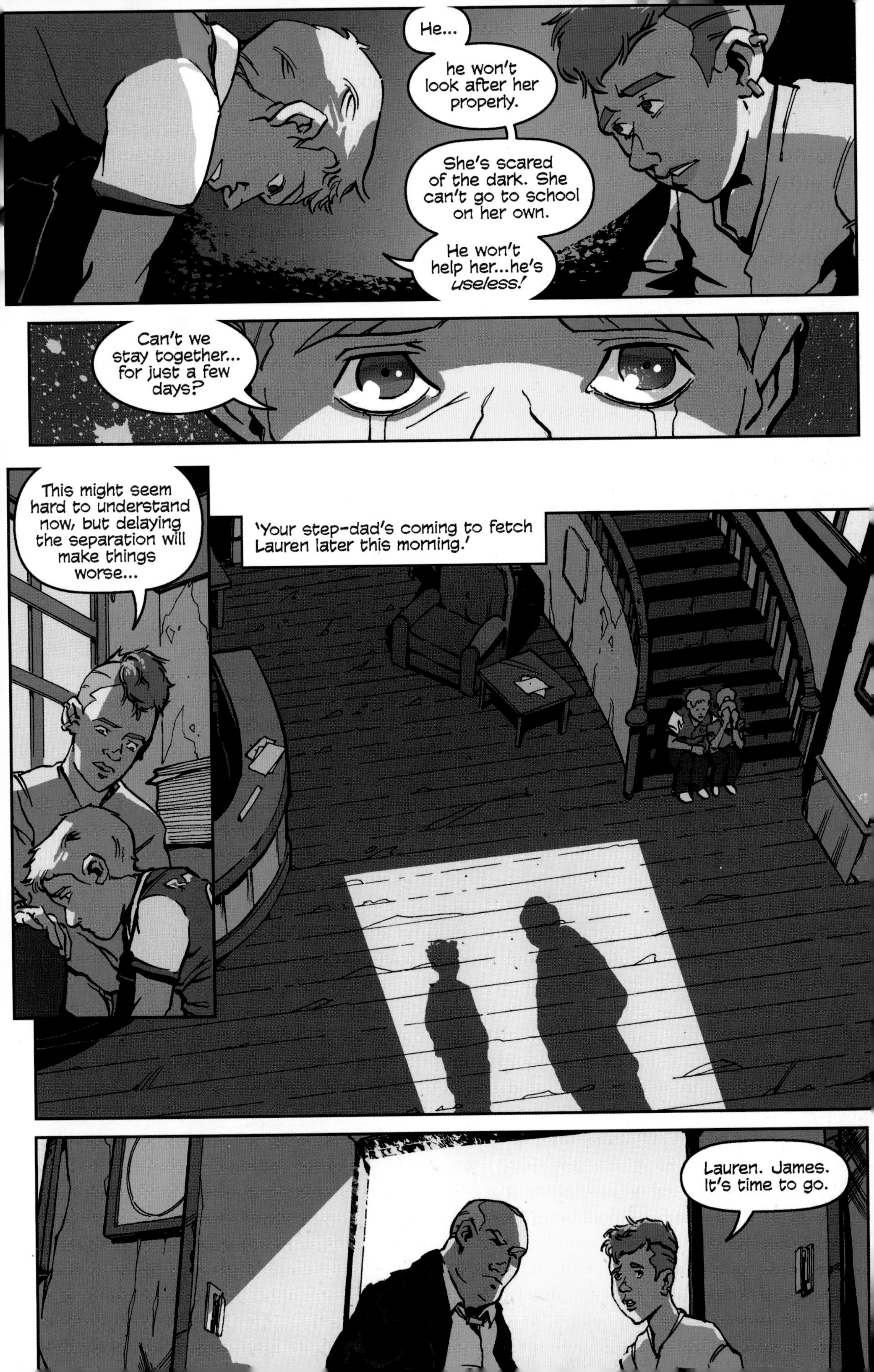
He...
he won't look after her properly.
She's scared of the dark. She can't go to school on her own.
He won't help her...he's *useless!*
Can't we stay together... for just a few days?
This might seem hard to understand now, but delaying the separation will make things worse...
'Your step-dad's coming to fetch Lauren later this morning.'
Lauren. James. It's time to go.

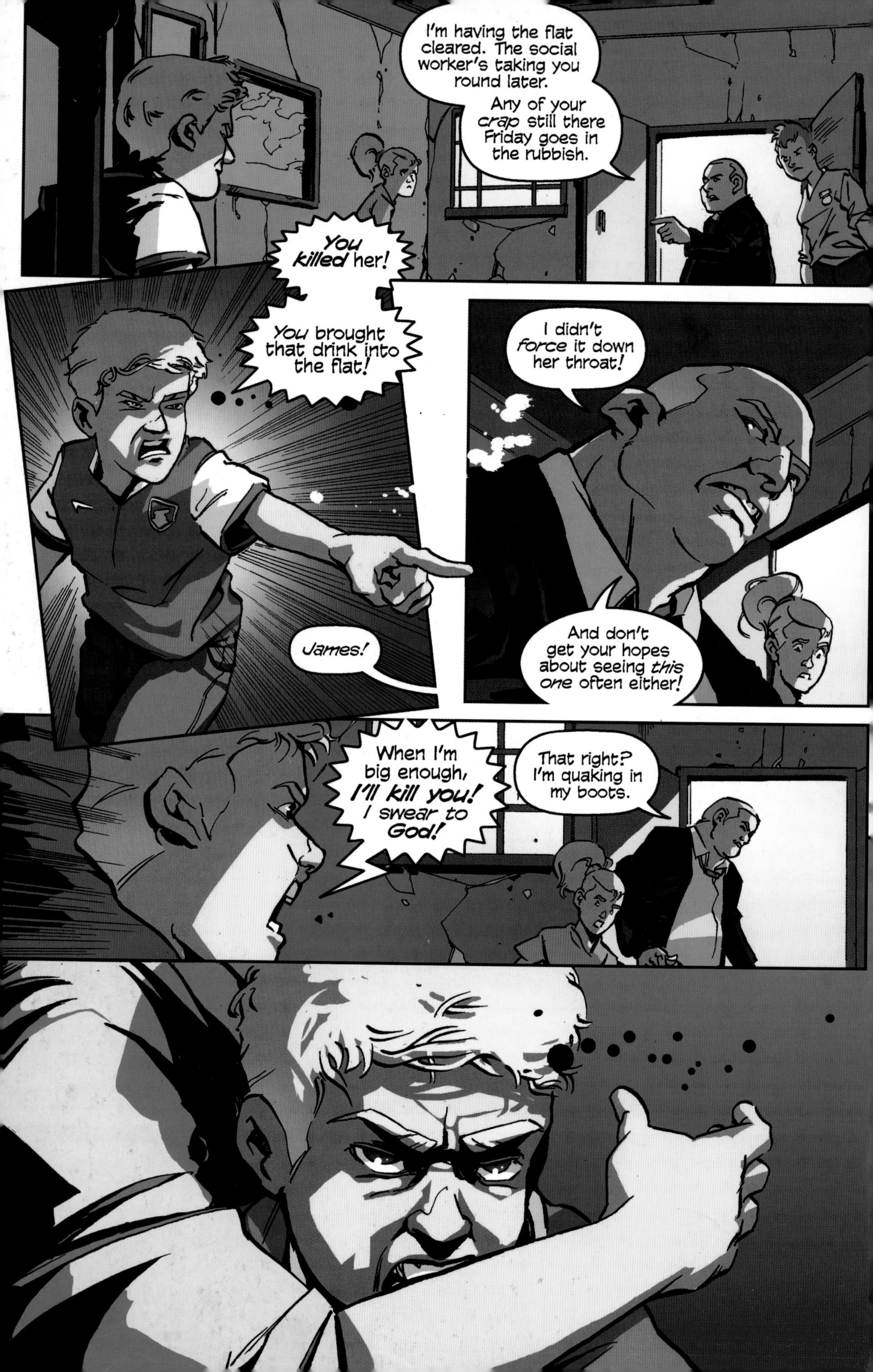
I'm having the flat cleared. The social worker's taking you round later.
Any of your *crap* still there Friday goes in the rubbish.
You killed her!
You brought that drink into the flat!
I didn't *force* it down her throat!
James!
And don't get your hopes about seeing *this one* often either!
When I'm big enough, ***I'll kill you!*** *I swear to* ***God!***
That right? I'm quaking in my boots.

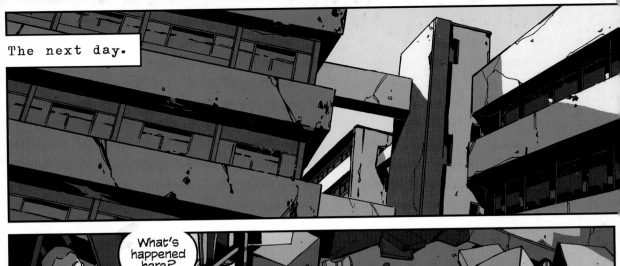

The next day.

What's happened here?

I half expected this, Ron's been here. He's stripped the place.

You're not gonna be able to take all this. We've only got fifteen minutes, then I've got to do a school run.

Your mum must've been *loaded!*

It's all *nicked.* She'd have it all stolen to order, then sell it on.

Bloody hell!

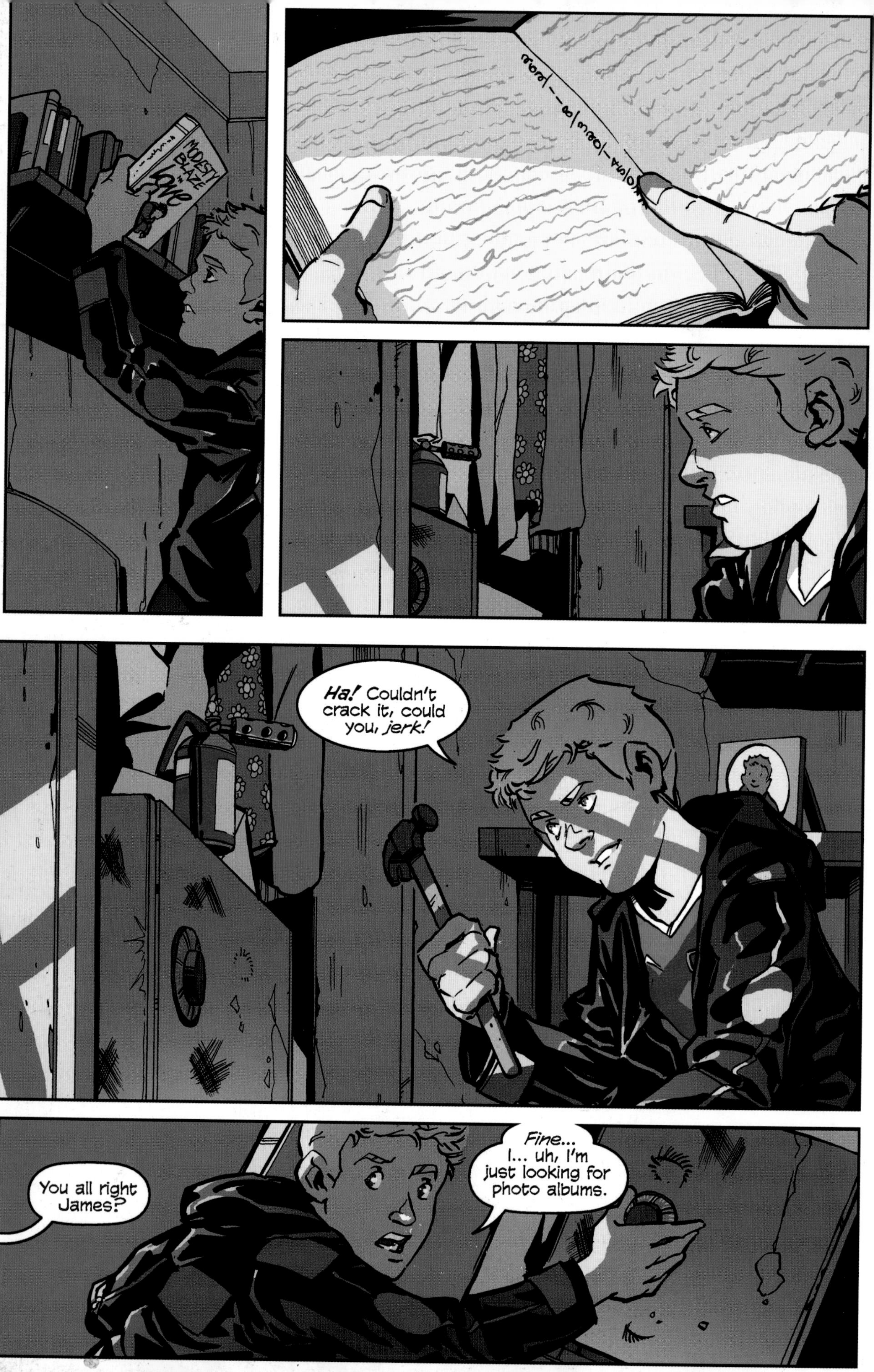
Ha! Couldn't crack it, could you, *jerk!*
You all right James?
Fine... I... uh, I'm just looking for photo albums.

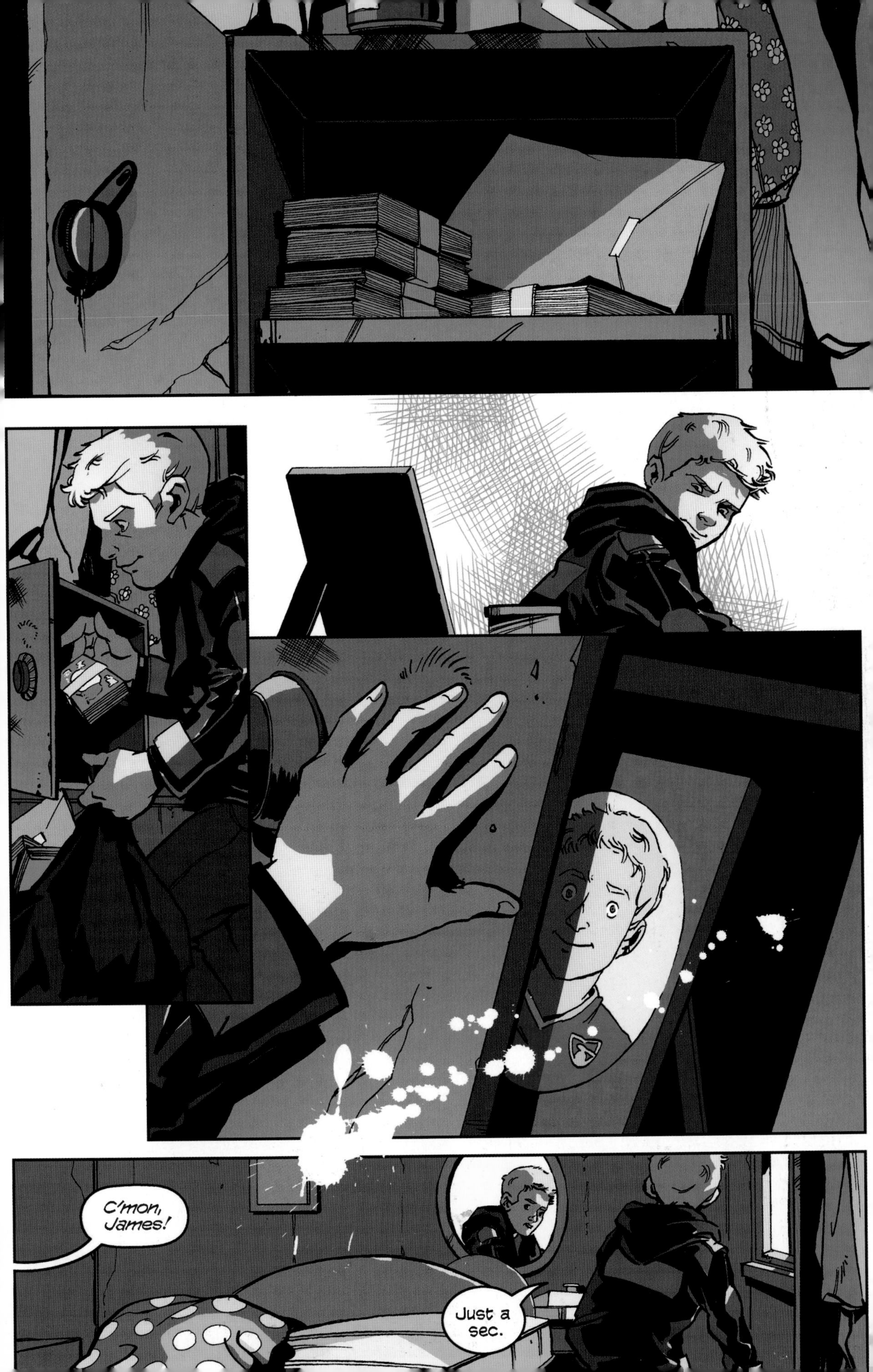
C'mon, James!
Just a sec.

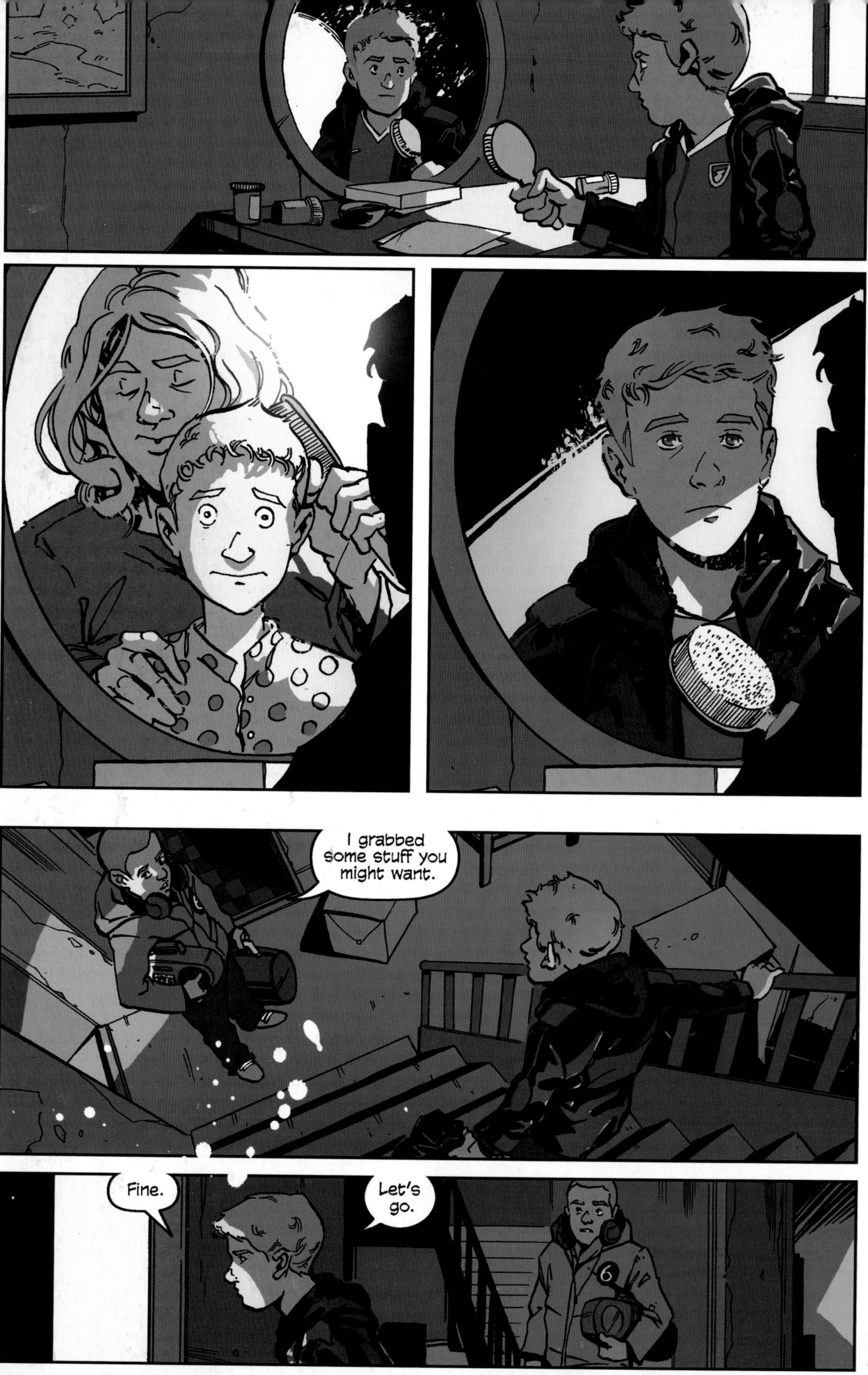
I grabbed some stuff you might want.
Fine.
Let's go.

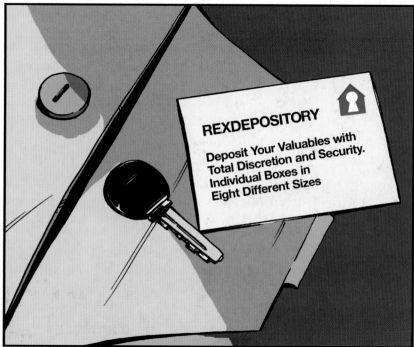

REXDEPOSITORY

Deposit Your Valuables with
Total Discretion and Security.
Individual Boxes in
Eight Different Sizes

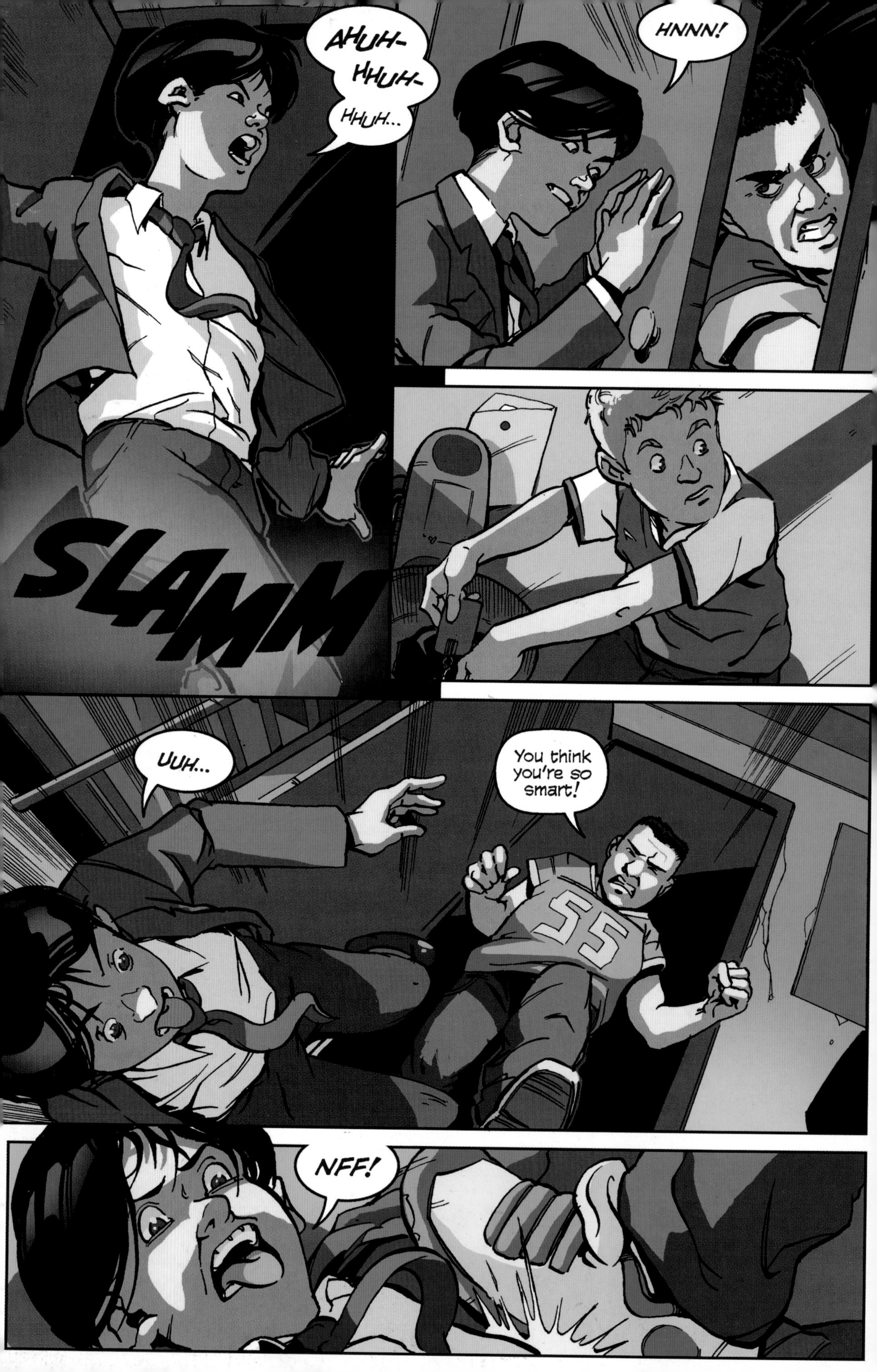
AHUH-
HHUH-
HHUH...
HNNN!
SLAMM
UUH...
You think you're so smart!
NFF!

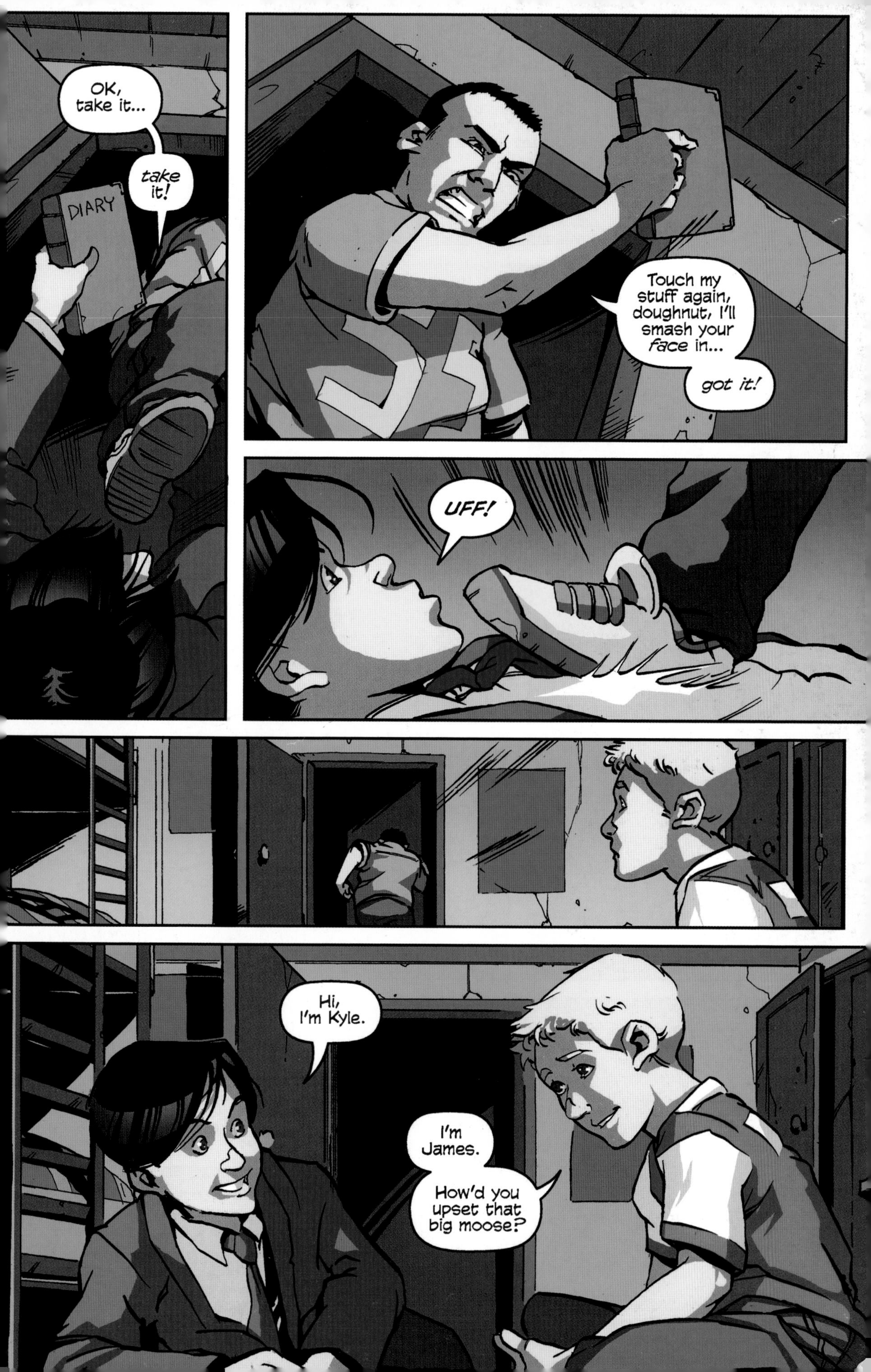
DIARY
OK, take it...
take it!
Touch my stuff again, doughnut, I'll smash your face in...
got it!
UFF!
Hi, I'm Kyle.
I'm James.
How'd you upset that big moose?

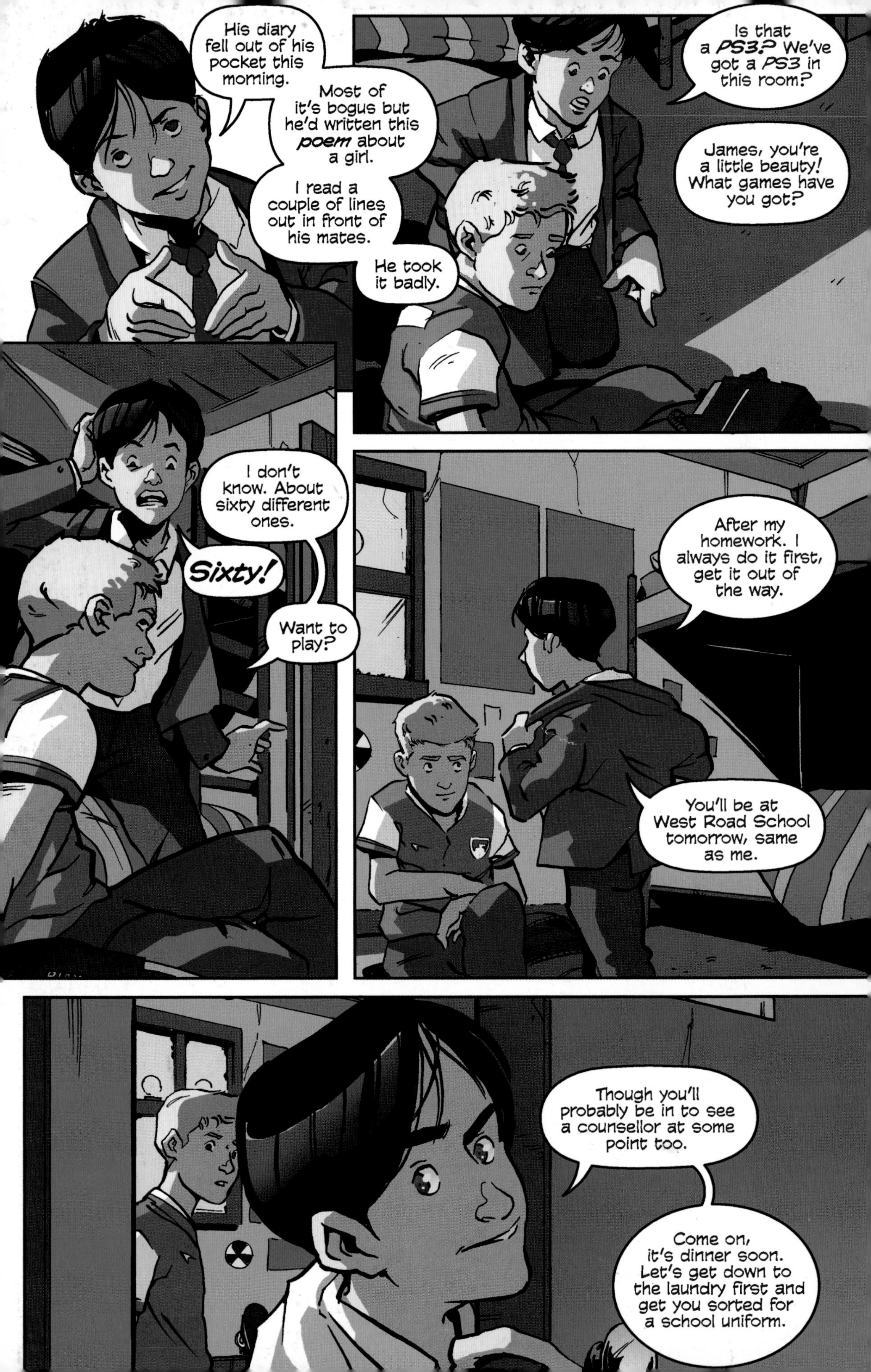
His diary fell out of his pocket this morning.
Most of it's bogus but he'd written this *poem* about a girl.
I read a couple of lines out in front of his mates.
He took it badly.
Is that a *PS3?* We've got a *PS3* in this room?
James, you're a little beauty! What games have you got?
I don't know. About sixty different ones.
Sixty!
Want to play?
After my homework. I always do it first, get it out of the way.
You'll be at West Road School tomorrow, same as me.
Though you'll probably be in to see a counsellor at some point too.
Come on, it's dinner soon. Let's get down to the laundry first and get you sorted for a school uniform.

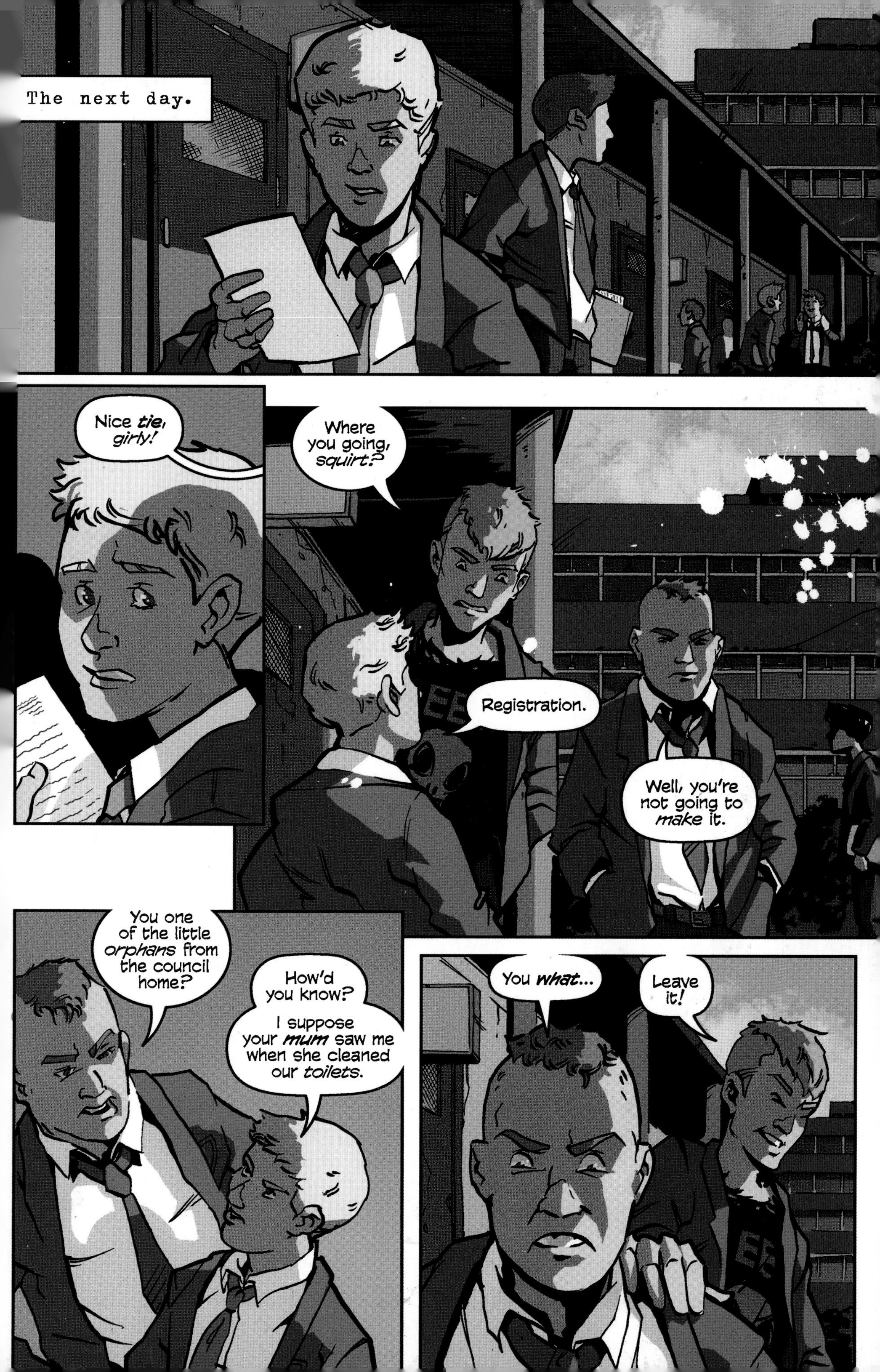

The next day.
Nice tie, girly!
Where you going, squirt?
Registration.
Well, you're not going to make it.
You one of the little orphans from the council home?
How'd you know?
I suppose your mum saw me when she cleaned our toilets.
You what...
Leave it!

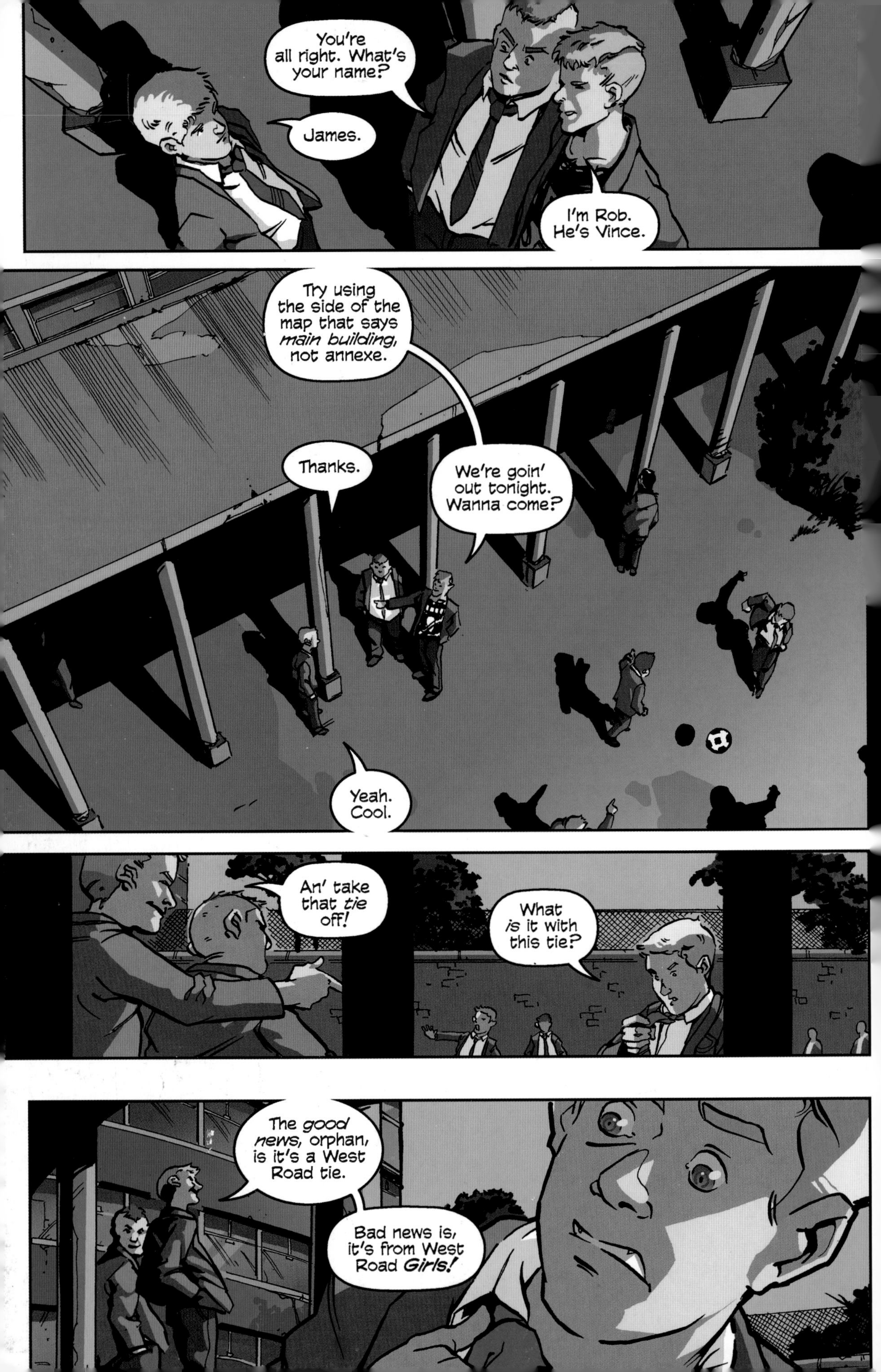
You're all right. What's your name?
James.
I'm Rob. He's Vince.
Try using the side of the map that says *main building,* not annexe.
Thanks.
We're goin' out tonight. Wanna come?
Yeah. Cool.
An' take that *tie* off!
What *is* it with this tie?
The *good news,* orphan, is it's a West Road tie.
Bad news is, it's from West Road *Girls!*

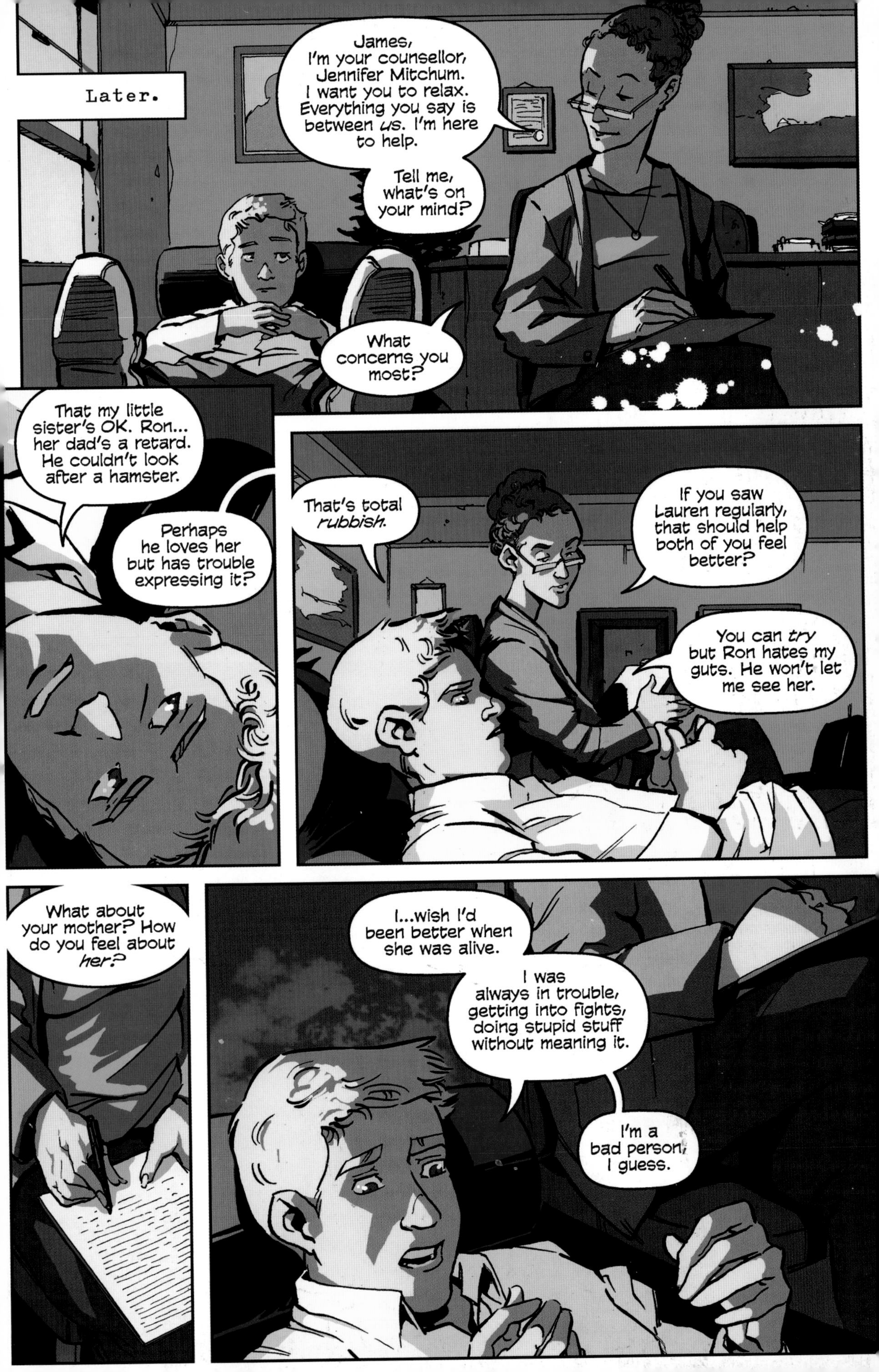

Later.
James, I'm your counsellor, Jennifer Mitchum. I want you to relax. Everything you say is between us. I'm here to help.
Tell me, what's on your mind?
What concerns you most?
That my little sister's OK. Ron... her dad's a retard. He couldn't look after a hamster.
Perhaps he loves her but has trouble expressing it?
That's total rubbish.
If you saw Lauren regularly, that should help both of you feel better?
You can try but Ron hates my guts. He won't let me see her.
What about your mother? How do you feel about her?
I...wish I'd been better when she was alive.
I was always in trouble, getting into fights, doing stupid stuff without meaning it.
I'm a bad person, I guess.

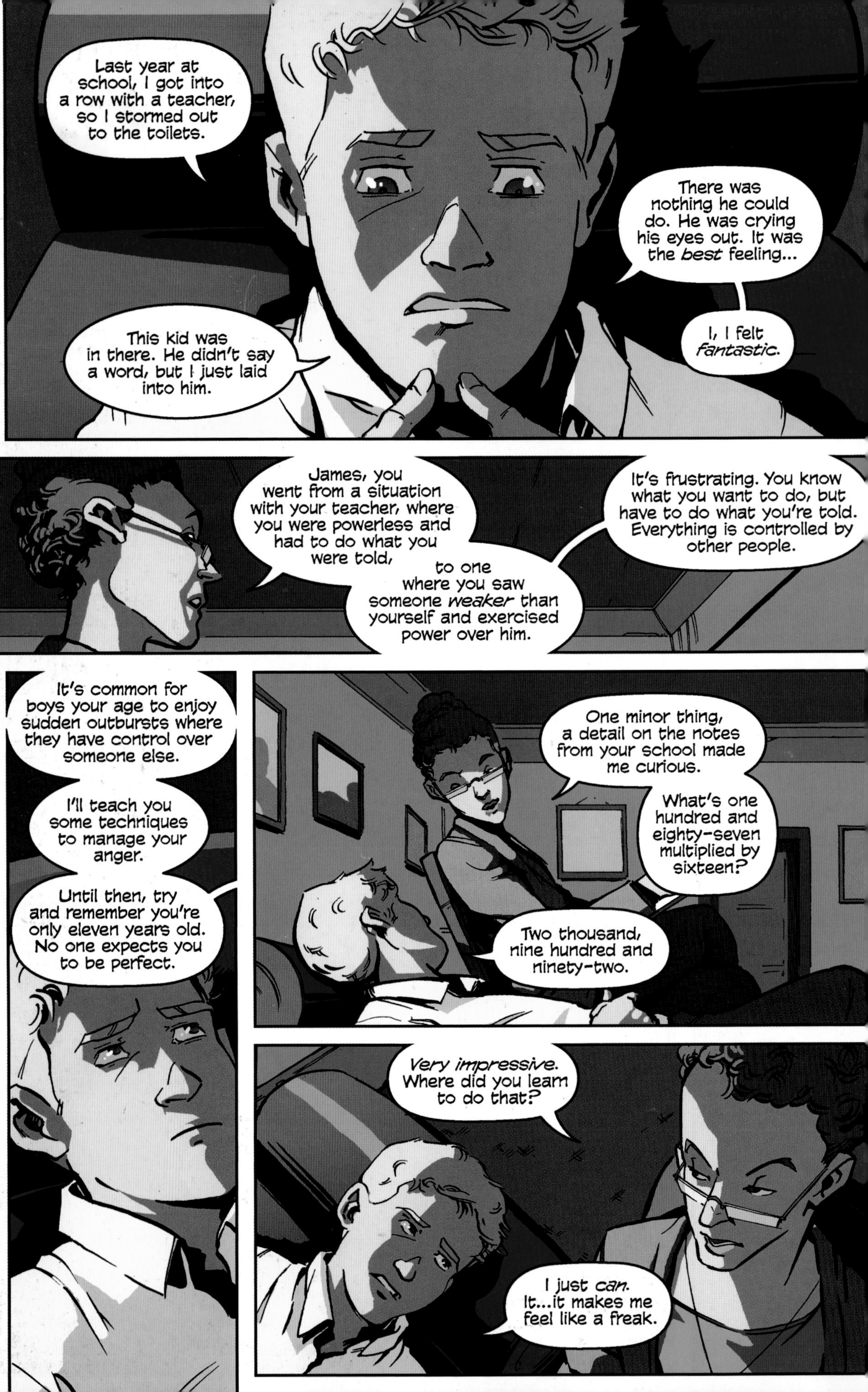

Last year at school, I got into a row with a teacher, so I stormed out to the toilets.
This kid was in there. He didn't say a word, but I just laid into him.
There was nothing he could do. He was crying his eyes out. It was the *best* feeling...
I, I felt *fantastic*.
James, you went from a situation with your teacher, where you were powerless and had to do what you were told,
to one where you saw someone *weaker* than yourself and exercised power over him.
It's frustrating. You know what you want to do, but have to do what you're told. Everything is controlled by other people.
It's common for boys your age to enjoy sudden outbursts where they have control over someone else.
I'll teach you some techniques to manage your anger.
Until then, try and remember you're only eleven years old. No one expects you to be perfect.
One minor thing, a detail on the notes from your school made me curious.
What's one hundred and eighty-seven multiplied by sixteen?
Two thousand, nine hundred and ninety-two.
Very impressive. Where did you learn to do that?
I just *can*. It...it makes me feel like a freak.

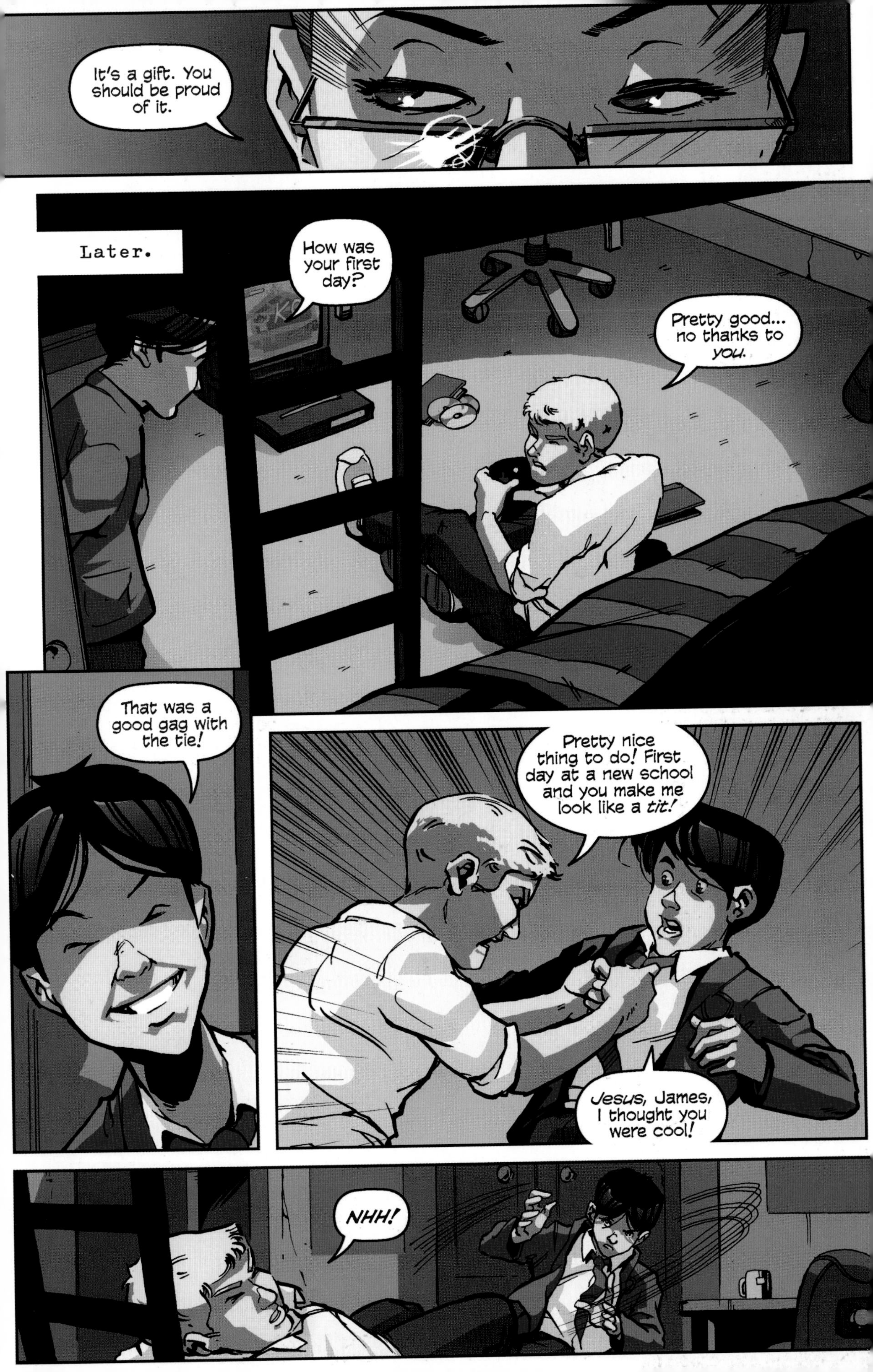
It's a gift. You should be proud of it.
Later.
How was your first day?
Pretty good... no thanks to *you*.
That was a good gag with the tie!
Pretty nice thing to do! First day at a new school and you make me look like a *tit!*
Jesus, James, I thought you were cool!
NHH!

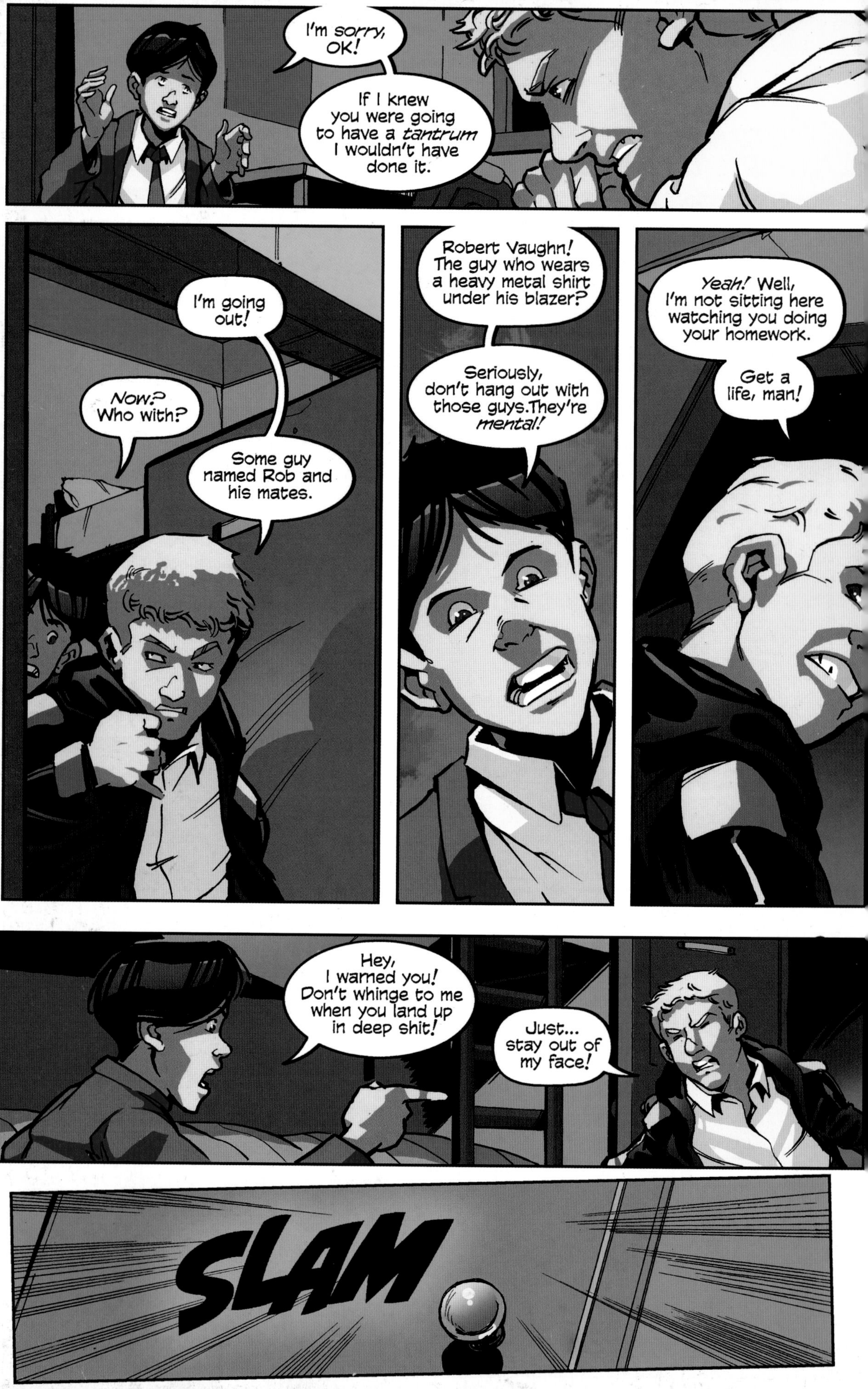

I'm sorry, OK!
If I knew you were going to have a tantrum I wouldn't have done it.
I'm going out!
Now? Who with?
Some guy named Rob and his mates.
Robert Vaughn! The guy who wears a heavy metal shirt under his blazer?
Seriously, don't hang out with those guys. They're mental!
Yeah! Well, I'm not sitting here watching you doing your homework.
Get a life, man!
Hey, I warned you! Don't whinge to me when you land up in deep shit!
Just... stay out of my face!
SLAM

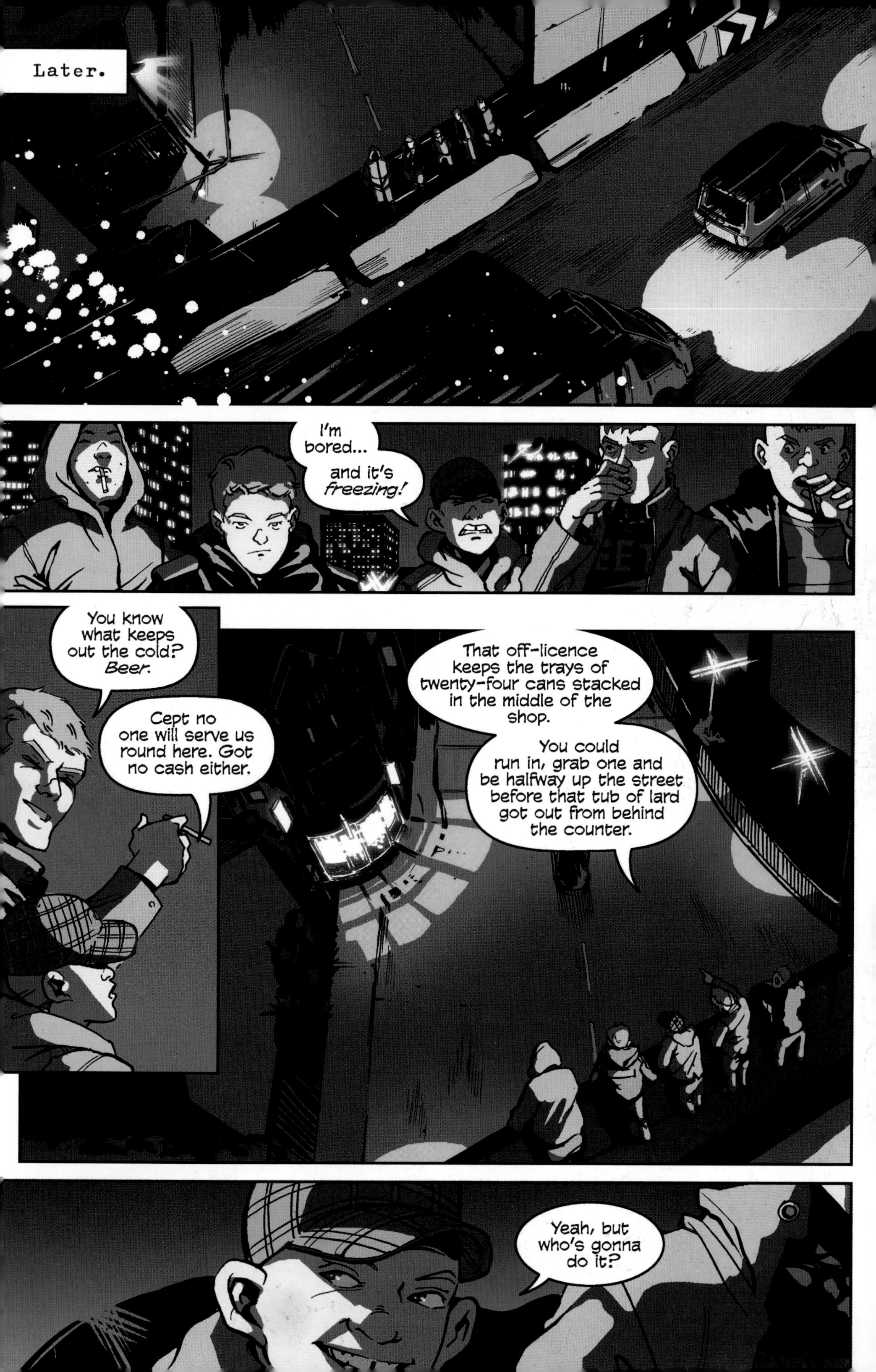
Later.
I'm bored...
and it's *freezing!*
You know what keeps out the cold? *Beer.*
Cept no one will serve us round here. Got no cash either.
That off-licence keeps the trays of twenty-four cans stacked in the middle of the shop.
You could run in, grab one and be halfway up the street before that tub of lard got out from behind the counter.
Yeah, but who's gonna do it?

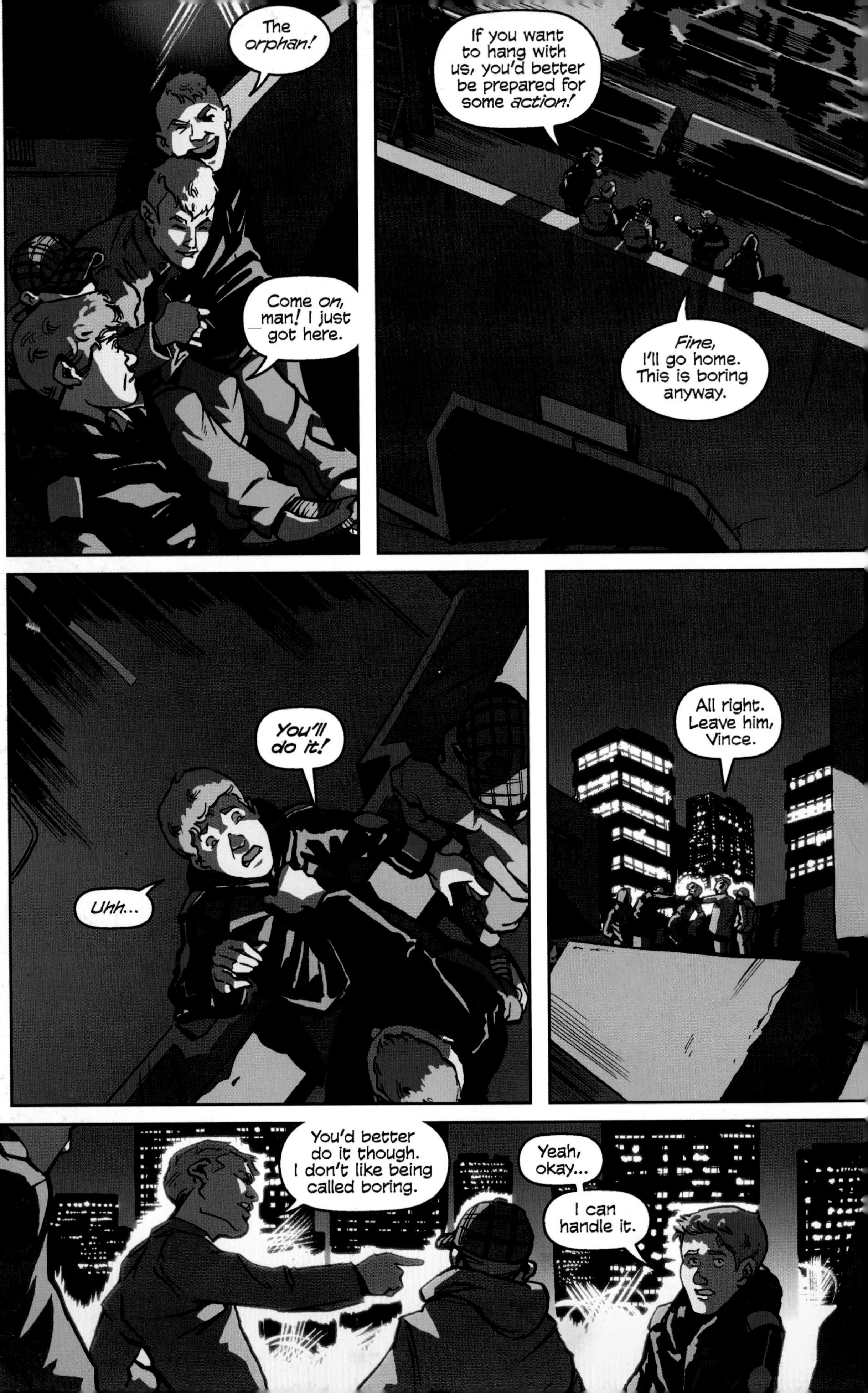

The *orphan!*
Come *on*, man! I just got here.
If you want to hang with us, you'd better be prepared for some *action!*
Fine, I'll go home. This is boring anyway.
You'll do it!
Uhh...
All right. Leave him, Vince.
You'd better do it though. I don't like being called boring.
Yeah, okay...
I can handle it.

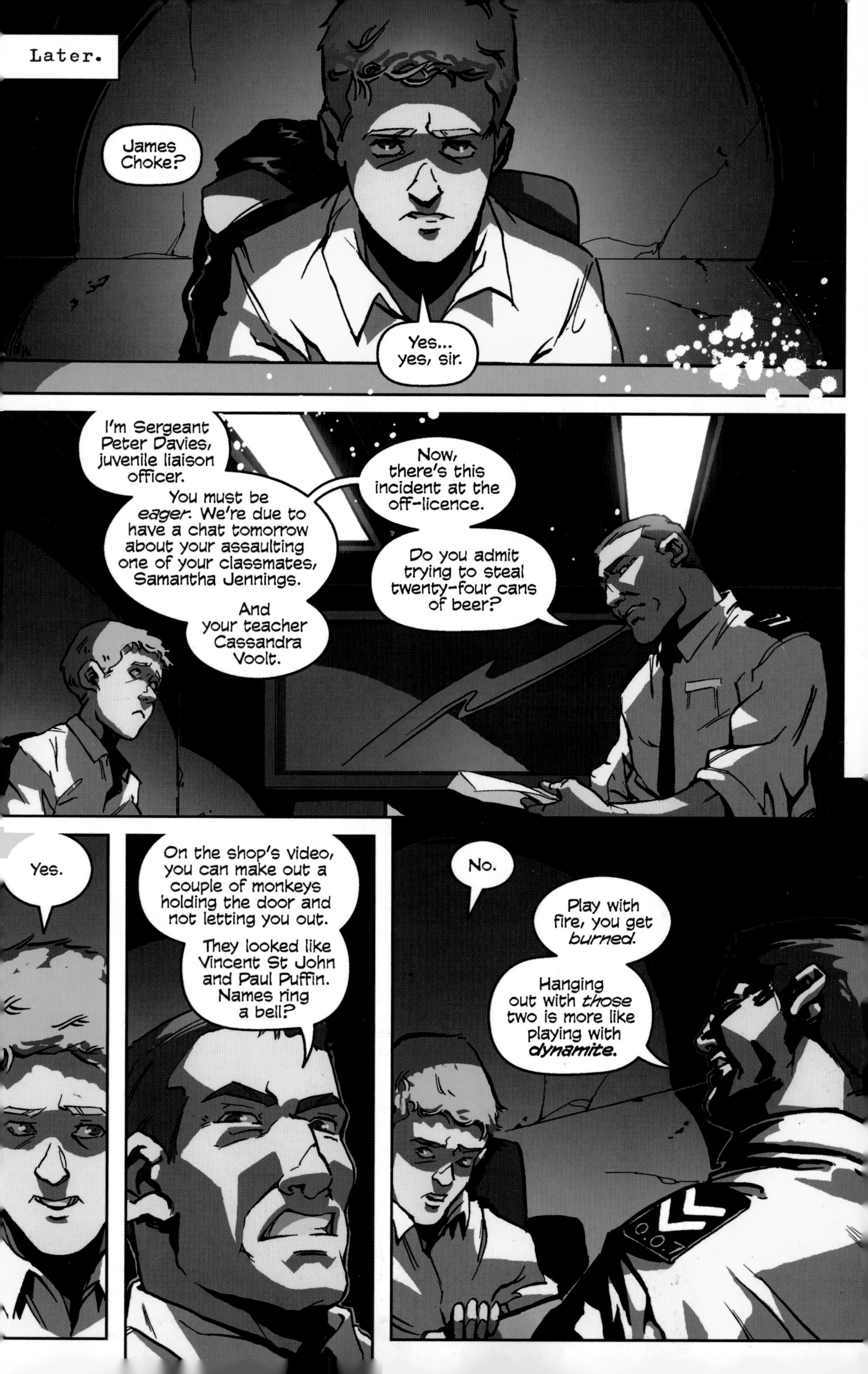
Later.
James Choke?
Yes... yes, sir.
I'm Sergeant Peter Davies, juvenile liaison officer.
You must be *eager*. We're due to have a chat tomorrow about your assaulting one of your classmates, Samantha Jennings.
And your teacher Cassandra Voolt.
Now, there's this incident at the off-licence.
Do you admit trying to steal twenty-four cans of beer?
Yes.
On the shop's video, you can make out a couple of monkeys holding the door and not letting you out.
They looked like Vincent St John and Paul Puffin. Names ring a bell?
No.
Play with fire, you get *burned*.
Hanging out with *those* two is more like playing with ***dynamite***.

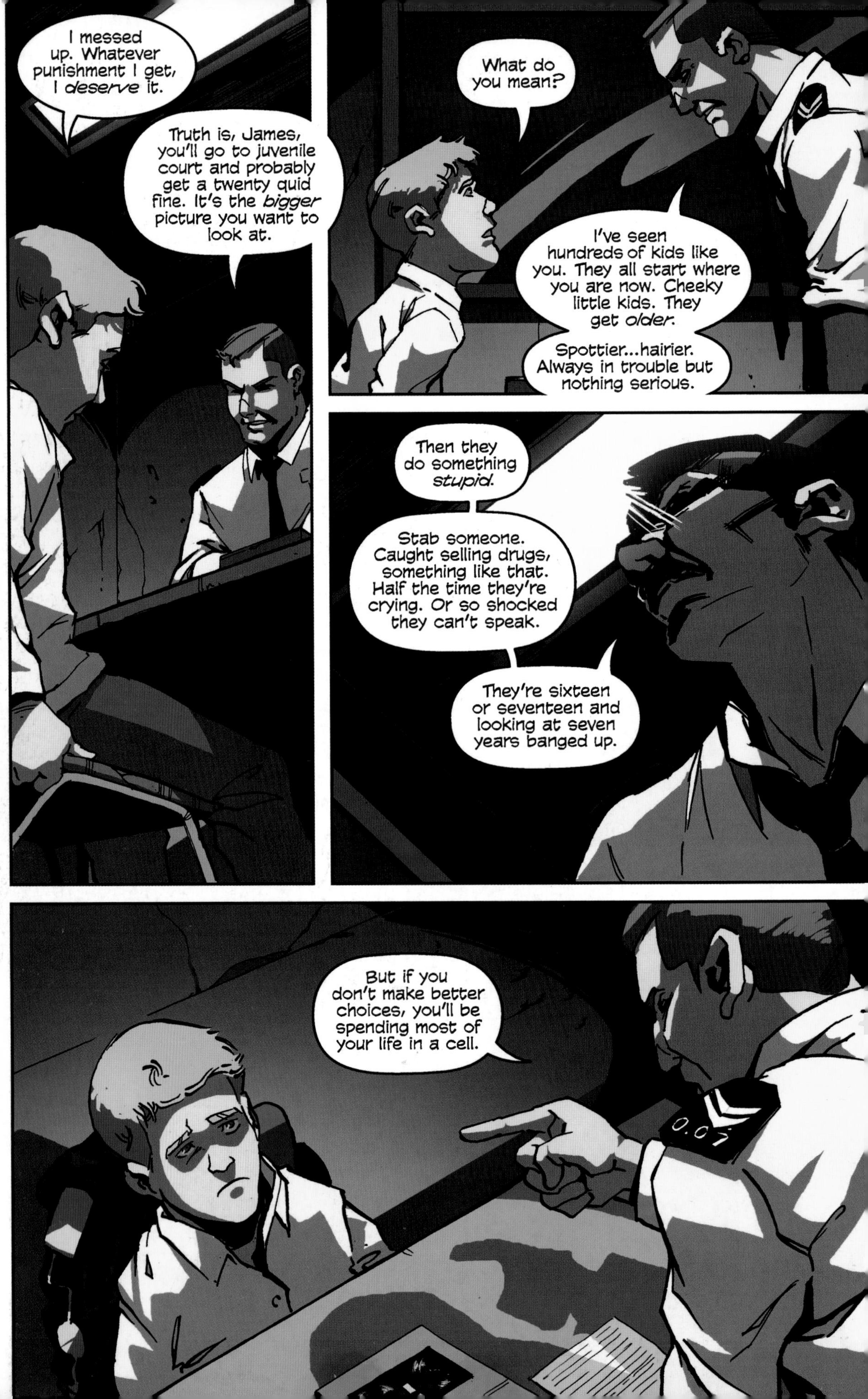
I messed up. Whatever punishment I get, I *deserve* it.
Truth is, James, you'll go to juvenile court and probably get a twenty quid fine. It's the *bigger* picture you want to look at.
What do you mean?
I've seen hundreds of kids like you. They all start where you are now. Cheeky little kids. They get *older*.
Spottier...hairier. Always in trouble but nothing serious.
Then they do something *stupid*.
Stab someone. Caught selling drugs, something like that. Half the time they're crying. Or so shocked they can't speak.
They're sixteen or seventeen and looking at seven years banged up.
But if you don't make better choices, you'll be spending most of your life in a cell.
0.07

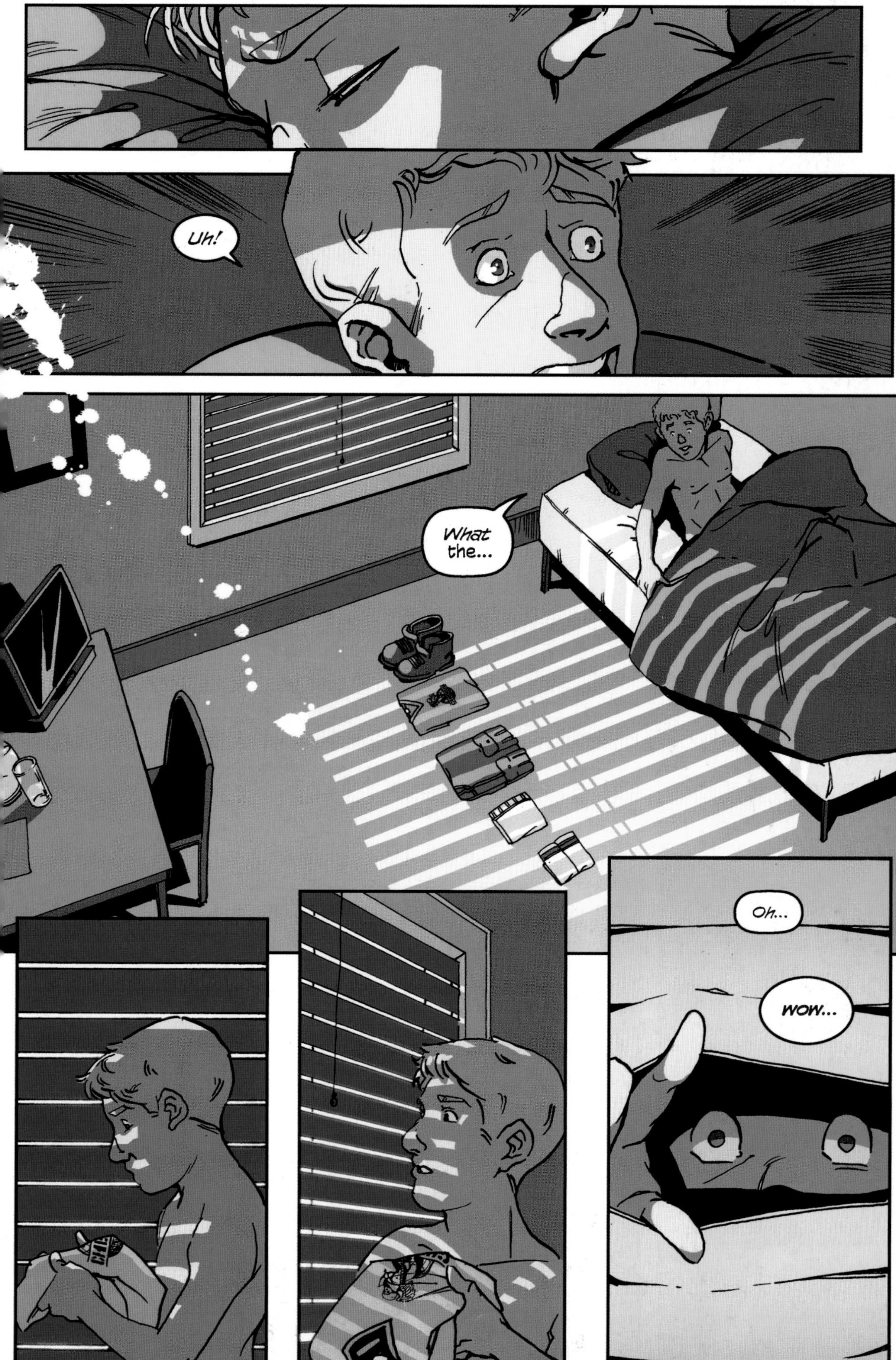
Uh!
What the...
Oh...
wow...

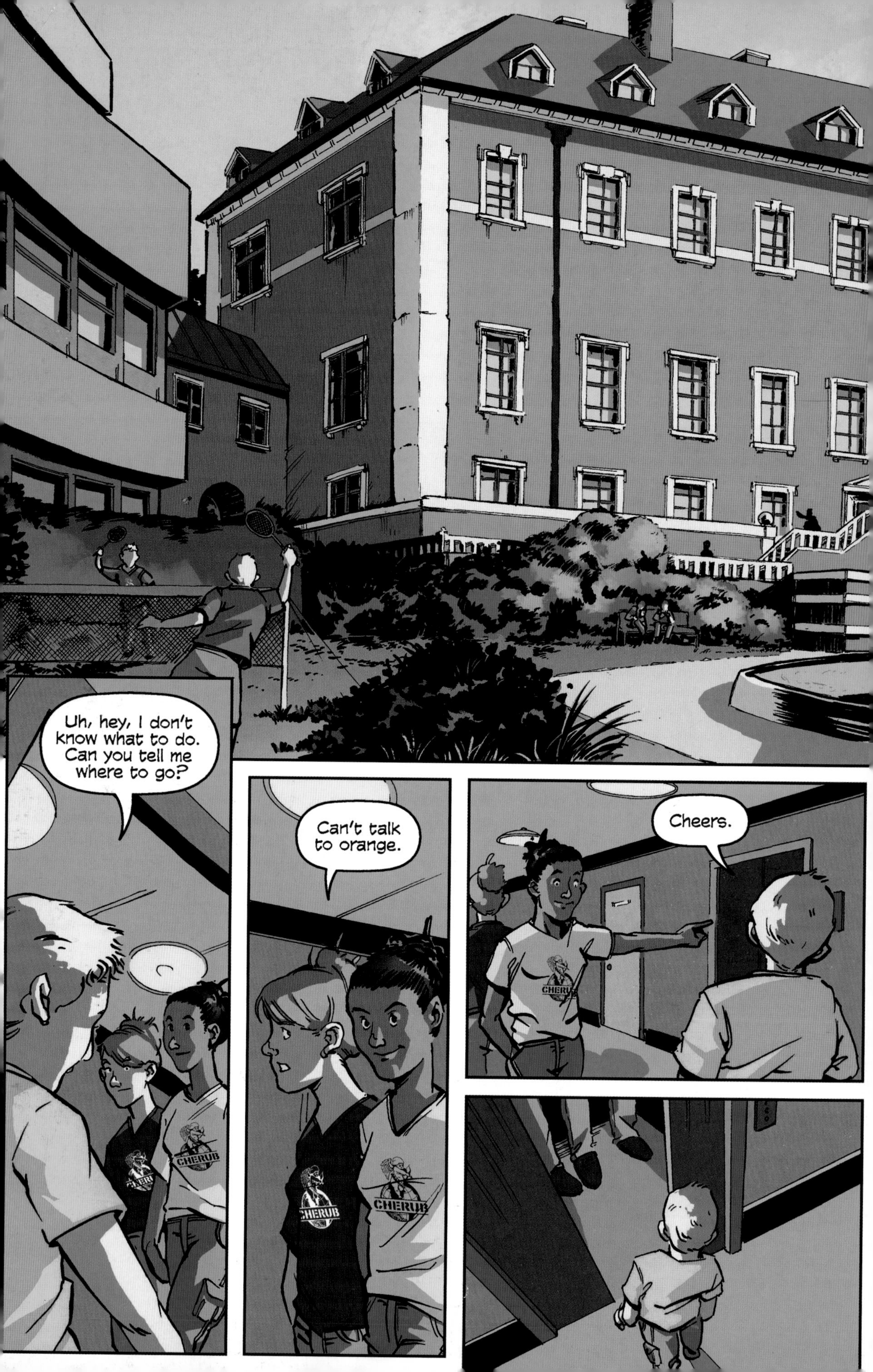
Uh, hey, I don't know what to do. Can you tell me where to go?
Can't talk to orange.
Cheers.
CHERUB

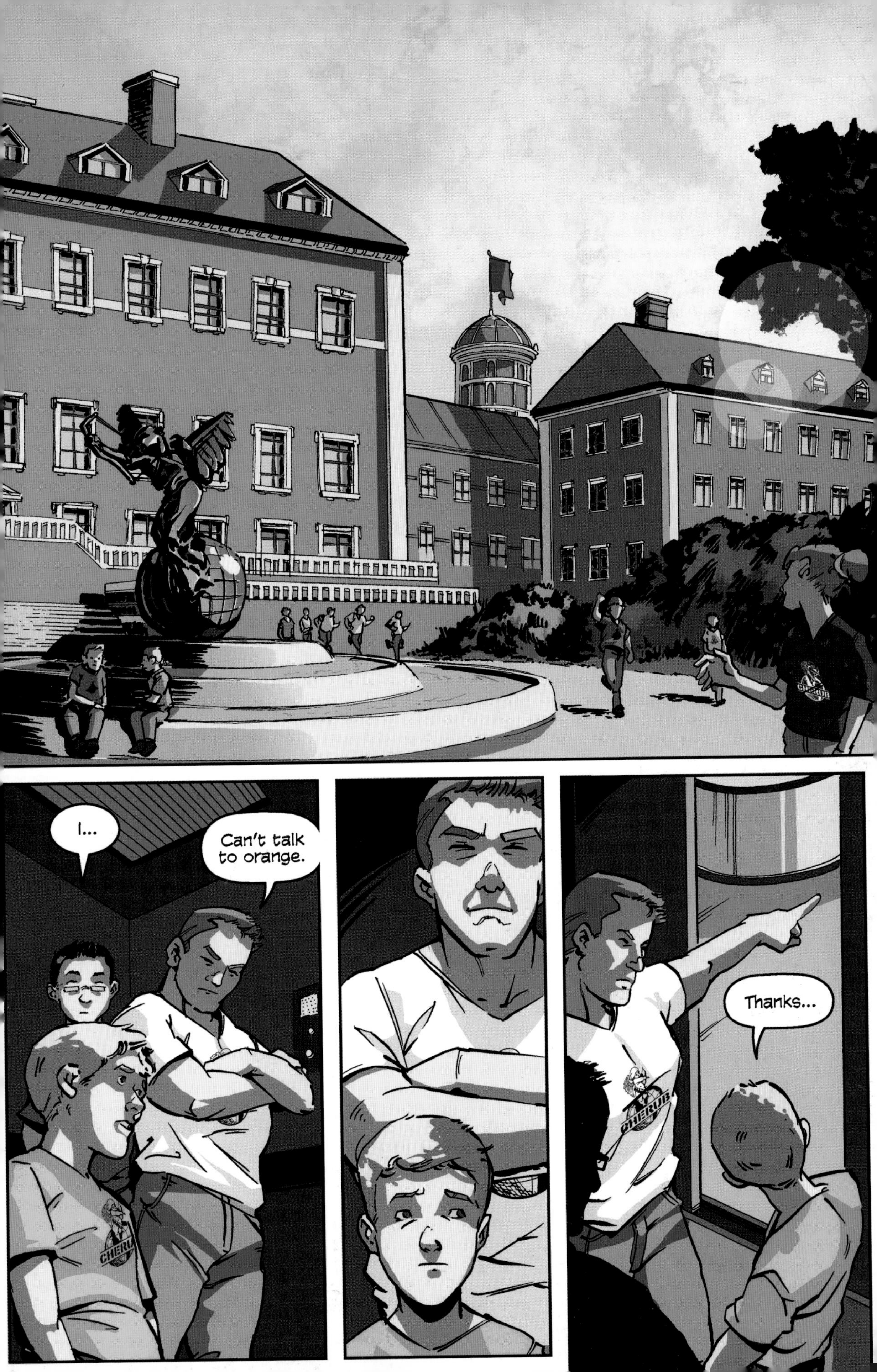
I...
Can't talk to orange.
Thanks...

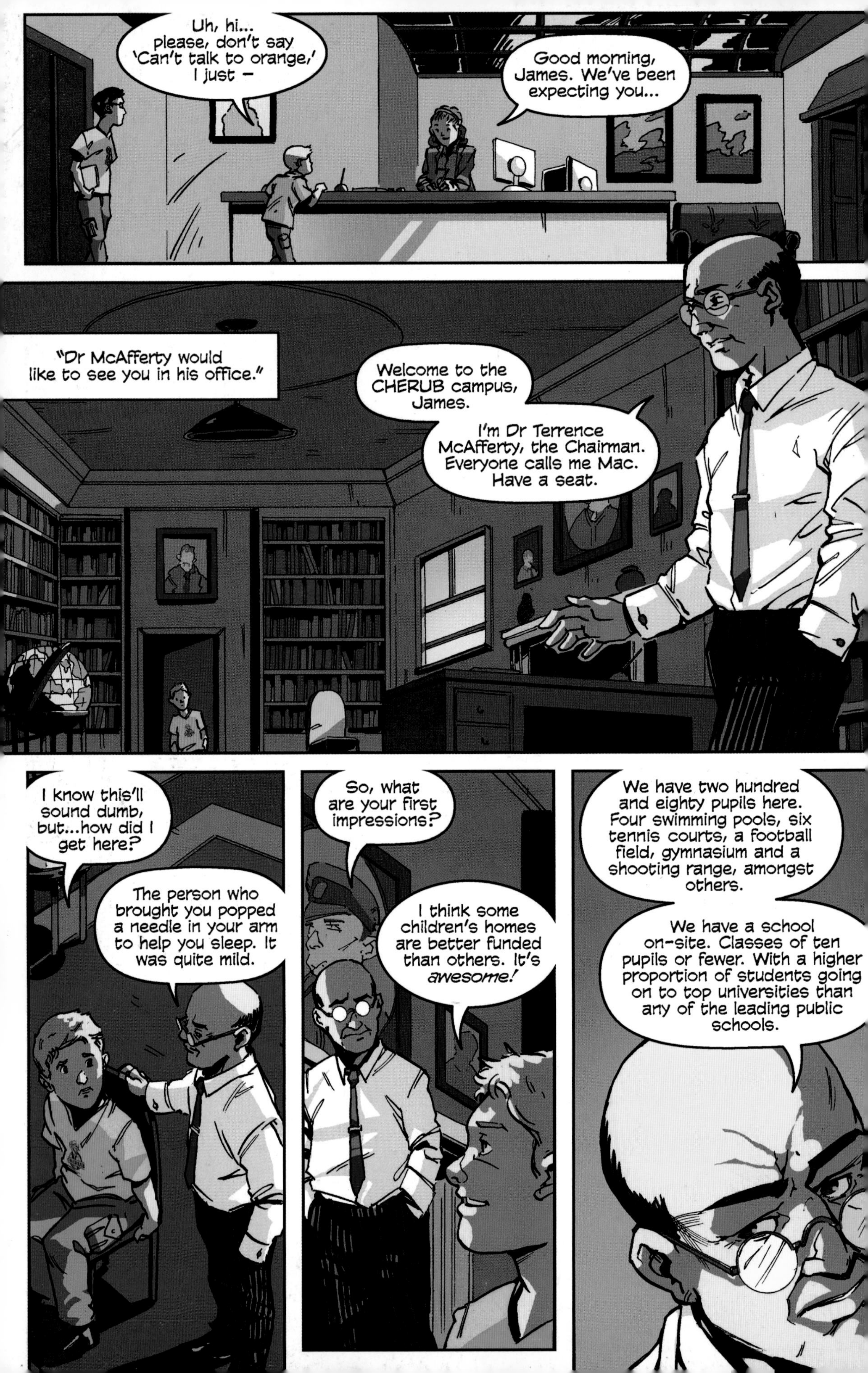

Uh, hi... please, don't say 'Can't talk to orange,' I just –
Good morning, James. We've been expecting you...
"Dr McAfferty would like to see you in his office."
Welcome to the CHERUB campus, James.
I'm Dr Terrence McAfferty, the Chairman. Everyone calls me Mac. Have a seat.
I know this'll sound dumb, but...how did I get here?
The person who brought you popped a needle in your arm to help you sleep. It was quite mild.
So, what are your first impressions?
I think some children's homes are better funded than others. It's *awesome!*
We have two hundred and eighty pupils here. Four swimming pools, six tennis courts, a football field, gymnasium and a shooting range, amongst others.
We have a school on-site. Classes of ten pupils or fewer. With a higher proportion of students going on to top universities than any of the leading public schools.

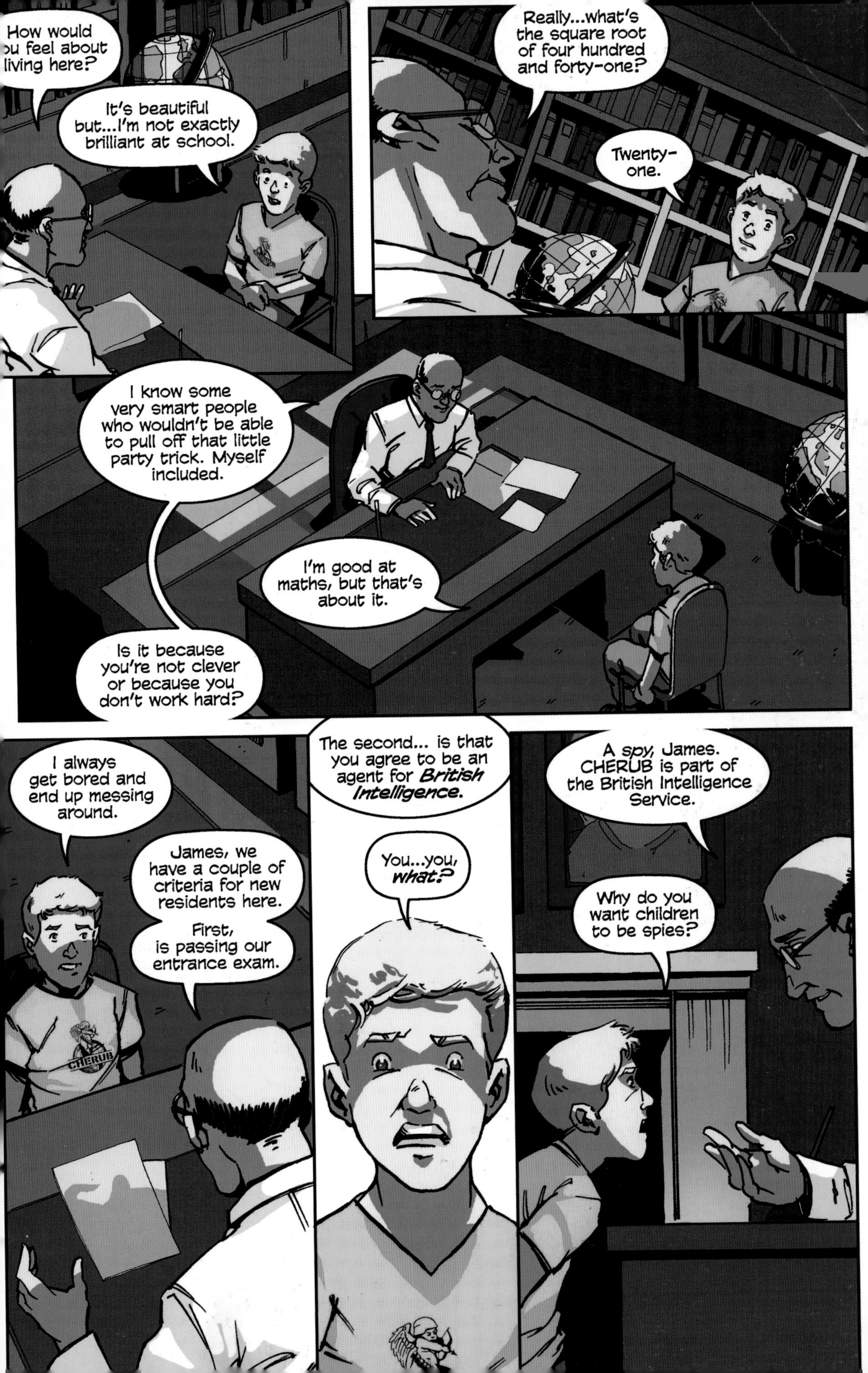
How would
ou feel about
living here?
It's beautiful but...I'm not exactly brilliant at school.
Really...what's the square root of four hundred and forty-one?
Twenty-one.
I know some very smart people who wouldn't be able to pull off that little party trick. Myself included.
I'm good at maths, but that's about it.
Is it because you're not clever or because you don't work hard?
I always get bored and end up messing around.
James, we have a couple of criteria for new residents here.
First, is passing our entrance exam.
The second... is that you agree to be an agent for *British Intelligence*.
You...you, *what?*
A *spy*, James. CHERUB is part of the British Intelligence Service.
Why do you want children to be spies?
CHERUB

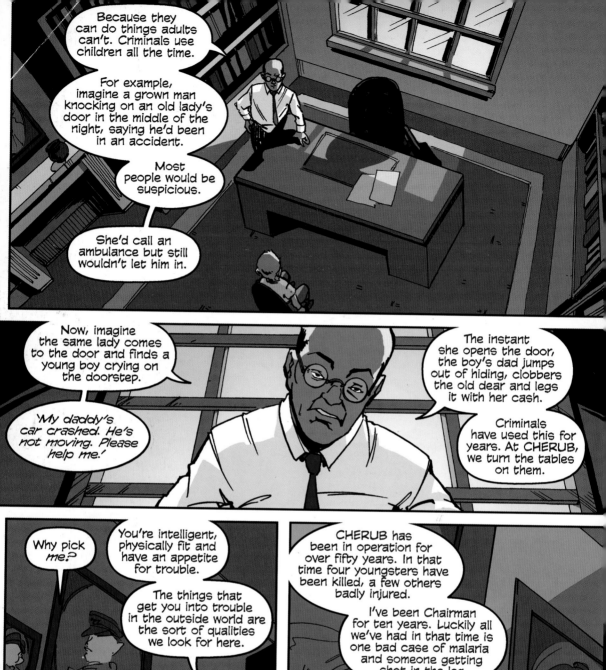

Because they can do things adults can't. Criminals use children all the time.

For example, imagine a grown man knocking on an old lady's door in the middle of the night, saying he'd been in an accident.

Most people would be suspicious.

She'd call an ambulance but still wouldn't let him in.

Now, imagine the same lady comes to the door and finds a young boy crying on the doorstep.

'My daddy's car crashed. He's not moving. Please help me.'

The instant she opens the door, the boy's dad jumps out of hiding, clobbers the old dear and legs it with her cash.

Criminals have used this for years. At CHERUB, we turn the tables on them.

Why pick me?

You're intelligent, physically fit and have an appetite for trouble.

The things that get you into trouble in the outside world are the sort of qualities we look for here.

CHERUB has been in operation for over fifty years. In that time four youngsters have been killed, a few others badly injured.

I've been Chairman for ten years. Luckily all we've had in that time is one bad case of malaria and someone getting shot in the leg.

We never send you on a mission that could be done by an adult. All missions go to an ethics approval committee first.

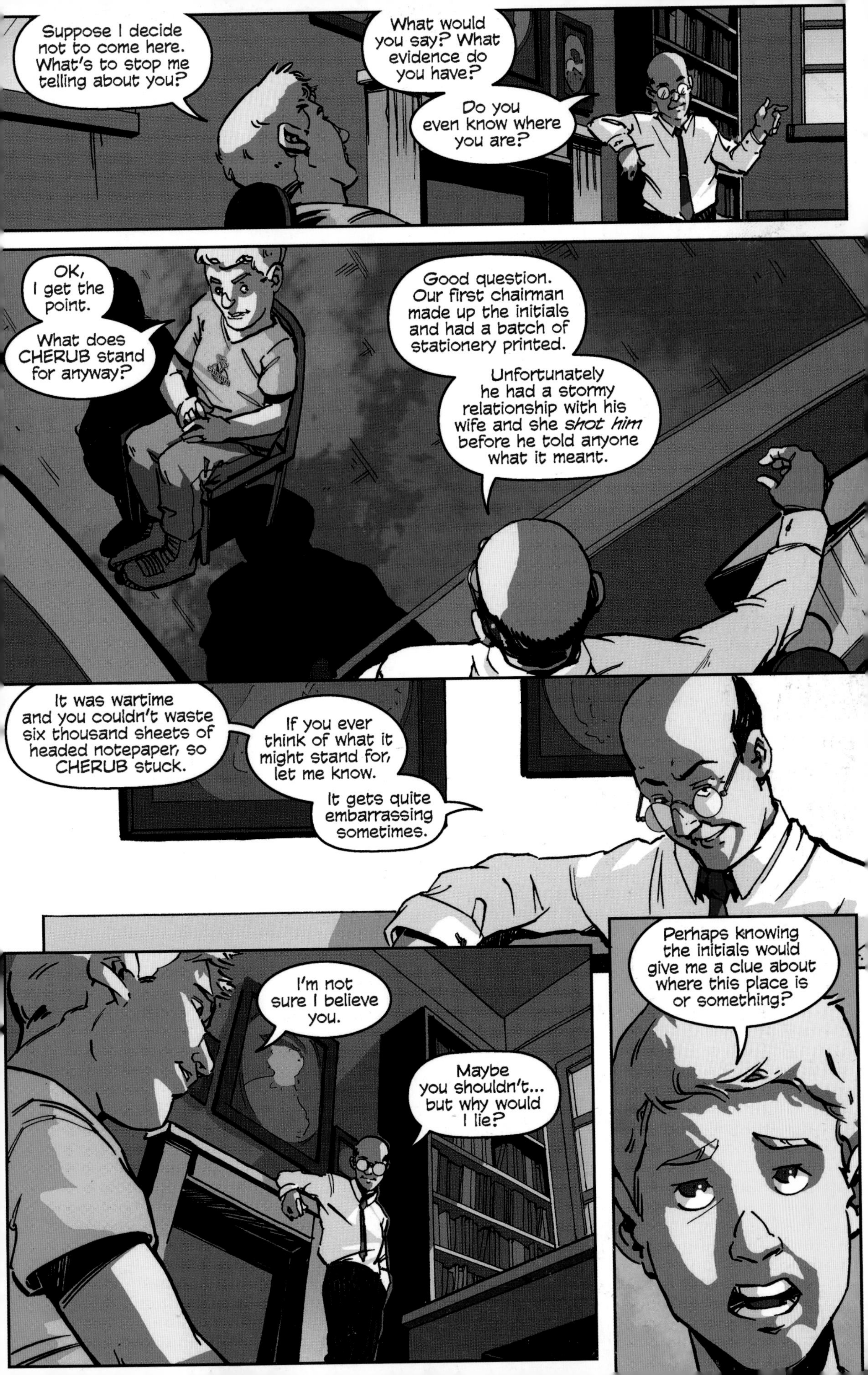
Suppose I decide not to come here. What's to stop me telling about you?
What would you say? What evidence do you have?
Do you even know where you are?
OK, I get the point.
What does CHERUB stand for anyway?
Good question. Our first chairman made up the initials and had a batch of stationery printed.
Unfortunately he had a stormy relationship with his wife and she *shot him* before he told anyone what it meant.
It was wartime and you couldn't waste six thousand sheets of headed notepaper, so CHERUB stuck.
If you ever think of what it might stand for, let me know.
It gets quite embarrassing sometimes.
I'm not sure I believe you.
Maybe you shouldn't... but why would I lie?
Perhaps knowing the initials would give me a clue about where this place is or something?

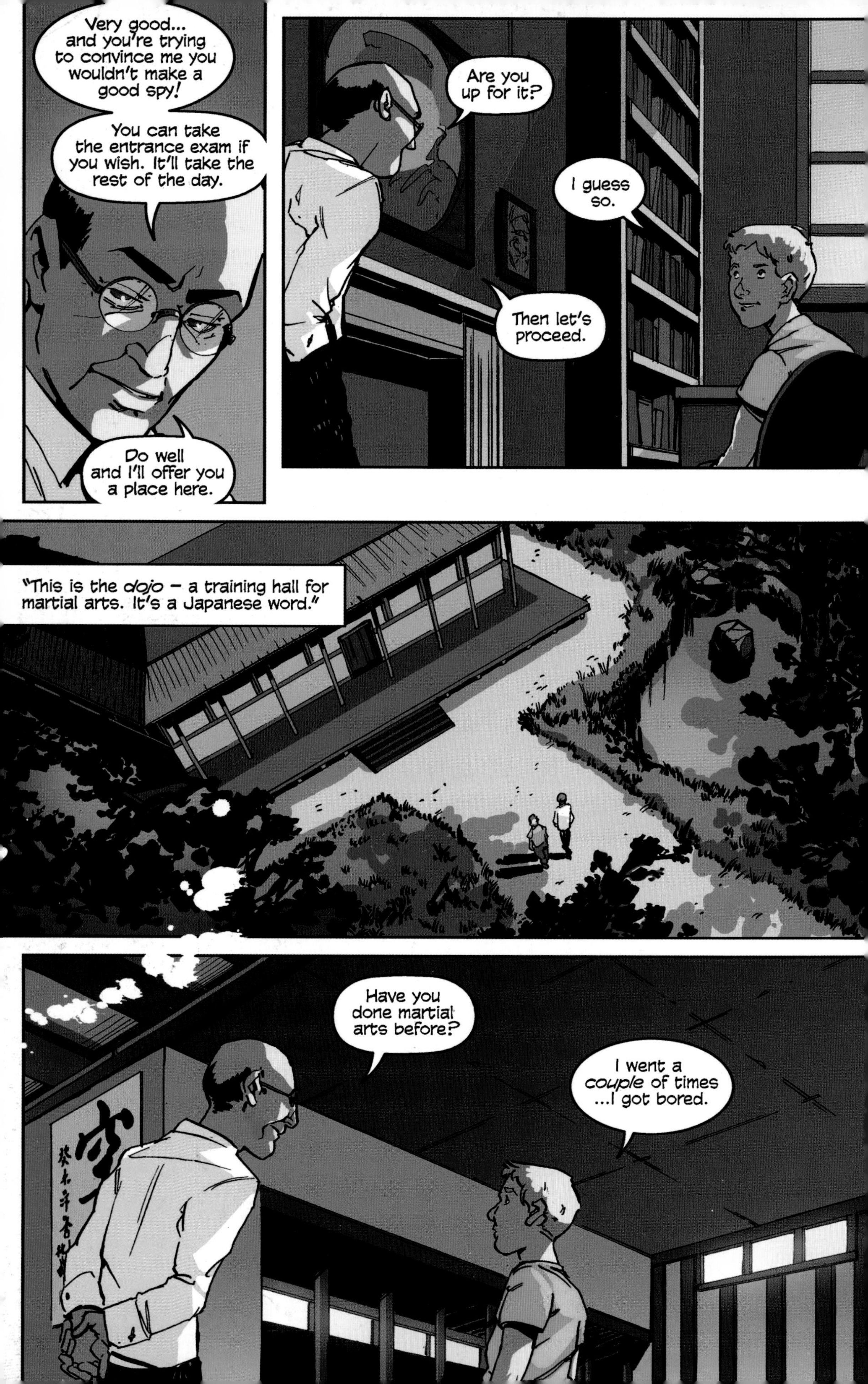
Very good... and you're trying to convince me you wouldn't make a good spy!
You can take the entrance exam if you wish. It'll take the rest of the day.
Do well and I'll offer you a place here.
Are you up for it?
I guess so.
Then let's proceed.
"This is the *dojo* – a training hall for martial arts. It's a Japanese word."
Have you done martial arts before?
I went a *couple* of times ...I got bored.

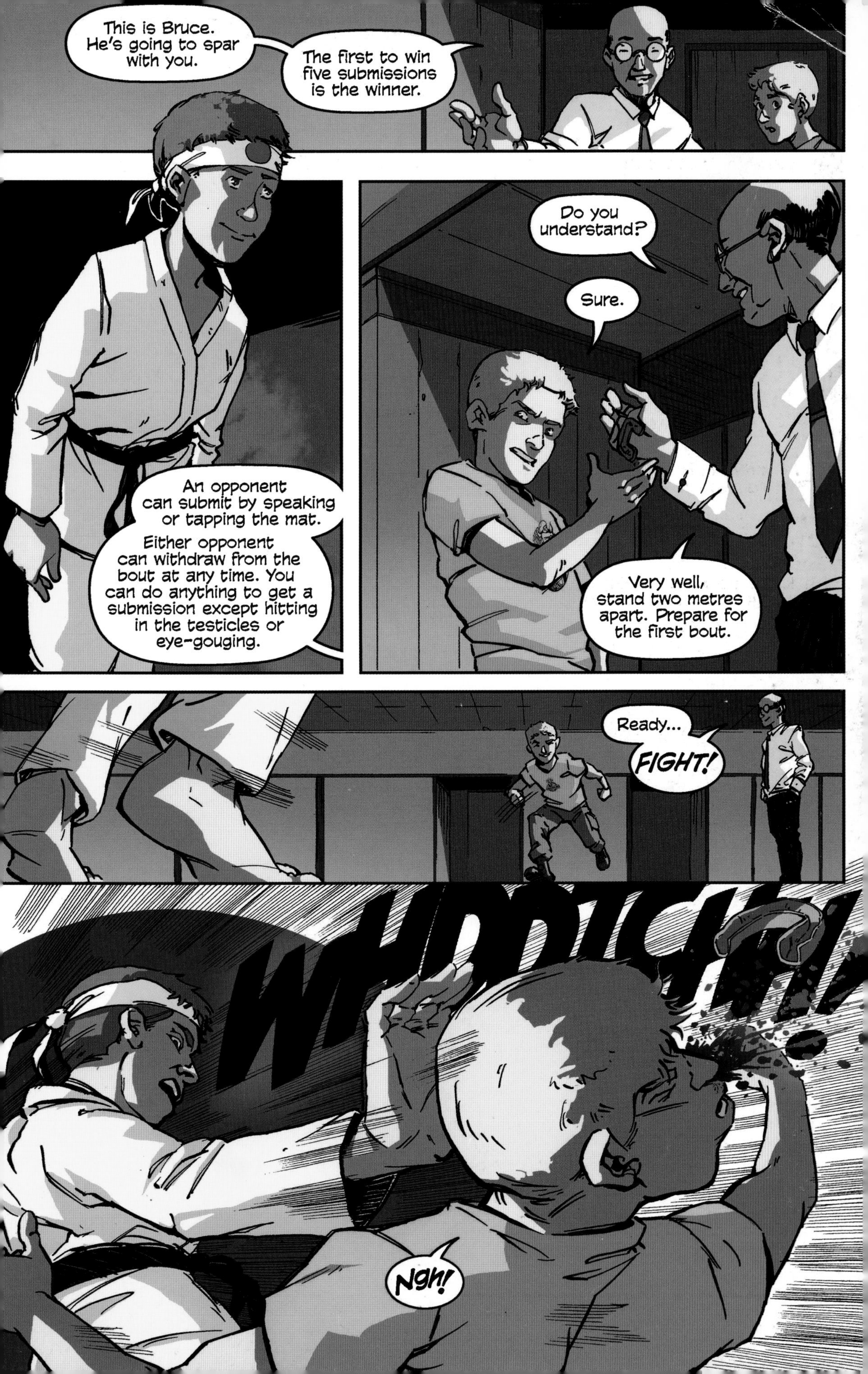
This is Bruce. He's going to spar with you.
The first to win five submissions is the winner.
An opponent can submit by speaking or tapping the mat.
Either opponent can withdraw from the bout at any time. You can do anything to get a submission except hitting in the testicles or eye-gouging.
Do you understand?
Sure.
Very well, stand two metres apart. Prepare for the first bout.
Ready...
FIGHT!
Ngh!

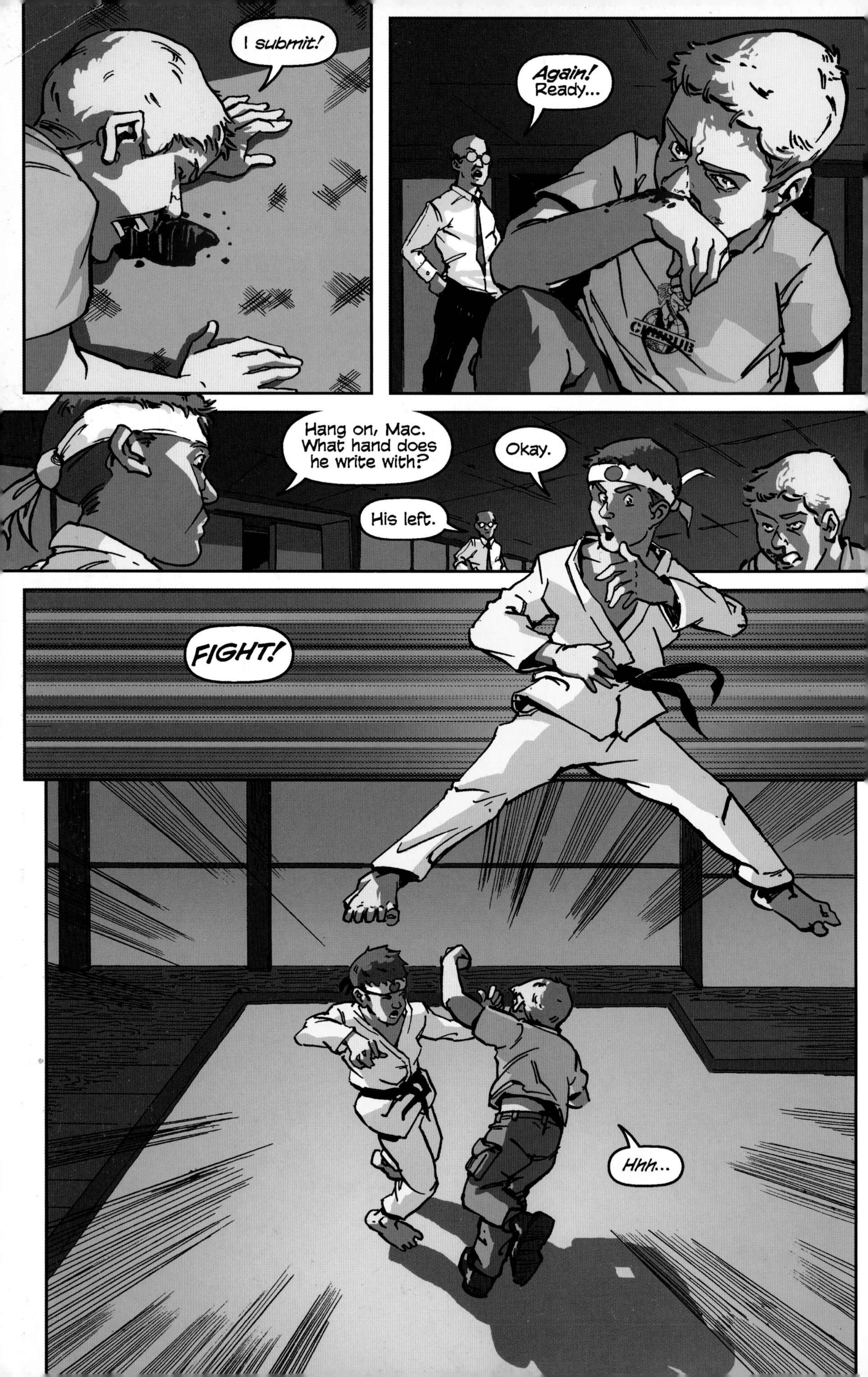
I submit!
Again! Ready...
Hang on, Mac. What hand does he write with?
His left.
Okay.
FIGHT!
Hhh...

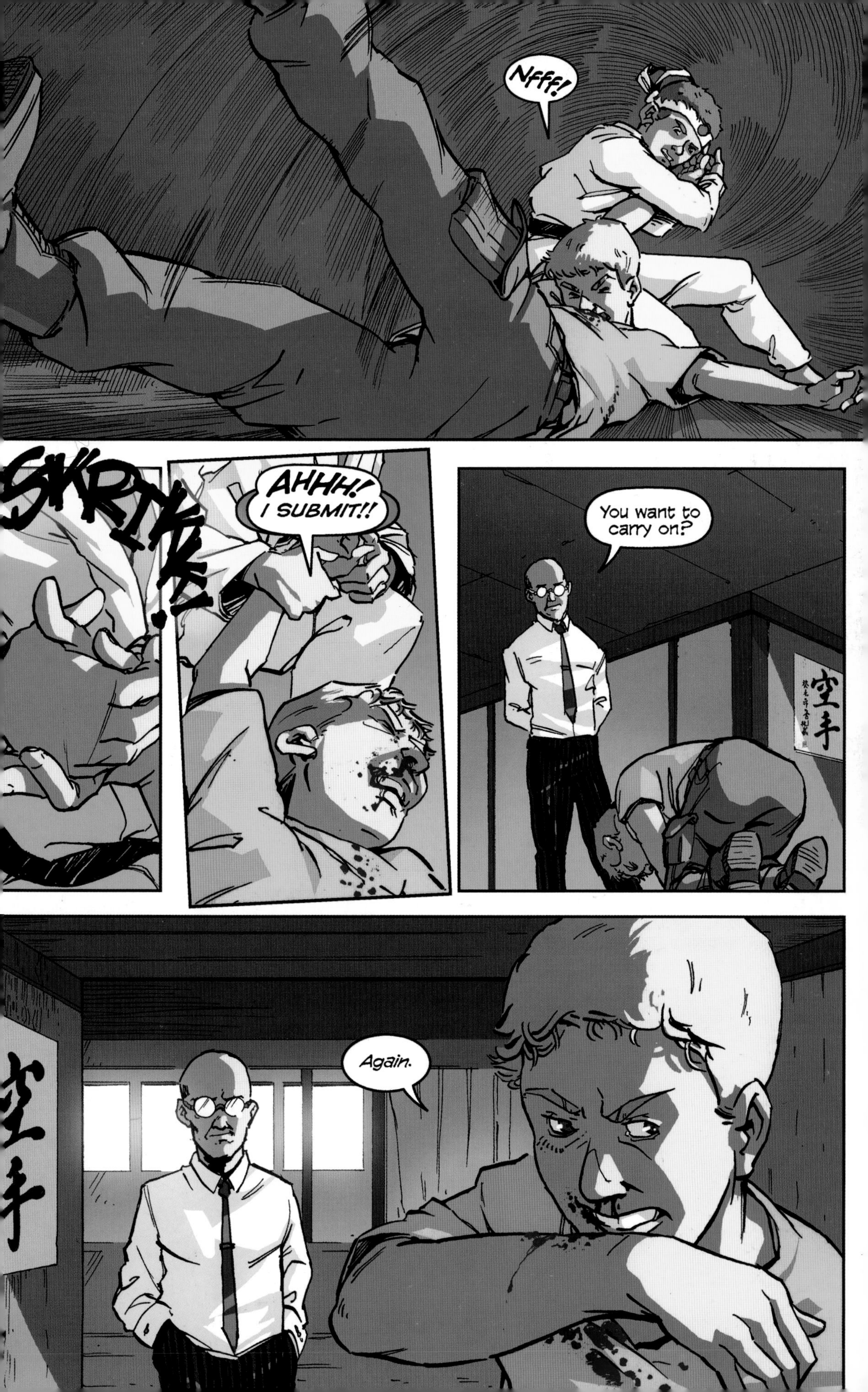
Nfff!
SKRIKK!
AHHH! I SUBMIT!!
You want to carry on?
空手
Again.
空手

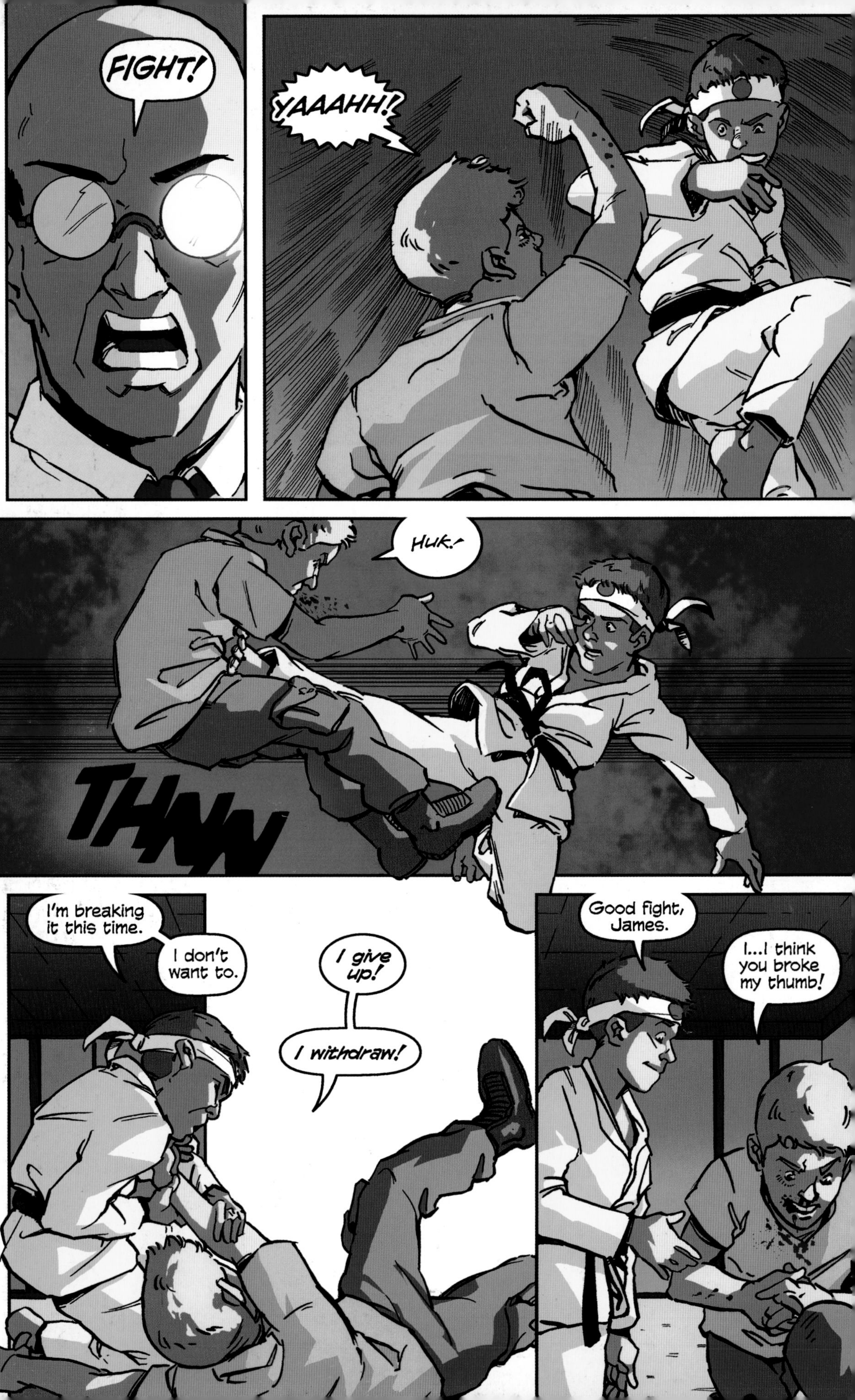

FIGHT!
YAAAHH!
HUK!
THNN
I'm breaking it this time.
I don't want to.
I give up!
I withdraw!
Good fight, James.
I...I think you broke my thumb!

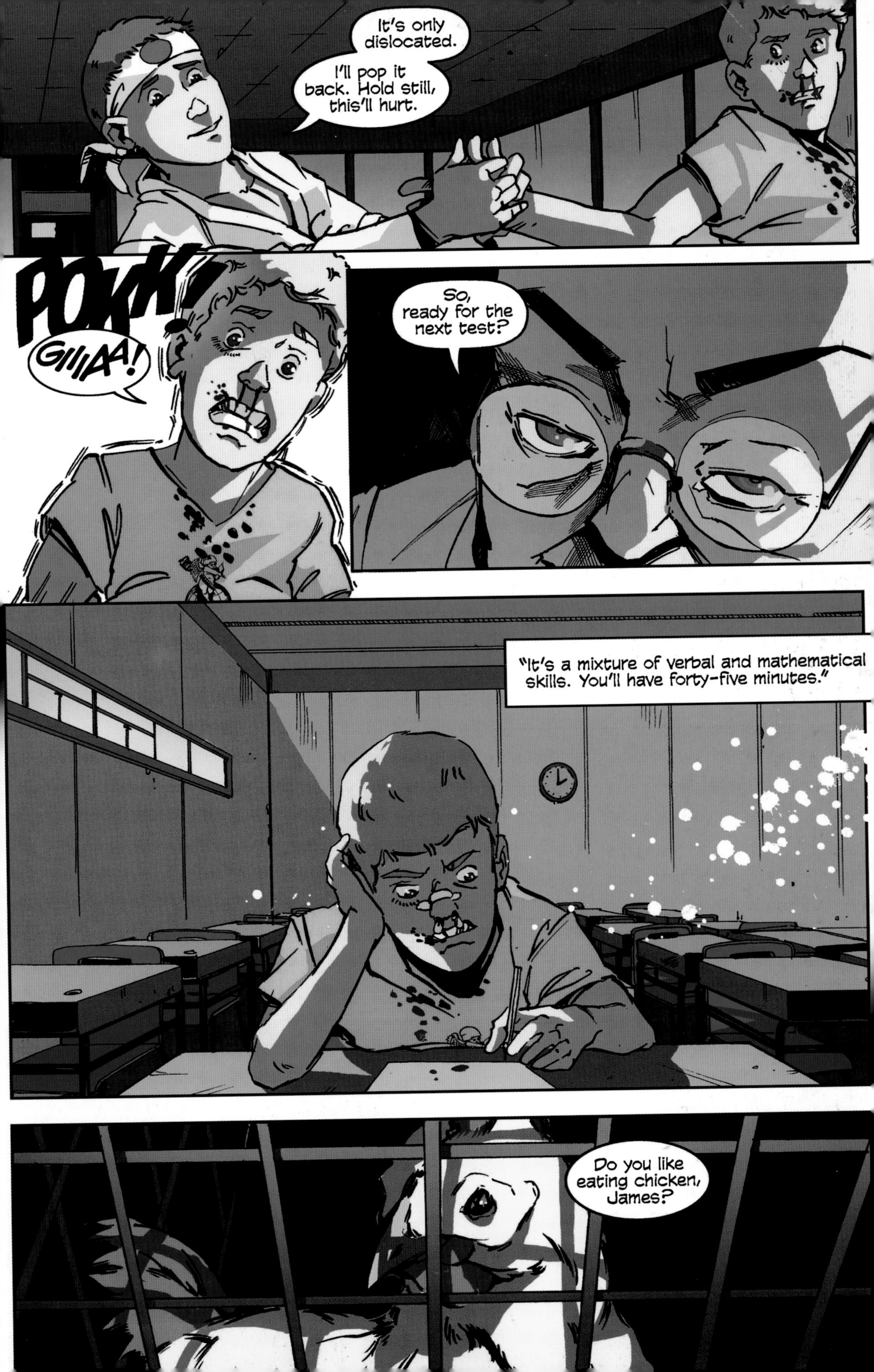
It's only dislocated.
I'll pop it back. Hold still, this'll hurt.
POKK!
GIIIAA!
So, ready for the next test?
"It's a mixture of verbal and mathematical skills. You'll have forty-five minutes."
Do you like eating chicken, James?

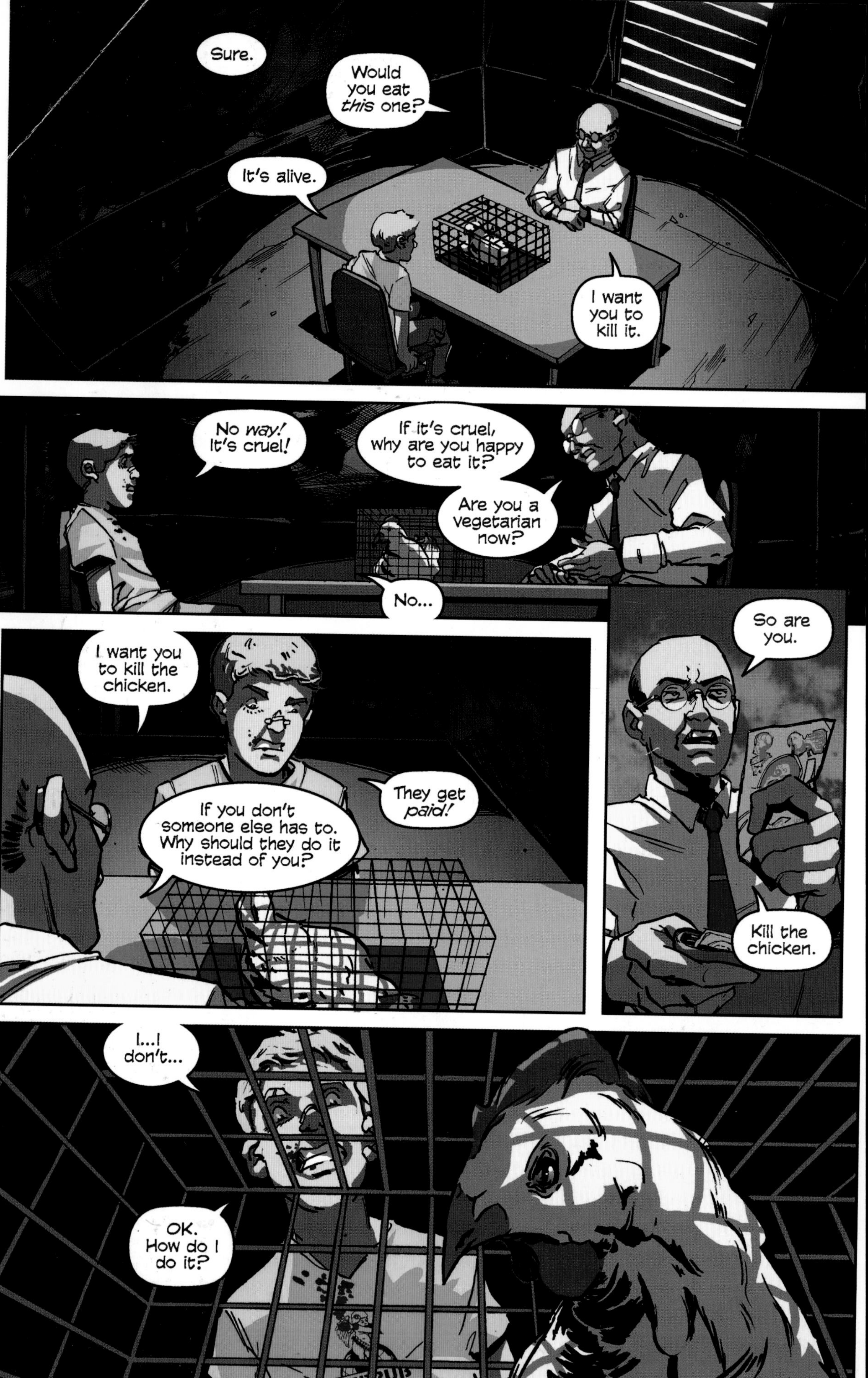

Sure.
Would you eat *this* one?
It's alive.
I want you to kill it.
No *way!* It's cruel!
If it's cruel, why are you happy to eat it?
Are you a vegetarian now?
No...
I want you to kill the chicken.
They get *paid!*
If you don't someone else has to. Why should they do it instead of you?
So are you.
Kill the chicken.
I...I don't...
OK. How do I do it?

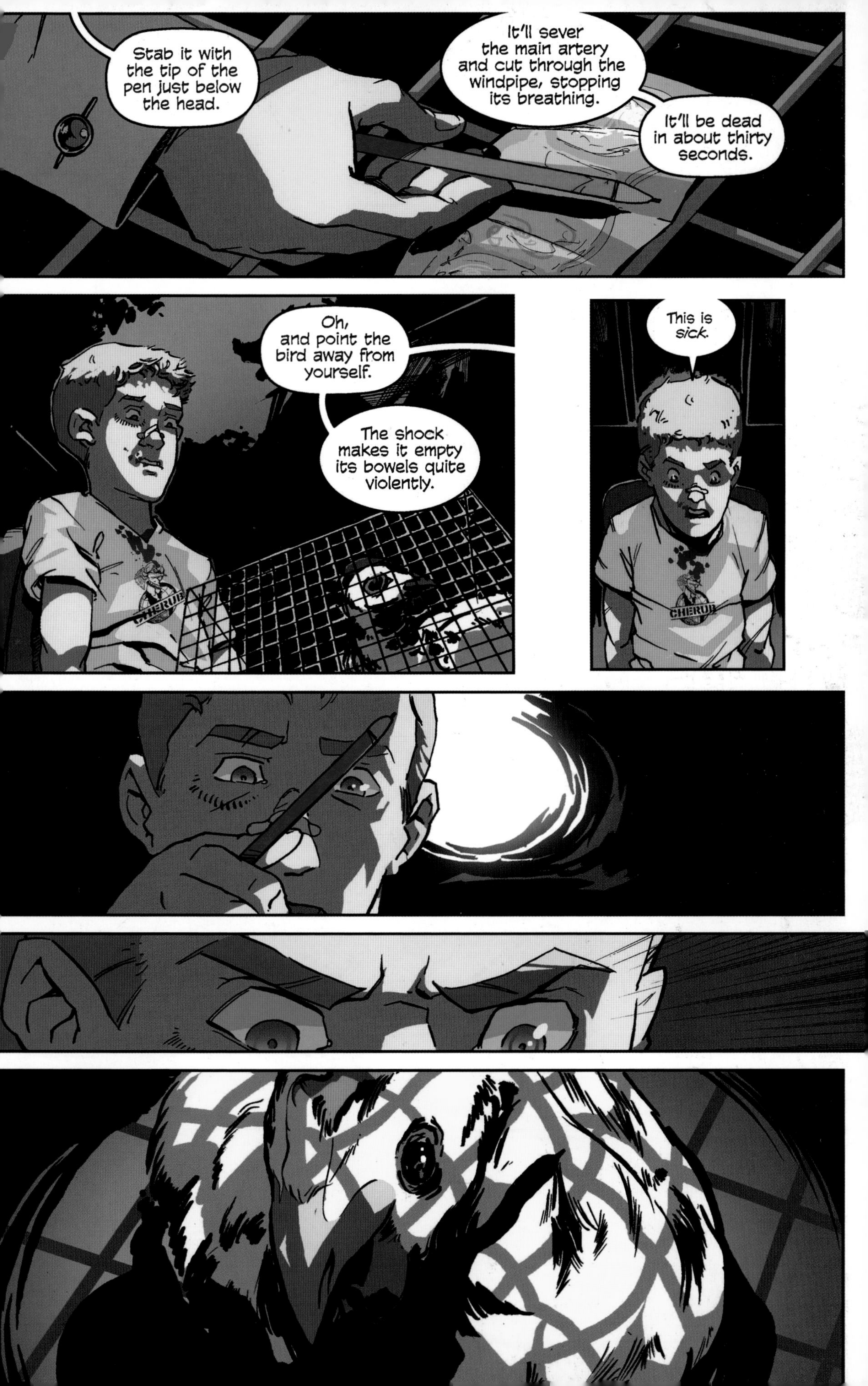

Stab it with the tip of the pen just below the head.
It'll sever the main artery and cut through the windpipe, stopping its breathing.
It'll be dead in about thirty seconds.
Oh, and point the bird away from yourself.
The shock makes it empty its bowels quite violently.
This is *sick*.
CHERUB
CHERUB

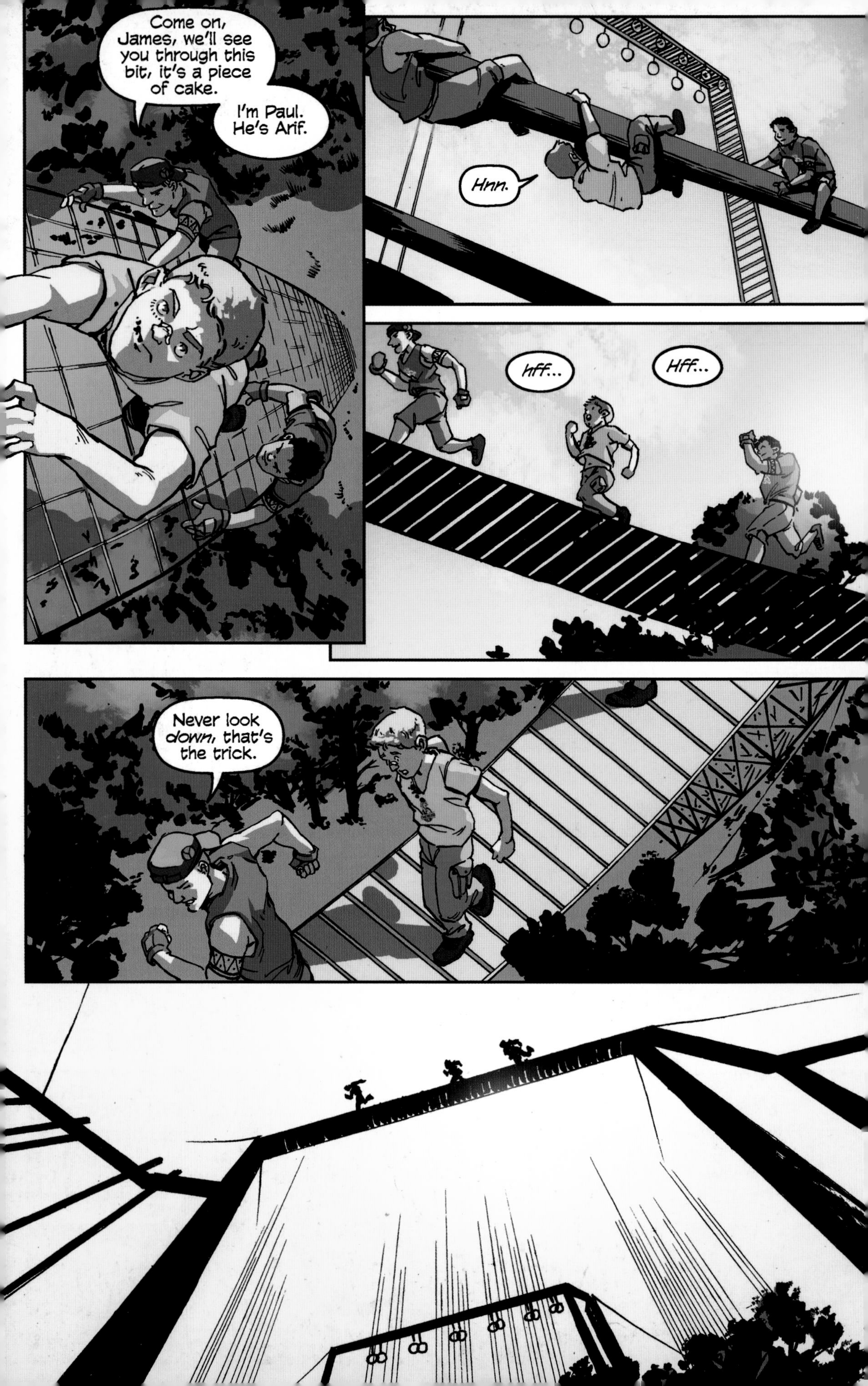
Come on, James, we'll see you through this bit, it's a piece of cake.
I'm Paul. He's Arif.
Hnn.
hff...
Hff...
Never look *down*, that's the trick.

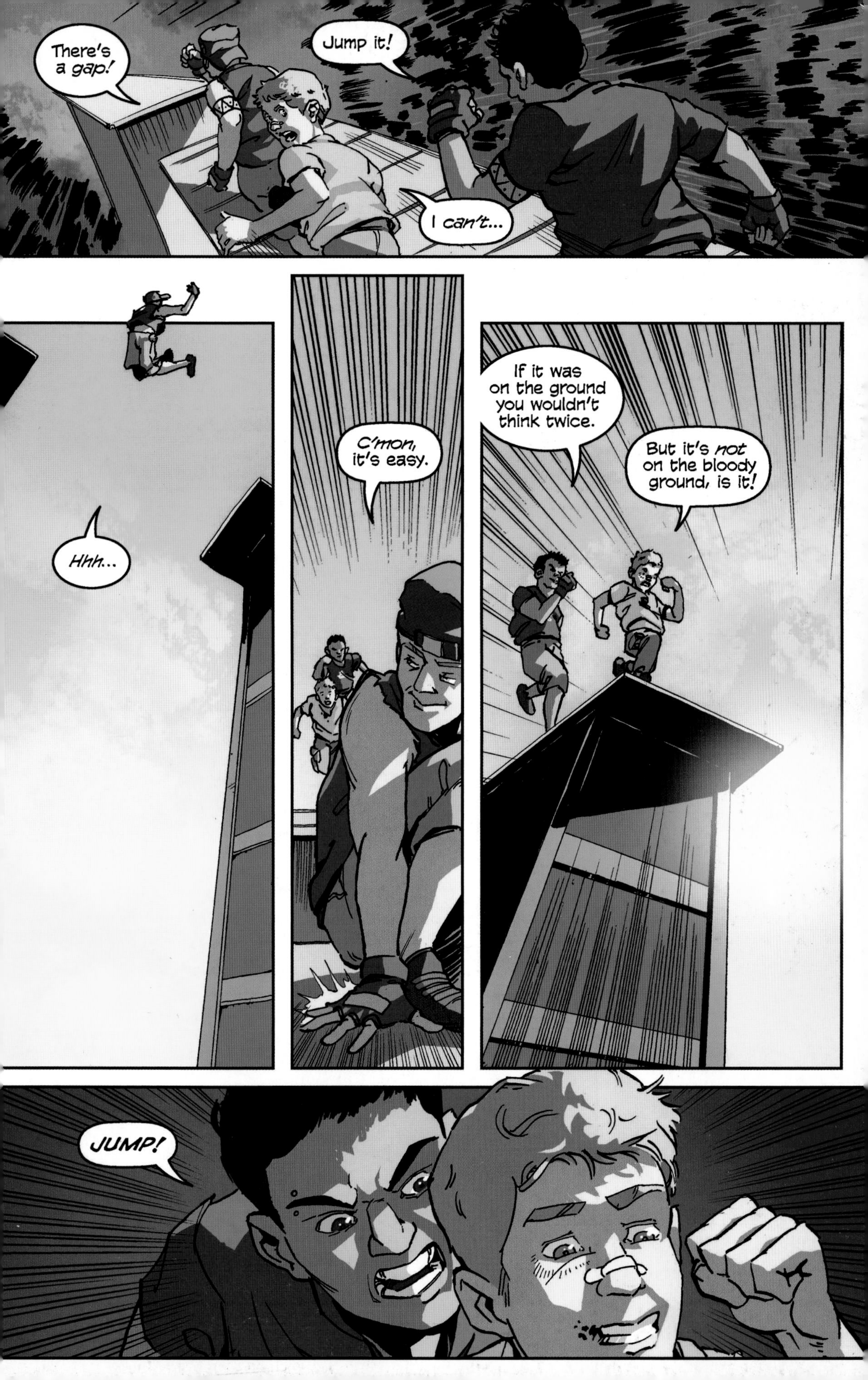
There's a gap!
Jump it!
I can't...
Hhh...
C'mon, it's easy.
If it was on the ground you wouldn't think twice.
But it's not on the bloody ground, is it!
JUMP!

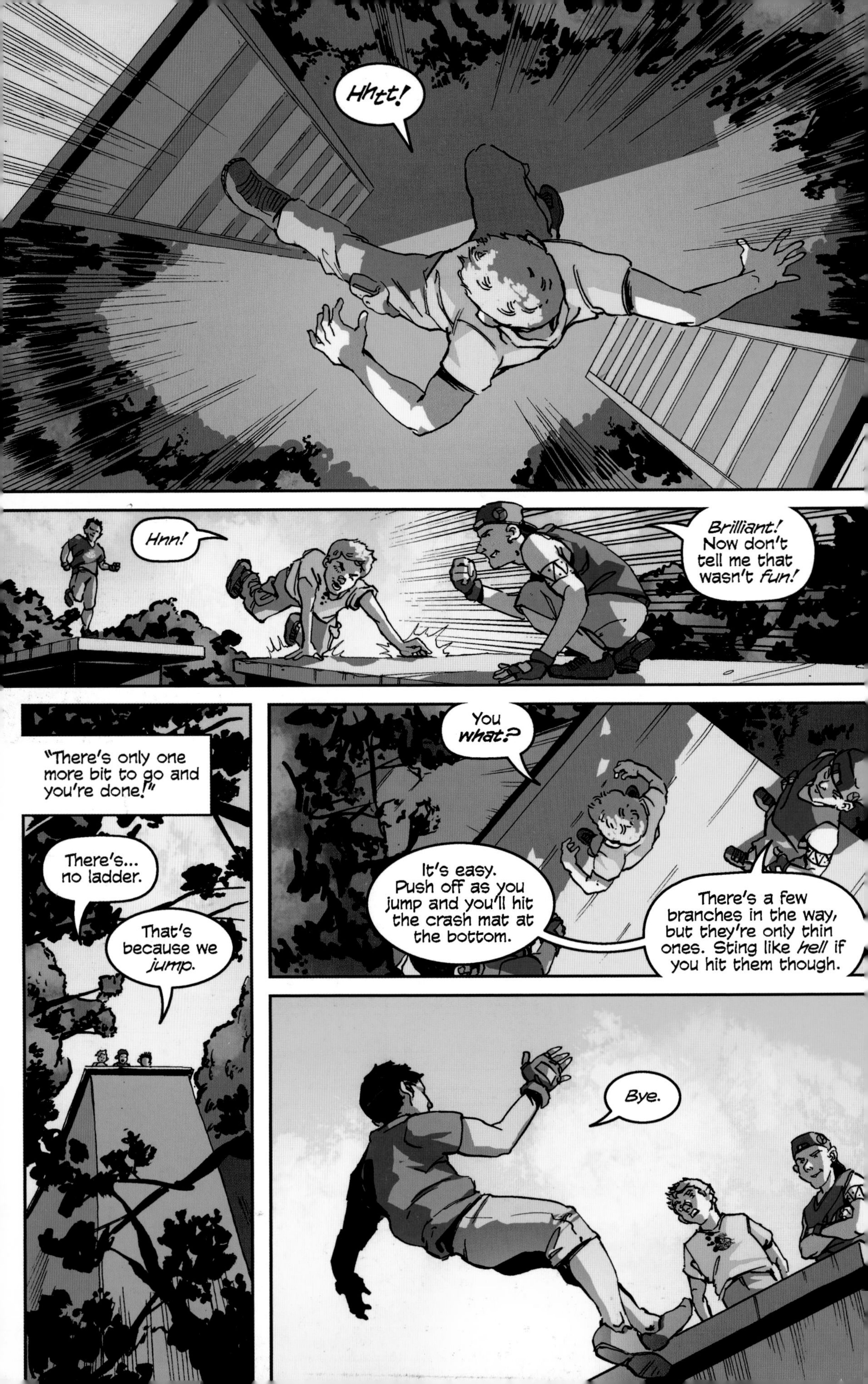
Hhtt!
Hnn!
Brilliant! Now don't tell me that wasn't fun!
"There's only one more bit to go and you're done!"
There's... no ladder.
That's because we jump.
You what?
It's easy. Push off as you jump and you'll hit the crash mat at the bottom.
There's a few branches in the way, but they're only thin ones. Sting like hell if you hit them though.
Bye.

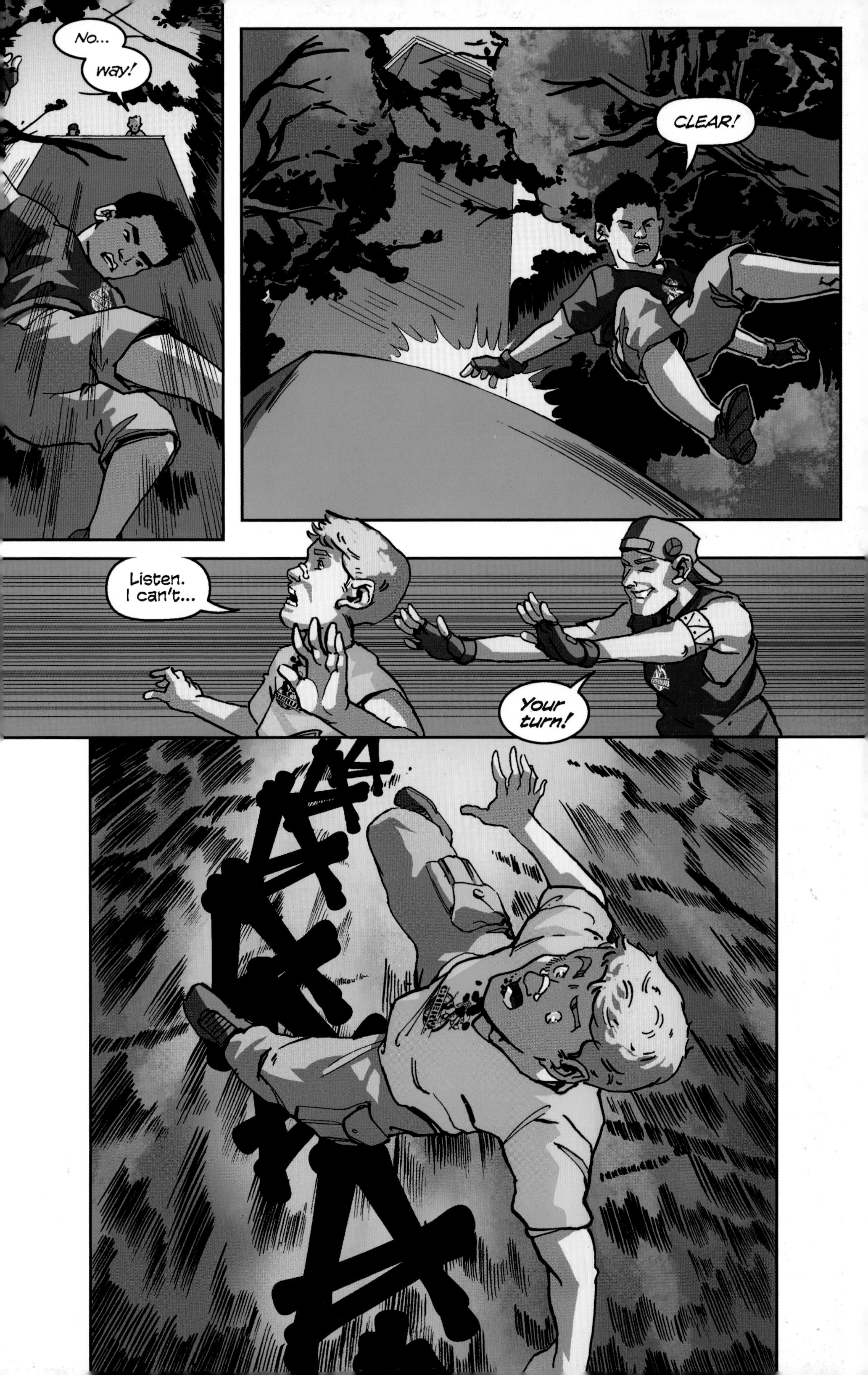
No... way!
CLEAR!
Listen. I can't...
Your turn!

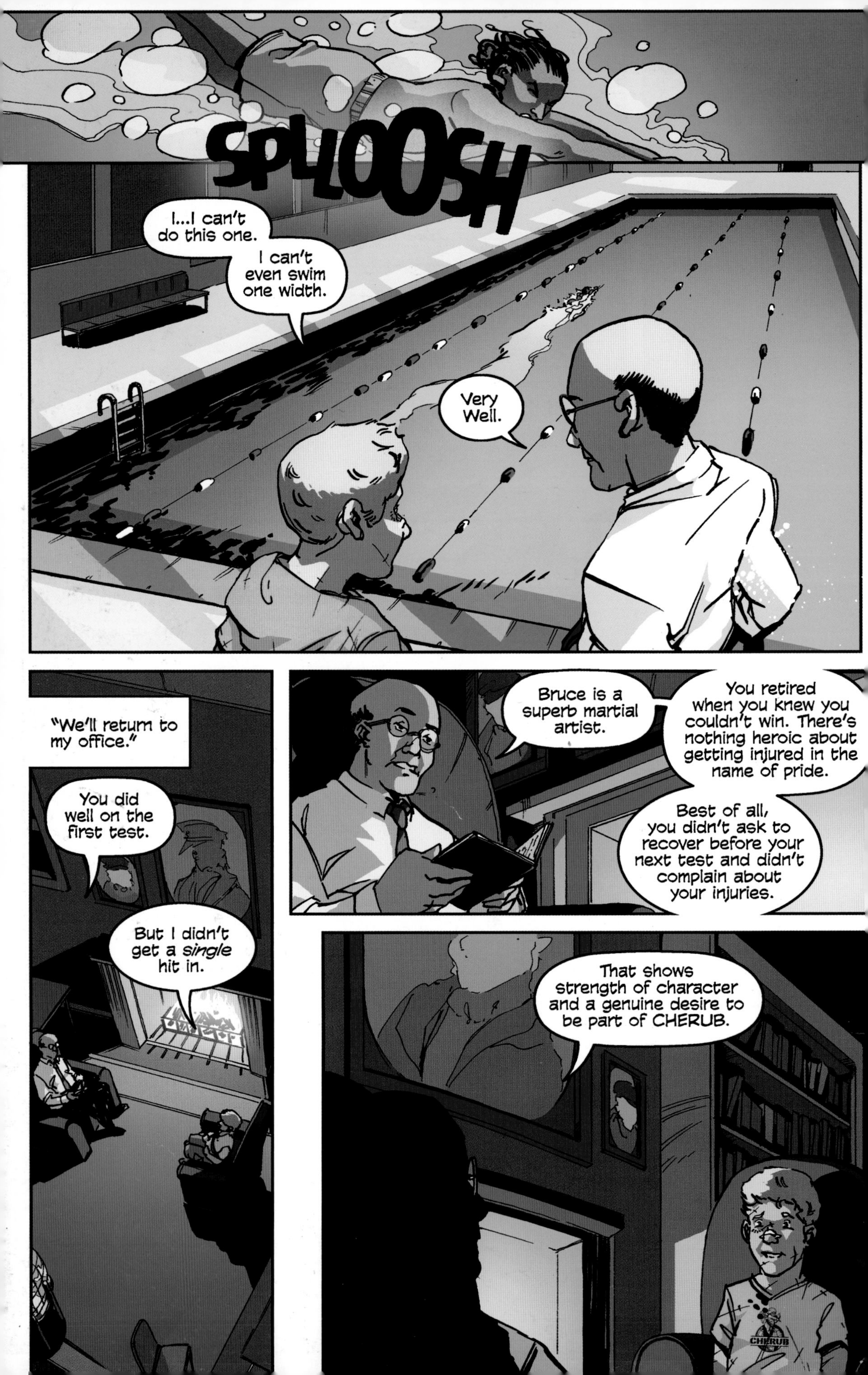
SPLLOOSH
I...I can't do this one.
I can't even swim one width.
Very Well.
"We'll return to my office."
You did well on the first test.
But I didn't get a single hit in.
Bruce is a superb martial artist.
You retired when you knew you couldn't win. There's nothing heroic about getting injured in the name of pride.
Best of all, you didn't ask to recover before your next test and didn't complain about your injuries.
That shows strength of character and a genuine desire to be part of CHERUB.
CHERUB

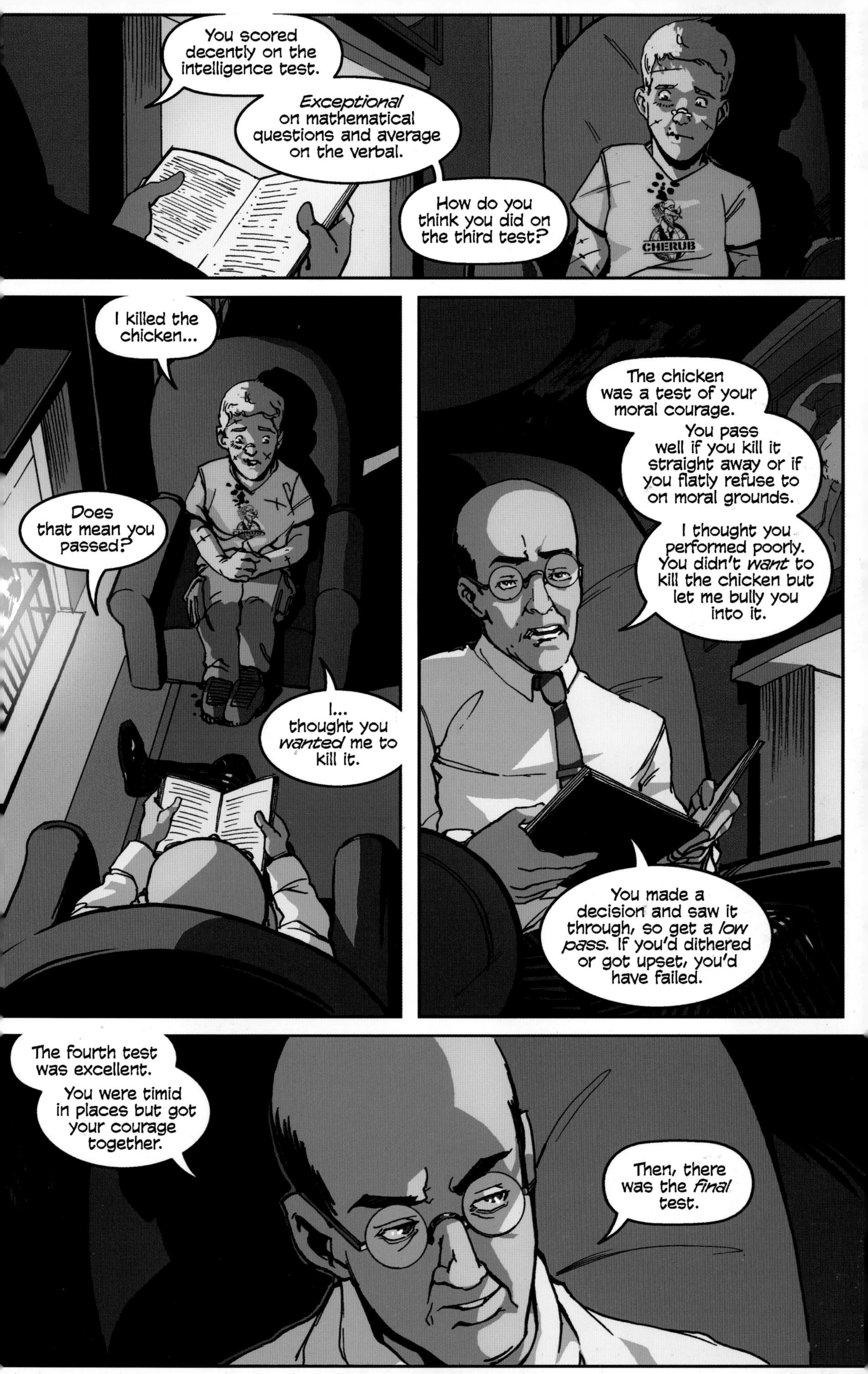
You scored decently on the intelligence test.
Exceptional on mathematical questions and average on the verbal.
How do you think you did on the third test?
I killed the chicken...
Does that mean you passed?
I... thought you *wanted* me to kill it.
The chicken was a test of your moral courage.
You pass well if you kill it straight away or if you flatly refuse to on moral grounds.
I thought you performed poorly. You didn't *want* to kill the chicken but let me bully you into it.
You made a decision and saw it through, so get a *low pass*. If you'd dithered or got upset, you'd have failed.
The fourth test was excellent.
You were timid in places but got your courage together.
Then, there was the *final* test.

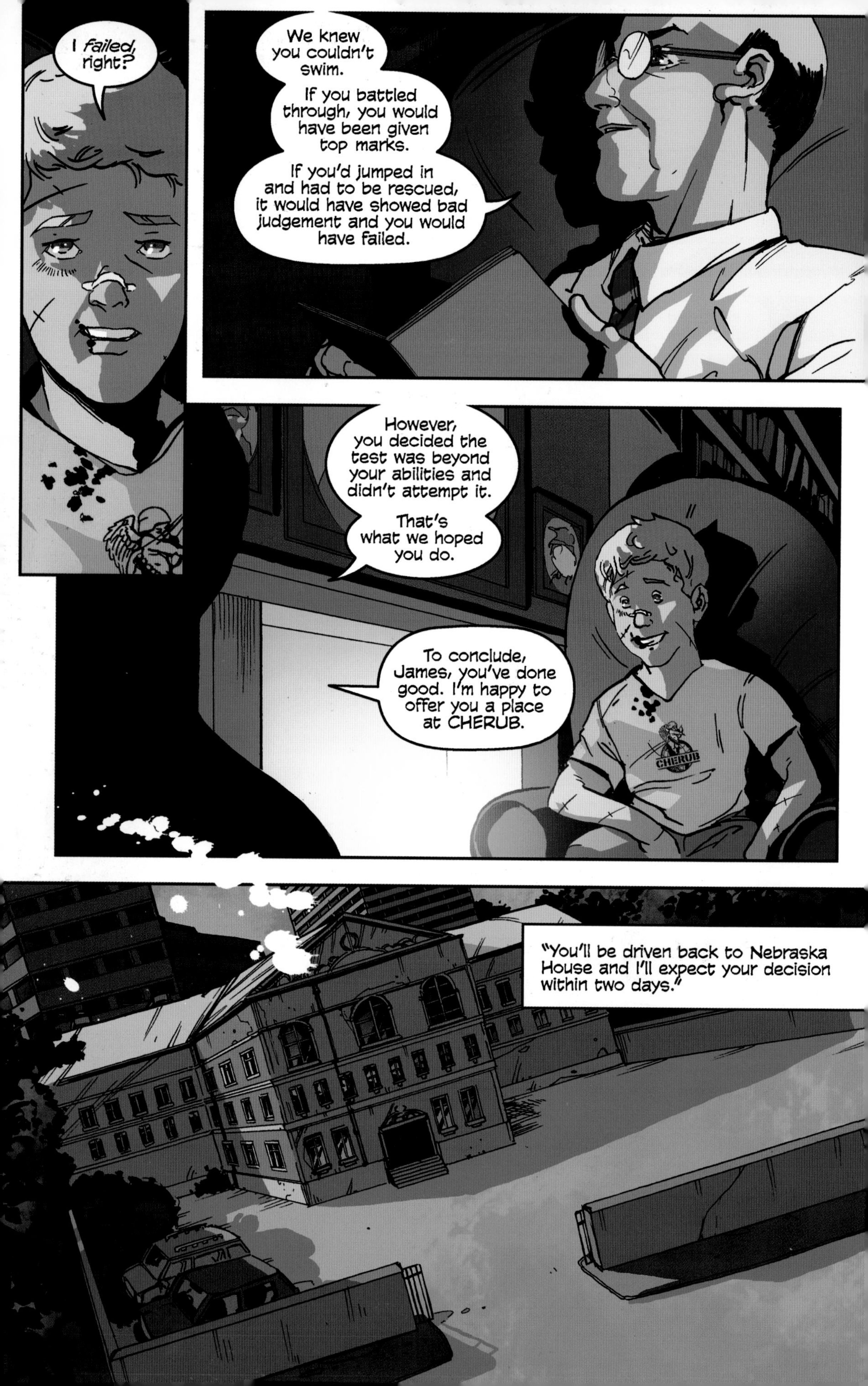
I *failed*, right?
We knew you couldn't swim.
If you battled through, you would have been given top marks.
If you'd jumped in and had to be rescued, it would have showed bad judgement and you would have failed.
However, you decided the test was beyond your abilities and didn't attempt it.
That's what we hoped you do.
To conclude, James, you've done good. I'm happy to offer you a place at CHERUB.
CHERUB
"You'll be driven back to Nebraska House and I'll expect your decision within two days."

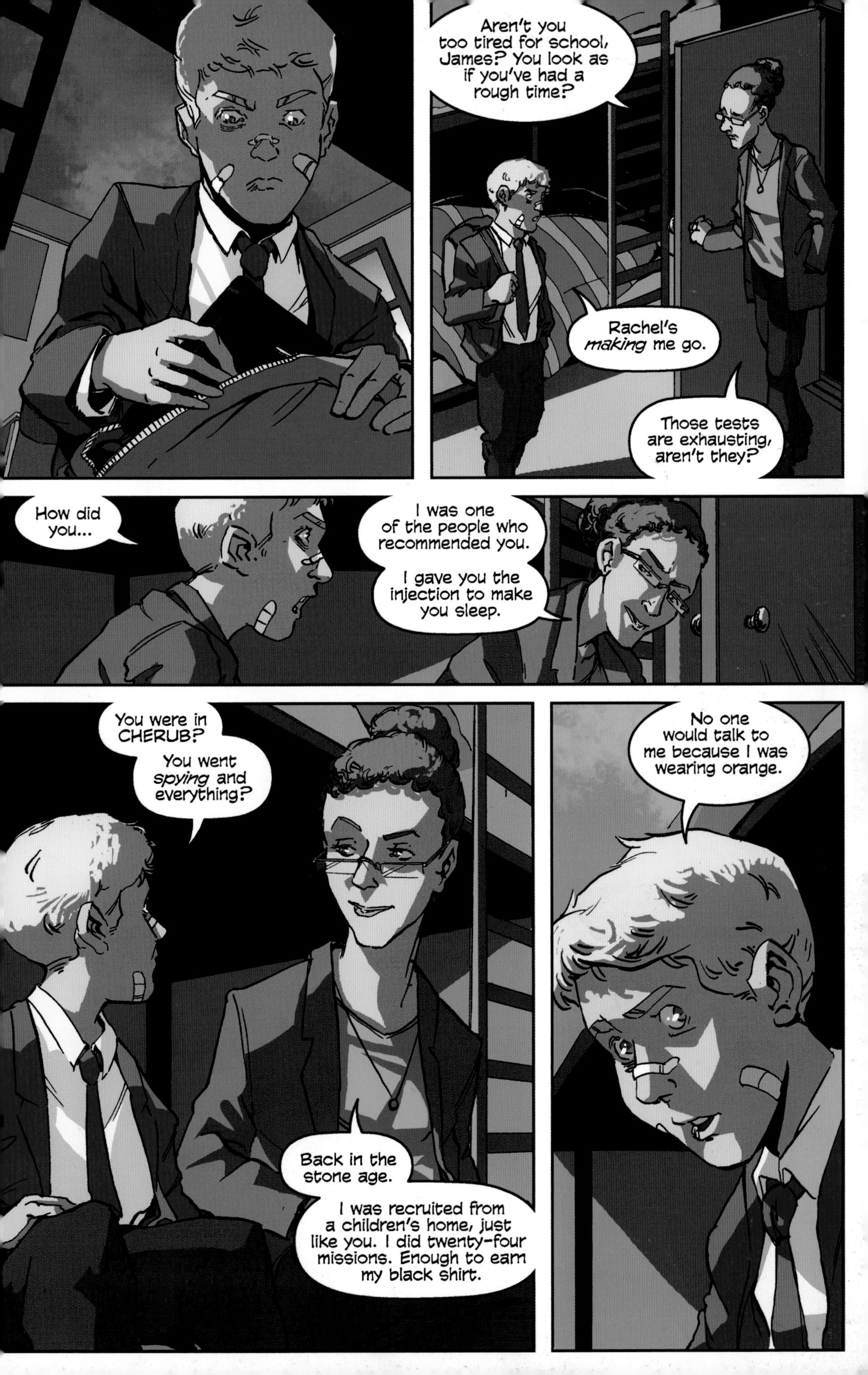

Aren't you too tired for school, James? You look as if you've had a rough time?
Rachel's *making* me go.
Those tests are exhausting, aren't they?
How did you...
I was one of the people who recommended you.
I gave you the injection to make you sleep.
You were in CHERUB?
You went *spying* and everything?
Back in the stone age.
I was recruited from a children's home, just like you. I did twenty-four missions. Enough to earn my black shirt.
No one would talk to me because I was wearing orange.

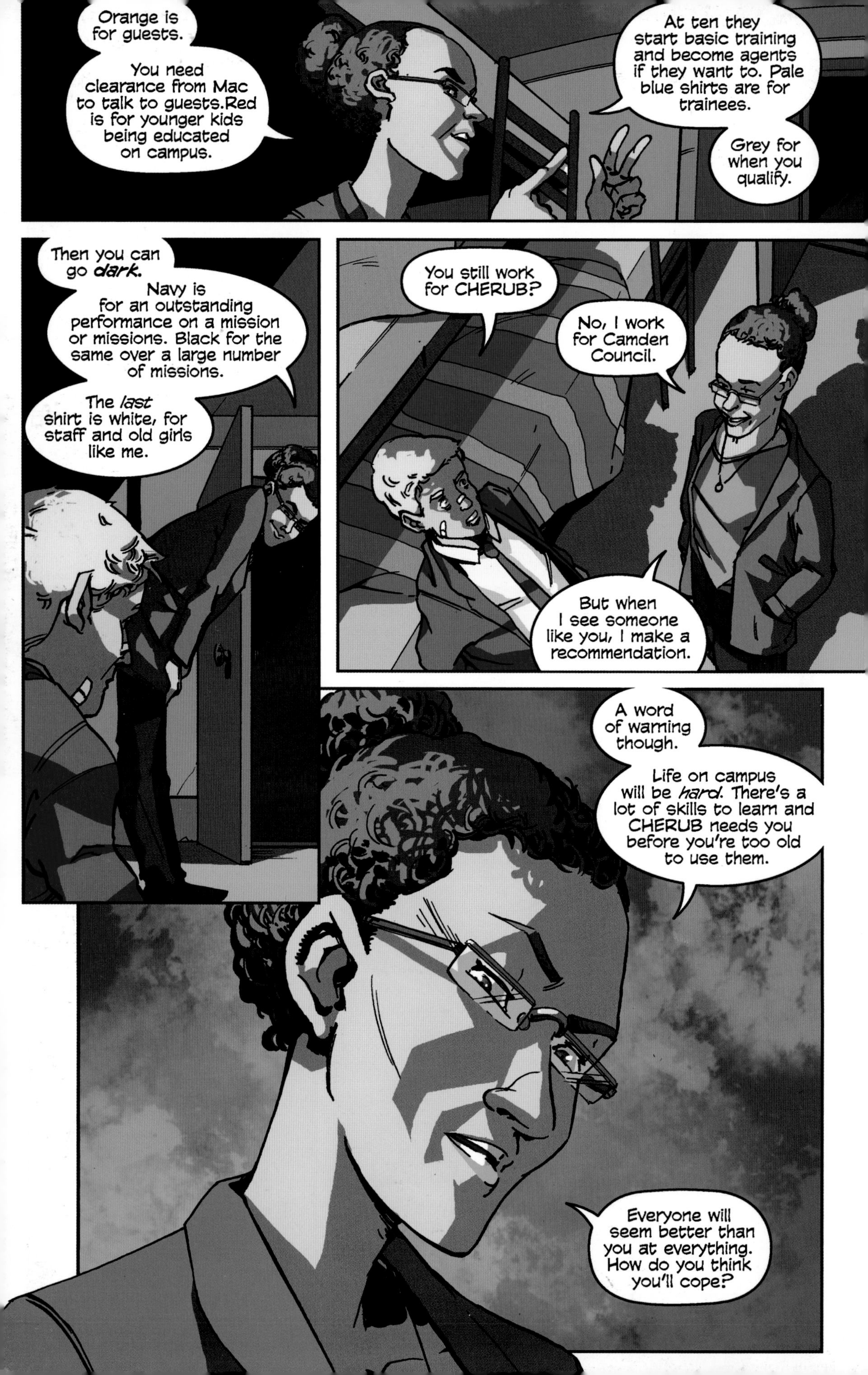
Orange is for guests.
You need clearance from Mac to talk to guests.Red is for younger kids being educated on campus.
At ten they start basic training and become agents if they want to. Pale blue shirts are for trainees.
Grey for when you qualify.
Then you can go *dark*.
Navy is for an outstanding performance on a mission or missions. Black for the same over a large number of missions.
The *last* shirt is white, for staff and old girls like me.
You still work for CHERUB?
No, I work for Camden Council.
But when I see someone like you, I make a recommendation.
A word of warning though.
Life on campus will be *hard*. There's a lot of skills to learn and CHERUB needs you before you're too old to use them.
Everyone will seem better than you at everything. How do you think you'll cope?

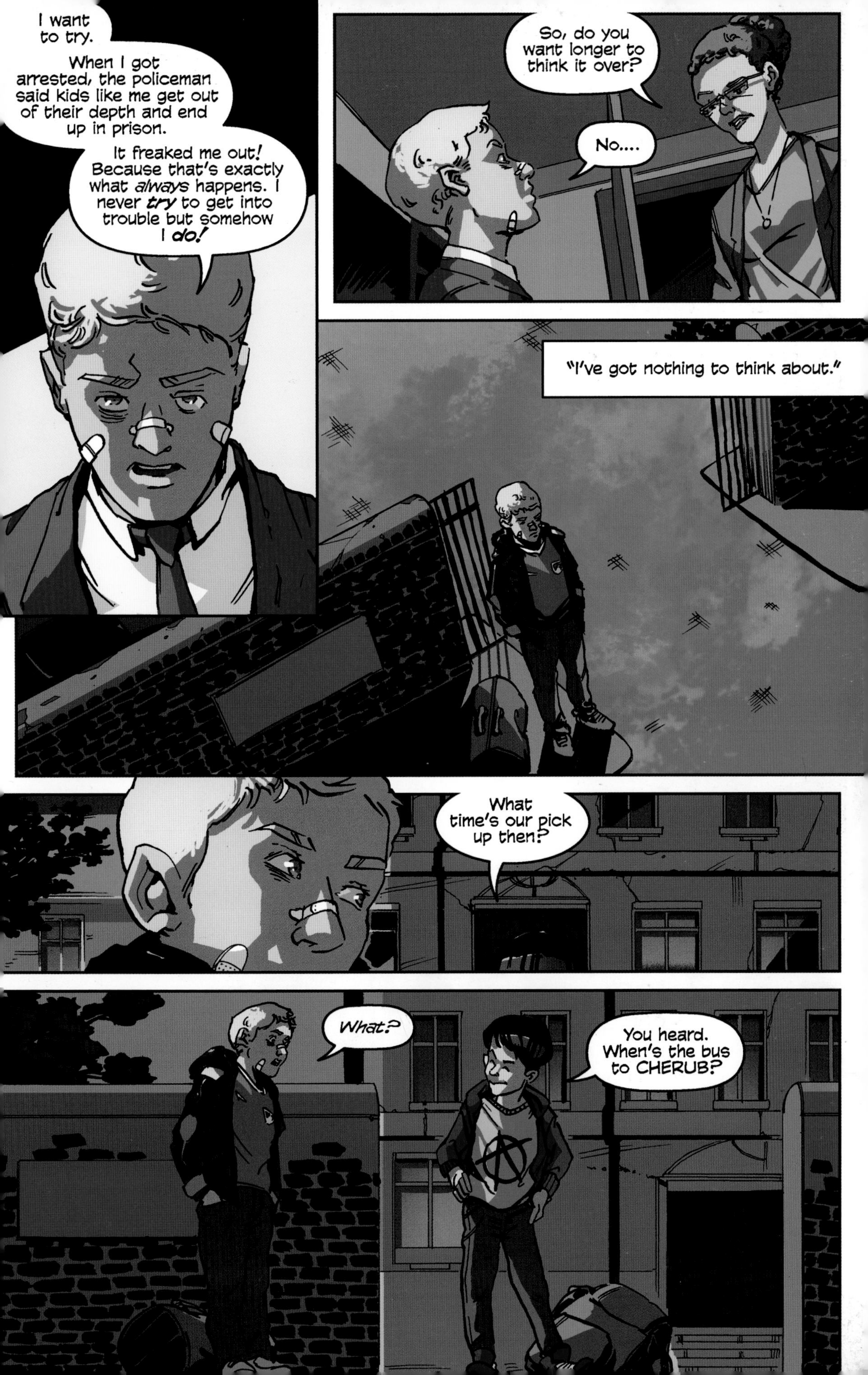
I want to try.
When I got arrested, the policeman said kids like me get out of their depth and end up in prison.
It freaked me out! Because that's exactly what *always* happens. I never ***try*** to get into trouble but somehow I ***do!***
So, do you want longer to think it over?
No....
"I've got nothing to think about."
What time's our pick up then?
What?
You heard. When's the bus to CHERUB?

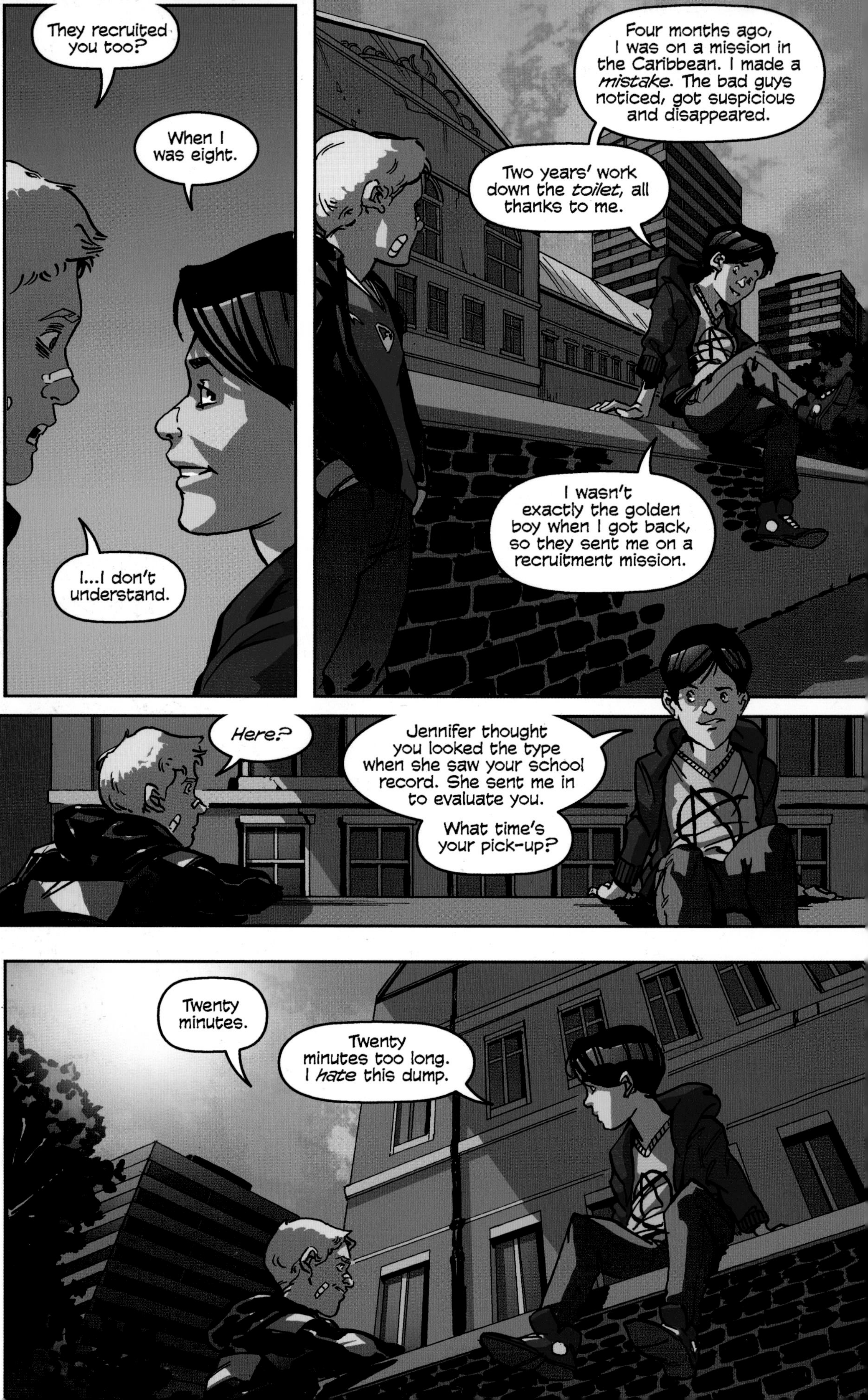
They recruited you too?
When I was eight.
I...I don't understand.
Four months ago, I was on a mission in the Caribbean. I made a *mistake*. The bad guys noticed, got suspicious and disappeared.
Two years' work down the *toilet*, all thanks to me.
I wasn't exactly the golden boy when I got back, so they sent me on a recruitment mission.
Here?
Jennifer thought you looked the type when she saw your school record. She sent me in to evaluate you.
What time's your pick-up?
Twenty minutes.
Twenty minutes too long. I *hate* this dump.

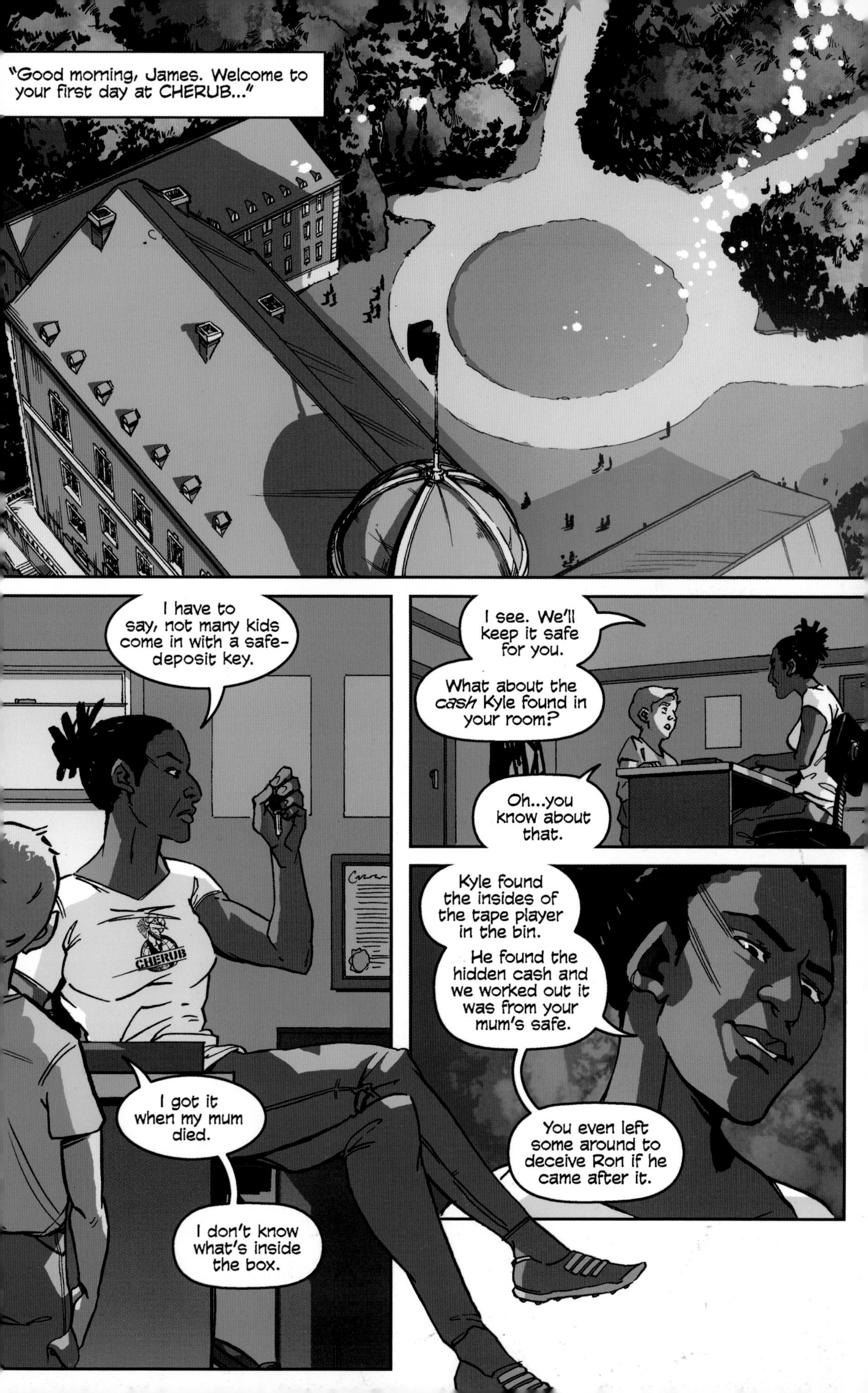
"Good morning, James. Welcome to your first day at CHERUB..."
I have to say, not many kids come in with a safe-deposit key.
I got it when my mum died.
I don't know what's inside the box.
I see. We'll keep it safe for you.
What about the *cash* Kyle found in your room?
Oh...you know about that.
Kyle found the insides of the tape player in the bin.
He found the hidden cash and we worked out it was from your mum's safe.
You even left some around to deceive Ron if he came after it.
CHERUB

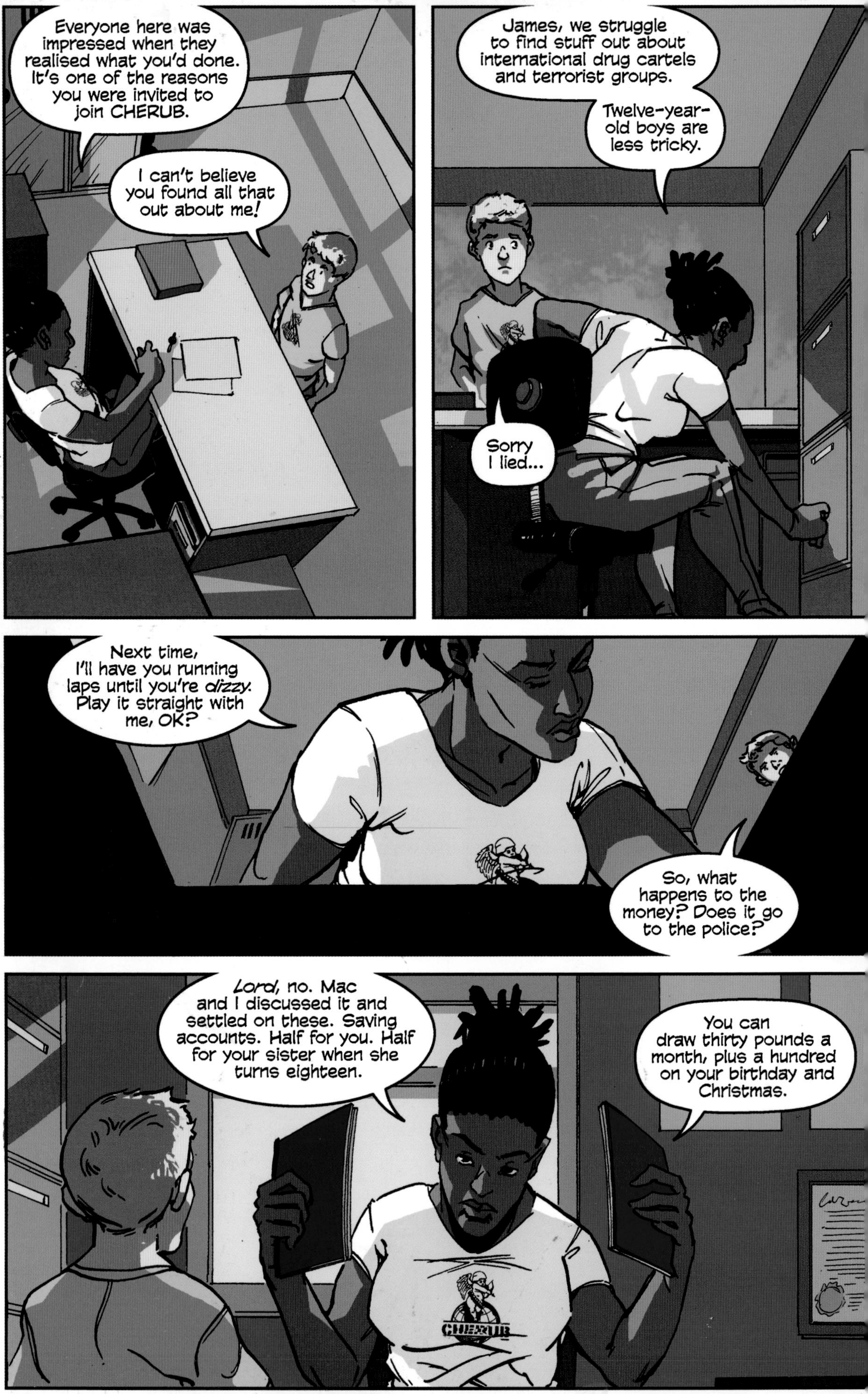
Everyone here was impressed when they realised what you'd done. It's one of the reasons you were invited to join CHERUB.
I can't believe you found all that out about me!
James, we struggle to find stuff out about international drug cartels and terrorist groups.
Twelve-year-old boys are less tricky.
Sorry I lied...
Next time, I'll have you running laps until you're *dizzy*. Play it straight with me, OK?
So, what happens to the money? Does it go to the police?
Lord, no. Mac and I discussed it and settled on these. Saving accounts. Half for you. Half for your sister when she turns eighteen.
You can draw thirty pounds a month, plus a hundred on your birthday and Christmas.
CHERUB

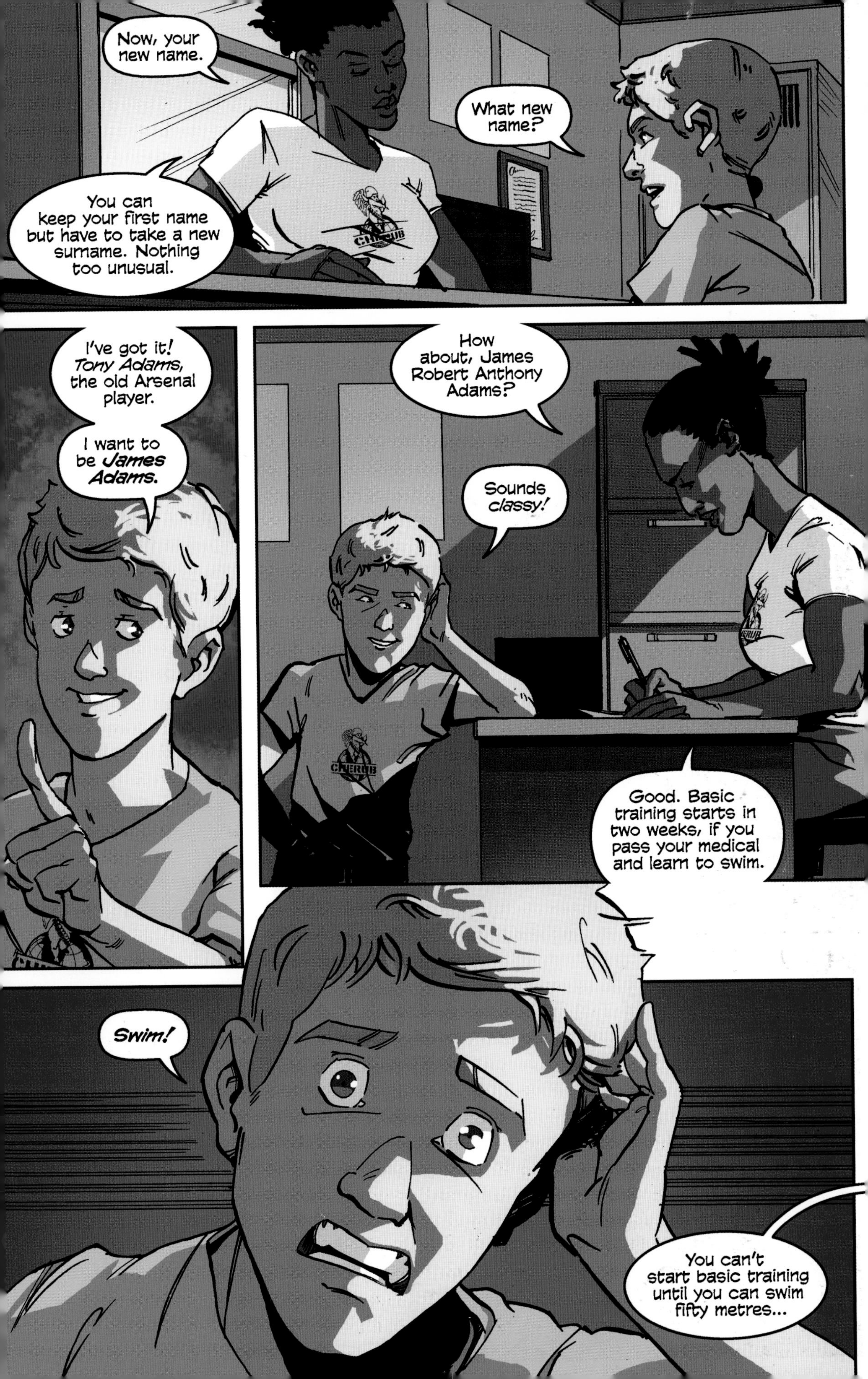
Now, your new name.
What new name?
You can keep your first name but have to take a new surname. Nothing too unusual.
I've got it! *Tony Adams*, the old Arsenal player.
I want to be ***James Adams.***
How about, James Robert Anthony Adams?
Sounds *classy!*
Good. Basic training starts in two weeks, if you pass your medical and learn to swim.
Swim!
You can't start basic training until you can swim fifty metres...

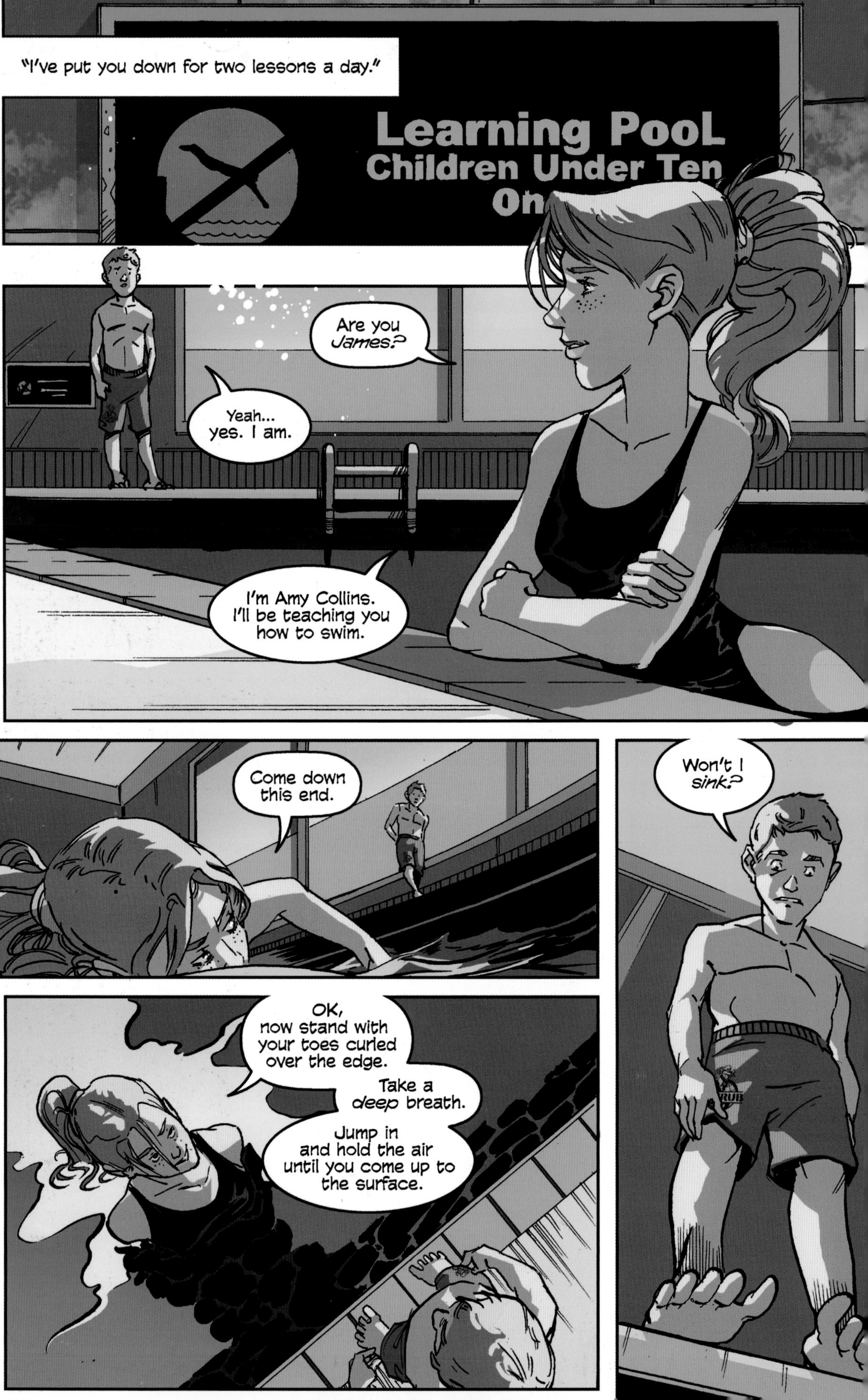
"I've put you down for two lessons a day."
Learning PooL
Children Under Ten
On
Are you *James?*
Yeah... yes. I am.
I'm Amy Collins. I'll be teaching you how to swim.
Come down this end.
Won't I *sink?*
OK, now stand with your toes curled over the edge.
Take a *deep* breath.
Jump in and hold the air until you come up to the surface.

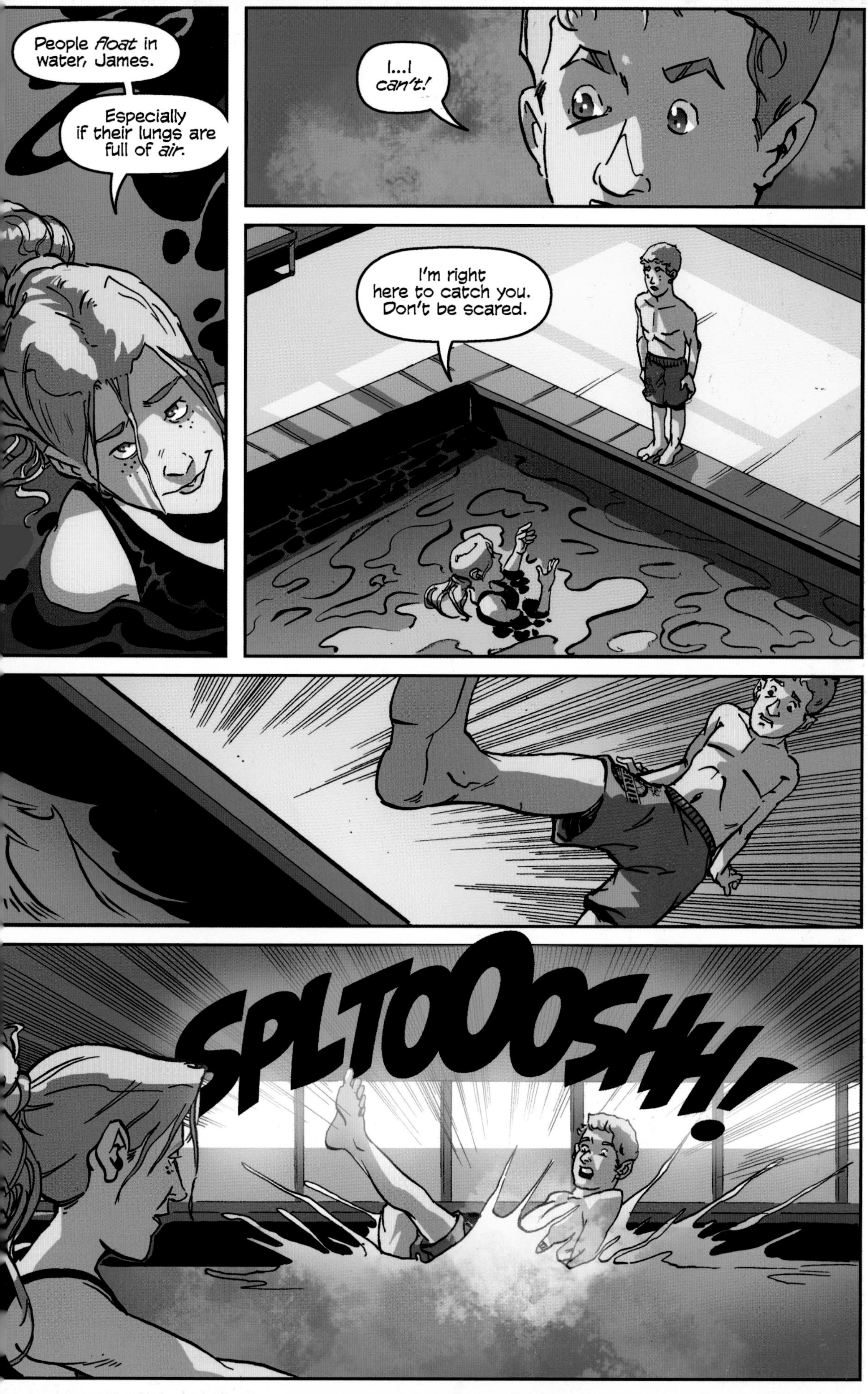
People *float* in water, James.
Especially if their lungs are full of *air*.
I...I *can't!*
I'm right here to catch you. Don't be scared.
SPLTOOOSH!

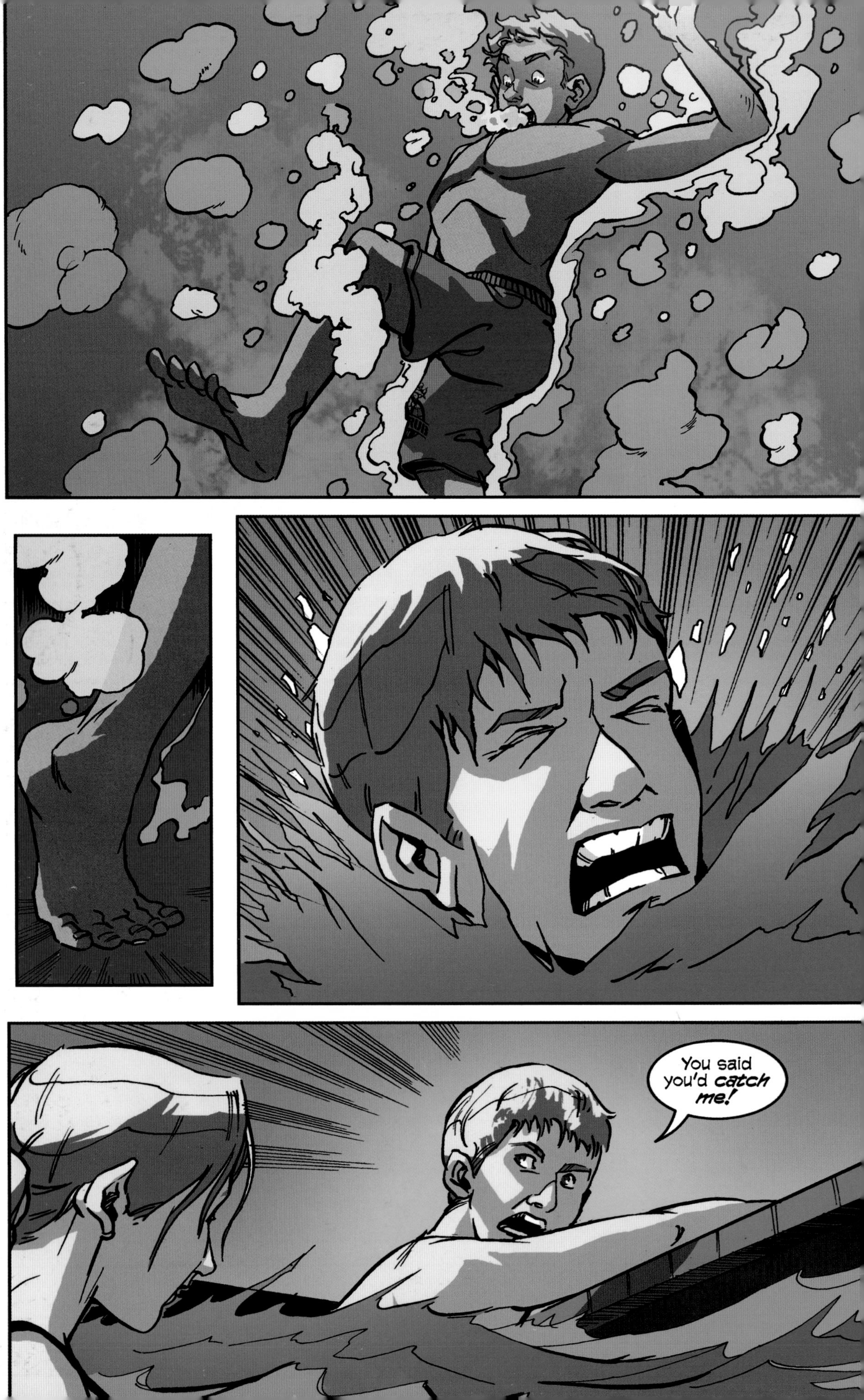
You said you'd *catch* *me!*

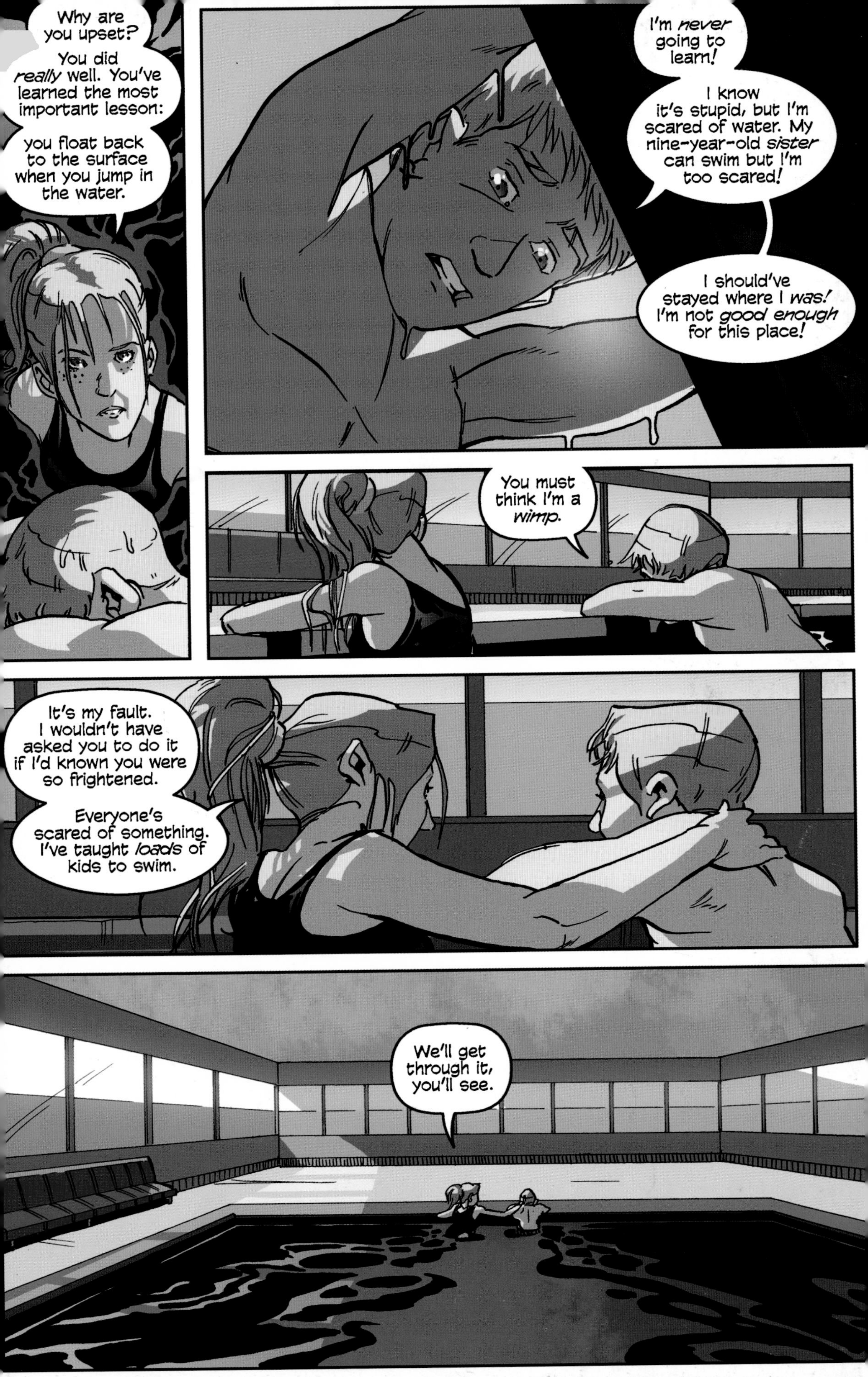
Why are you upset?
You did *really* well. You've learned the most important lesson:
you float back to the surface when you jump in the water.
I'm *never* going to learn!
I know it's stupid, but I'm scared of water. My nine-year-old *sister* can swim but I'm too scared!
I should've stayed where I *was!* I'm not *good enough* for this place!
You must think I'm a *wimp*.
It's my fault. I wouldn't have asked you to do it if I'd known you were so frightened.
Everyone's scared of something. I've taught *loads* of kids to swim.
We'll get through it, you'll see.

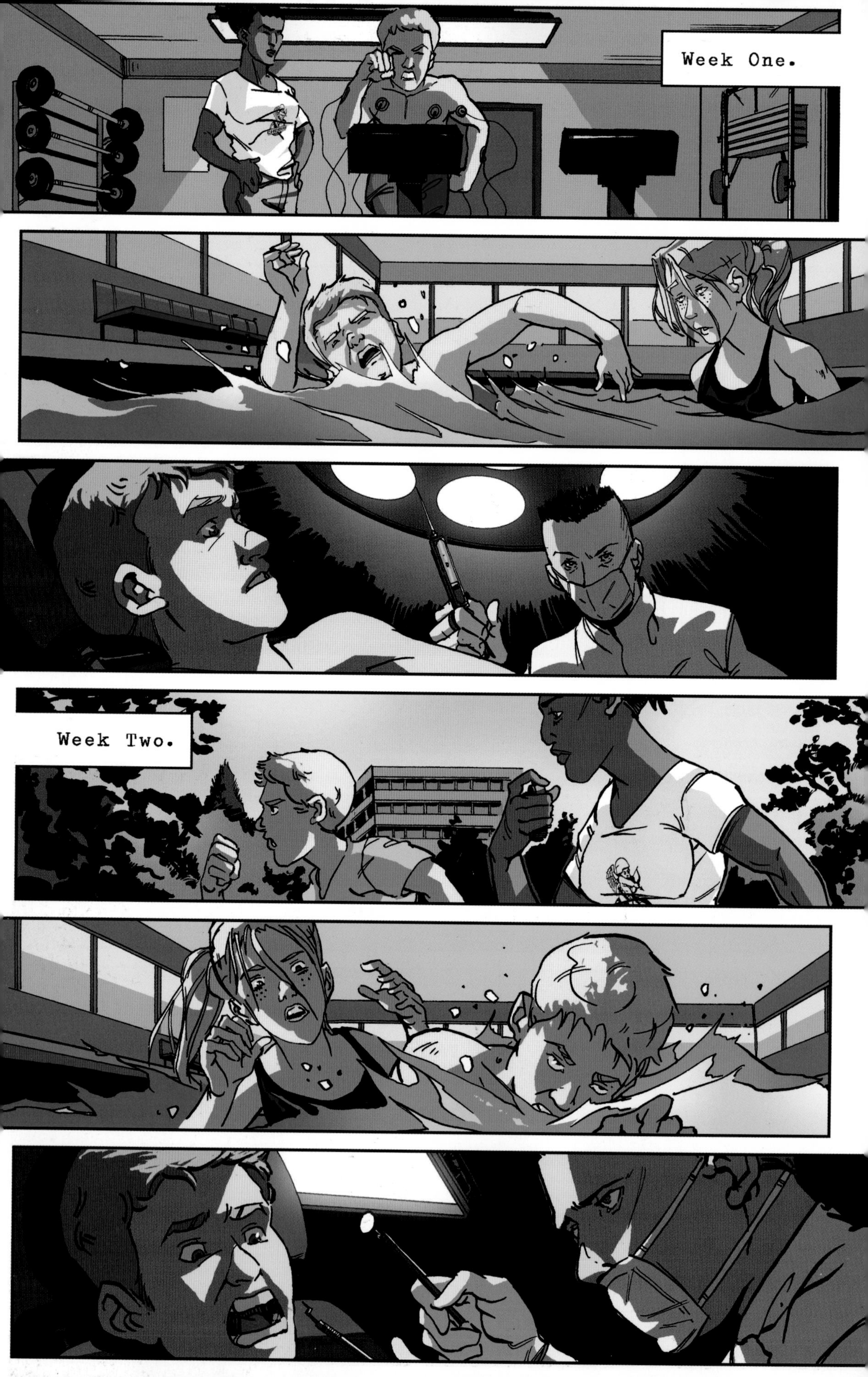
Week One.
Week Two.

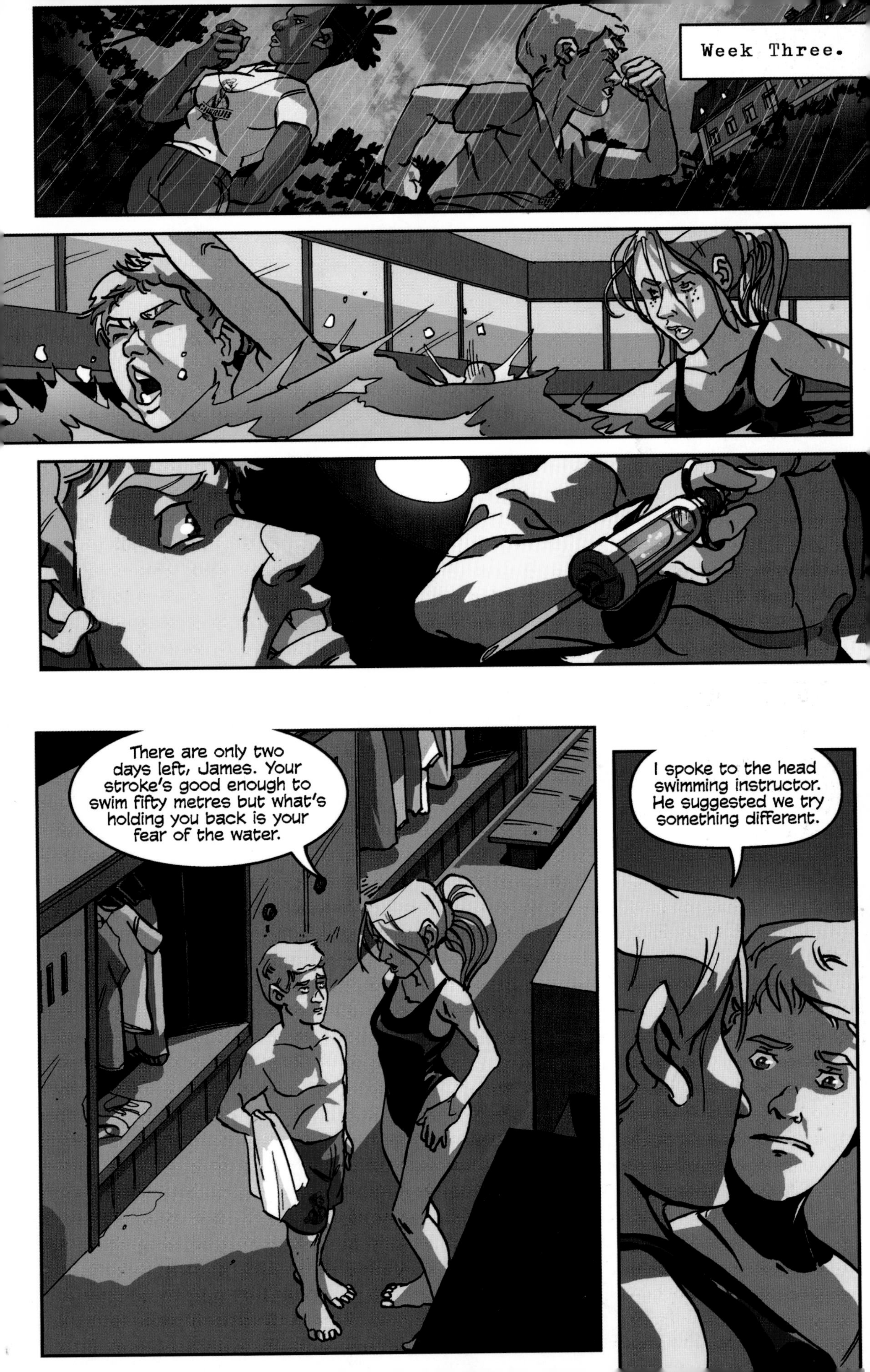
Week Three.
There are only two days left, James. Your stroke's good enough to swim fifty metres but what's holding you back is your fear of the water.
I spoke to the head swimming instructor. He suggested we try something different.

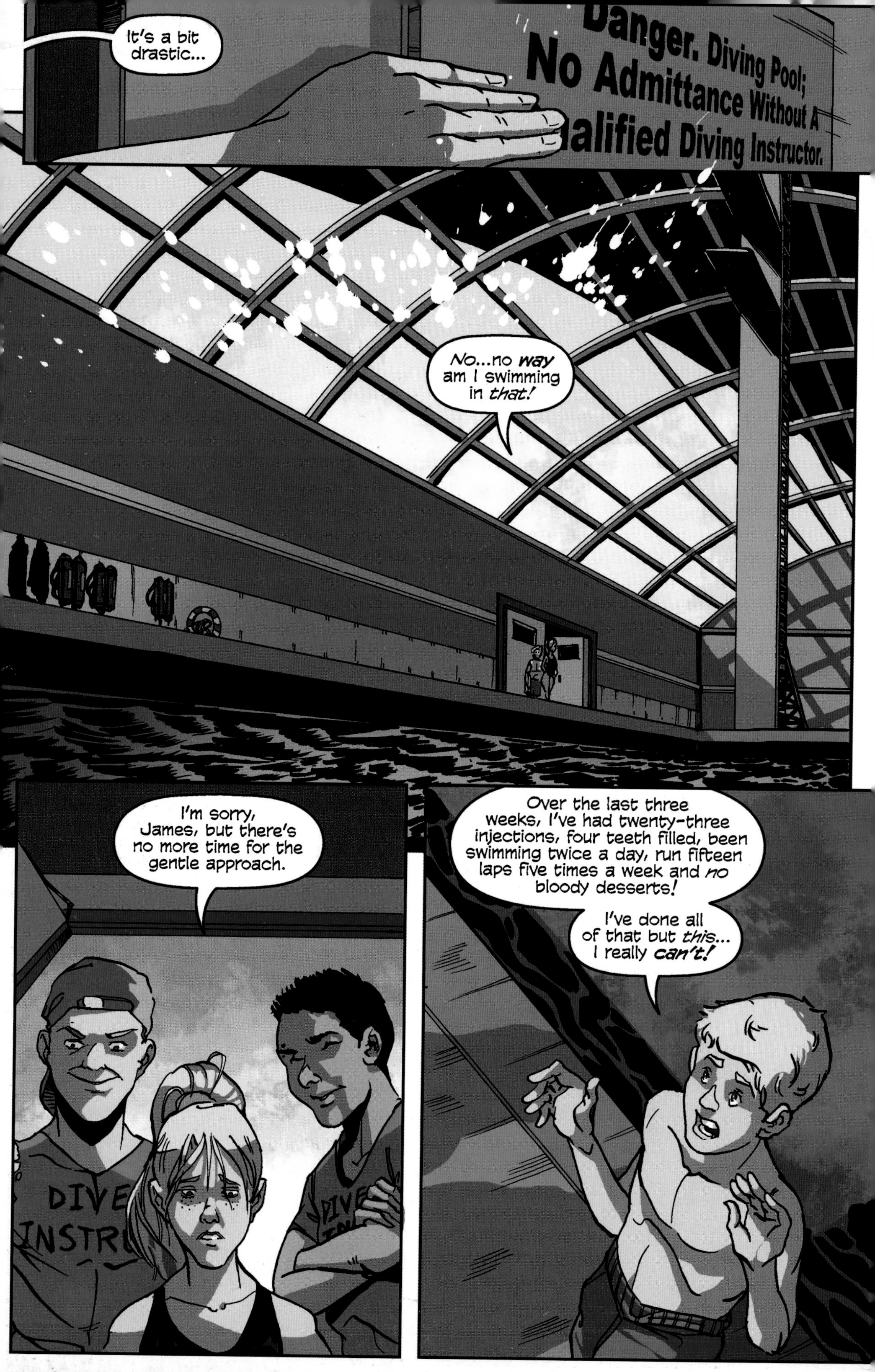
It's a bit drastic...
Danger. Diving Pool; No Admittance Without A ualified Diving Instructor.
No...no *way* am I swimming in *that!*
I'm sorry, James, but there's no more time for the gentle approach.
Over the last three weeks, I've had twenty-three injections, four teeth filled, been swimming twice a day, run fifteen laps five times a week and *no* bloody desserts!
I've done all of that but *this*... I really ***can't!***

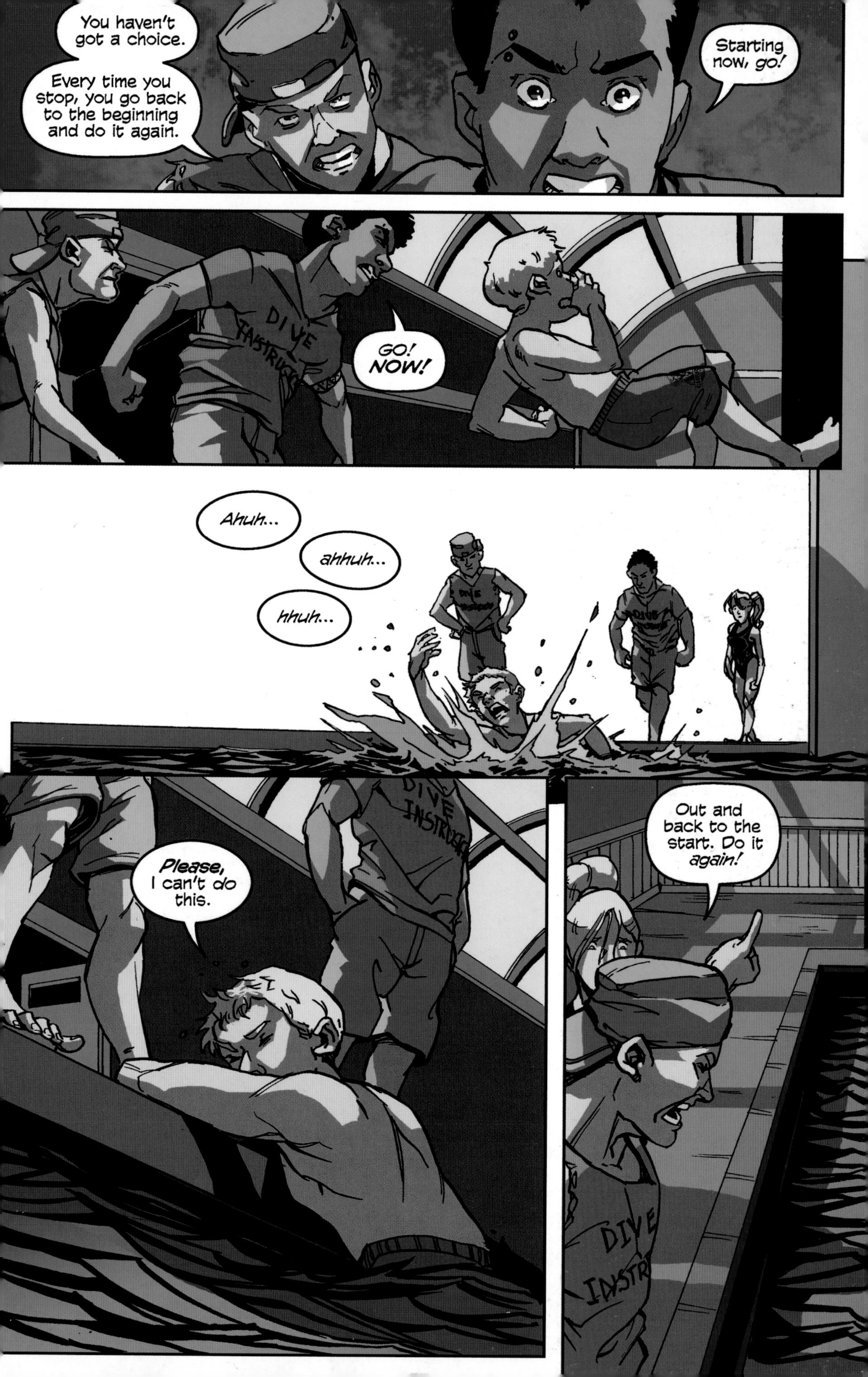

You haven't got a choice.
Every time you stop, you go back to the beginning and do it again.
Starting now, go!
DIVE INSTRUCT
GO! NOW!
Ahuh...
ahhuh...
hhuh...
DIVE INSTRUCT
Please, I can't do this.
Out and back to the start. Do it again!
DIVE INSTR

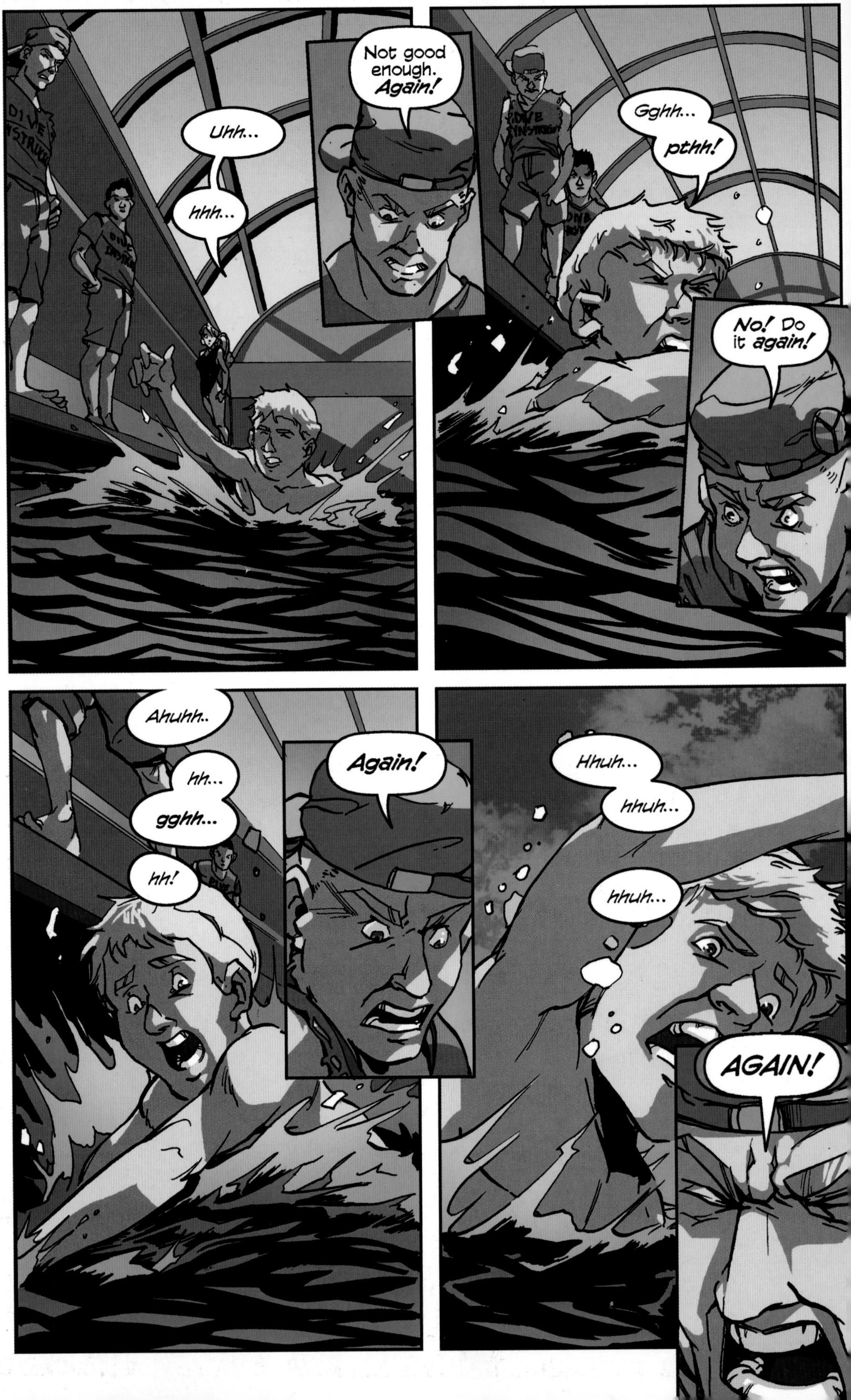
Uhh...
hhh...
Not good enough. Again!
Gghh...
pthh!
No! Do it again!
Ahuhh..
hh...
gghh...
hh!
Again!
Hhuh...
hhuh...
hhuh...
AGAIN!

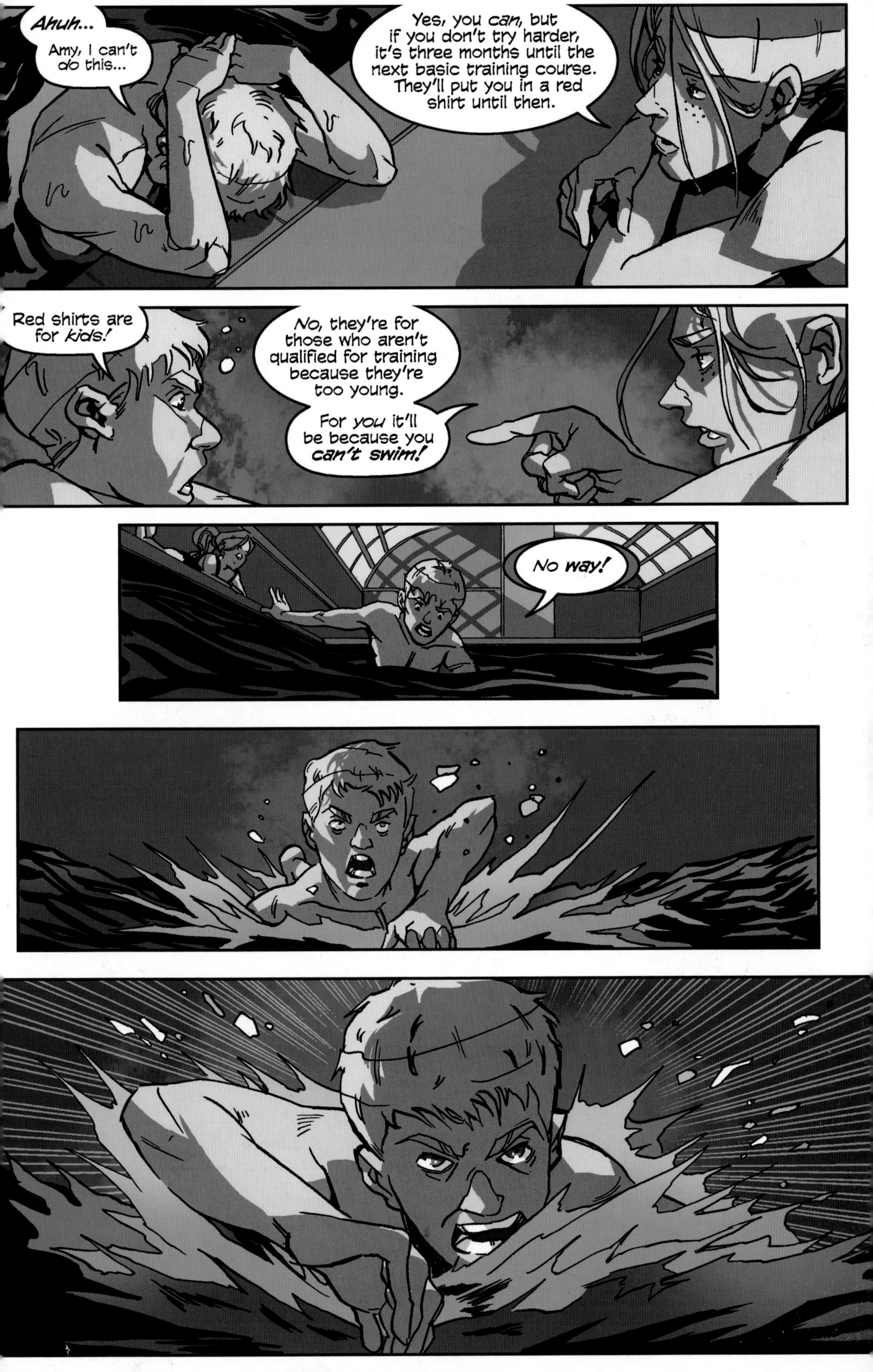
Ahuh...
Amy, I can't do this...
Yes, you can, but if you don't try harder, it's three months until the next basic training course. They'll put you in a red shirt until then.
Red shirts are for kids!
No, they're for those who aren't qualified for training because they're too young.
For you it'll be because you can't swim!
No way!

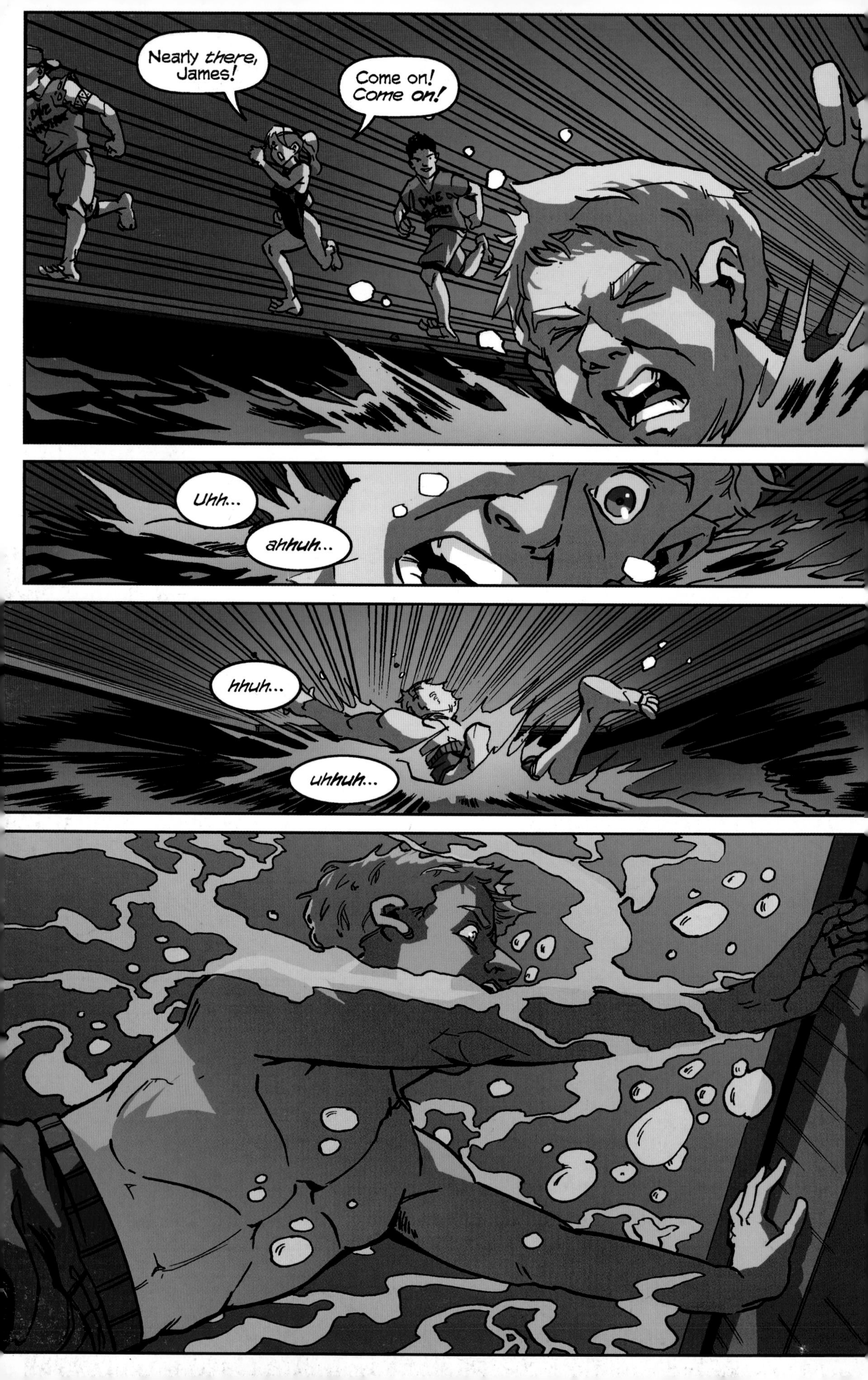
Nearly there, James!
Come on! Come on!
Uhh...
ahhuh...
hhuh...
uhhuh...

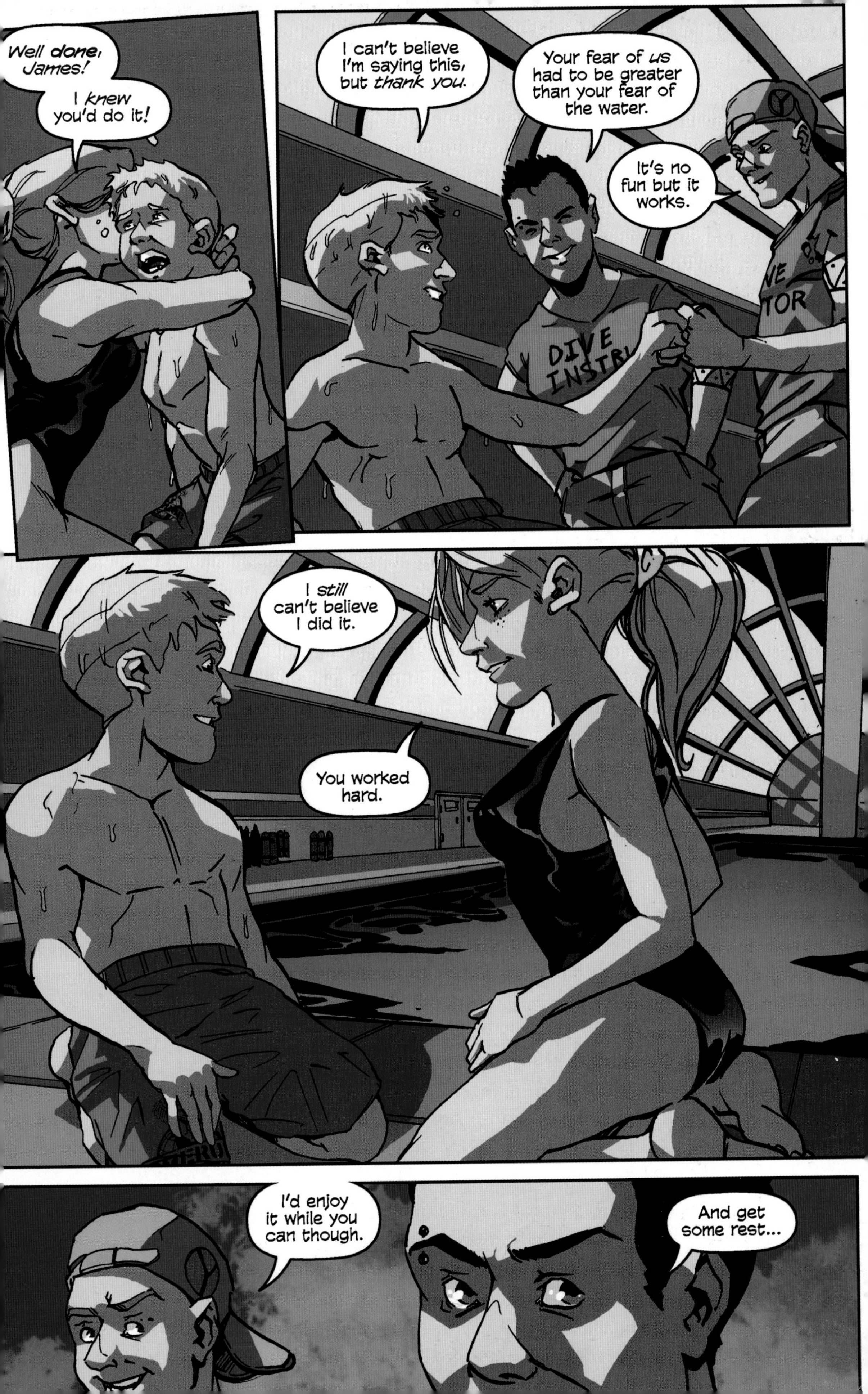
Well done, James!
I knew you'd do it!
I can't believe I'm saying this, but thank you.
Your fear of us had to be greater than your fear of the water.
It's no fun but it works.
I still can't believe I did it.
You worked hard.
I'd enjoy it while you can though.
And get some rest...

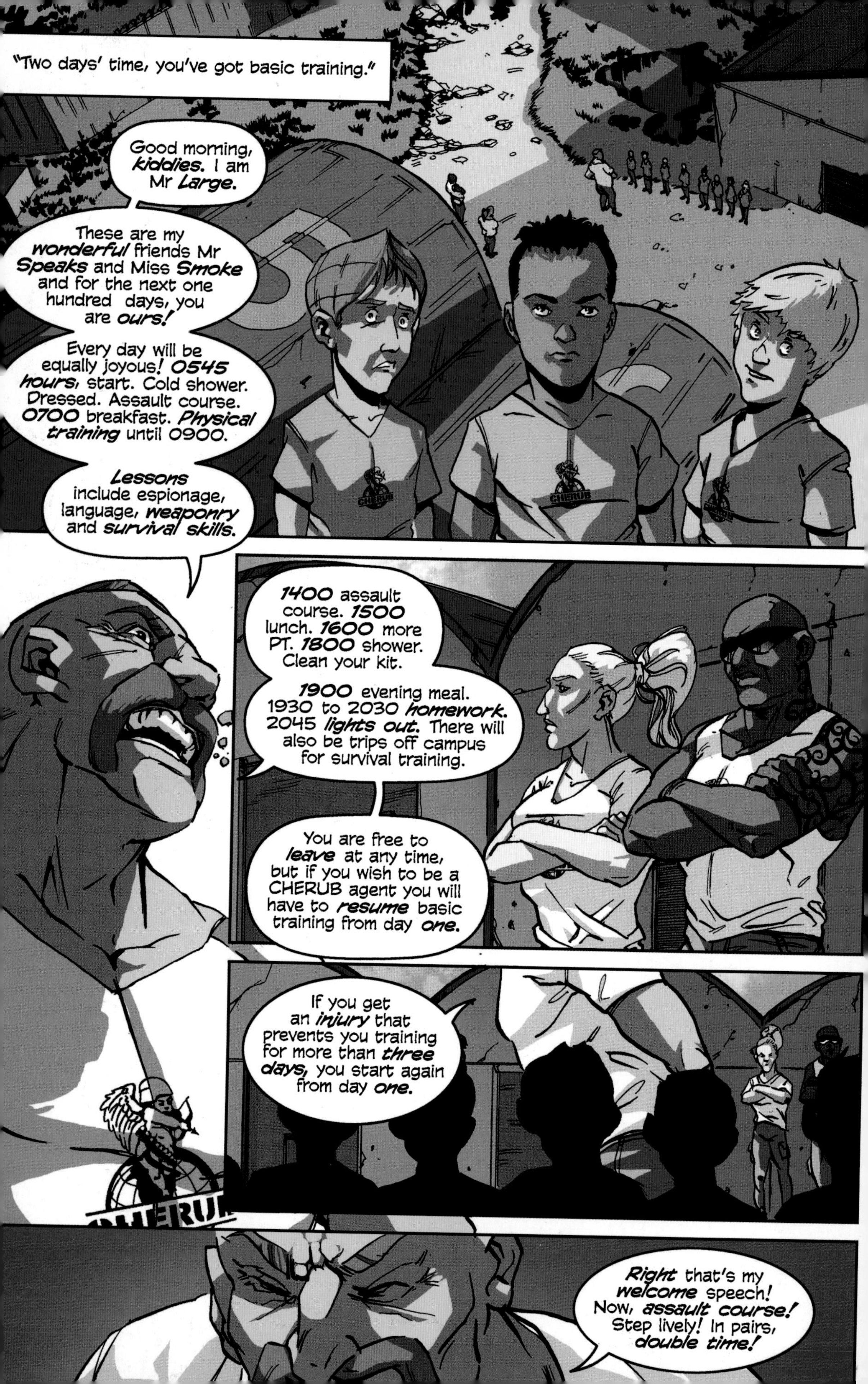
"Two days' time, you've got basic training."
Good morning, kiddies. I am Mr Large.
These are my wonderful friends Mr Speaks and Miss Smoke and for the next one hundred days, you are ours!
Every day will be equally joyous! 0545 hours, start. Cold shower. Dressed. Assault course. 0700 breakfast. Physical training until 0900.
Lessons include espionage, language, weaponry and survival skills.
CHERUB
1400 assault course. 1500 lunch. 1600 more PT. 1800 shower. Clean your kit.
1900 evening meal. 1930 to 2030 homework. 2045 lights out. There will also be trips off campus for survival training.
You are free to leave at any time, but if you wish to be a CHERUB agent you will have to resume basic training from day one.
If you get an injury that prevents you training for more than three days, you start again from day one.
Right that's my welcome speech! Now, assault course! Step lively! In pairs, double time!

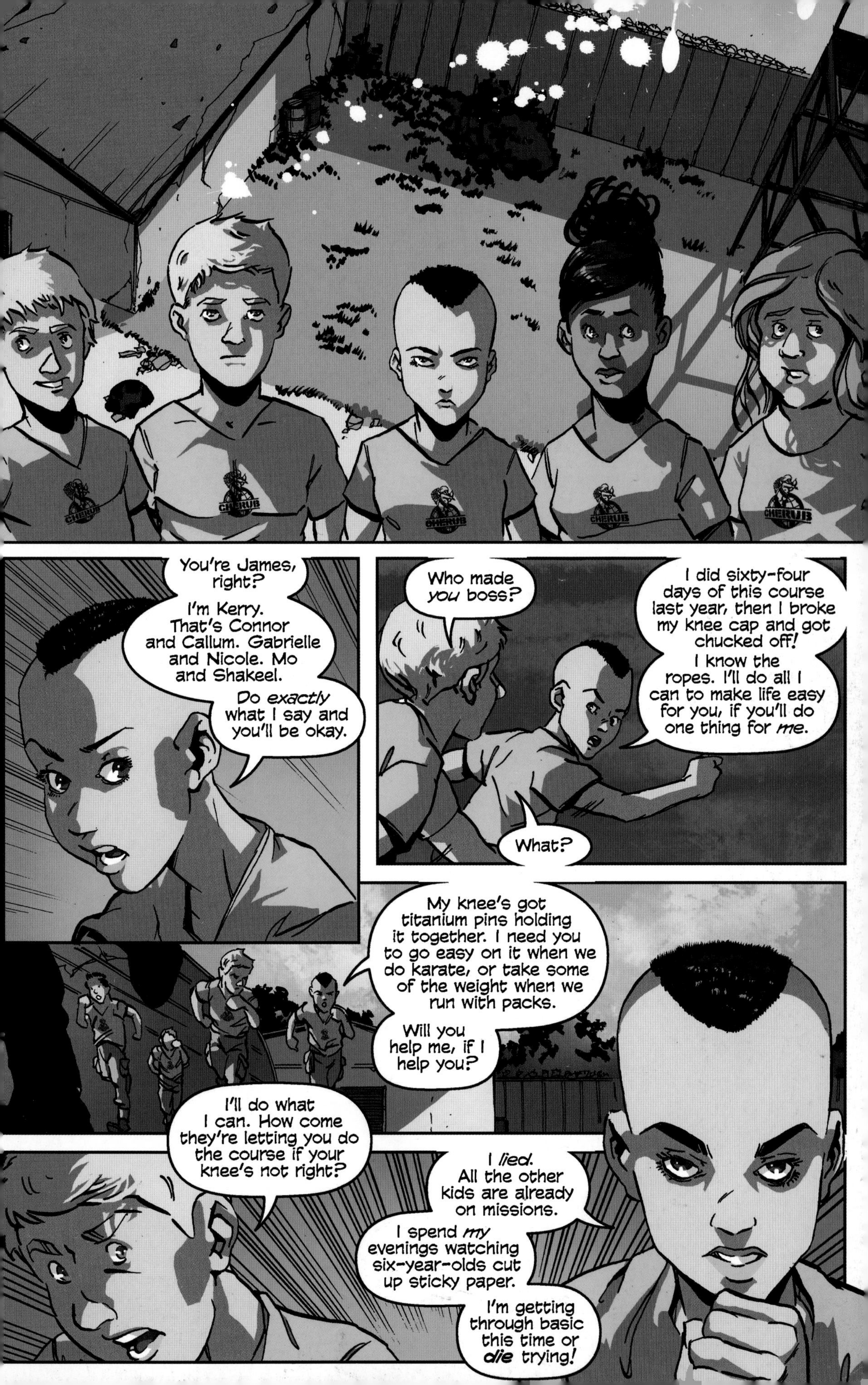
CHERUB
You're James, right?
I'm Kerry. That's Connor and Callum. Gabrielle and Nicole. Mo and Shakeel.
Do *exactly* what I say and you'll be okay.
Who made *you* boss?
I did sixty-four days of this course last year, then I broke my knee cap and got chucked off!
I know the ropes. I'll do all I can to make life easy for you, if you'll do one thing for *me*.
What?
My knee's got titanium pins holding it together. I need you to go easy on it when we do karate, or take some of the weight when we run with packs.
Will you help me, if I help you?
I'll do what I can. How come they're letting you do the course if your knee's not right?
I *lied*. All the other kids are already on missions.
I spend *my* evenings watching six-year-olds cut up sticky paper.
I'm getting through basic this time or ***die*** trying!

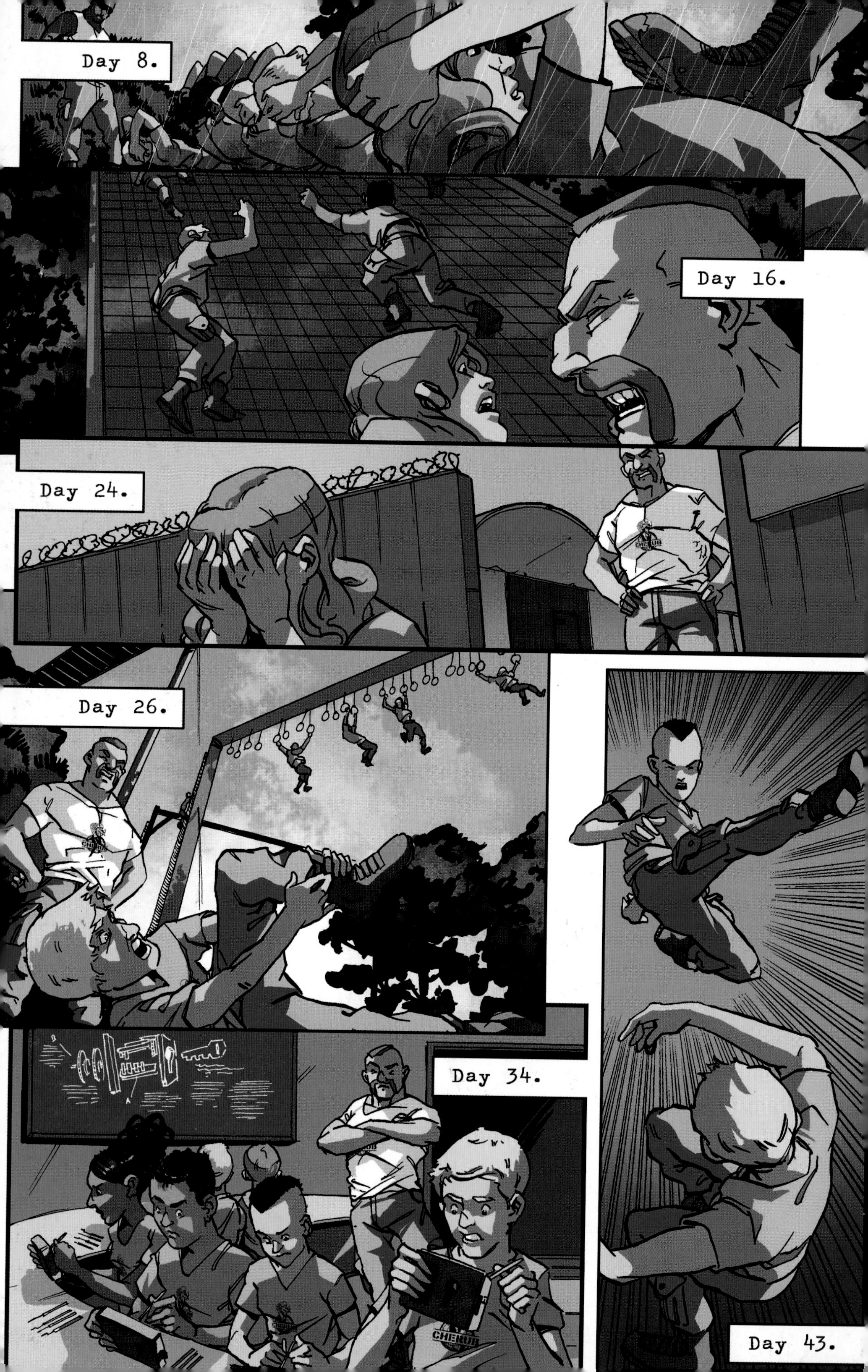

Day 8.
Day 16.
Day 24.
CHERUB
Day 26.
CHERUB
Day 34.
CHERUB
Day 43.

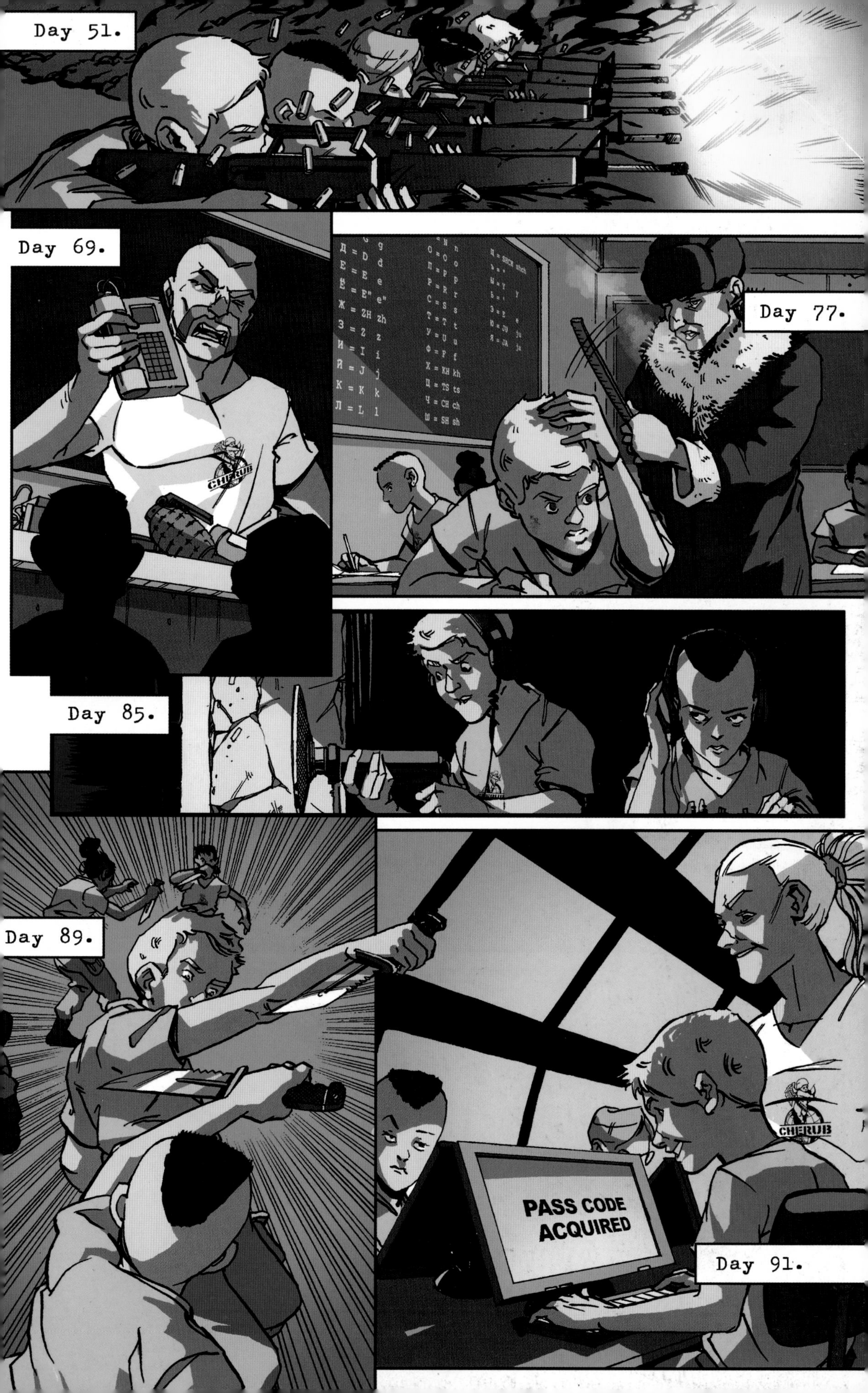
Day 51.
Day 69.
Day 77.
Day 85.
Day 89.
PASS CODE ACQUIRED
Day 91.

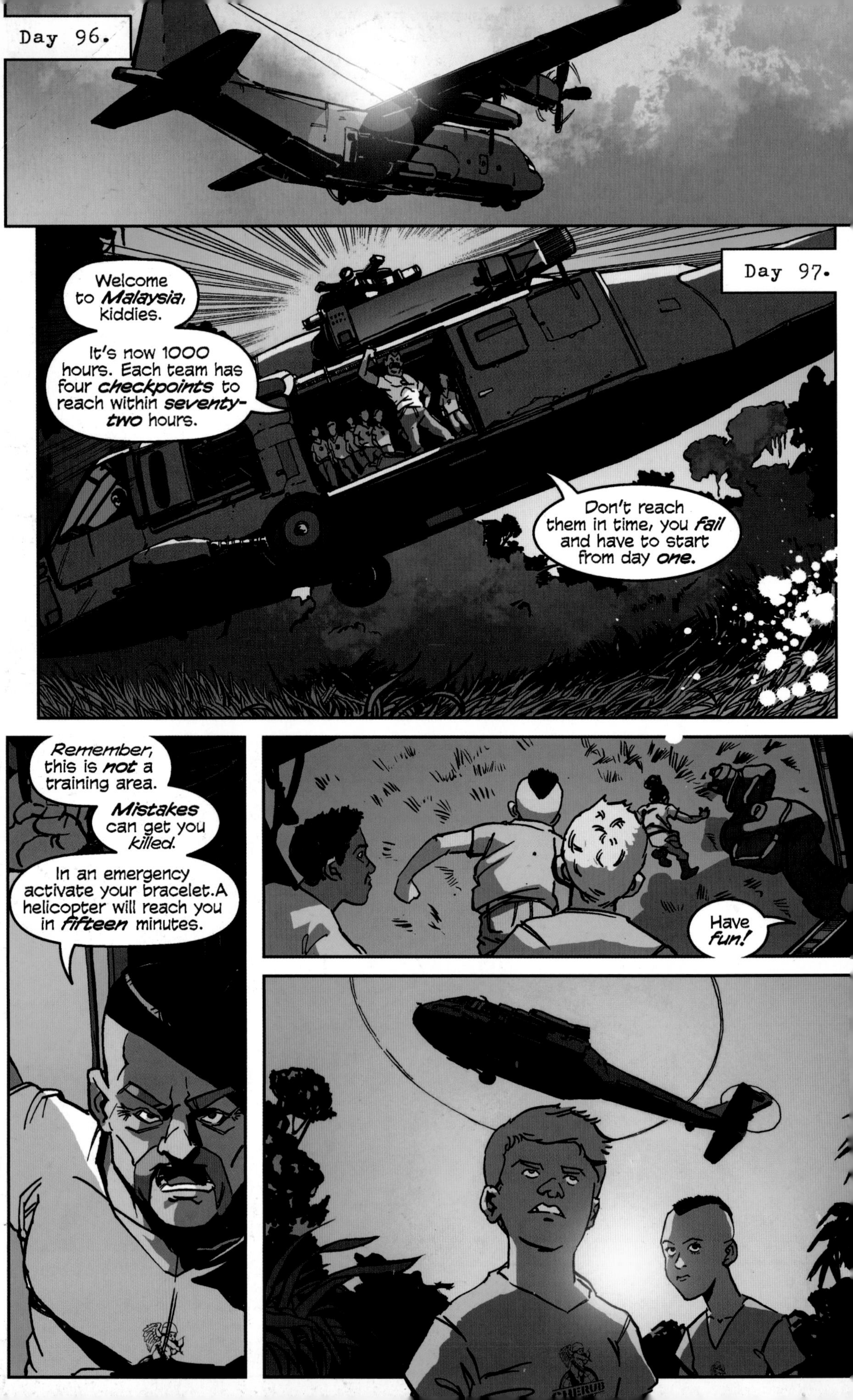
Day 96.
Day 97.
Welcome to Malaysia, kiddies.
It's now 1000 hours. Each team has four checkpoints to reach within seventy-two hours.
Don't reach them in time, you fail and have to start from day one.
Remember, this is not a training area.
Mistakes can get you killed.
In an emergency activate your bracelet.A helicopter will reach you in fifteen minutes.
Have fun!

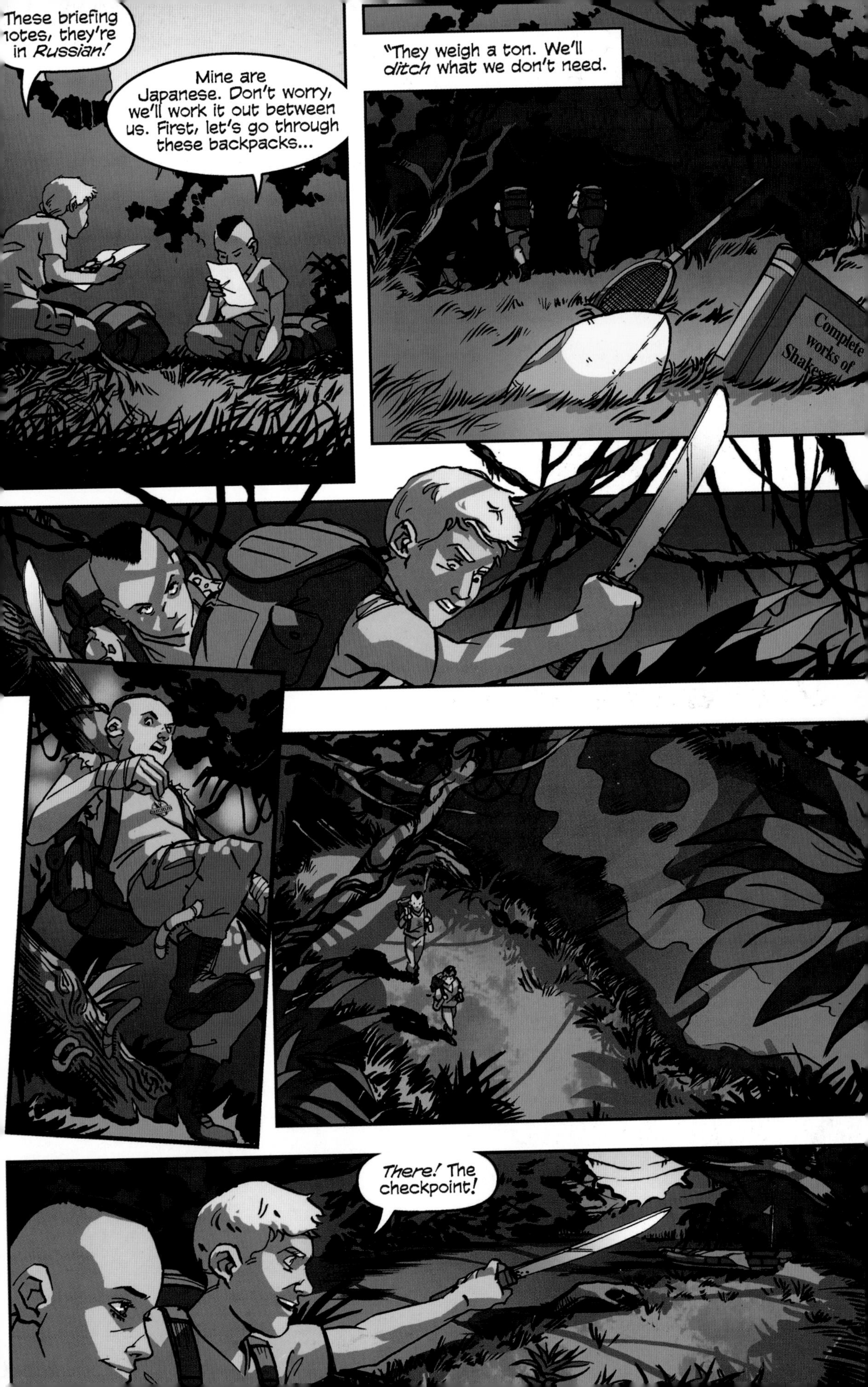
These briefing notes, they're in *Russian!*
Mine are Japanese. Don't worry, we'll work it out between us. First, let's go through these backpacks...
"They weigh a ton. We'll *ditch* what we don't need.
Complete works of Shakes
There! The checkpoint!

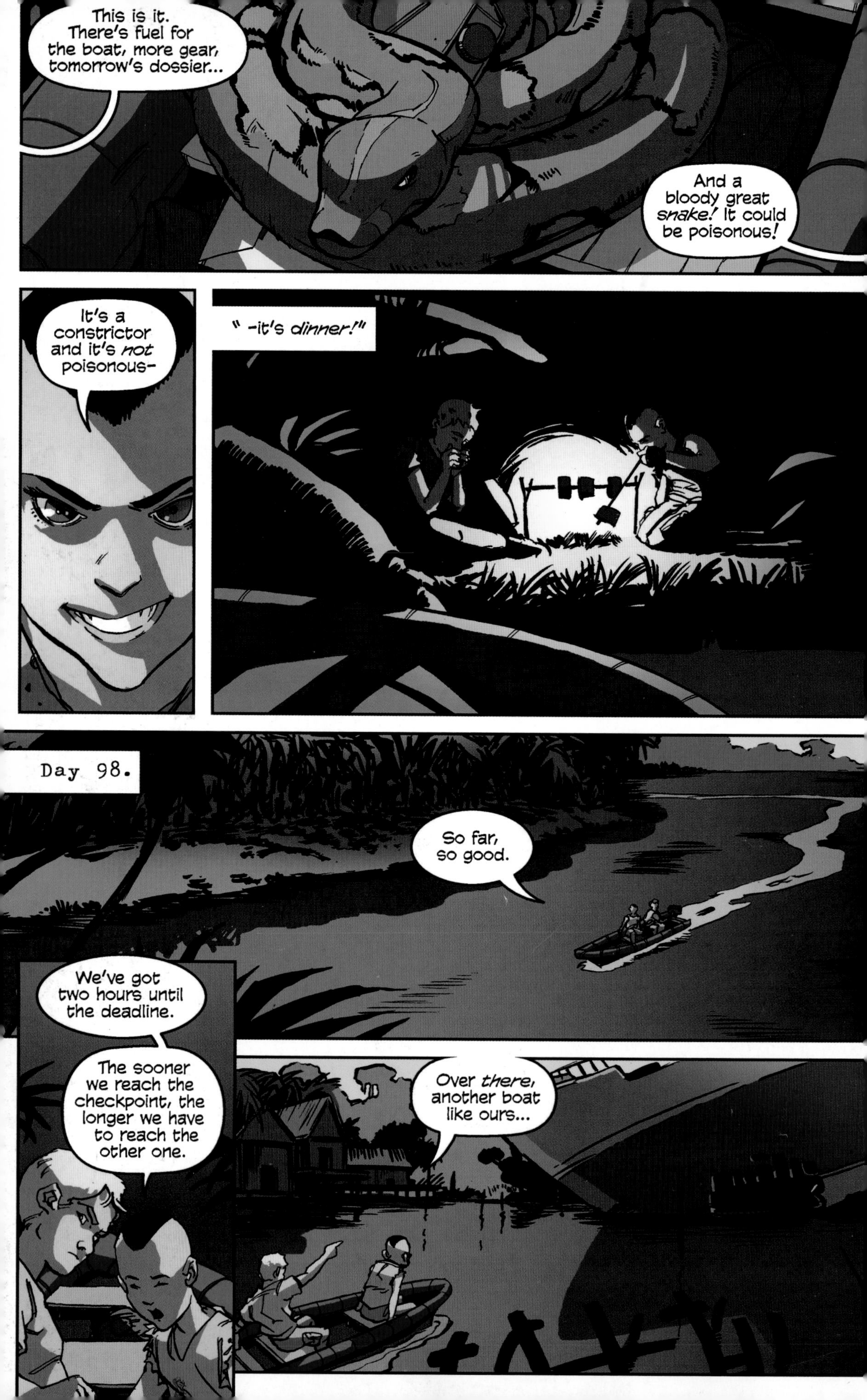
This is it. There's fuel for the boat, more gear, tomorrow's dossier...
And a bloody great *snake!* It could be poisonous!
It's a constrictor and it's *not* poisonous-
" -it's *dinner!*"
Day 98.
So far, so good.
We've got two hours until the deadline.
The sooner we reach the checkpoint, the longer we have to reach the other one.
Over *there,* another boat like ours...

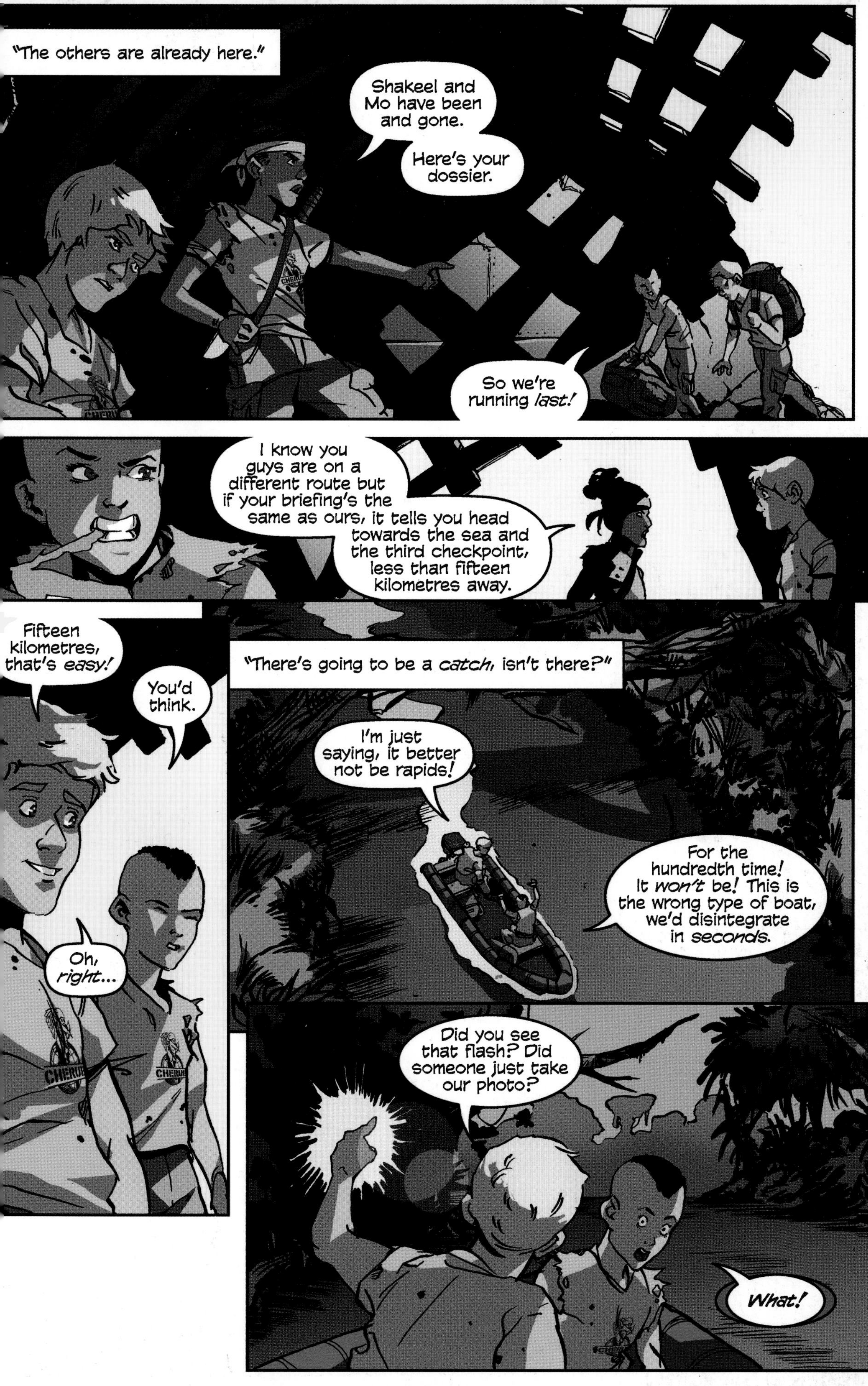
"The others are already here."
Shakeel and Mo have been and gone.
Here's your dossier.
So we're running *last!*
I know you guys are on a different route but if your briefing's the same as ours, it tells you head towards the sea and the third checkpoint, less than fifteen kilometres away.
Fifteen kilometres, that's *easy!*
You'd think.
Oh, *right*...
"There's going to be a *catch*, isn't there?"
I'm just saying, it better not be rapids!
For the hundredth time! It *won't* be! This is the wrong type of boat, we'd disintegrate in *seconds*.
Did you see that flash? Did someone just take our photo?
What!

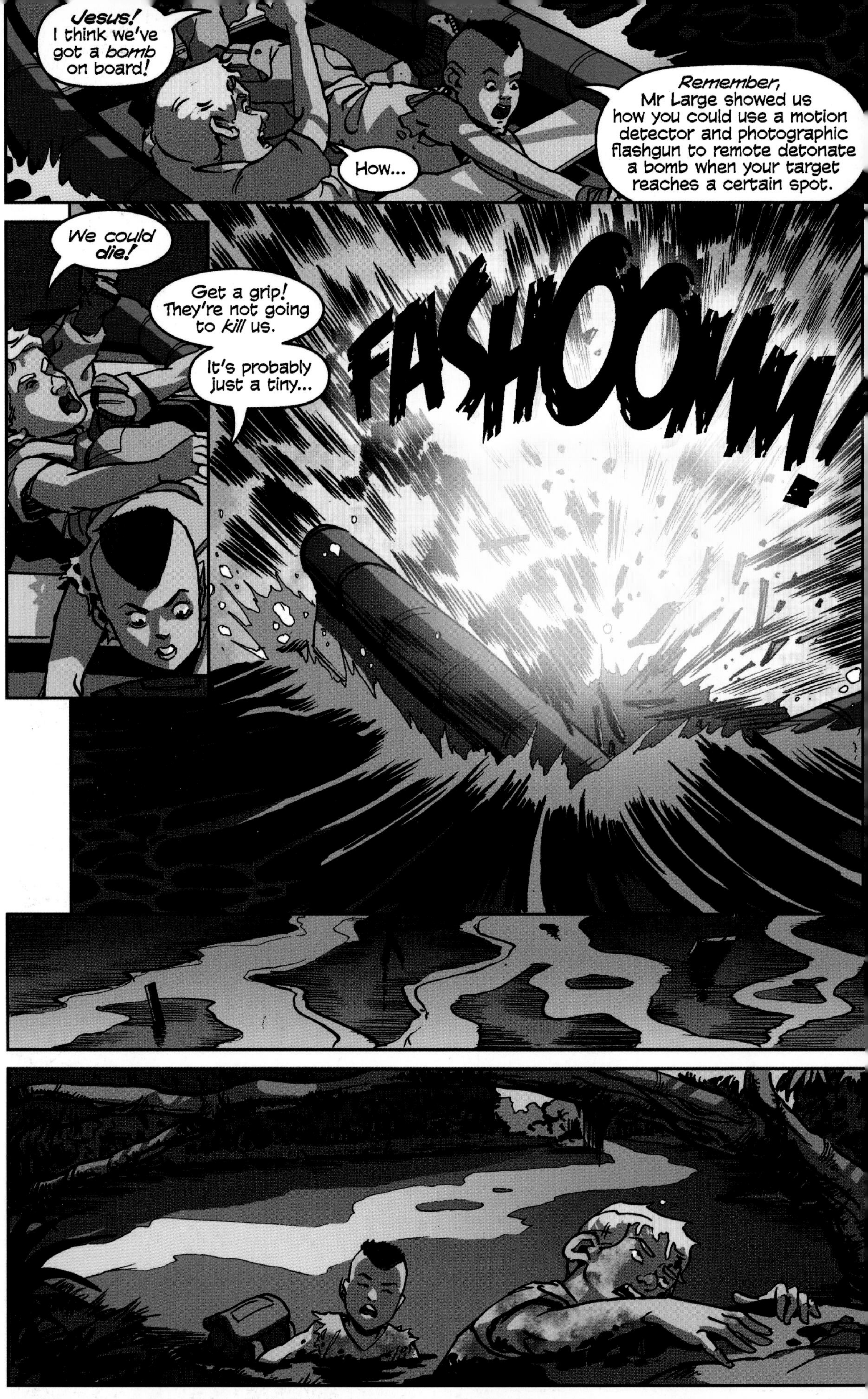
Jesus! I think we've got a bomb on board!
How...
Remember, Mr Large showed us how you could use a motion detector and photographic flashgun to remote detonate a bomb when your target reaches a certain spot.
We could die!
Get a grip! They're not going to kill us.
It's probably just a tiny...
FASHOOMM!

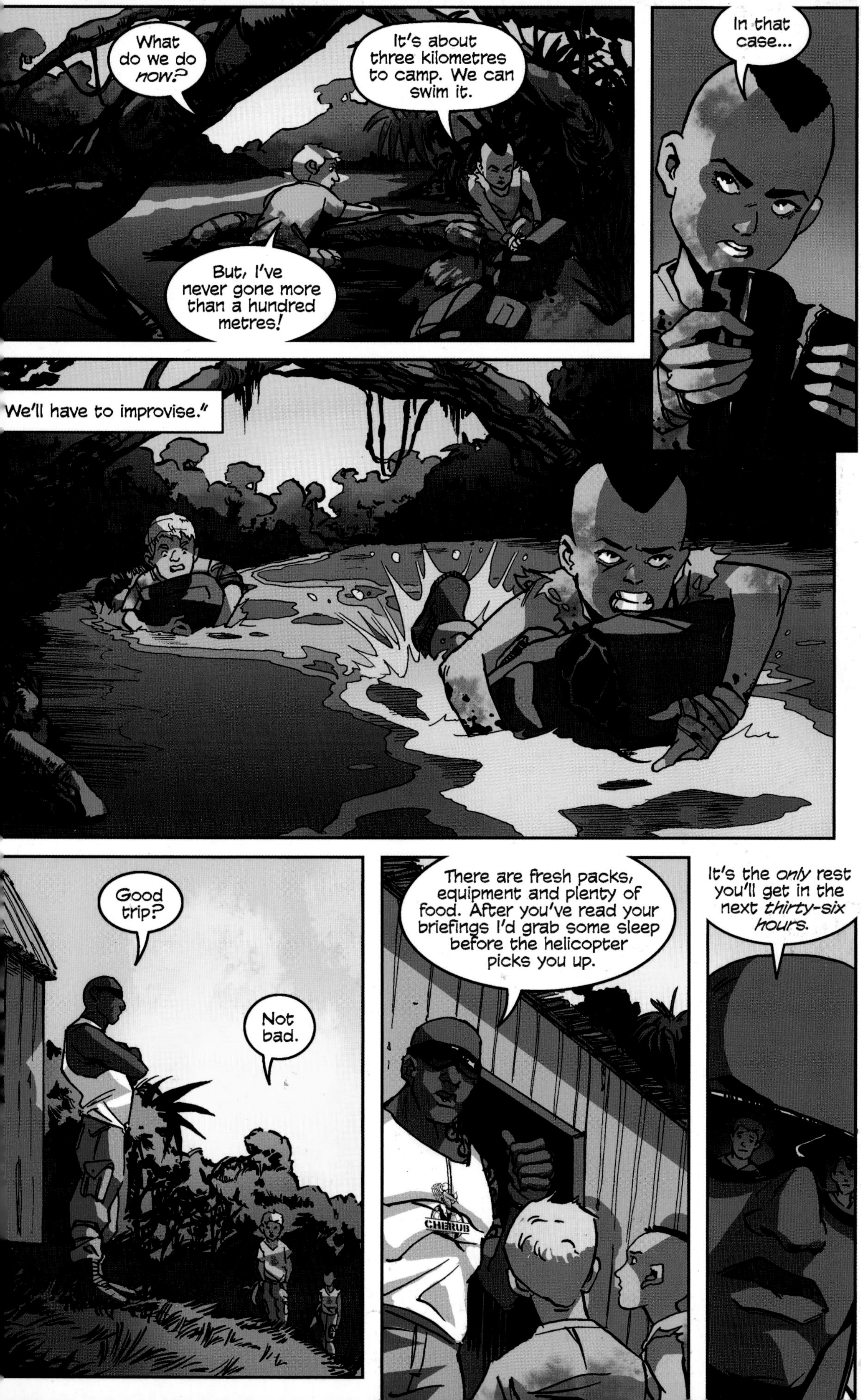
What do we do *now?*
It's about three kilometres to camp. We can swim it.
But, I've never gone more than a hundred metres!
In that case...
We'll have to improvise."
Good trip?
Not bad.
There are fresh packs, equipment and plenty of food. After you've read your briefings I'd grab some sleep before the helicopter picks you up.
It's the *only* rest you'll get in the next *thirty-six hours.*
CHERUB

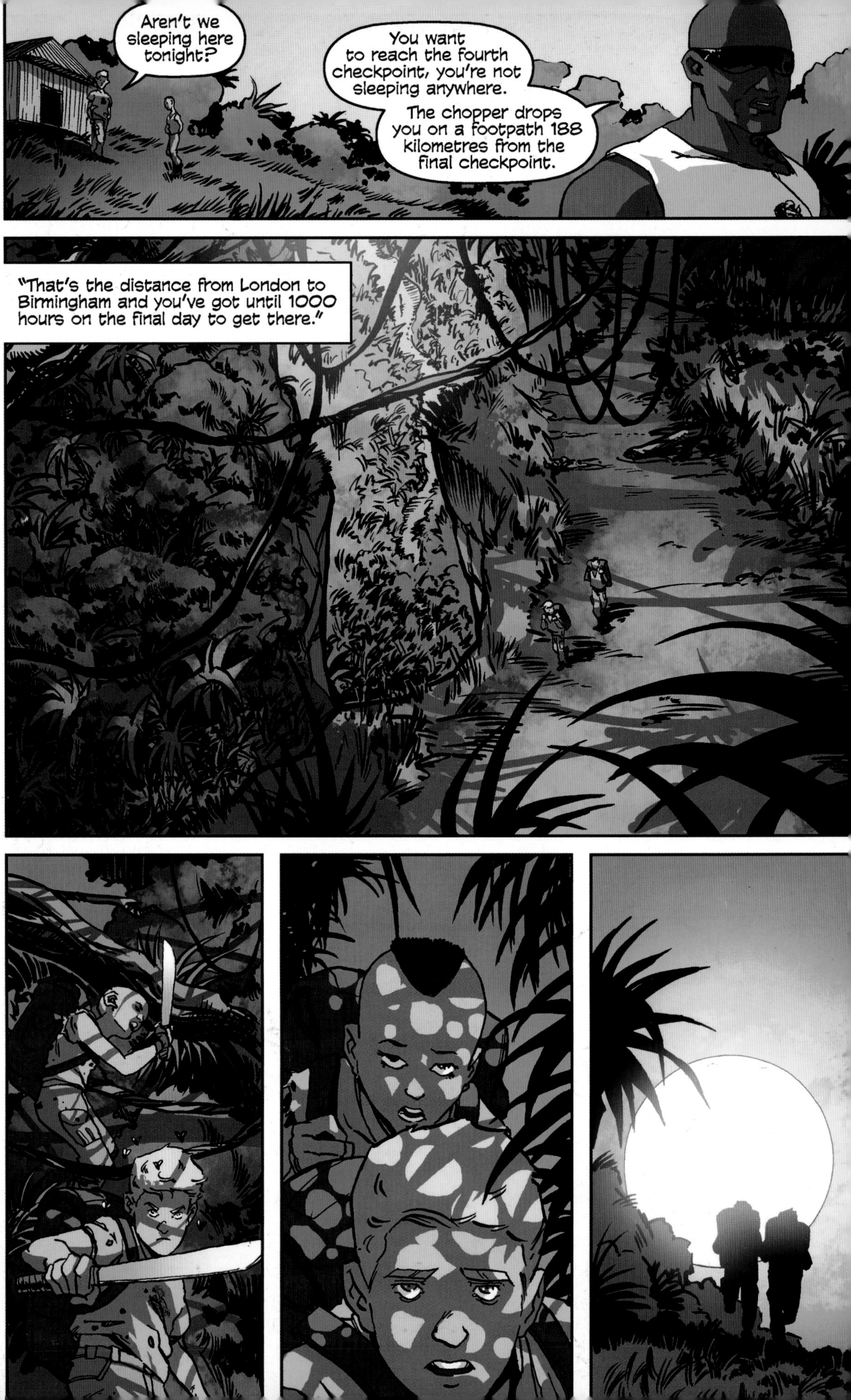
Aren't we sleeping here tonight?
You want to reach the fourth checkpoint, you're not sleeping anywhere.
The chopper drops you on a footpath 188 kilometres from the final checkpoint.
"That's the distance from London to Birmingham and you've got until 1000 hours on the final day to get there."

We were getting worried about you two. You cut it pretty close.

At least it's *over*.

Who says. It's only the *morning* of the last day.

"I bet the instructors have something else up their sleeves."

Welcome to the *ultimate test*. Before you six tired little bunnies become operatives we need to be sure you can cope with the worst thing that can happen to you.

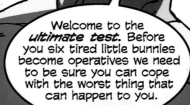

I am talking about *torture*.

We *hope* it never happens to you but we have to know you can take the *pain* if it does.

You each have *two* buckets in front of you. In the left, a *poisonous jellyfish*, in the right the *antidote*.

You'll each place your *hands* in the bucket.

The jellyfish will *grab* you. You will have to *tolerate* the pain for *one hour*.

The pain is *extreme*, hence the mouth guard to prevent you biting through your *tongues*.

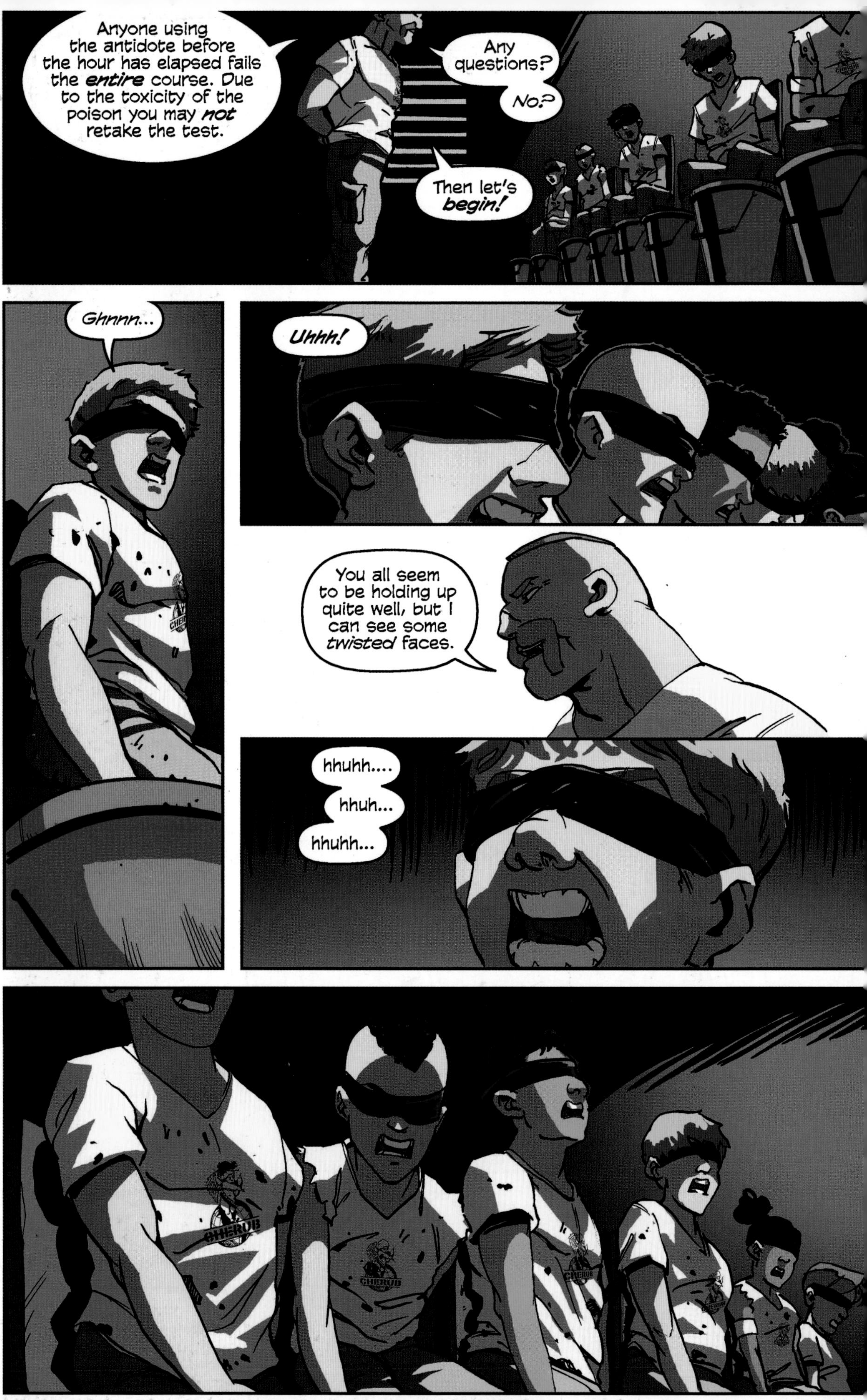
Anyone using the antidote before the hour has elapsed fails the *entire* course. Due to the toxicity of the poison you may *not* retake the test.
Any questions?
No?
Then let's *begin!*
Ghnnn...
Uhhh!
You all seem to be holding up quite well, but I can see some *twisted* faces.
hhuhh....
hhuh...
hhuhh...

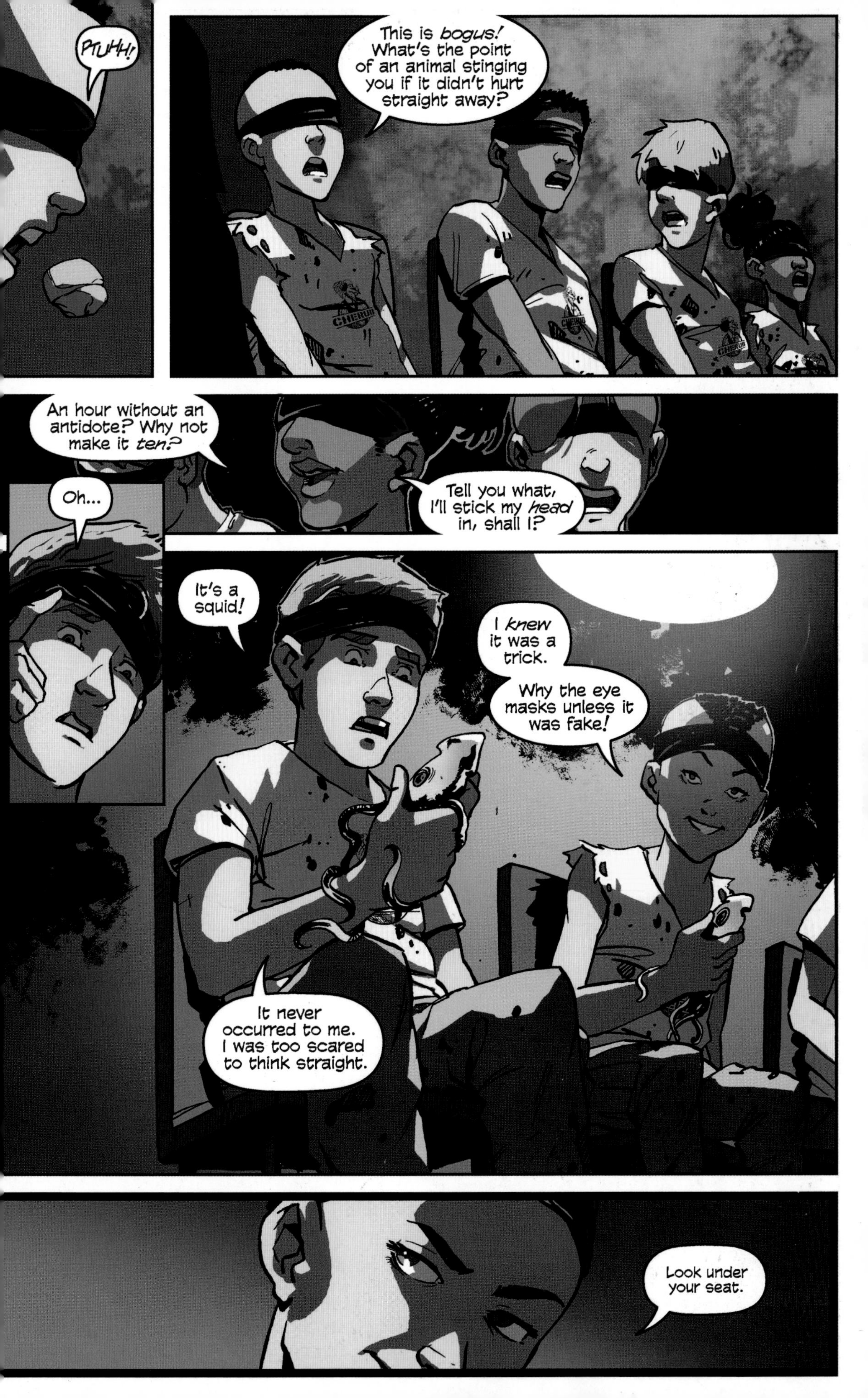
PTUHH!
This is *bogus!* What's the point of an animal stinging you if it didn't hurt straight away?
An hour without an antidote? Why not make it *ten?*
Tell you what, I'll stick my *head* in, shall I?
Oh...
It's a squid!
I *knew* it was a trick.
Why the eye masks unless it was fake!
It never occurred to me. I was too scared to think straight.
Look under your seat.

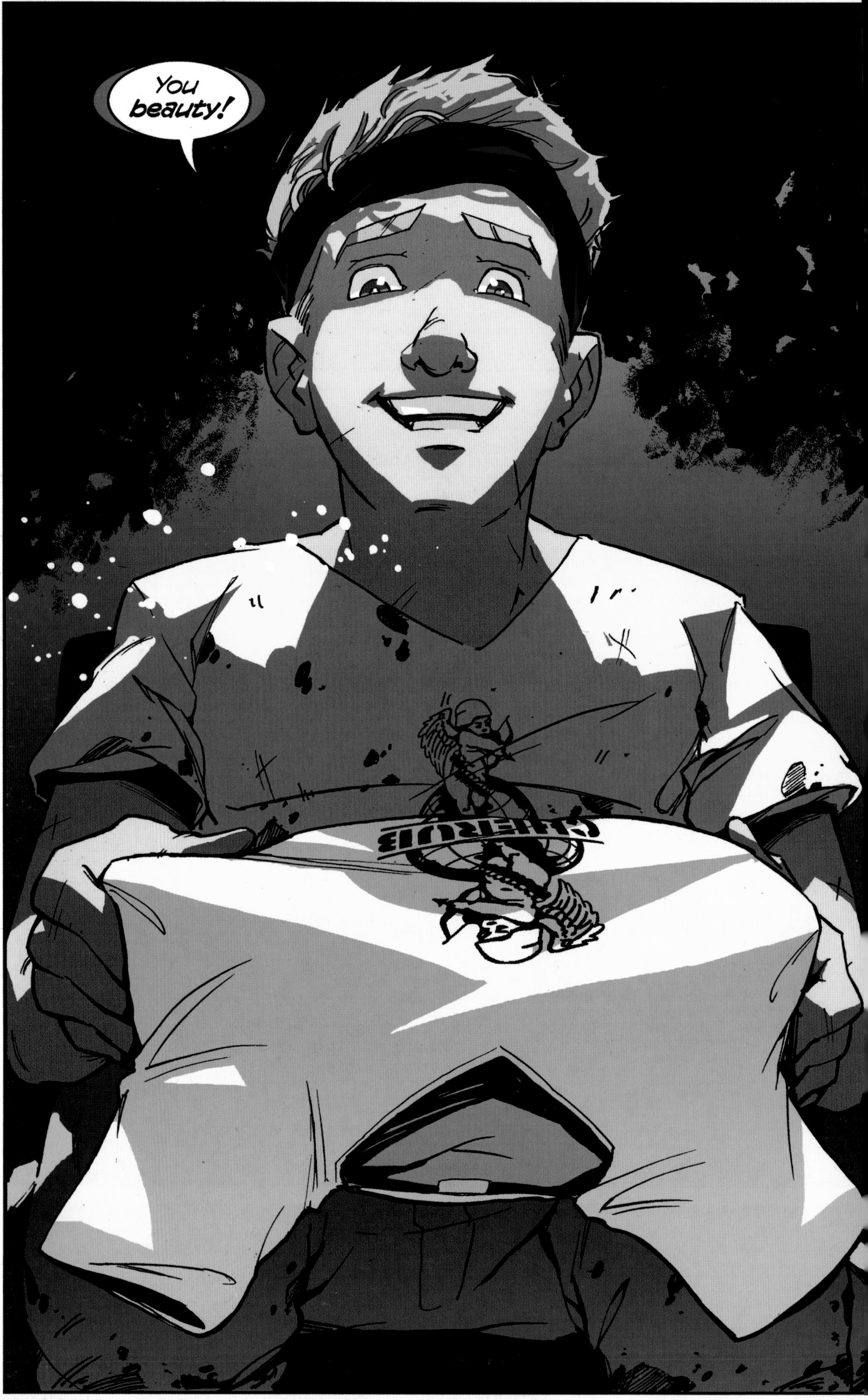
You beauty!

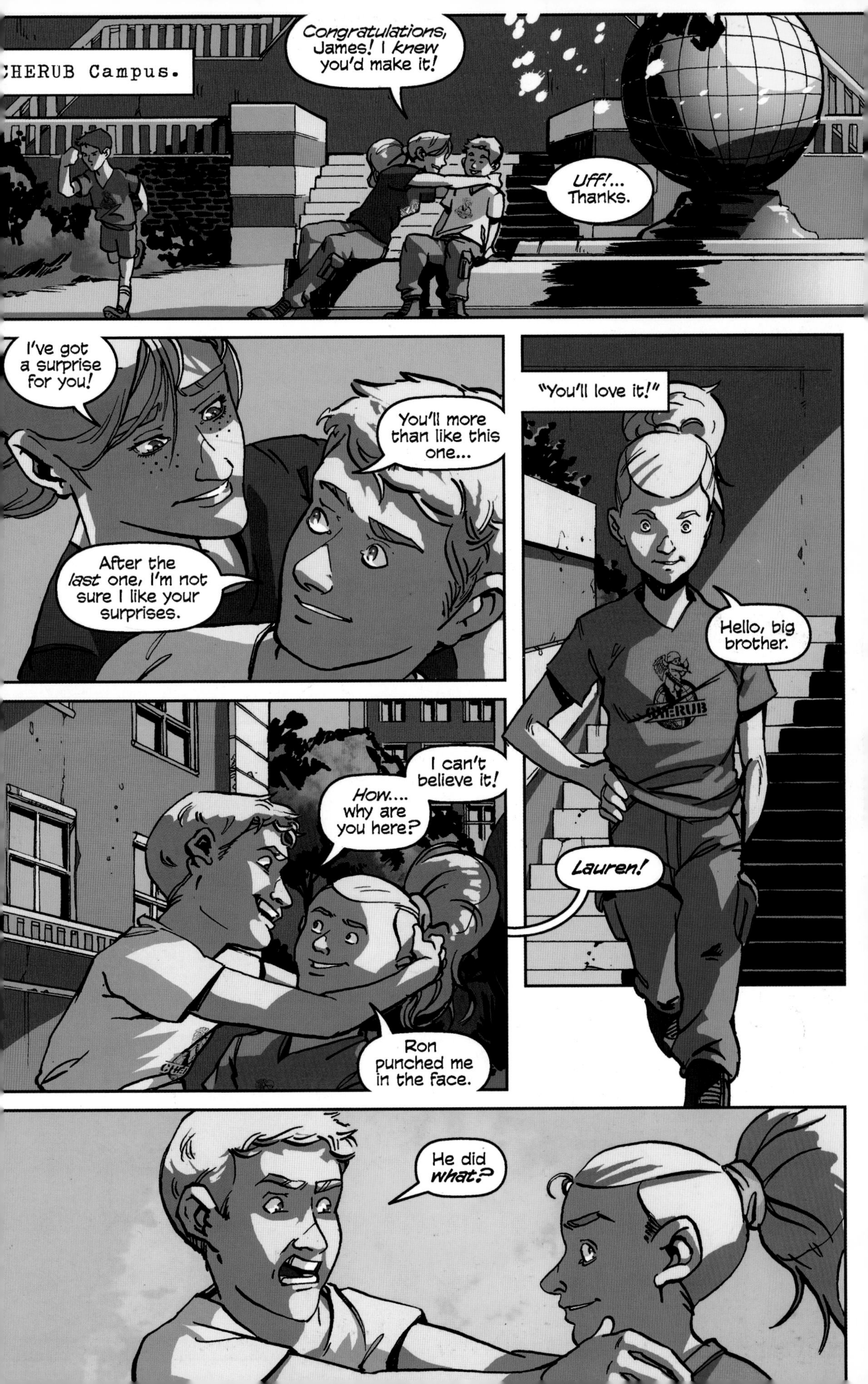
CHERUB Campus.
Congratulations, James! I *knew* you'd make it!
Uff!... Thanks.
I've got a surprise for you!
You'll more than like this one...
After the *last* one, I'm not sure I like your surprises.
"You'll love it!"
Hello, big brother.
Lauren!
I can't believe it!
How.... why are you here?
Ron punched me in the face.
He did *what?*

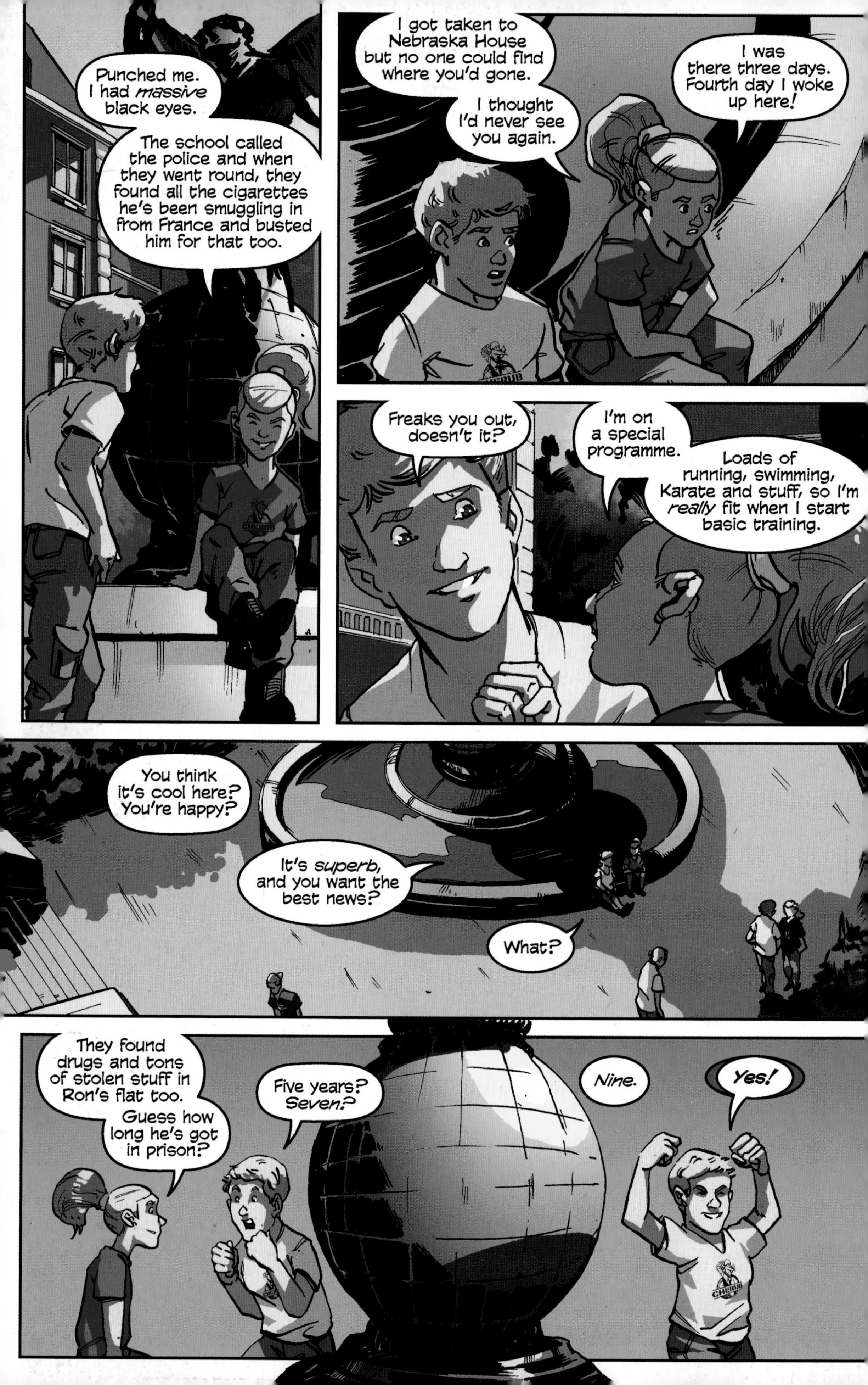
Punched me. I had *massive* black eyes.
The school called the police and when they went round, they found all the cigarettes he's been smuggling in from France and busted him for that too.
I got taken to Nebraska House but no one could find where you'd gone.
I thought I'd never see you again.
I was there three days. Fourth day I woke up here!
Freaks you out, doesn't it?
I'm on a special programme.
Loads of running, swimming, Karate and stuff, so I'm *really* fit when I start basic training.
You think it's cool here? You're happy?
It's *superb*, and you want the best news?
What?
They found drugs and tons of stolen stuff in Ron's flat too.
Guess how long he's got in prison?
Five years? *Seven?*
Nine.
Yes!

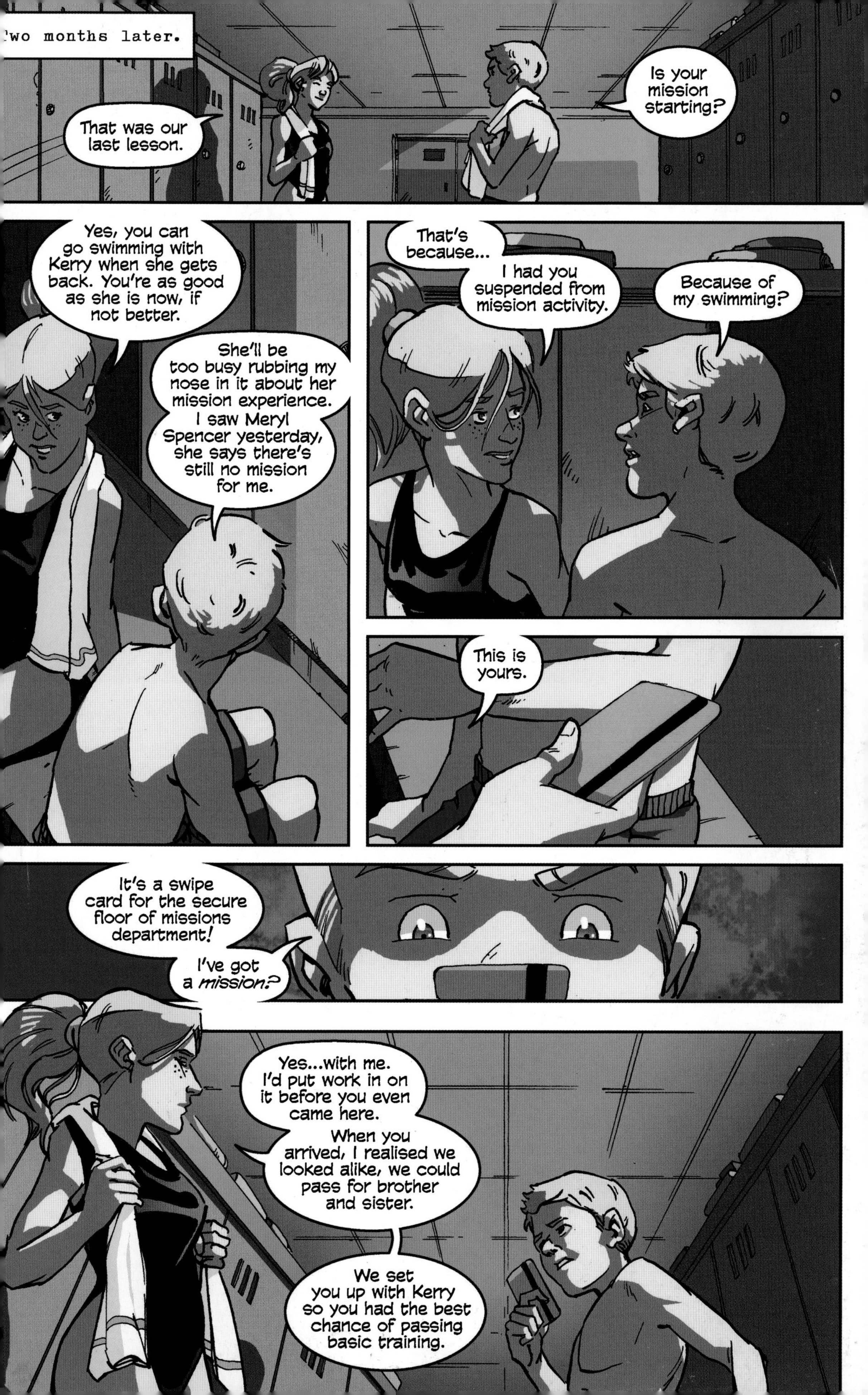
Two months later.
That was our last lesson.
Is your mission starting?
Yes, you can go swimming with Kerry when she gets back. You're as good as she is now, if not better.
She'll be too busy rubbing my nose in it about her mission experience.
I saw Meryl Spencer yesterday, she says there's still no mission for me.
That's because...
I had you suspended from mission activity.
Because of my swimming?
This is yours.
It's a swipe card for the secure floor of missions department!
I've got a *mission?*
Yes...with me. I'd put work in on it before you even came here.
When you arrived, I realised we looked alike, we could pass for brother and sister.
We set you up with Kerry so you had the best chance of passing basic training.

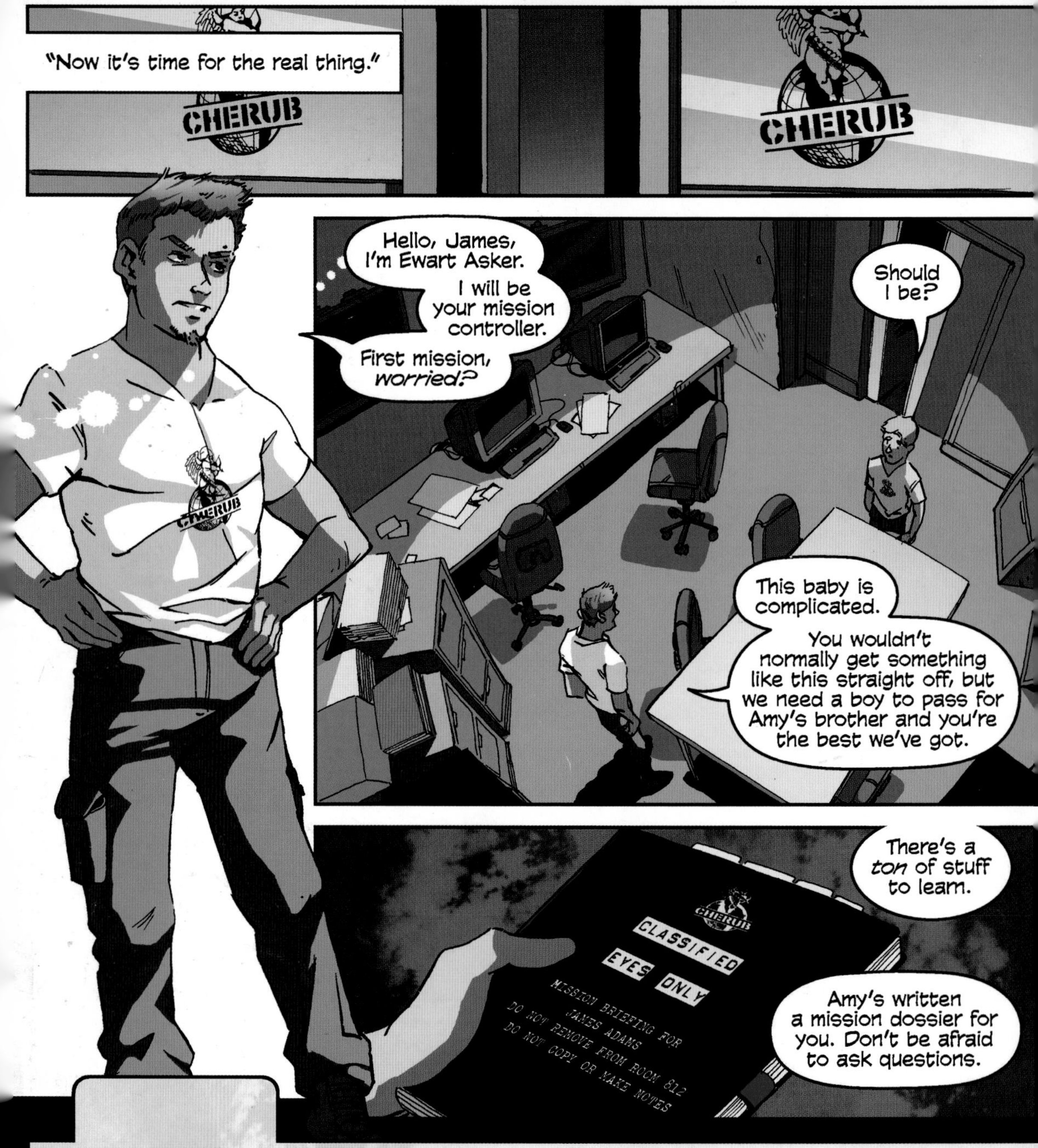
"Now it's time for the real thing."
CHERUB
CHERUB
Hello, James, I'm Ewart Asker.
I will be your mission controller.
First mission, *worried?*
Should I be?
This baby is complicated.
You wouldn't normally get something like this straight off, but we need a boy to pass for Amy's brother and you're the best we've got.
There's a *ton* of stuff to learn.
CHERUB
CLASSIFIED
EYES ONLY
MISSION BRIEFING FOR
JAMES ADAMS
DO NOT REMOVE FROM ROOM 812
DO NOT COPY OR MAKE NOTES
Amy's written a mission dossier for you. Don't be afraid to ask questions.

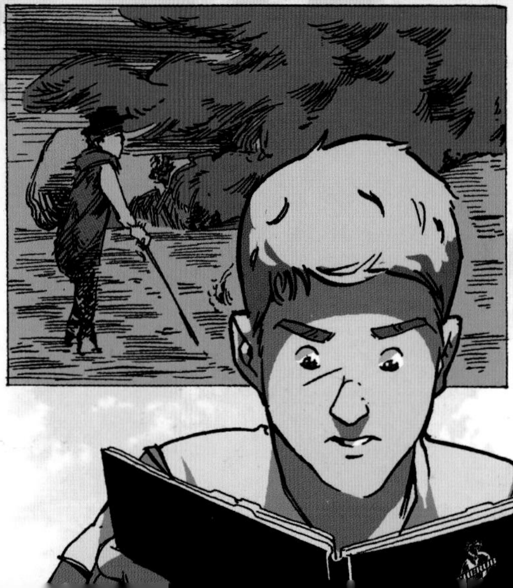

1) FORT HARMONY.

In 1612 King James made a fifty-square-metre area near the Welsh village of Craddogh into common land for people to graze animals and build a small shelter upon.

By the 1870s everyone living on the common had moved into the village, to work in the local mine. No one lived there for the next ninety-seven years.

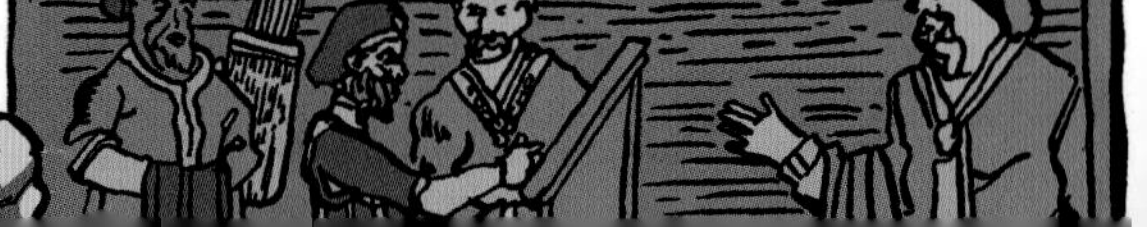

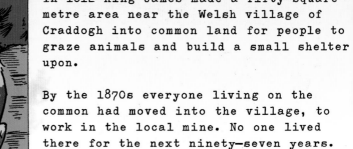

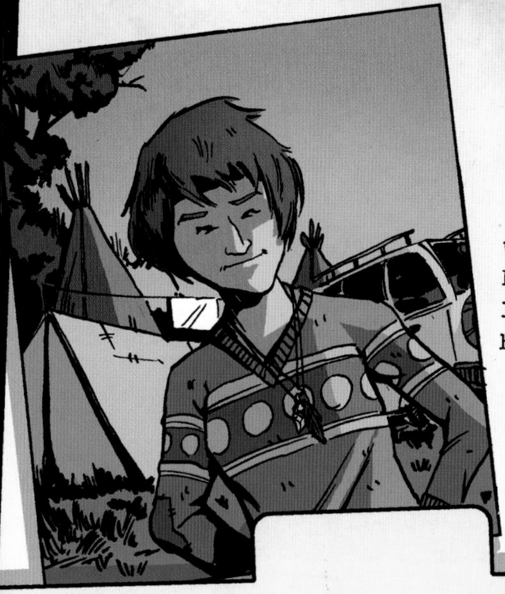

In 1950, Craddogh Common became part of West Monmouthshire National Park. In 196 a small group of hippies led by one **Gladys Dunn** settled there claiming right under the 1612 charter.

The High Court decided the charter ended when the common was made part of the National Park. The hippies refused to leave. In 1972 the police began destroying huts and arresting them.

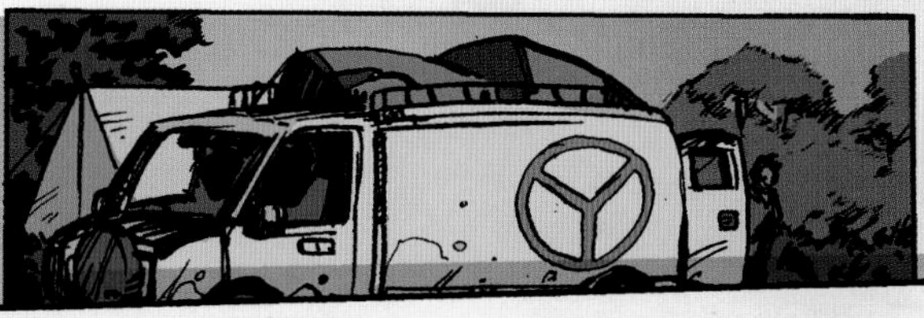

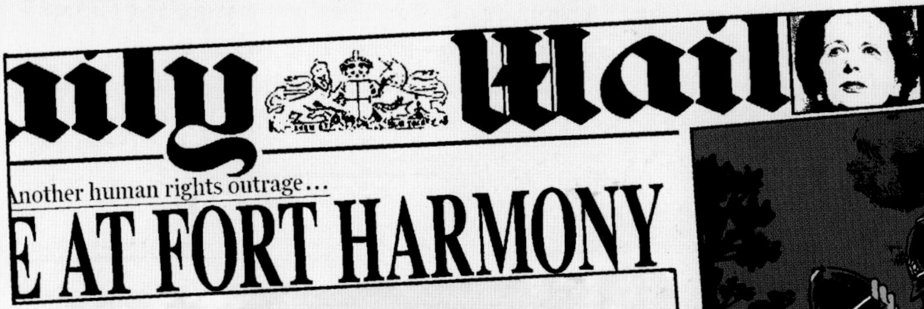

ily Mail
Another human rights outrage...
E AT FORT HARMONY

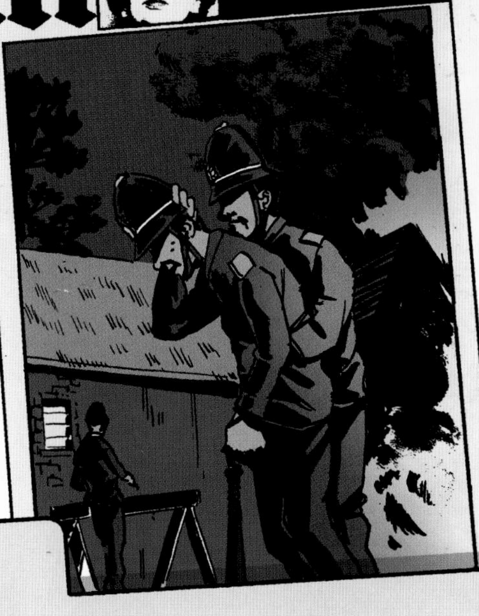

2) THE BATTLE.

The Fort Harmony residents fled every day while the police demolished their shelters, before returning each night to build new ones.

They also dug networks of tunnels and traps for the police to fall into. Newspaper coverage attracted dozens of new residents.

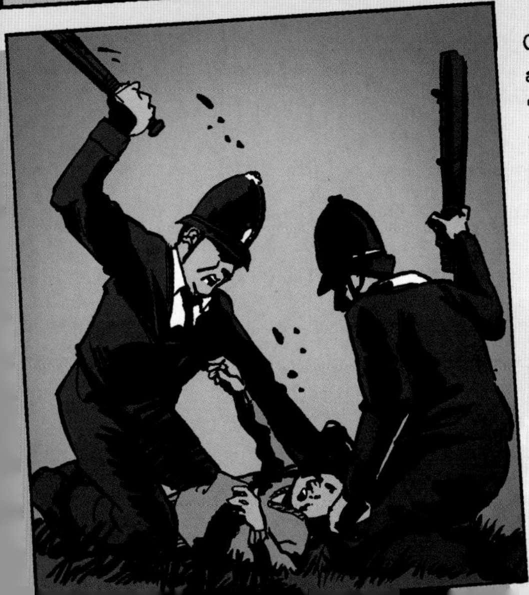

On **26 August 1973**, police launched an all-out effort to destroy Fort Harmony. Television and newspaper journalists watched as they pulled **Joshua Dunn**, aged nine, son of Gladys Dunn, from a tunnel and brutally beat him.

The incident caused a surge of public support for the hippies.

The police were exhausted, their lines broken. They withdrew, vowing to return. However, the **National Parks Authority** and the police hadn't the money to continue paying for such an operation, so nothing further was done.

3) FORT HARMONY

Thirty years later, Fort Harmony still exists. The camp has about **sixty** permanent residents. Gladys Dunn is now seventy-six. She wrote a best-selling **autobiography** in 1979. Her three sons — including Joshua who is brain damaged — still live on site as do many of her grand-children and great-grandchildren.

4) GREEN BROOKE

After the Craddogh mine closed in 1996, over half the population of the village were unemployed. In response, the National Park allowed the lavish **Green Brooke Conference Centre** to be built. Many of the residents of Craddogh and Fort Harmony work there.

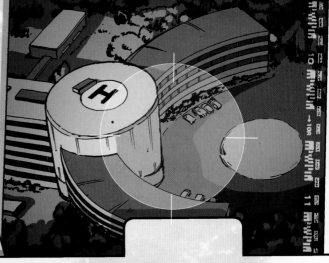

5) PETROCON

The most prestigious event in Green Brooke's brief history. Petrocon is a secretive, three-day meeting of global oil executives and politicians, the **United States Secretary of Energy** and the **Deputy Prime Minister of Great Britain** amongst them. Security will be handled by the **Diplomatic Protection Branch** of the police, with **MI5** and **CHERUB**.

6) HELP EARTH

A militant environmentalist group responsible for sending **mail bombs** to those who support the oil industry in the US and UK and the death of a **French oil executive.**

Despite this, nobody involved with **Help Earth** has been identified, although there are several violent suspects under suspicion. Four are currently resident at Fort Harmony. Given this, **an attack on Petrocon is likely.**

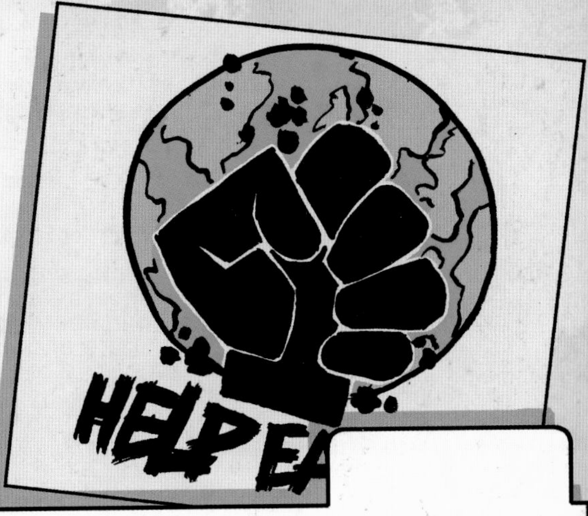
HELP EA

7) THE ROLE OF CHERUB

MI5 already has informers and **undercover agents** within the environmental movement but wants extra agents at Fort Harmony in the build up to Petrocon.

Any new adults arriving will be suspect. Therefore two **CHERUB** operatives posing as relatives of Fort Harmony resident **Cathy Dunn** will have the best chance of a successful undercover mission.

Dunn, a long-standing member of the Fort Harmony community turned **paid informer,** was briefly married to Gladys Dunn's son **Michael.**

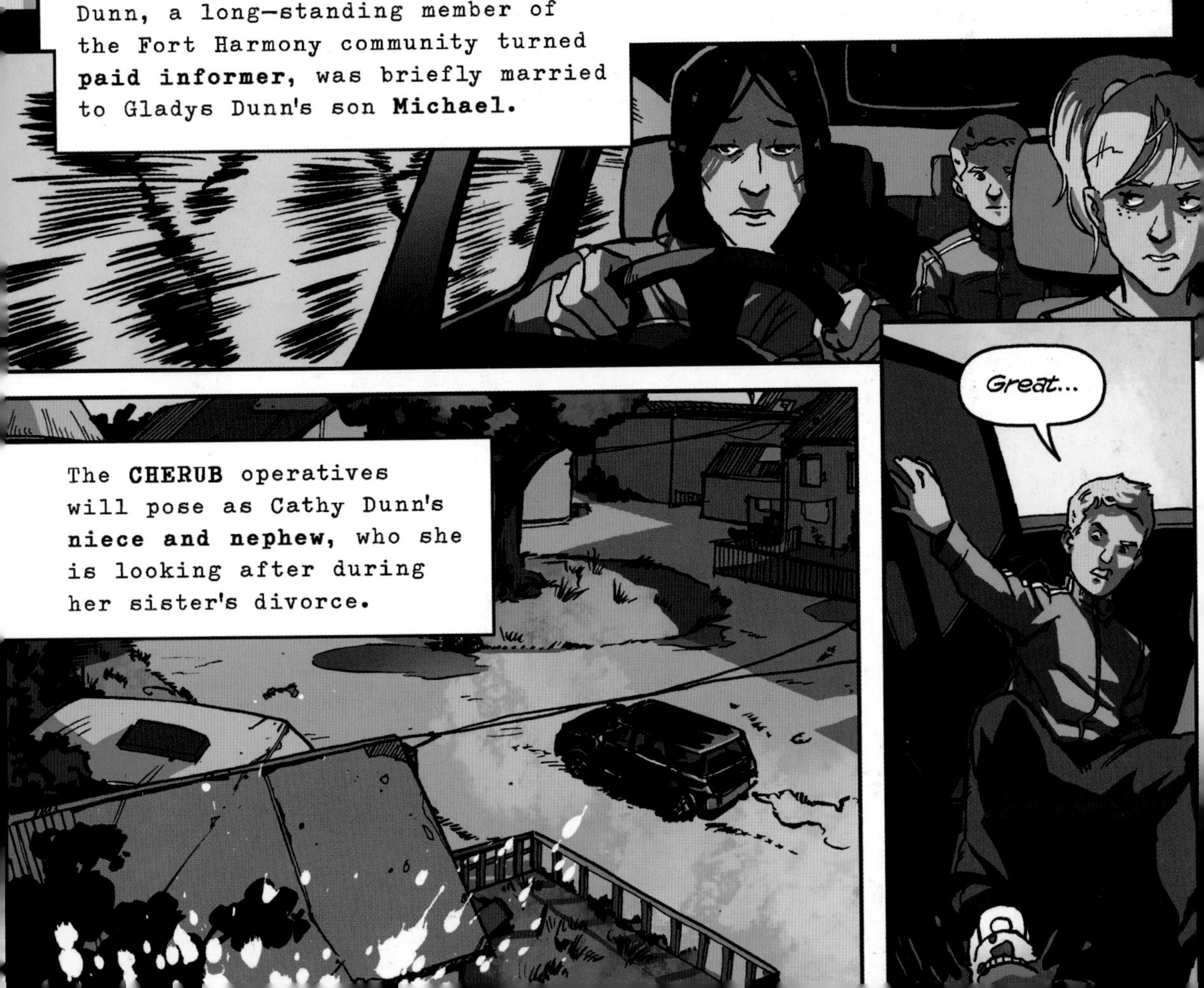
The CHERUB operatives will pose as Cathy Dunn's niece and nephew, who she is looking after during her sister's divorce.
Great...

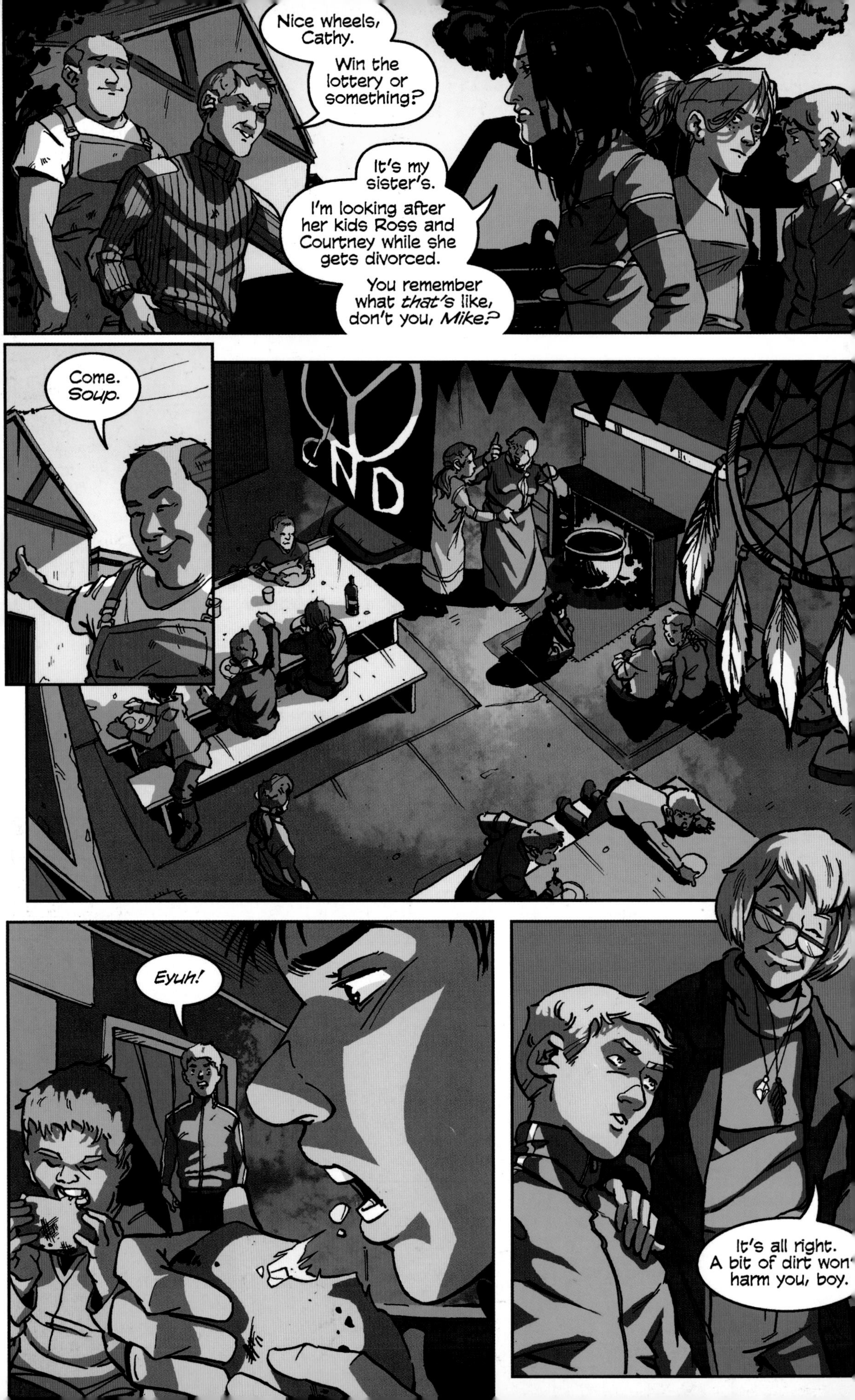
Nice wheels, Cathy.
Win the lottery or something?
It's my sister's.
I'm looking after her kids Ross and Courtney while she gets divorced.
You remember what *that's* like, don't you, *Mike?*
Come. Soup.
Eyuh!
It's all right. A bit of dirt won' harm you, boy.

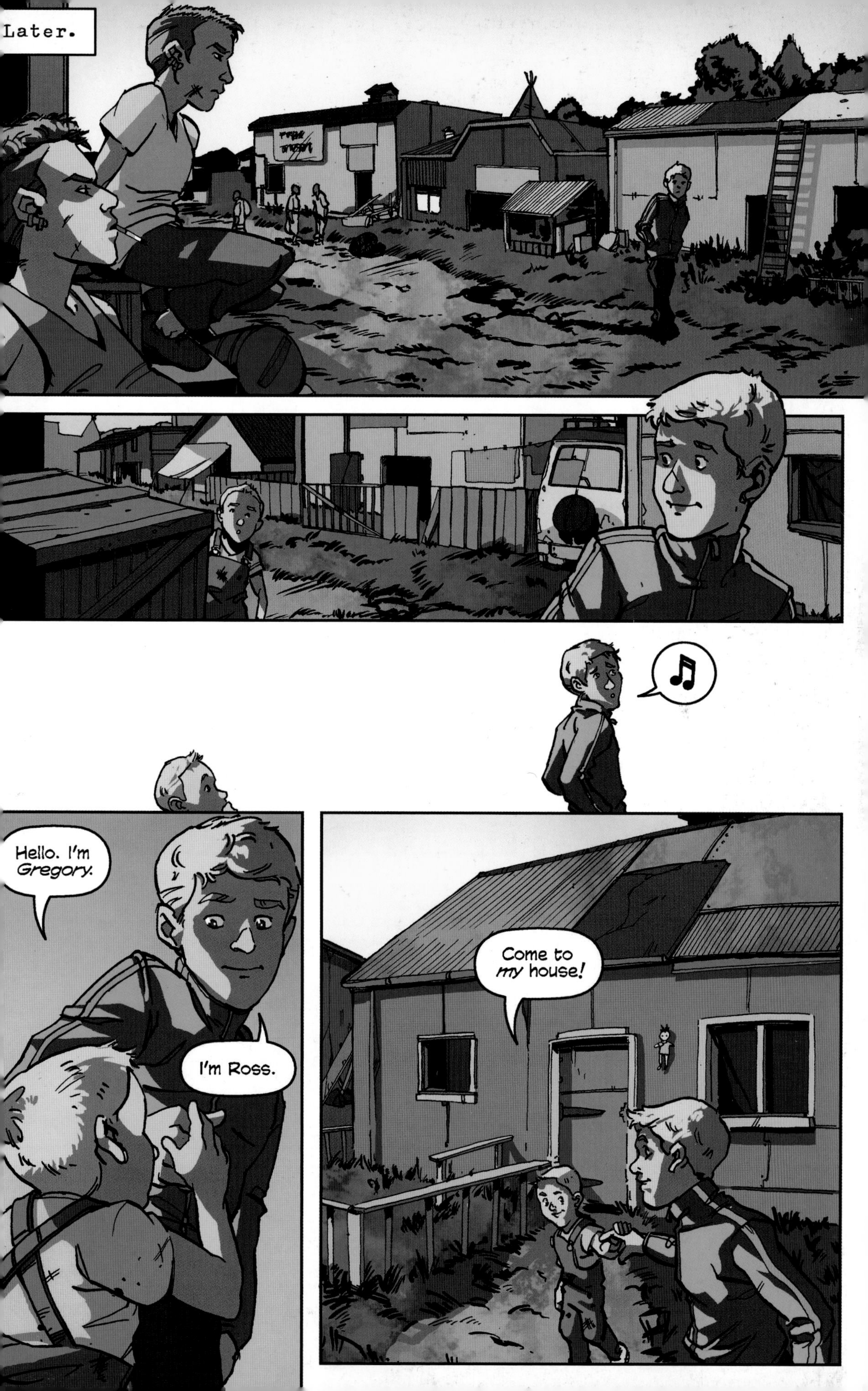
Later.
♫
Hello. I'm *Gregory.*
I'm Ross.
Come to *my* house!

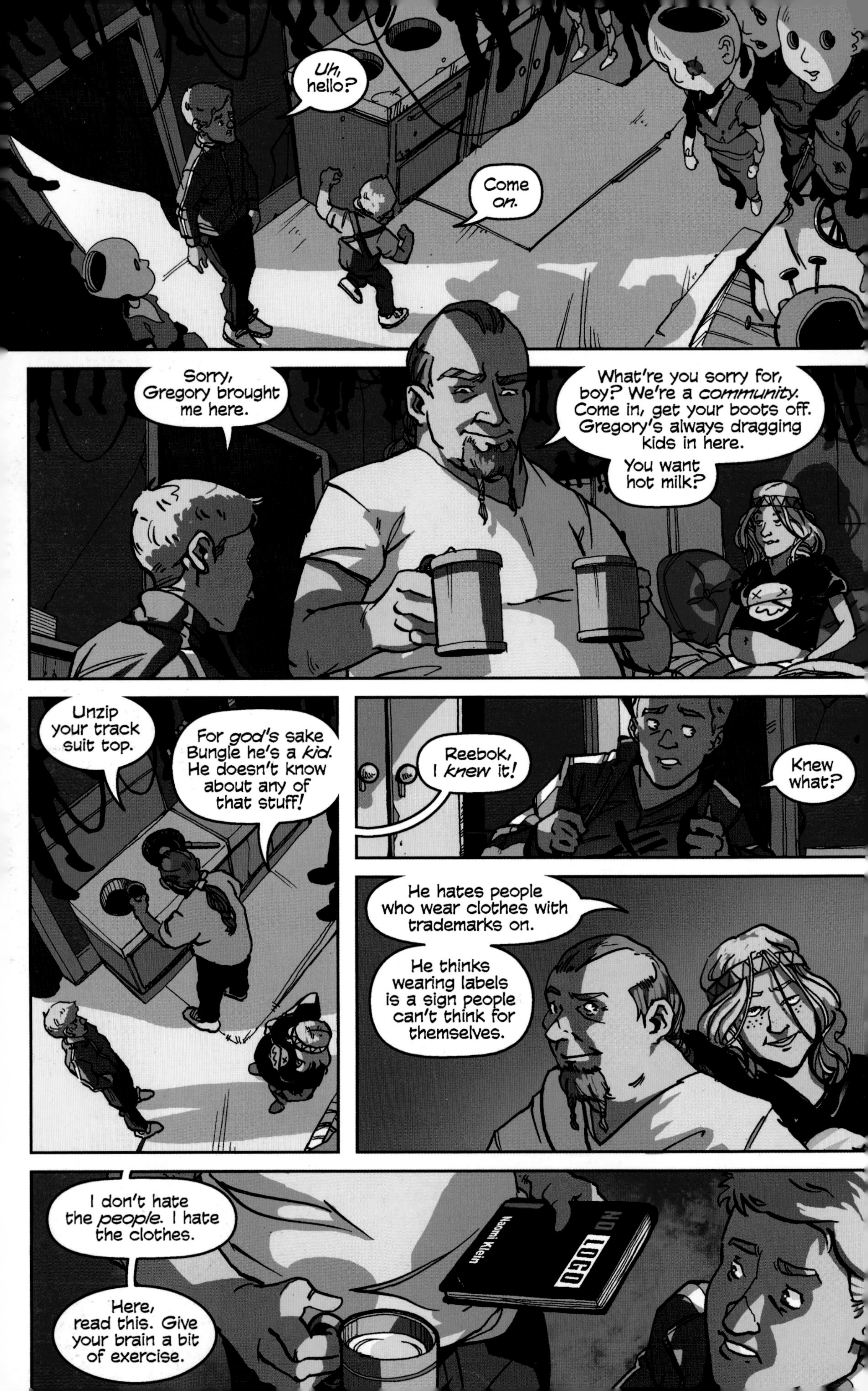
Uh, hello?
Come on.
Sorry, Gregory brought me here.
What're you sorry for, boy? We're a community. Come in, get your boots off. Gregory's always dragging kids in here.
You want hot milk?
Unzip your track suit top.
For god's sake Bungle he's a kid. He doesn't know about any of that stuff!
Reebok, I knew it!
Knew what?
He hates people who wear clothes with trademarks on.
He thinks wearing labels is a sign people can't think for themselves.
I don't hate the people. I hate the clothes.
Here, read this. Give your brain a bit of exercise.
NO LOGO
Naomi Klein

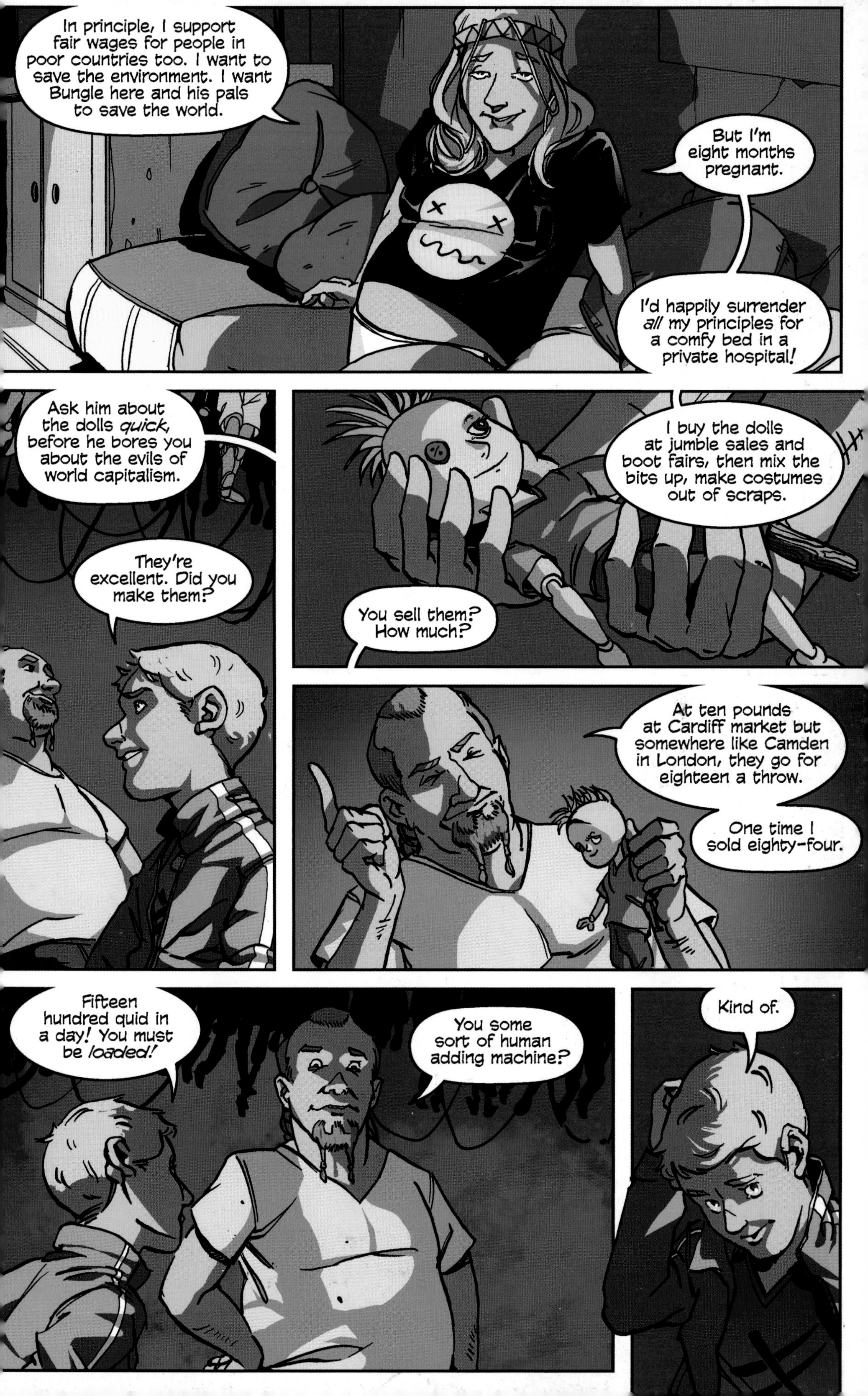

In principle, I support fair wages for people in poor countries too. I want to save the environment. I want Bungle here and his pals to save the world.
But I'm eight months pregnant.
I'd happily surrender *all* my principles for a comfy bed in a private hospital!
Ask him about the dolls *quick*, before he bores you about the evils of world capitalism.
They're excellent. Did you make them?
I buy the dolls at jumble sales and boot fairs, then mix the bits up, make costumes out of scraps.
You sell them? How much?
At ten pounds at Cardiff market but somewhere like Camden in London, they go for eighteen a throw.
One time I sold eighty-four.
Fifteen hundred quid in a day! You must be *loaded!*
You some sort of human adding machine?
Kind of.

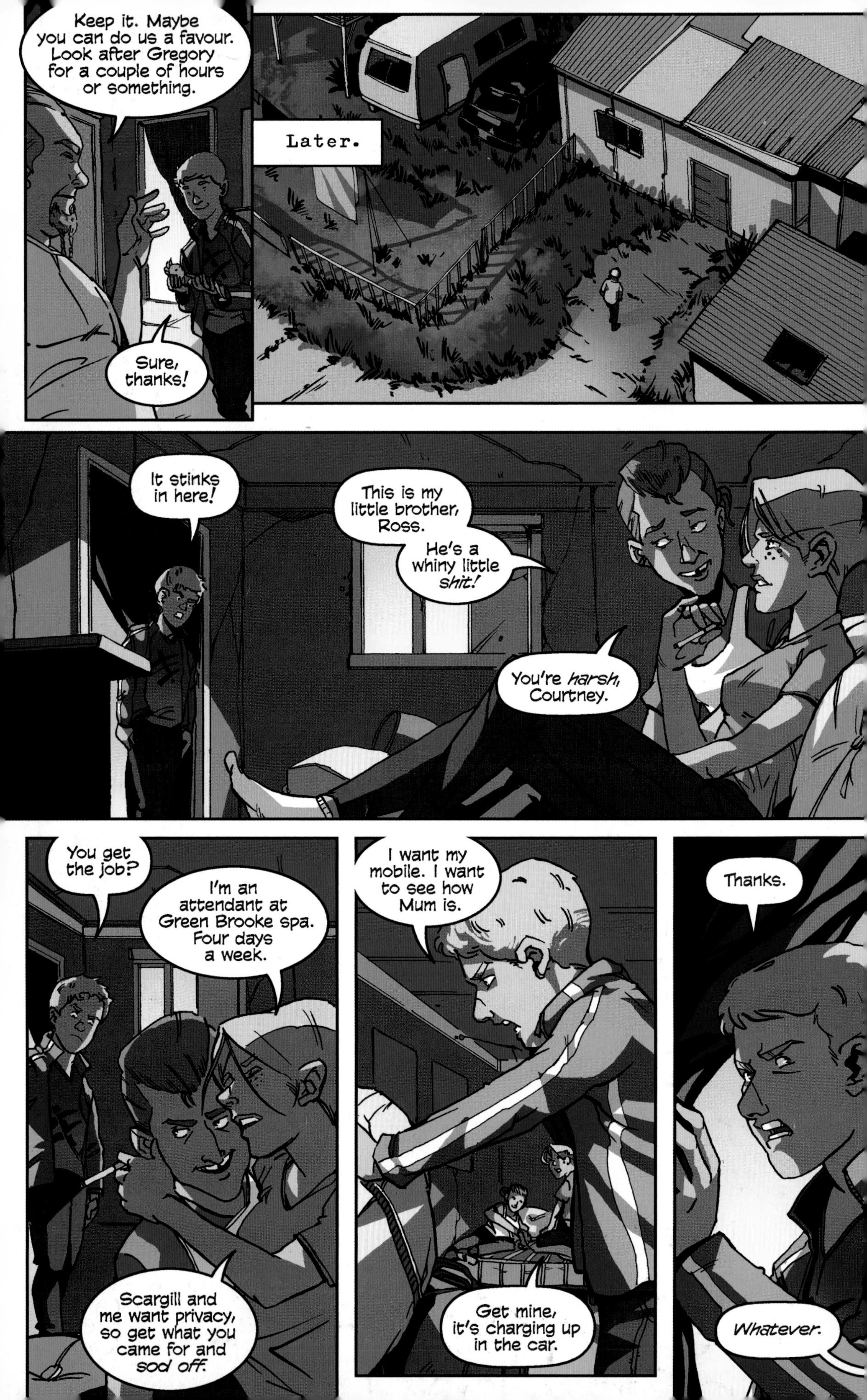
Keep it. Maybe you can do us a favour. Look after Gregory for a couple of hours or something.
Sure, thanks!
Later.
It stinks in here!
This is my little brother, Ross.
He's a whiny little *shit!*
You're *harsh*, Courtney.
You get the job?
I'm an attendant at Green Brooke spa. Four days a week.
Scargill and me want privacy, so get what you came for and *sod off.*
I want my mobile. I want to see how Mum is.
Get mine, it's charging up in the car.
Thanks.
Whatever.

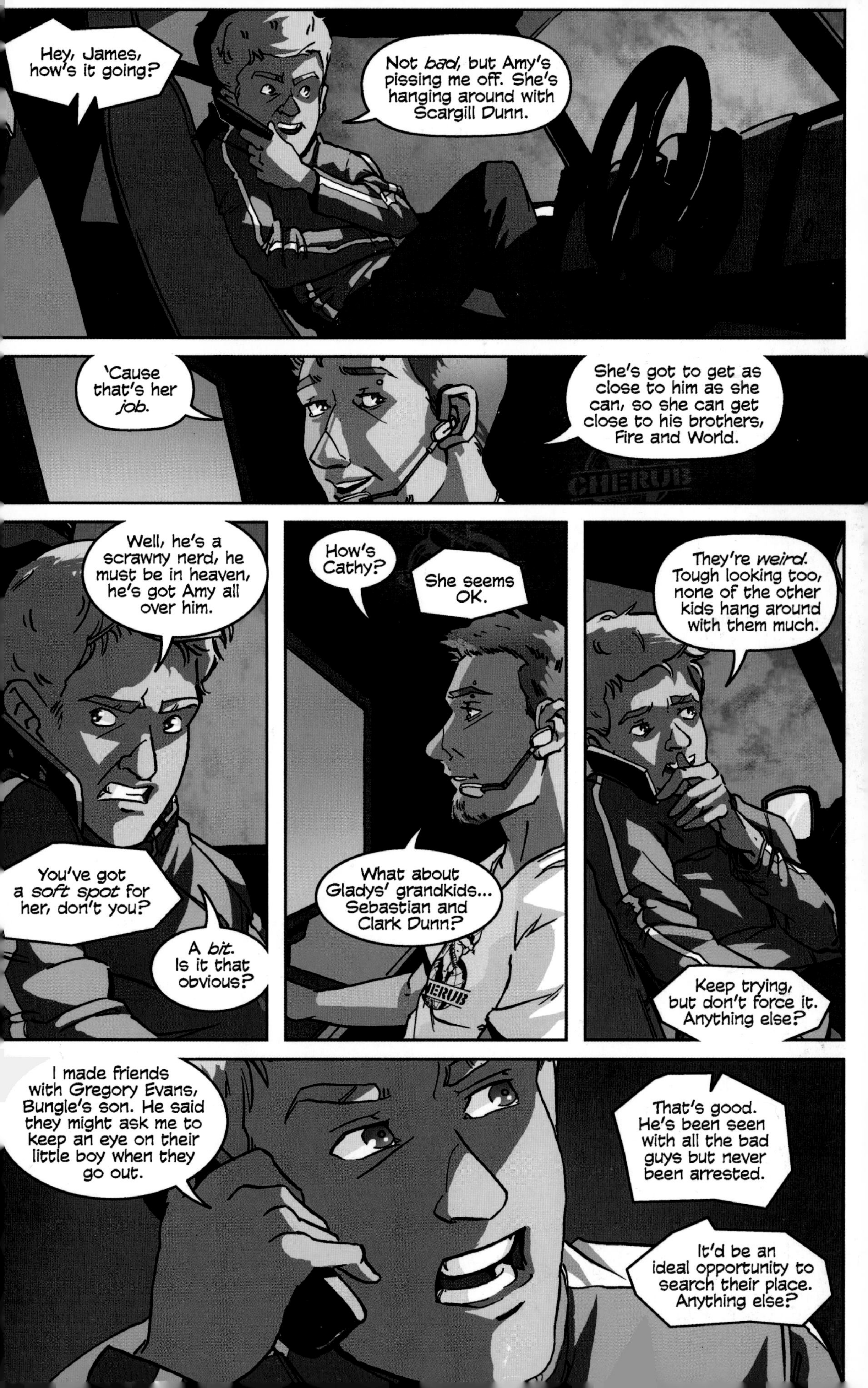
Hey, James, how's it going?
Not *bad*, but Amy's pissing me off. She's hanging around with Scargill Dunn.
'Cause that's her *job*.
She's got to get as close to him as she can, so she can get close to his brothers, Fire and World.
CHERUB
Well, he's a scrawny nerd, he must be in heaven, he's got Amy all over him.
You've got a *soft spot* for her, don't you?
A *bit*. Is it that obvious?
How's Cathy?
She seems OK.
What about Gladys' grandkids... Sebastian and Clark Dunn?
They're *weird*. Tough looking too, none of the other kids hang around with them much.
Keep trying, but don't force it. Anything else?
I made friends with Gregory Evans, Bungle's son. He said they might ask me to keep an eye on their little boy when they go out.
That's good. He's been seen with all the bad guys but never been arrested.
It'd be an ideal opportunity to search their place. Anything else?

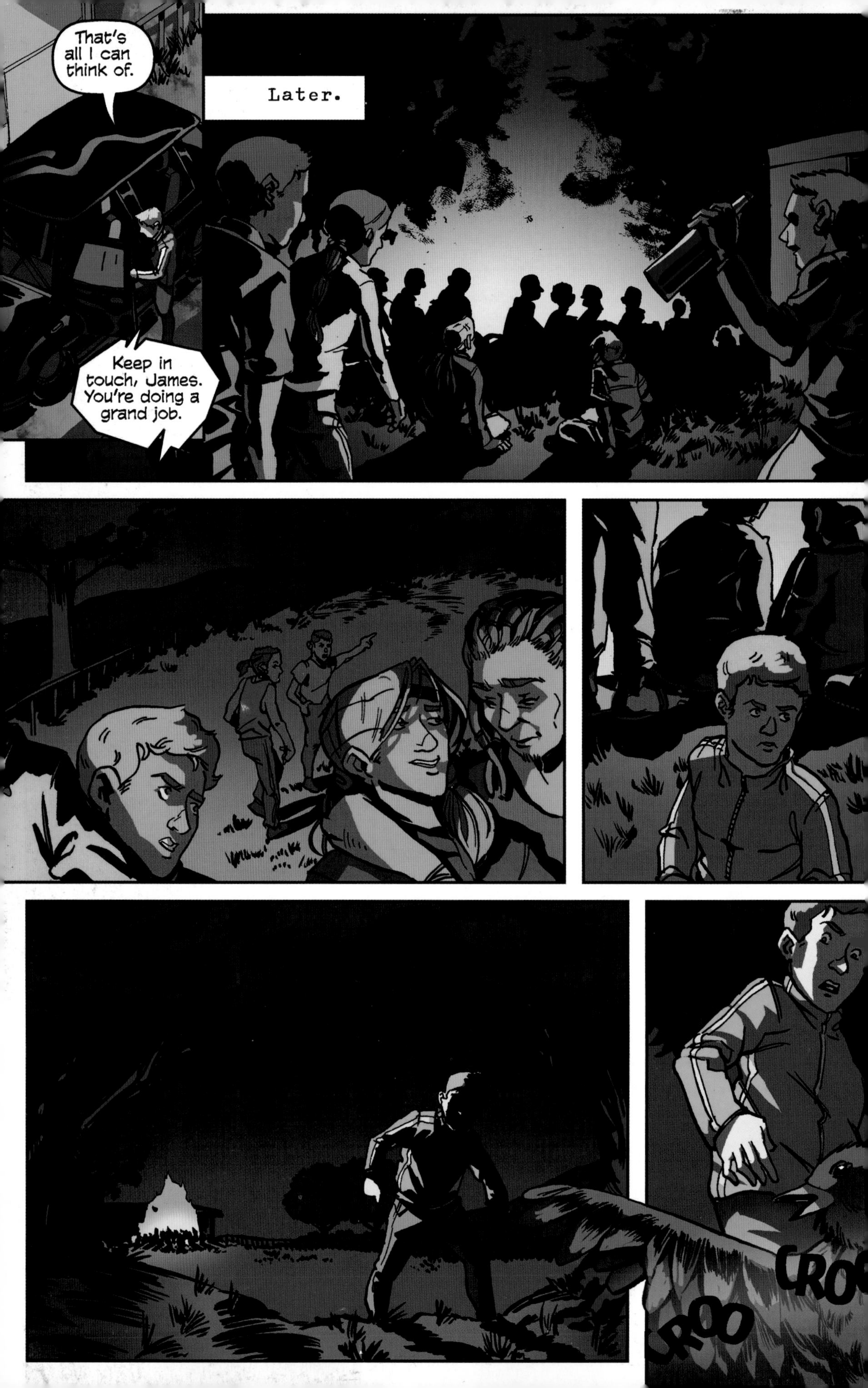
That's all I can think of.
Keep in touch, James. You're doing a grand job.
Later.
CROO
CROO

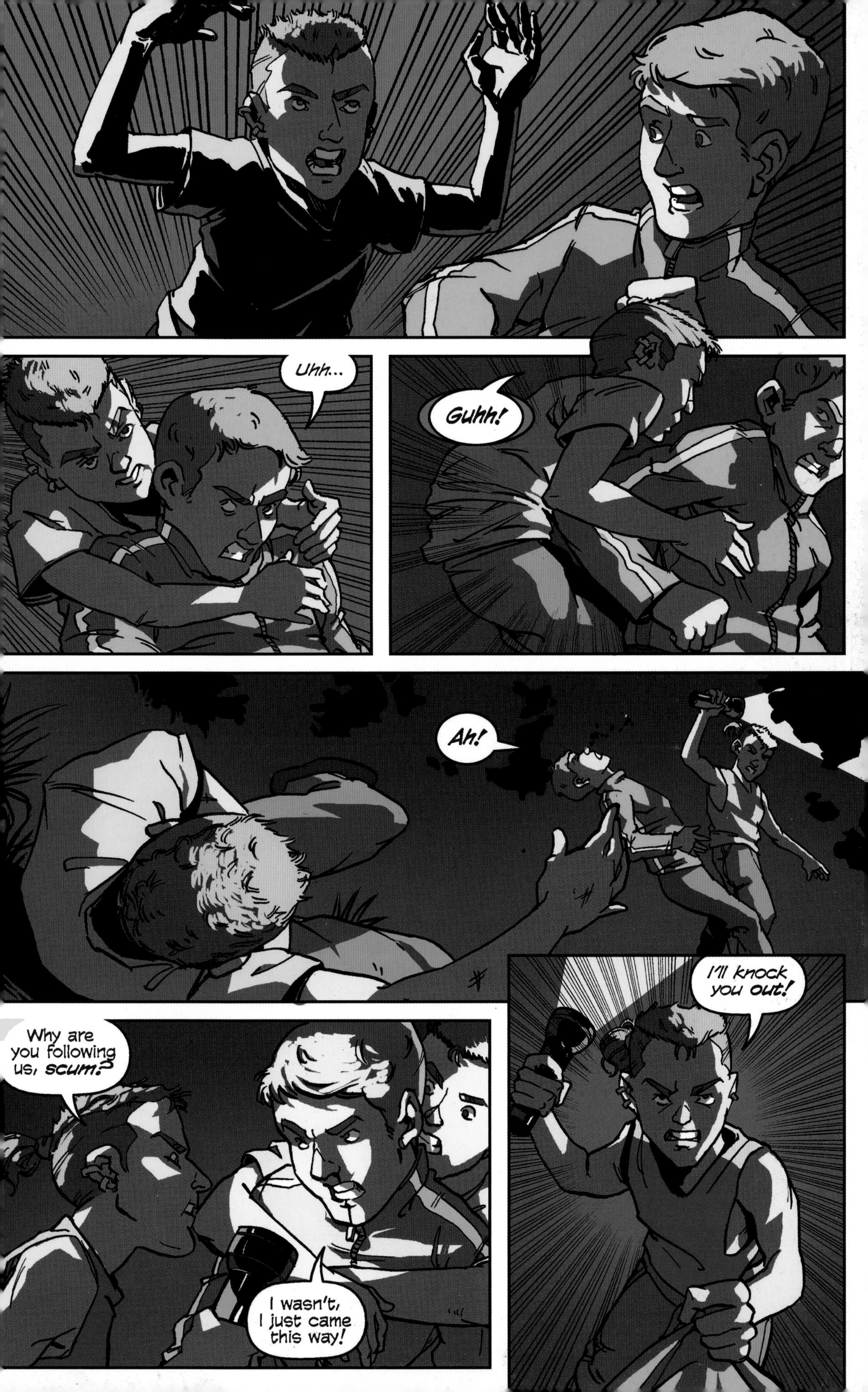
Uhh...
Guhh!
Ah!
I'll knock you out!
Why are you following us, scum?
I wasn't, I just came this way!

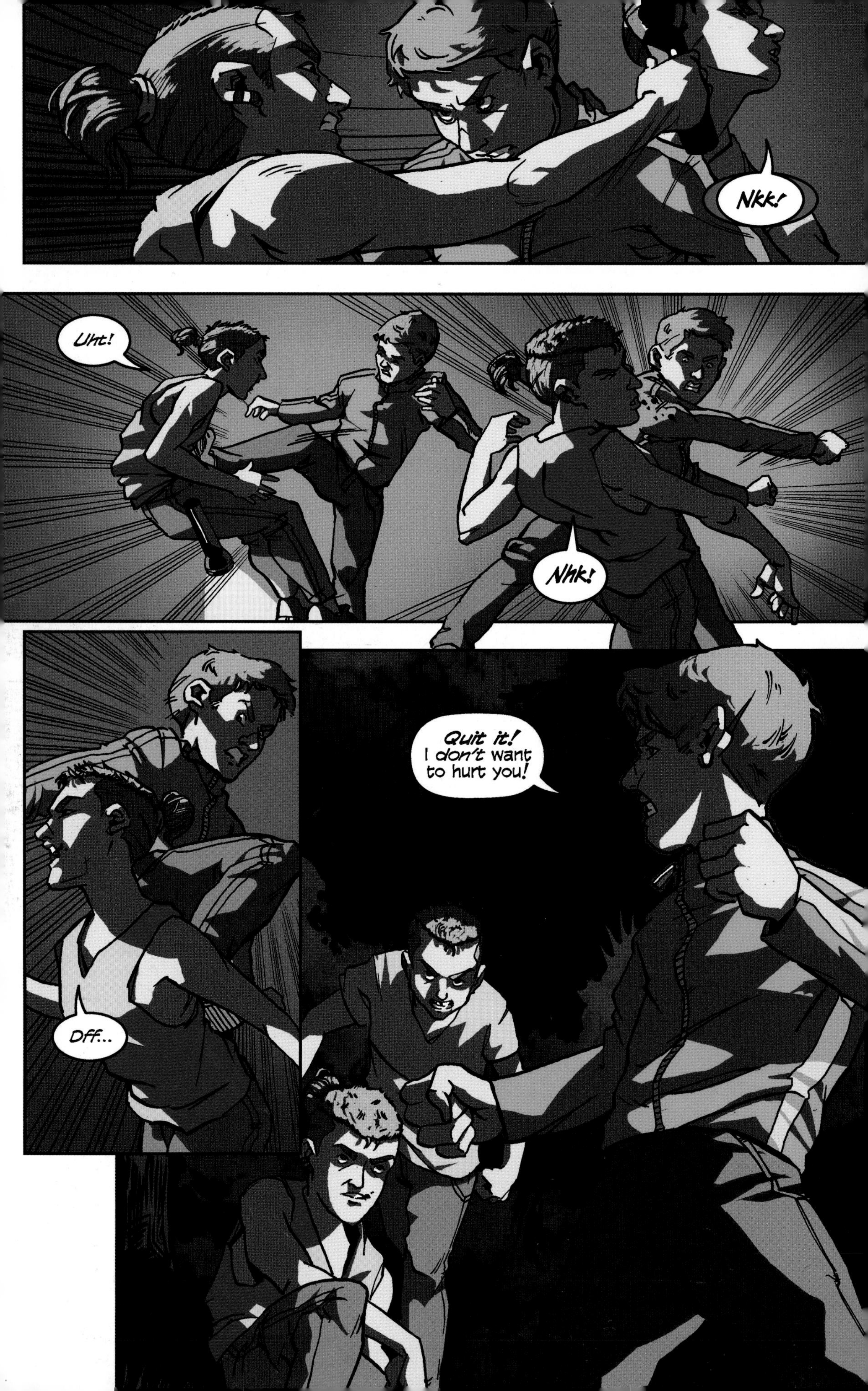
Nkk!
Uht!
Nhk!
Off...
Quit it! I don't want to hurt you!

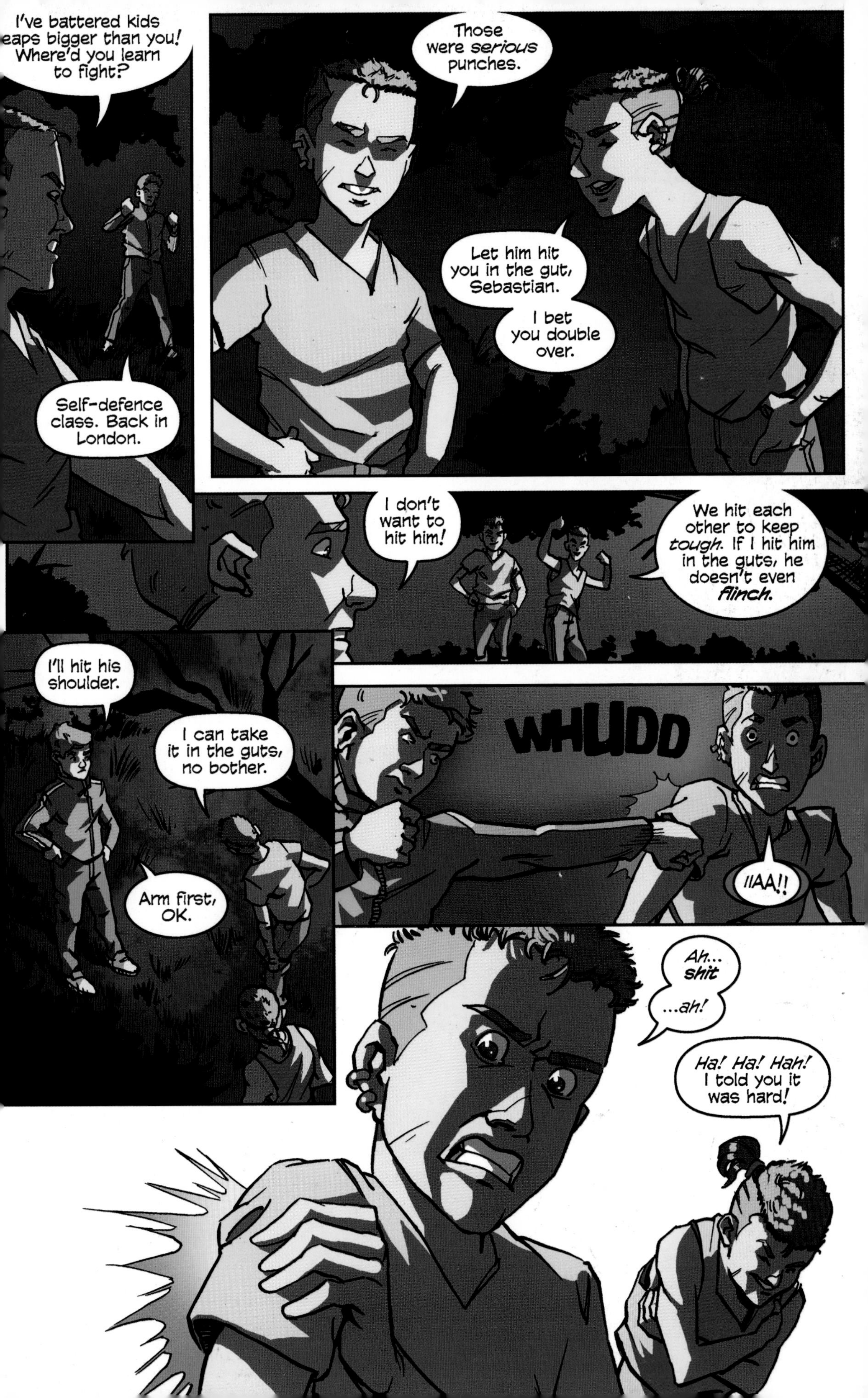
I've battered kids eaps bigger than you! Where'd you learn to fight?
Self-defence class. Back in London.
Those were serious punches.
Let him hit you in the gut, Sebastian.
I bet you double over.
I don't want to hit him!
We hit each other to keep tough. If I hit him in the guts, he doesn't even flinch.
I'll hit his shoulder.
I can take it in the guts, no bother.
Arm first, OK.
WHUDD
!!AA!!
Ah... shit
...ah!
Ha! Ha! Hah! I told you it was hard!

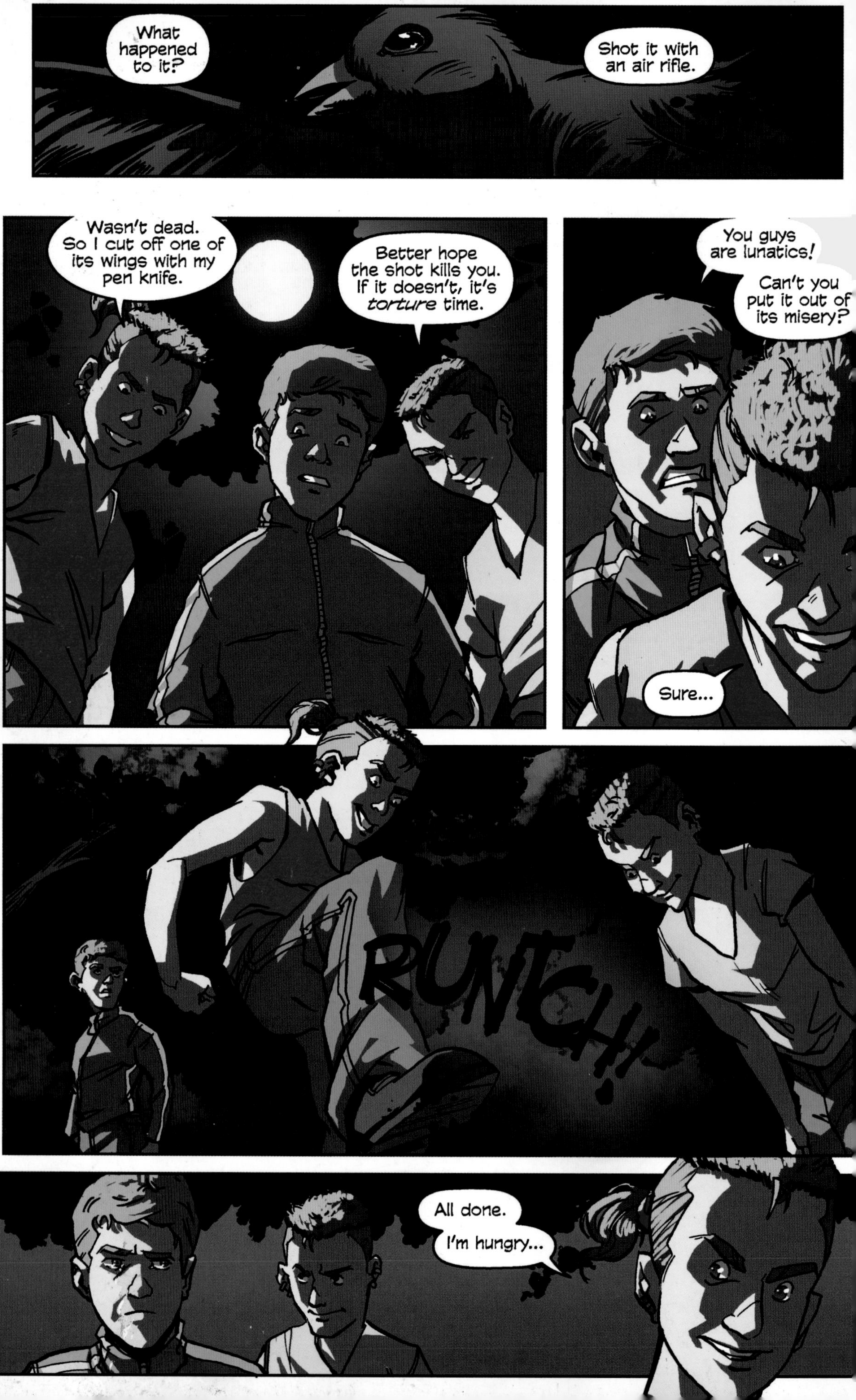
What happened to it?
Shot it with an air rifle.
Wasn't dead. So I cut off one of its wings with my pen knife.
Better hope the shot kills you. If it doesn't, it's *torture* time.
You guys are lunatics!
Can't you put it out of its misery?
Sure...
RUNTCH!!
All done.
I'm hungry...

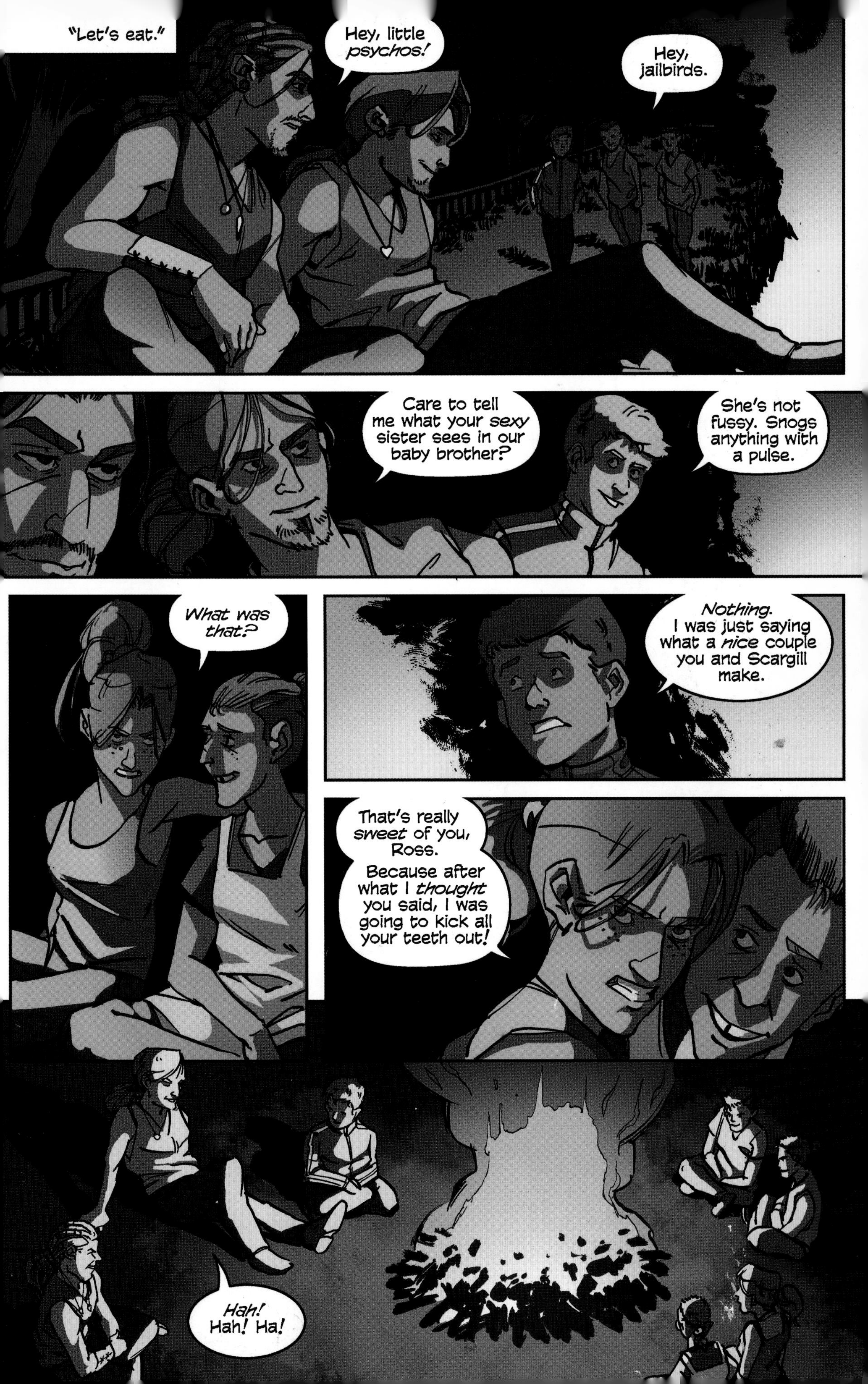
"Let's eat."
Hey, little *psychos!*
Hey, jailbirds.
Care to tell me what your *sexy* sister sees in our baby brother?
She's not fussy. Snogs anything with a pulse.
What was that?
Nothing. I was just saying what a *nice* couple you and Scargill make.
That's really *sweet* of you, Ross.
Because after what I *thought* you said, I was going to kick all your teeth out!
Hah! Hah! Ha!

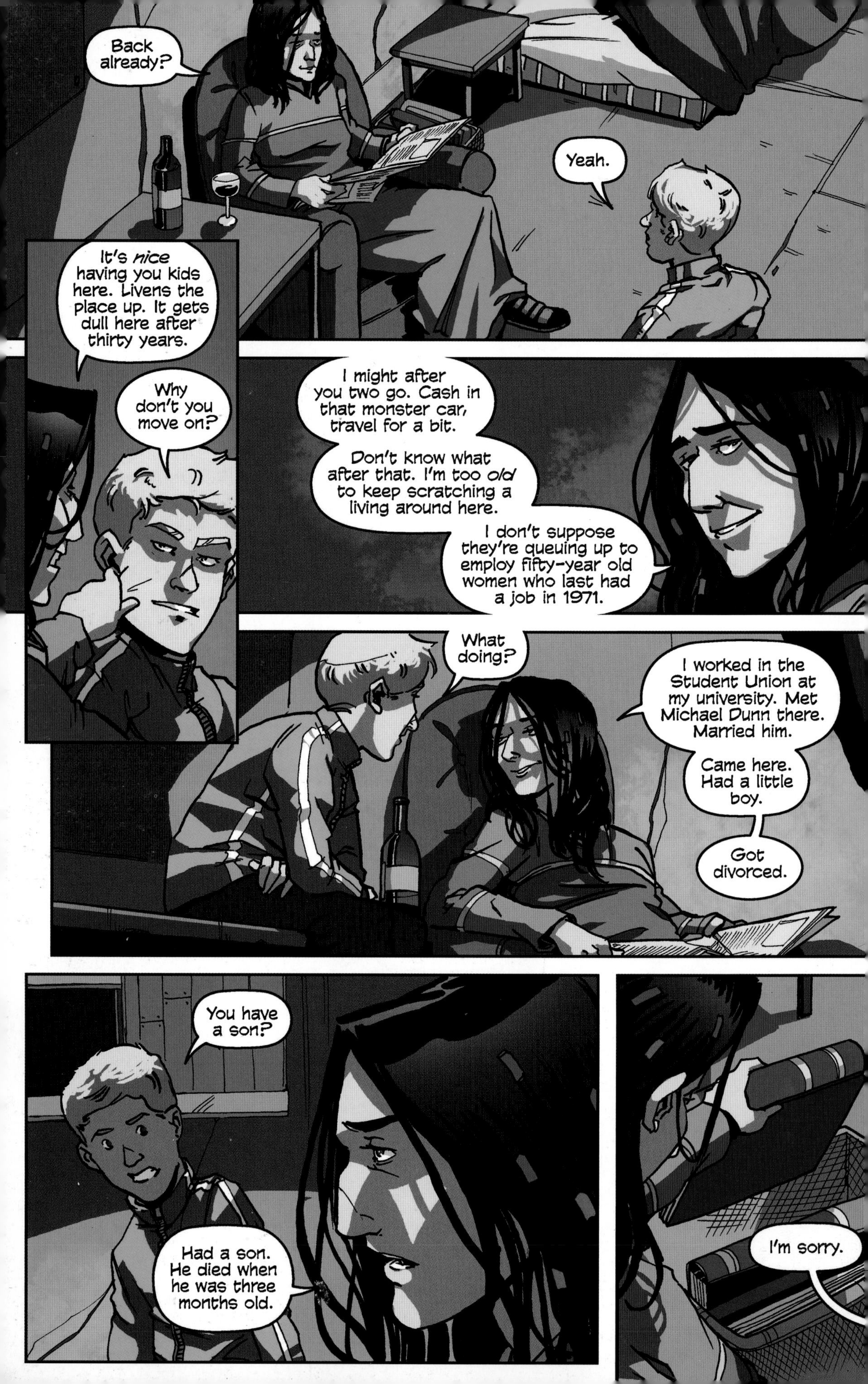
Back already?
Yeah.
It's *nice* having you kids here. Livens the place up. It gets dull here after thirty years.
Why don't you move on?
I might after you two go. Cash in that monster car, travel for a bit.
Don't know what after that. I'm too *old* to keep scratching a living around here.
I don't suppose they're queuing up to employ fifty-year old women who last had a job in 1971.
What doing?
I worked in the Student Union at my university. Met Michael Dunn there. Married him.
Came here. Had a little boy.
Got divorced.
You have a son?
Had a son. He died when he was three months old.
I'm sorry.

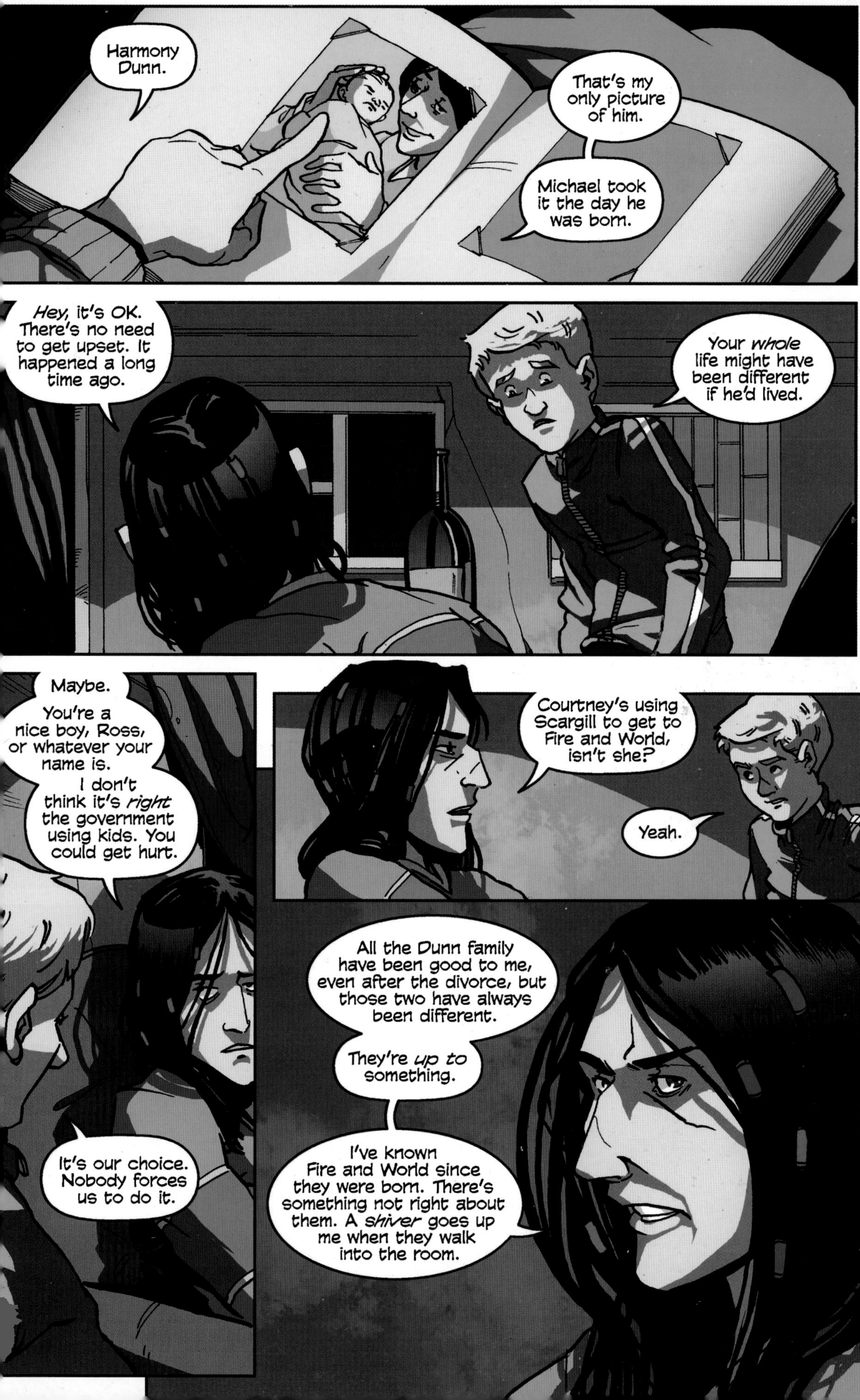

Harmony Dunn.
That's my only picture of him.
Michael took it the day he was born.
Hey, it's OK. There's no need to get upset. It happened a long time ago.
Your *whole* life might have been different if he'd lived.
Maybe.
You're a nice boy, Ross, or whatever your name is.
I don't think it's *right* the government using kids. You could get hurt.
It's our choice. Nobody forces us to do it.
Courtney's using Scargill to get to Fire and World, isn't she?
Yeah.
All the Dunn family have been good to me, even after the divorce, but those two have always been different.
They're *up to* something.
I've known Fire and World since they were born. There's something not right about them. A *shiver* goes up me when they walk into the room.

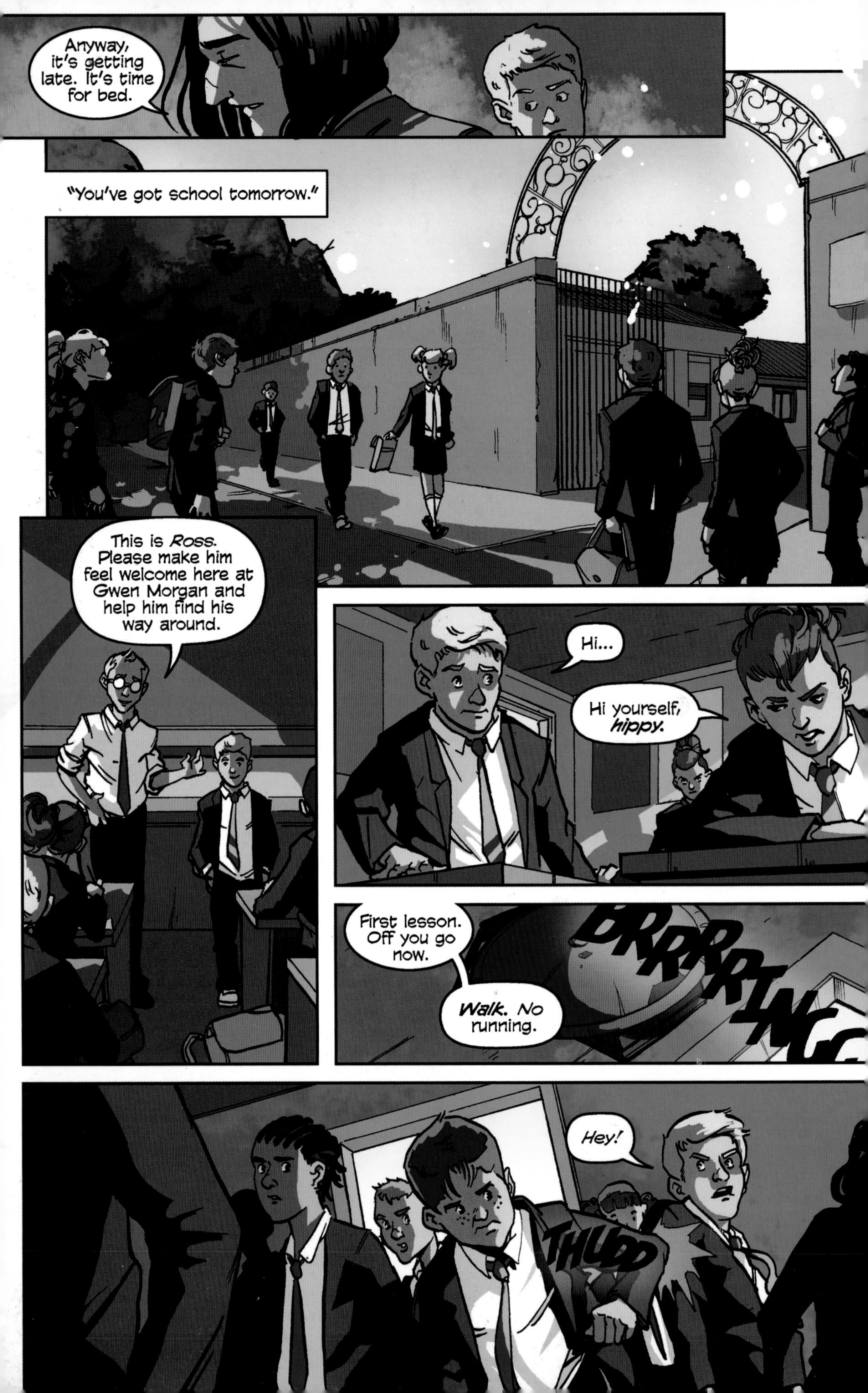
Anyway, it's getting late. It's time for bed.
"You've got school tomorrow."
This is *Ross*. Please make him feel welcome here at Gwen Morgan and help him find his way around.
Hi...
Hi yourself, ***hippy***.
First lesson. Off you go now.
Walk. No running.
BRRRRING
Hey!
THUDD

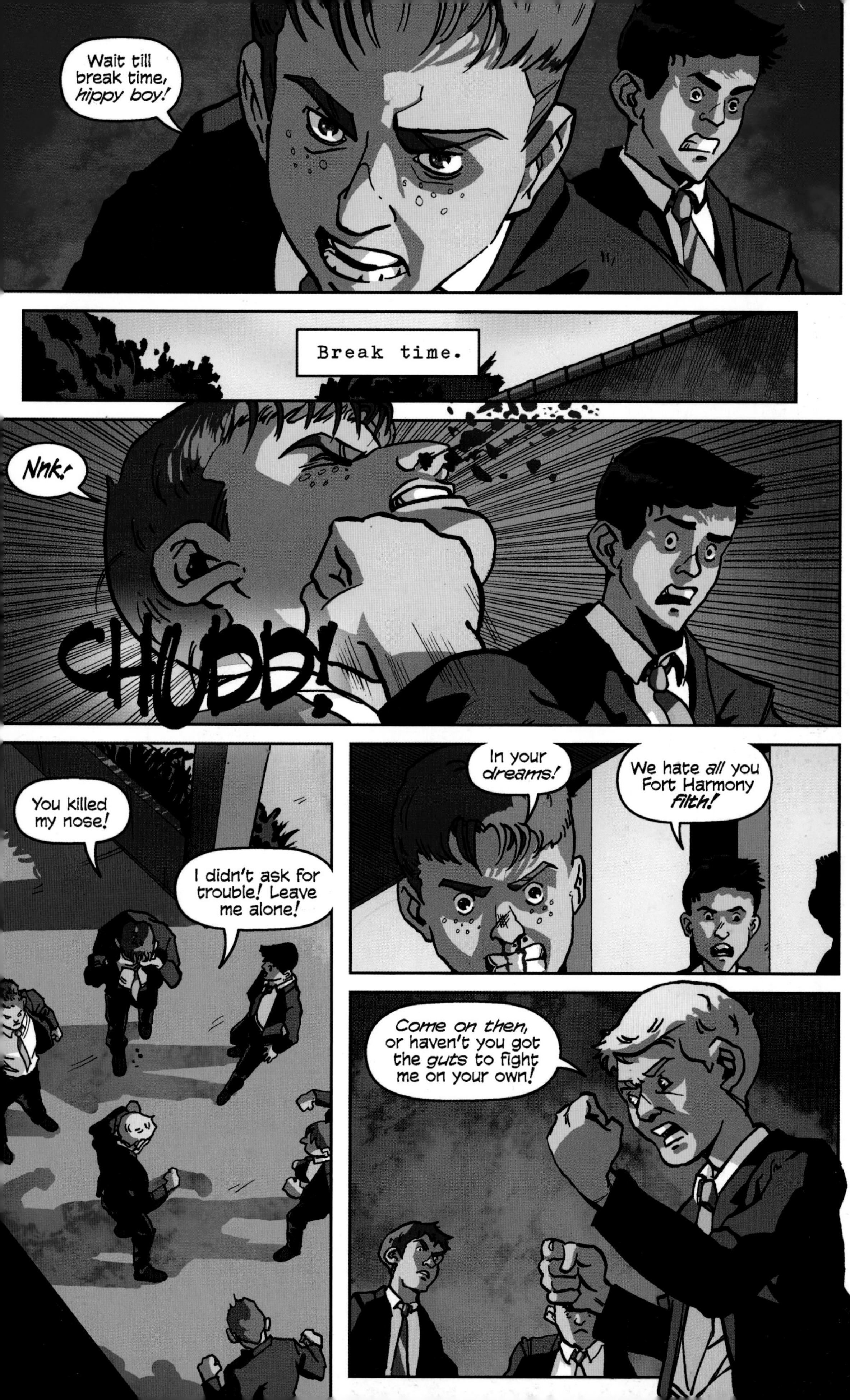
Wait till break time, *hippy boy!*
Break time.
Nnk!
CHUDD!
You killed my nose!
I didn't ask for trouble! Leave me alone!
In your *dreams!*
We hate *all* you Fort Harmony *filth!*
Come on then, or haven't you got the *guts* to fight me on your own!

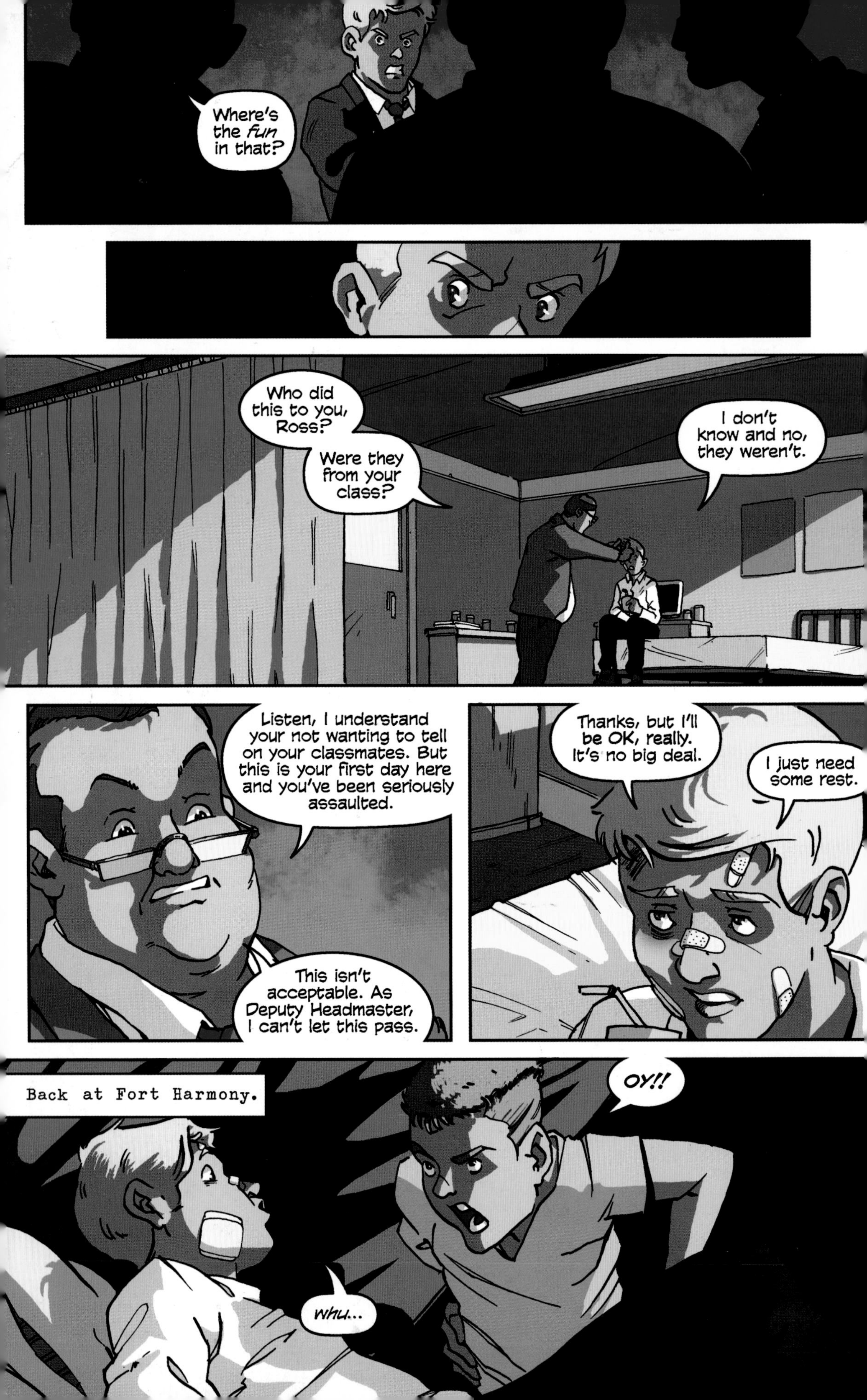
Where's the *fun* in that?
Who did this to you, Ross?
Were they from your class?
I don't know and no, they weren't.
Listen, I understand your not wanting to tell on your classmates. But this is your first day here and you've been seriously assaulted.
This isn't acceptable. As Deputy Headmaster, I can't let this pass.
Thanks, but I'll be OK, really. It's no big deal.
I just need some rest.
Back at Fort Harmony.
OY!!
whu...

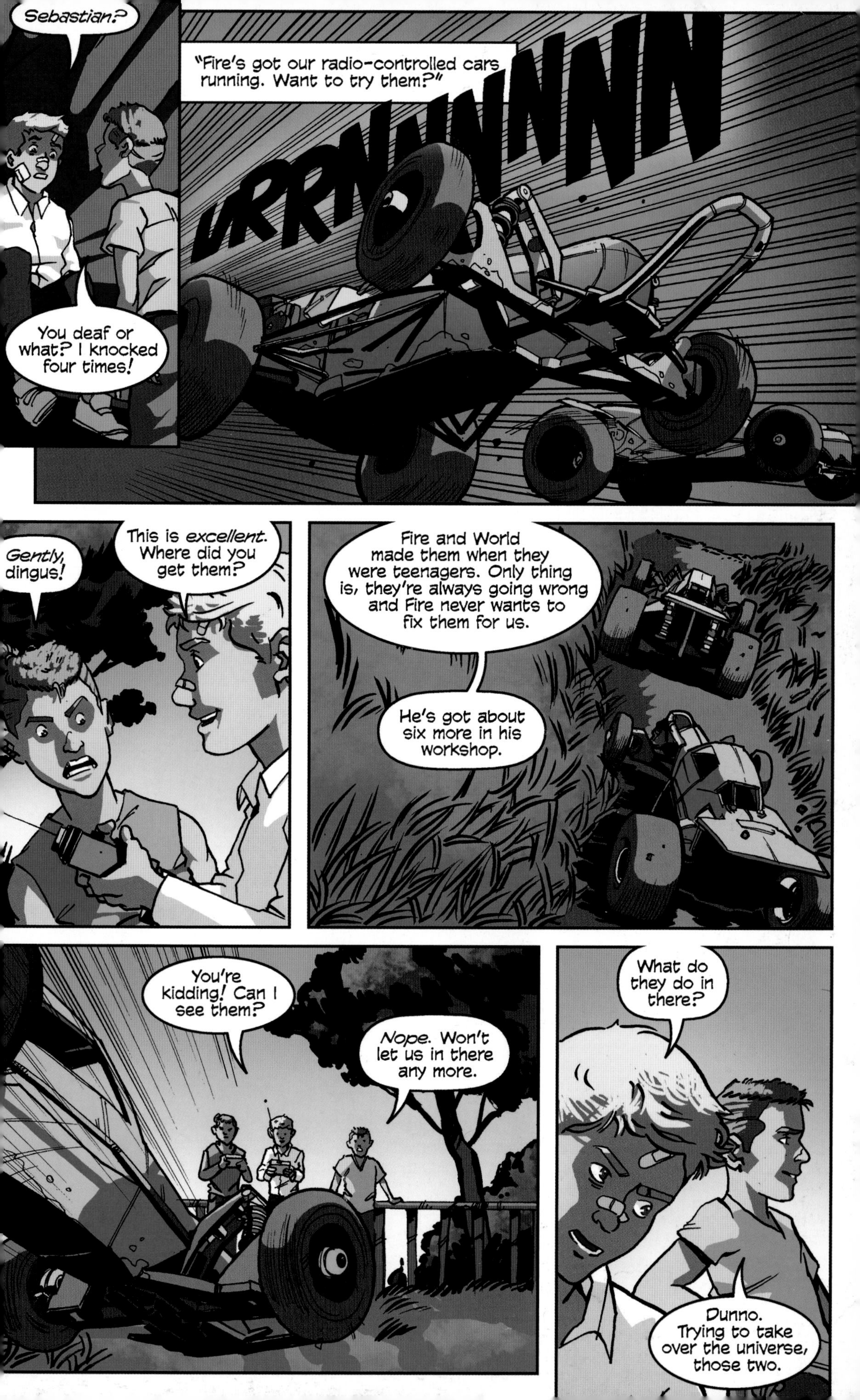
Sebastian?
"Fire's got our radio-controlled cars running. Want to try them?"
URRNNNNNNN
You deaf or what? I knocked four times!
Gently, dingus!
This is excellent. Where did you get them?
Fire and World made them when they were teenagers. Only thing is, they're always going wrong and Fire never wants to fix them for us.
He's got about six more in his workshop.
You're kidding! Can I see them?
Nope. Won't let us in there any more.
What do they do in there?
Dunno. Trying to take over the universe, those two.

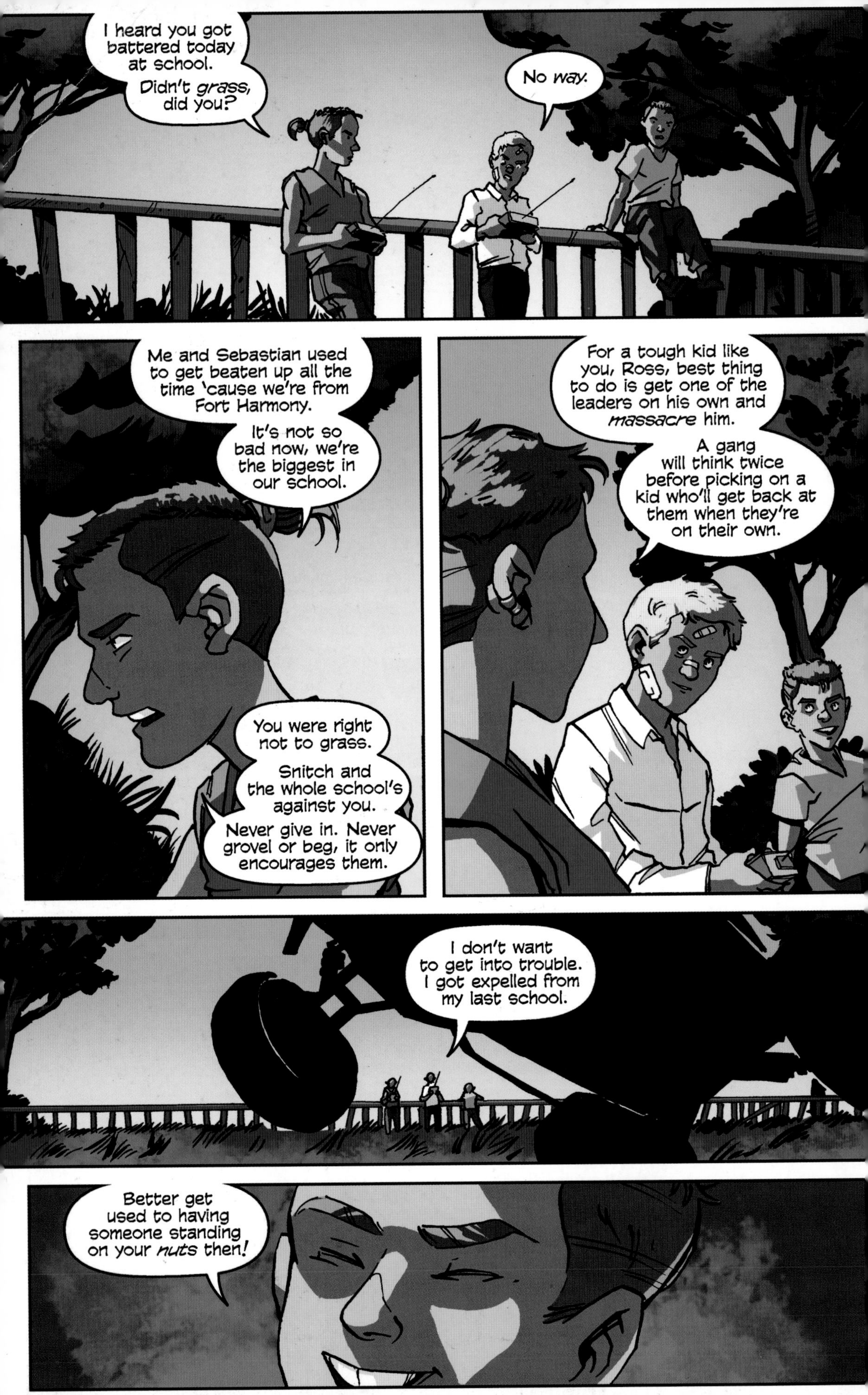
I heard you got battered today at school.
Didn't *grass*, did you?
No *way*.
Me and Sebastian used to get beaten up all the time 'cause we're from Fort Harmony.
It's not so bad now, we're the biggest in our school.
You were right not to grass.
Snitch and the whole school's against you.
Never give in. Never grovel or beg, it only encourages them.
For a tough kid like you, Ross, best thing to do is get one of the leaders on his own and *massacre* him.
A gang will think twice before picking on a kid who'll get back at them when they're on their own.
I don't want to get into trouble. I got expelled from my last school.
Better get used to having someone standing on your *nuts* then!

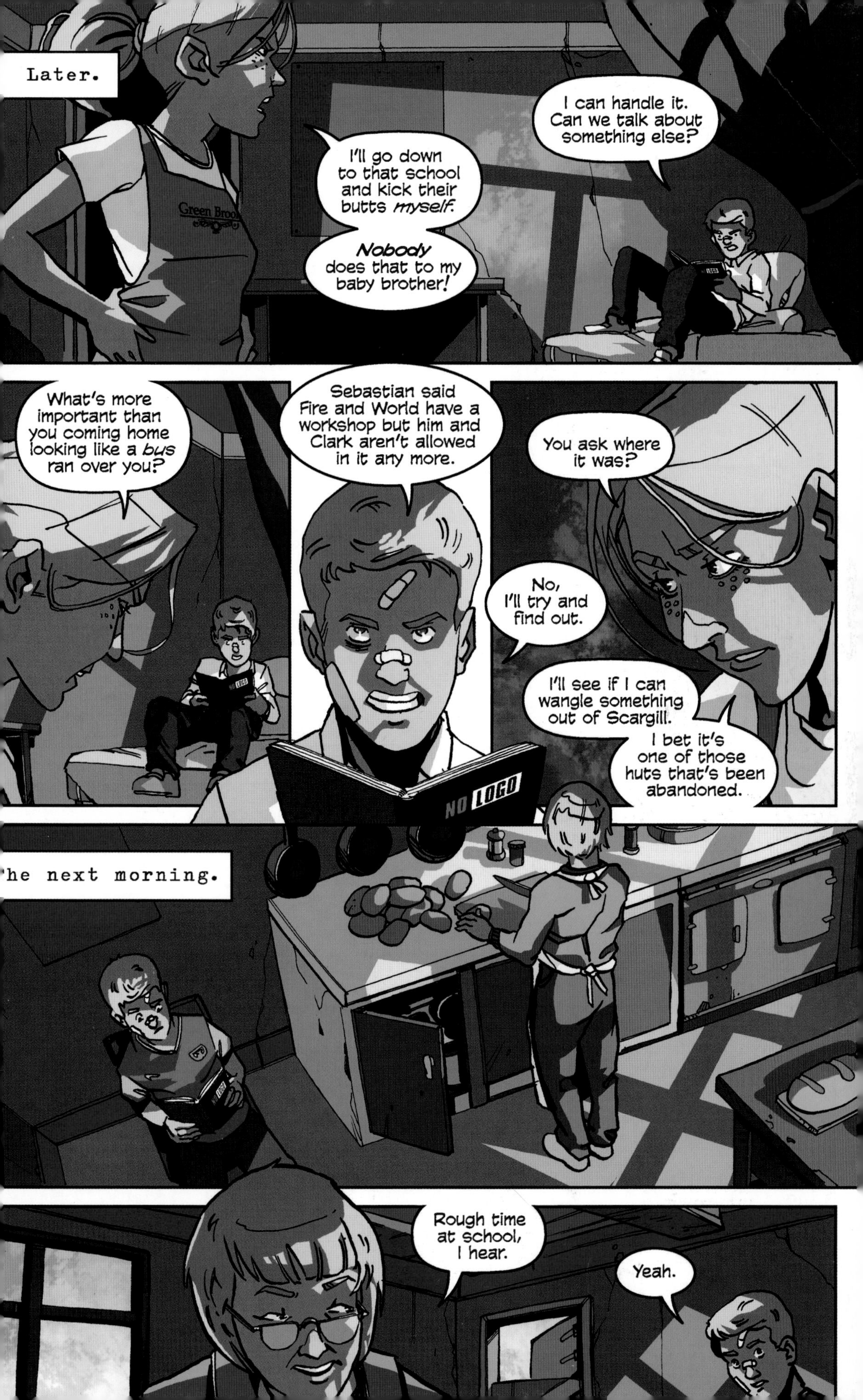
Later.
I'll go down to that school and kick their butts *myself*.
Nobody does that to my baby brother!
I can handle it. Can we talk about something else?
What's more important than you coming home looking like a *bus* ran over you?
Sebastian said Fire and World have a workshop but him and Clark aren't allowed in it any more.
You ask where it was?
No, I'll try and find out.
I'll see if I can wangle something out of Scargill.
I bet it's one of those huts that's been abandoned.
NO LOGO
he next morning.
Rough time at school, I hear.
Yeah.

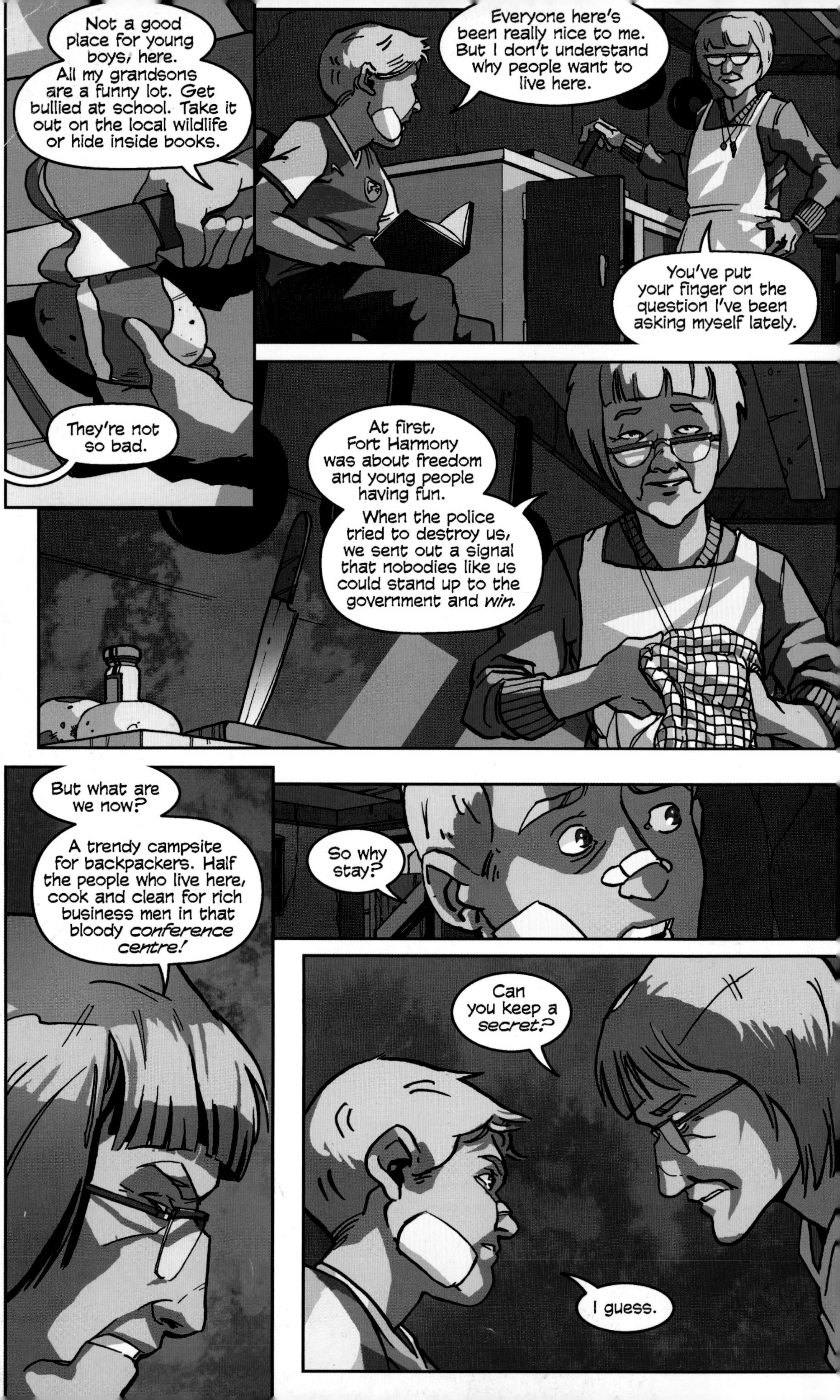
Not a good place for young boys, here. All my grandsons are a funny lot. Get bullied at school. Take it out on the local wildlife or hide inside books.
Everyone here's been really nice to me. But I don't understand why people want to live here.
You've put your finger on the question I've been asking myself lately.
They're not so bad.
At first, Fort Harmony was about freedom and young people having fun.
When the police tried to destroy us, we sent out a signal that nobodies like us could stand up to the government and *win.*
But what are we now?
A trendy campsite for backpackers. Half the people who live here, cook and clean for rich business men in that bloody *conference centre!*
So why stay?
Can you keep a *secret?*
I guess.

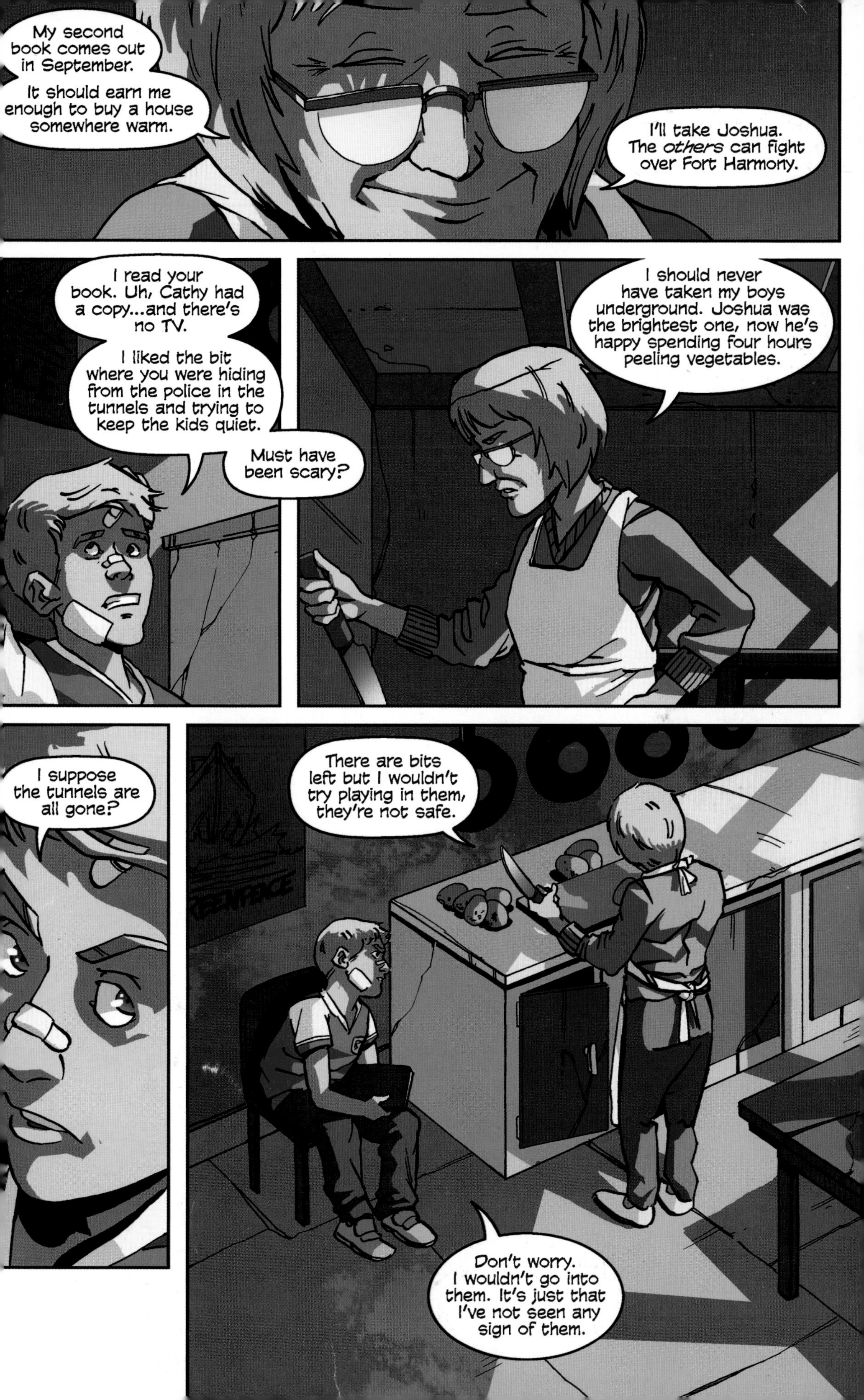
My second book comes out in September.
It should earn me enough to buy a house somewhere warm.
I'll take Joshua. The *others* can fight over Fort Harmony.
I read your book. Uh, Cathy had a copy...and there's no TV.
I liked the bit where you were hiding from the police in the tunnels and trying to keep the kids quiet.
Must have been scary?
I should never have taken my boys underground. Joshua was the brightest one, now he's happy spending four hours peeling vegetables.
I suppose the tunnels are all gone?
There are bits left but I wouldn't try playing in them, they're not safe.
Don't worry. I wouldn't go into them. It's just that I've not seen any sign of them.

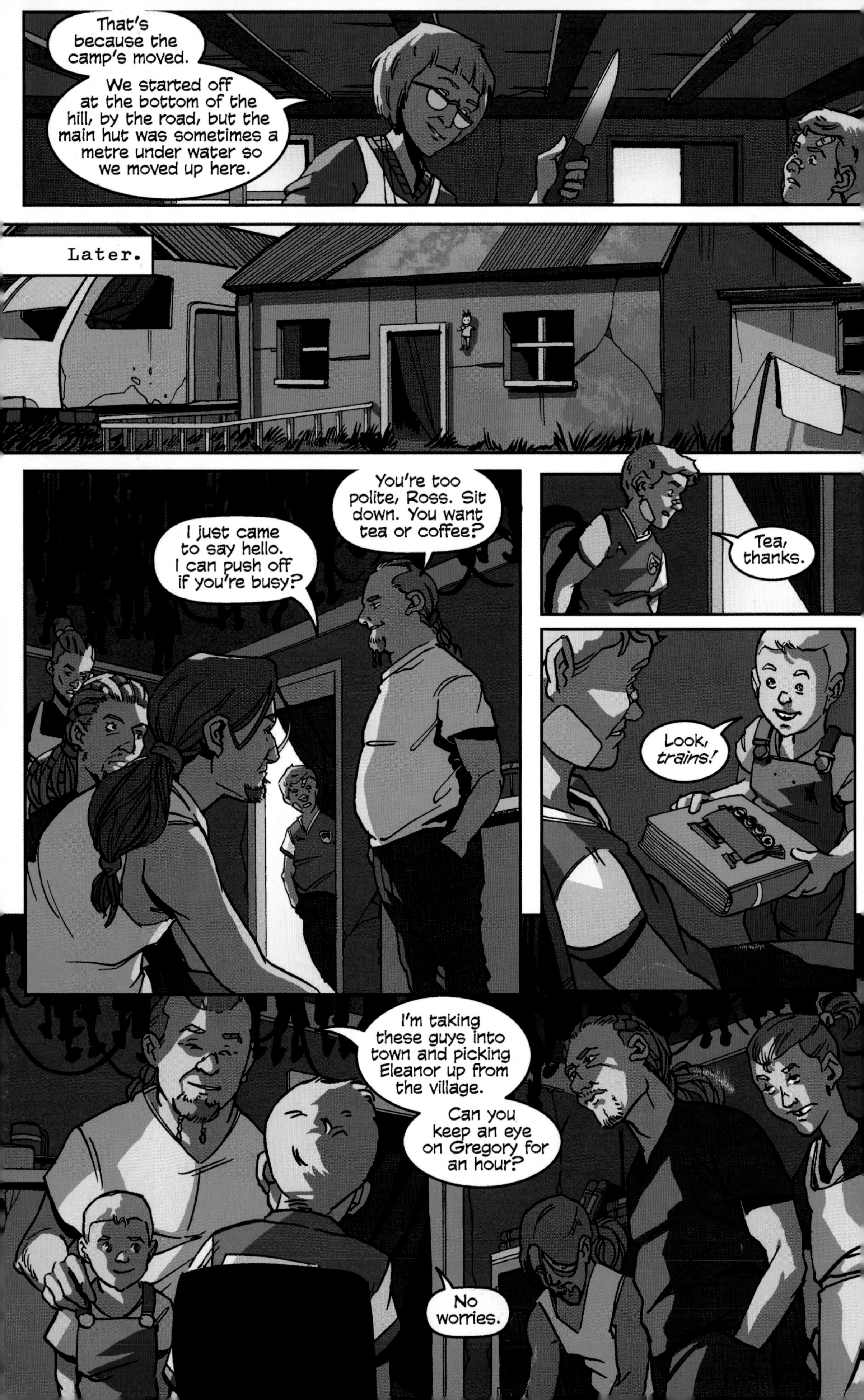
That's because the camp's moved.
We started off at the bottom of the hill, by the road, but the main hut was sometimes a metre under water so we moved up here.
Later.
I just came to say hello. I can push off if you're busy?
You're too polite, Ross. Sit down. You want tea or coffee?
Tea, thanks.
Look, trains!
I'm taking these guys into town and picking Eleanor up from the village.
Can you keep an eye on Gregory for an hour?
No worries.

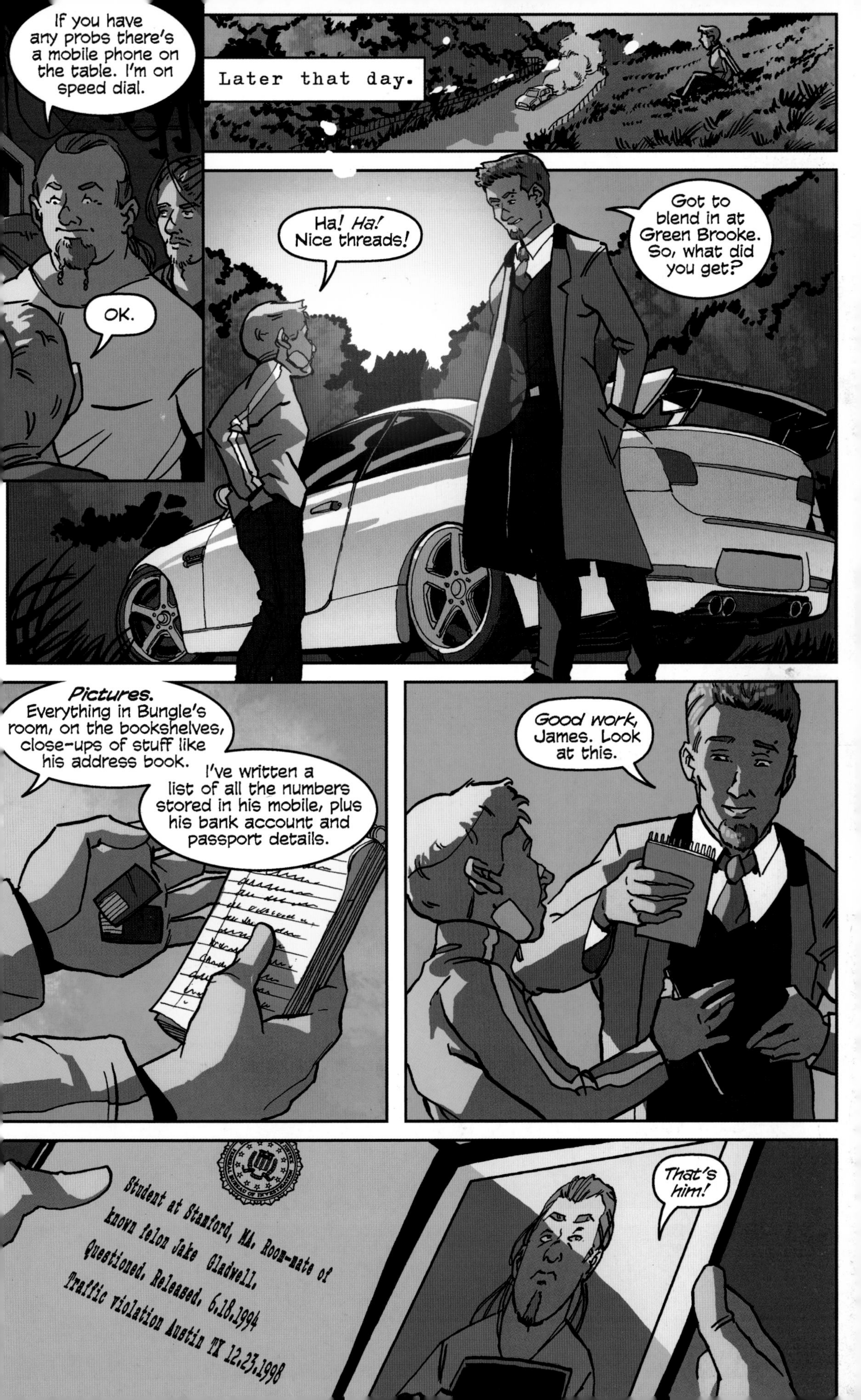
If you have any probs there's a mobile phone on the table. I'm on speed dial.
OK.
Later that day.
Ha! *Ha!* Nice threads!
Got to blend in at Green Brooke. So, what did you get?
Pictures. Everything in Bungle's room, on the bookshelves, close-ups of stuff like his address book.
I've written a list of all the numbers stored in his mobile, plus his bank account and passport details.
Good work, James. Look at this.
Student at Stamford, MA. Room-mate of
known felon Jake Gladwell.
Questioned. Released. 6.18.1994
Traffic violation Austin TX 12.23.1998
That's him!

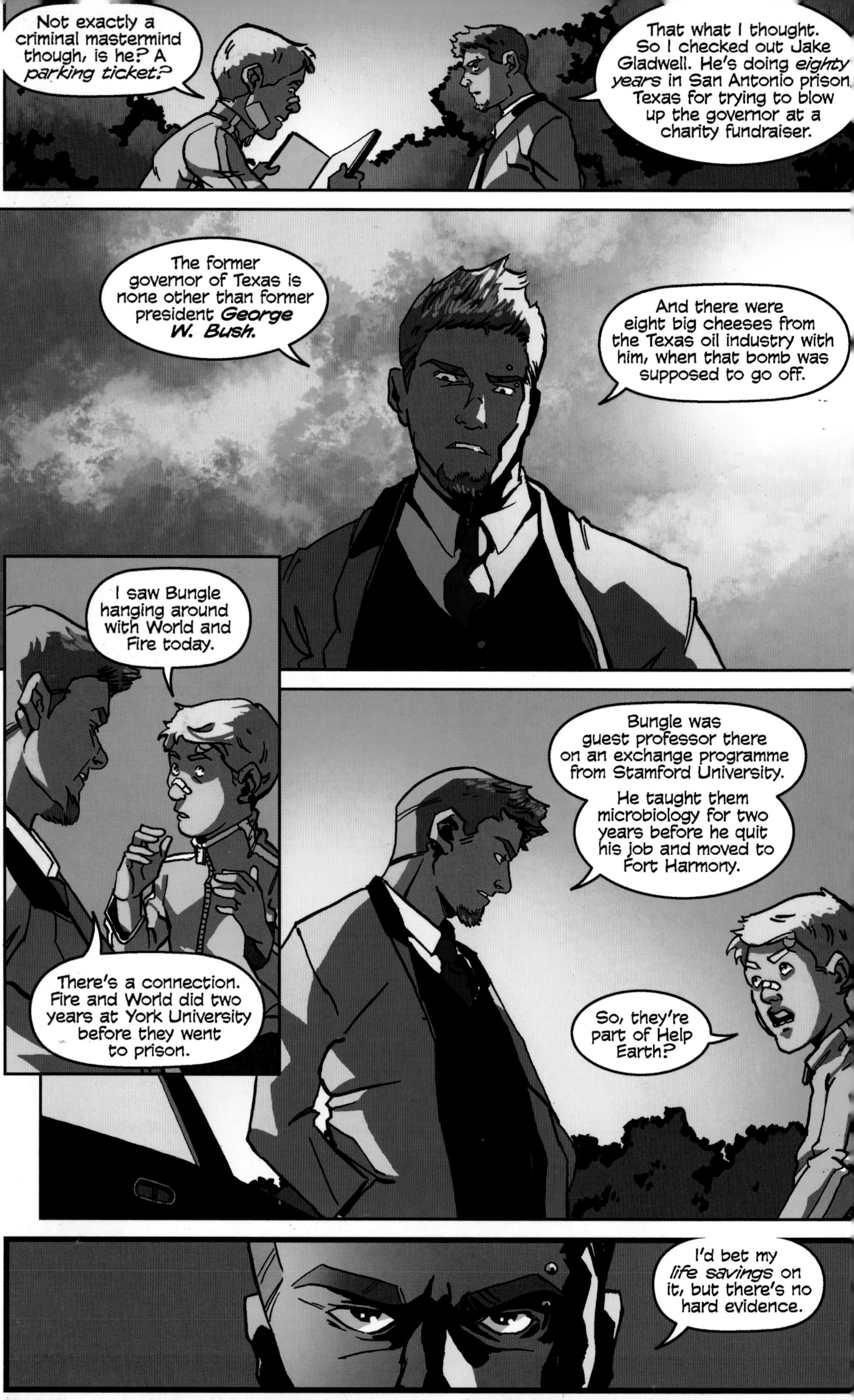
Not exactly a criminal mastermind though, is he? A *parking ticket?*
That what I thought. So I checked out Jake Gladwell. He's doing *eighty years* in San Antonio prison Texas for trying to blow up the governor at a charity fundraiser.
The former governor of Texas is none other than former president ***George W. Bush.***
And there were eight big cheeses from the Texas oil industry with him, when that bomb was supposed to go off.
I saw Bungle hanging around with World and Fire today.
There's a connection. Fire and World did two years at York University before they went to prison.
Bungle was guest professor there on an exchange programme from Stamford University.
He taught them microbiology for two years before he quit his job and moved to Fort Harmony.
So, they're part of Help Earth?
I'd bet my *life savings* on it, but there's no hard evidence.

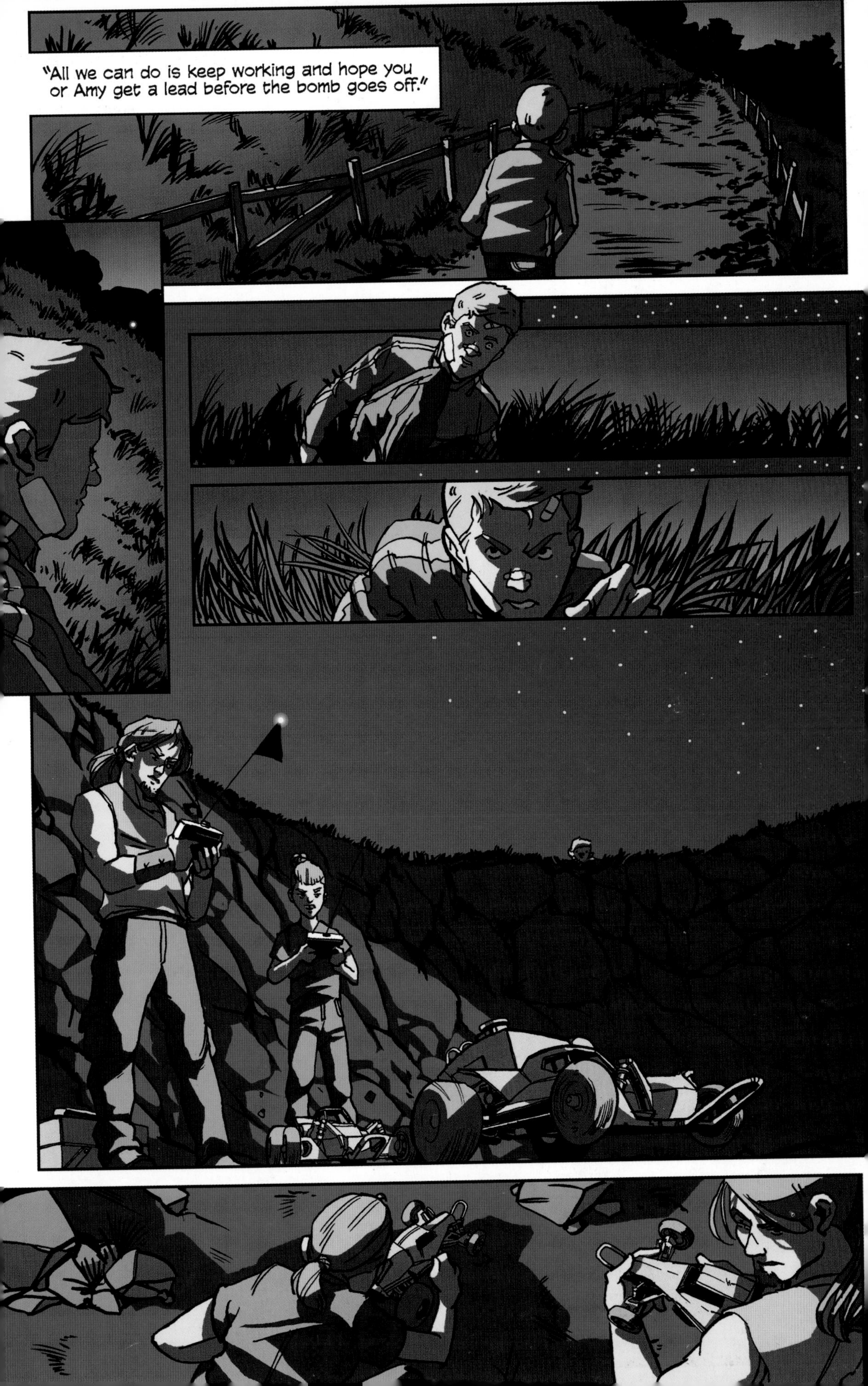
"All we can do is keep working and hope you or Amy get a lead before the bomb goes off."

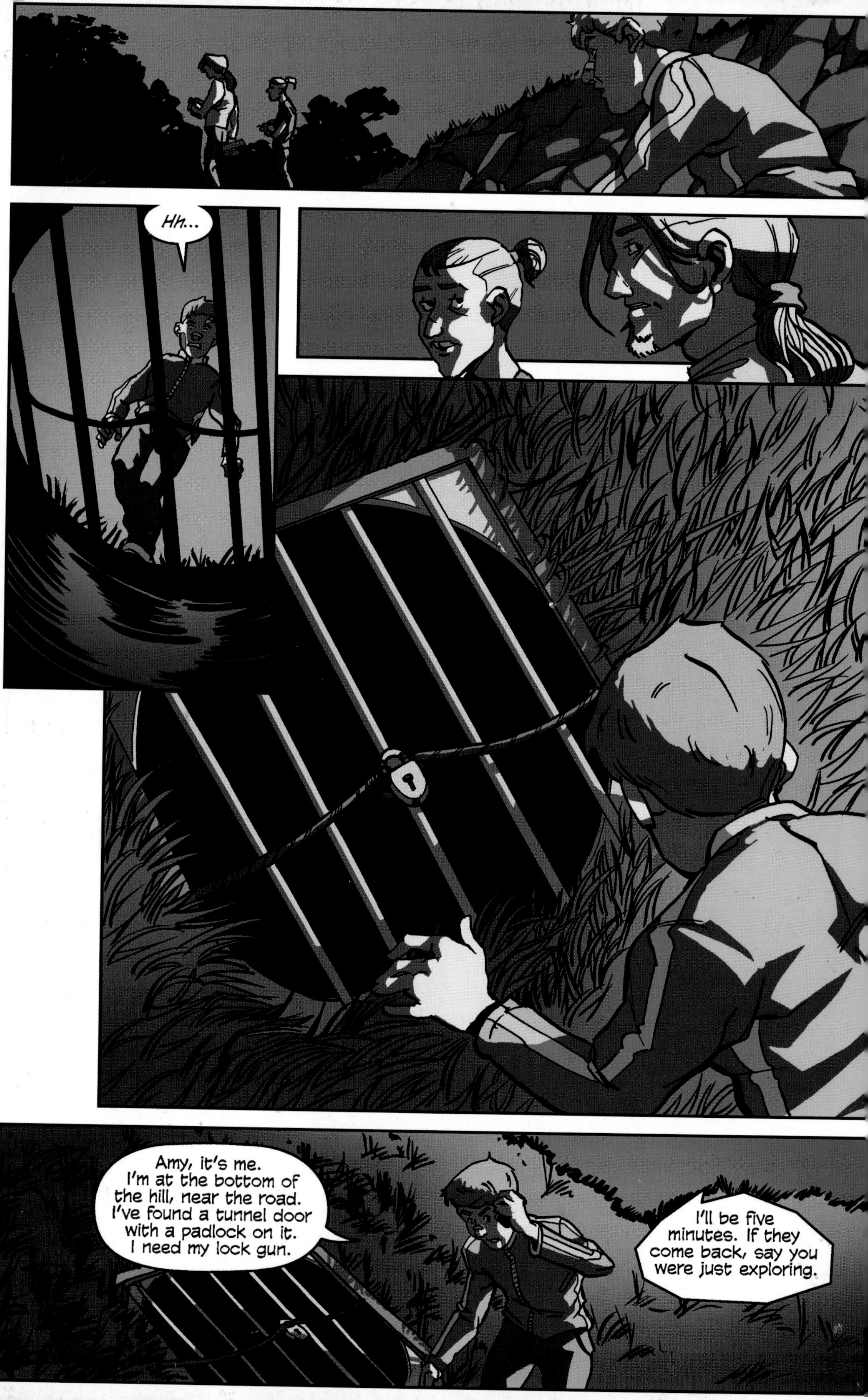
Hh...
Amy, it's me. I'm at the bottom of the hill, near the road. I've found a tunnel door with a padlock on it. I need my lock gun.
I'll be five minutes. If they come back, say you were just exploring.

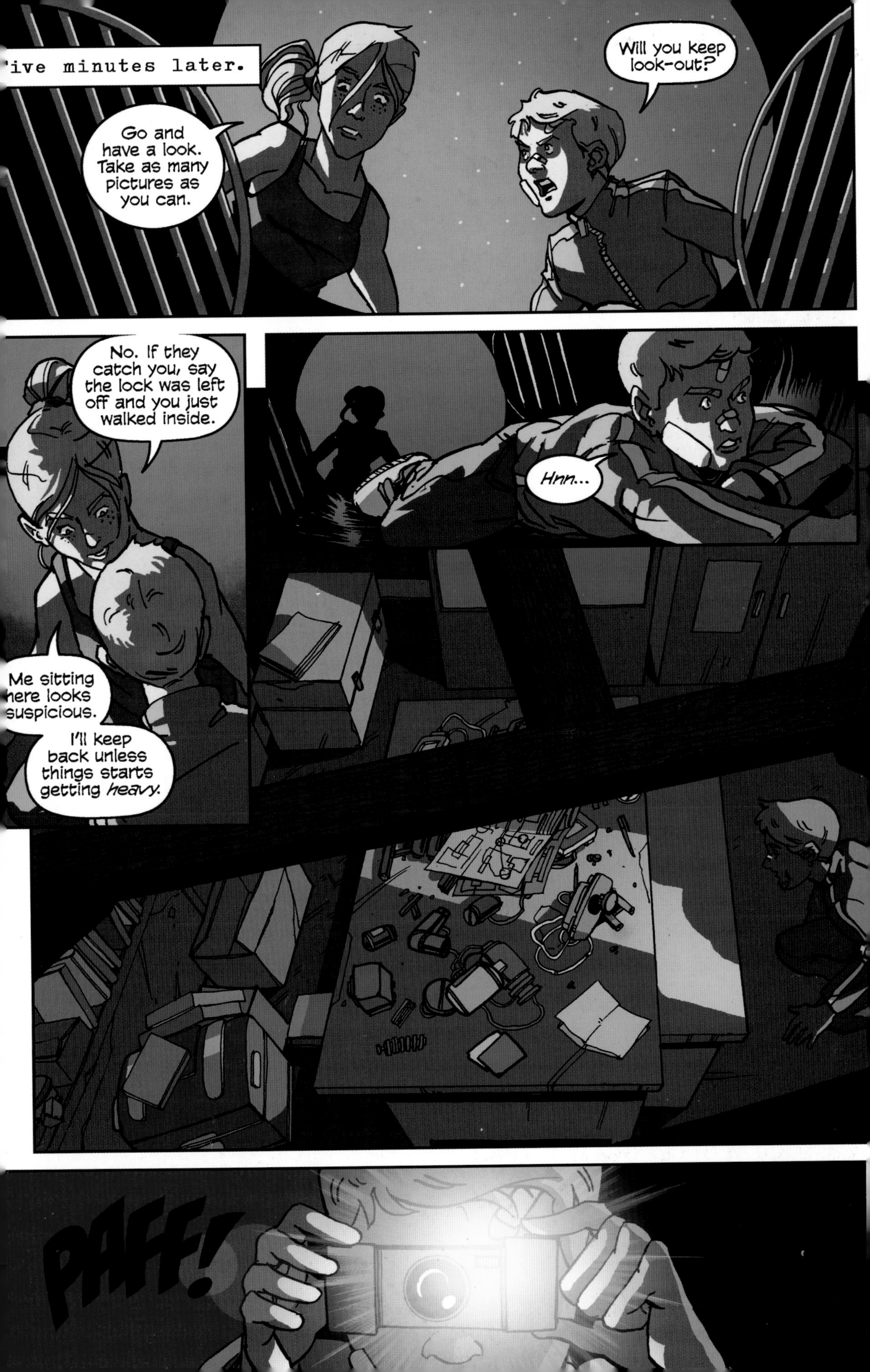
ive minutes later.
Go and have a look. Take as many pictures as you can.
Will you keep look-out?
No. If they catch you, say the lock was left off and you just walked inside.
Hnn...
Me sitting here looks suspicious.
I'll keep back unless things starts getting *heavy*.
PAFF!

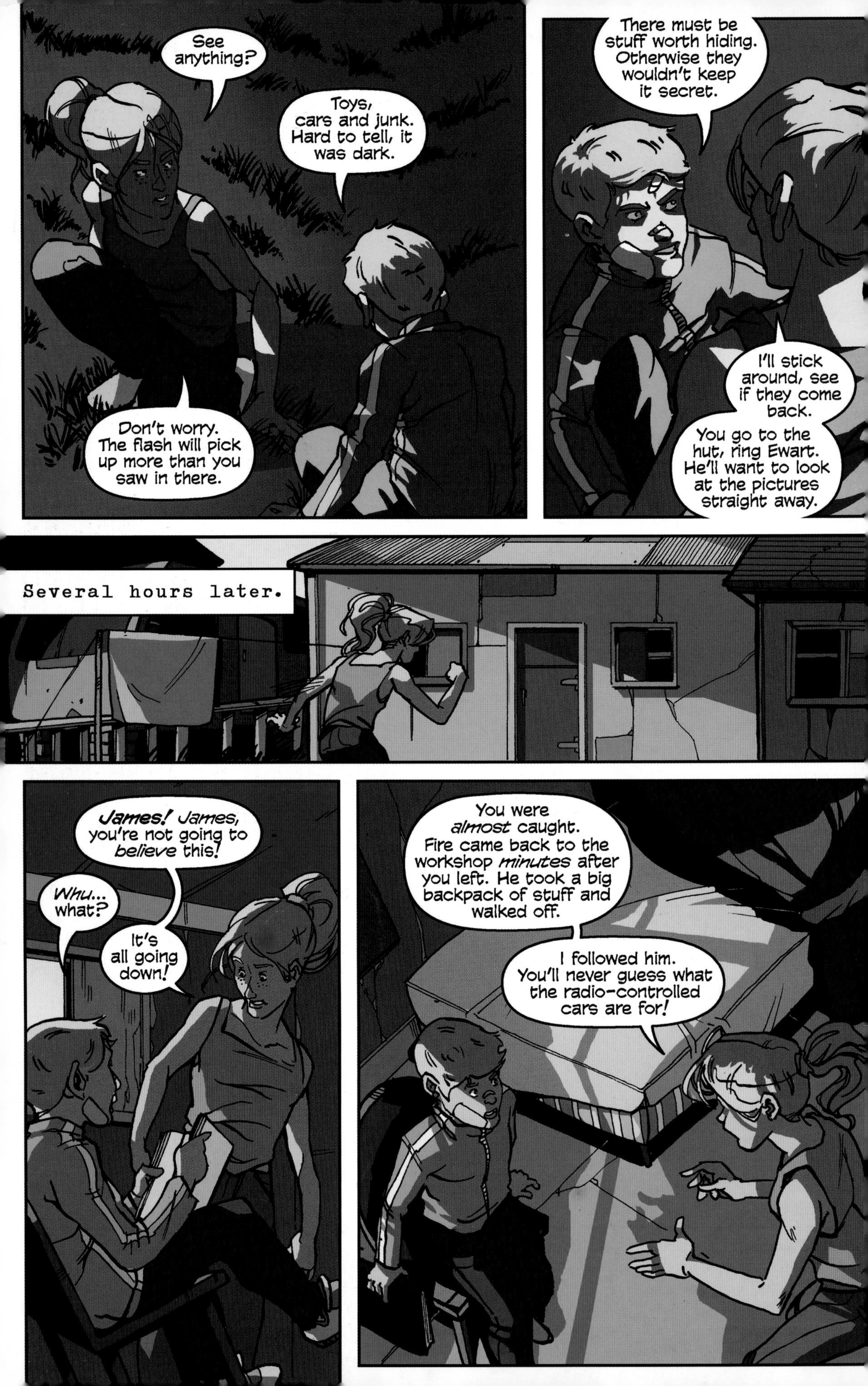
See anything?
Toys, cars and junk. Hard to tell, it was dark.
Don't worry. The flash will pick up more than you saw in there.
There must be stuff worth hiding. Otherwise they wouldn't keep it secret.
I'll stick around, see if they come back.
You go to the hut, ring Ewart. He'll want to look at the pictures straight away.
Several hours later.
James! James, you're not going to *believe* this!
Whu... what?
It's all going down!
You were *almost* caught. Fire came back to the workshop *minutes* after you left. He took a big backpack of stuff and walked off.
I followed him. You'll never guess what the radio-controlled cars are for!

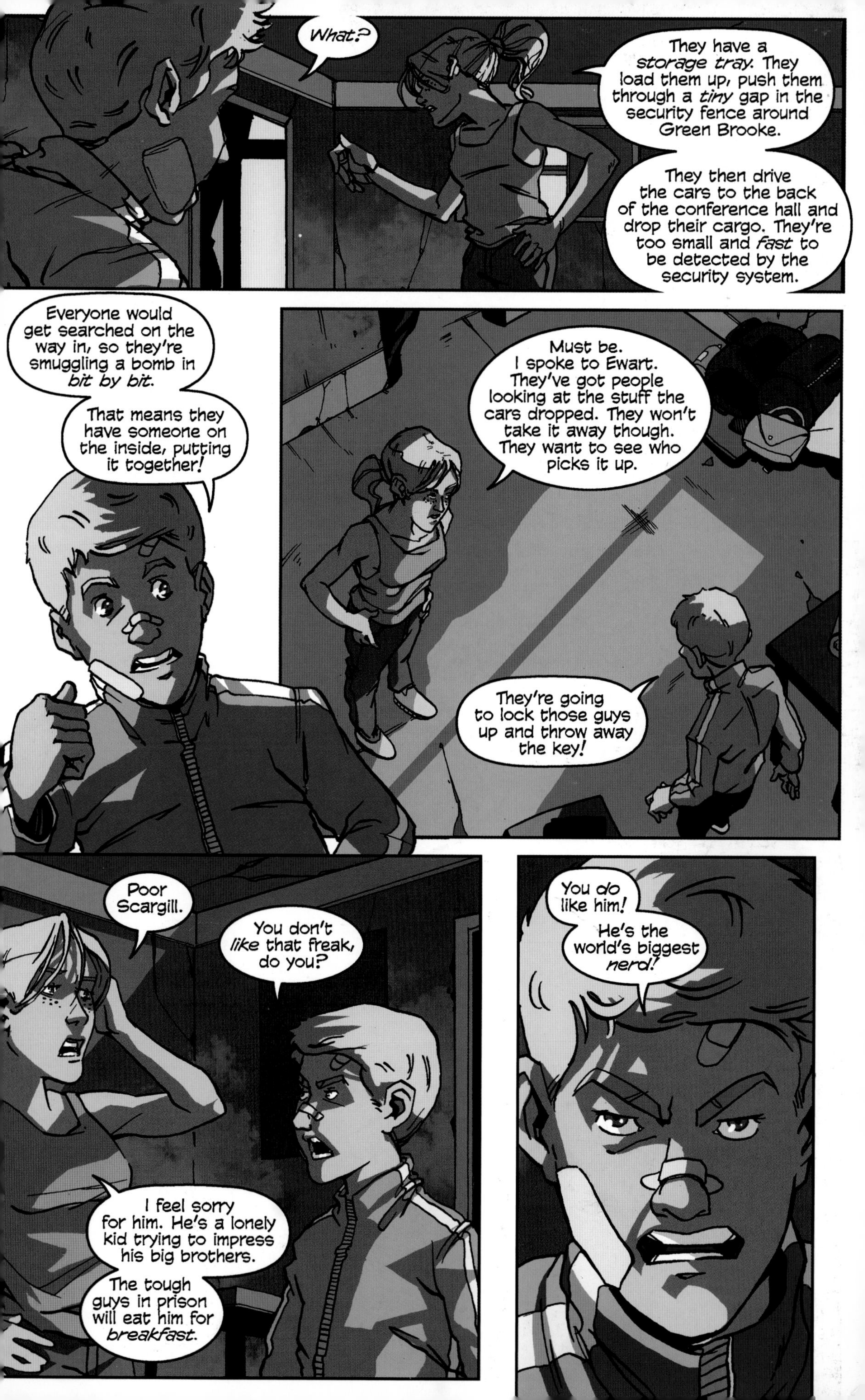
What?
They have a *storage tray.* They load them up, push them through a *tiny* gap in the security fence around Green Brooke.
They then drive the cars to the back of the conference hall and drop their cargo. They're too small and *fast* to be detected by the security system.
Everyone would get searched on the way in, so they're smuggling a bomb in *bit by bit.*
That means they have someone on the inside, putting it together!
Must be. I spoke to Ewart. They've got people looking at the stuff the cars dropped. They won't take it away though. They want to see who picks it up.
They're going to lock those guys up and throw away the key!
Poor Scargill.
You don't *like* that freak, do you?
I feel sorry for him. He's a lonely kid trying to impress his big brothers.
The tough guys in prison will eat him for *breakfast.*
You *do* like him!
He's the world's biggest *nerd!*

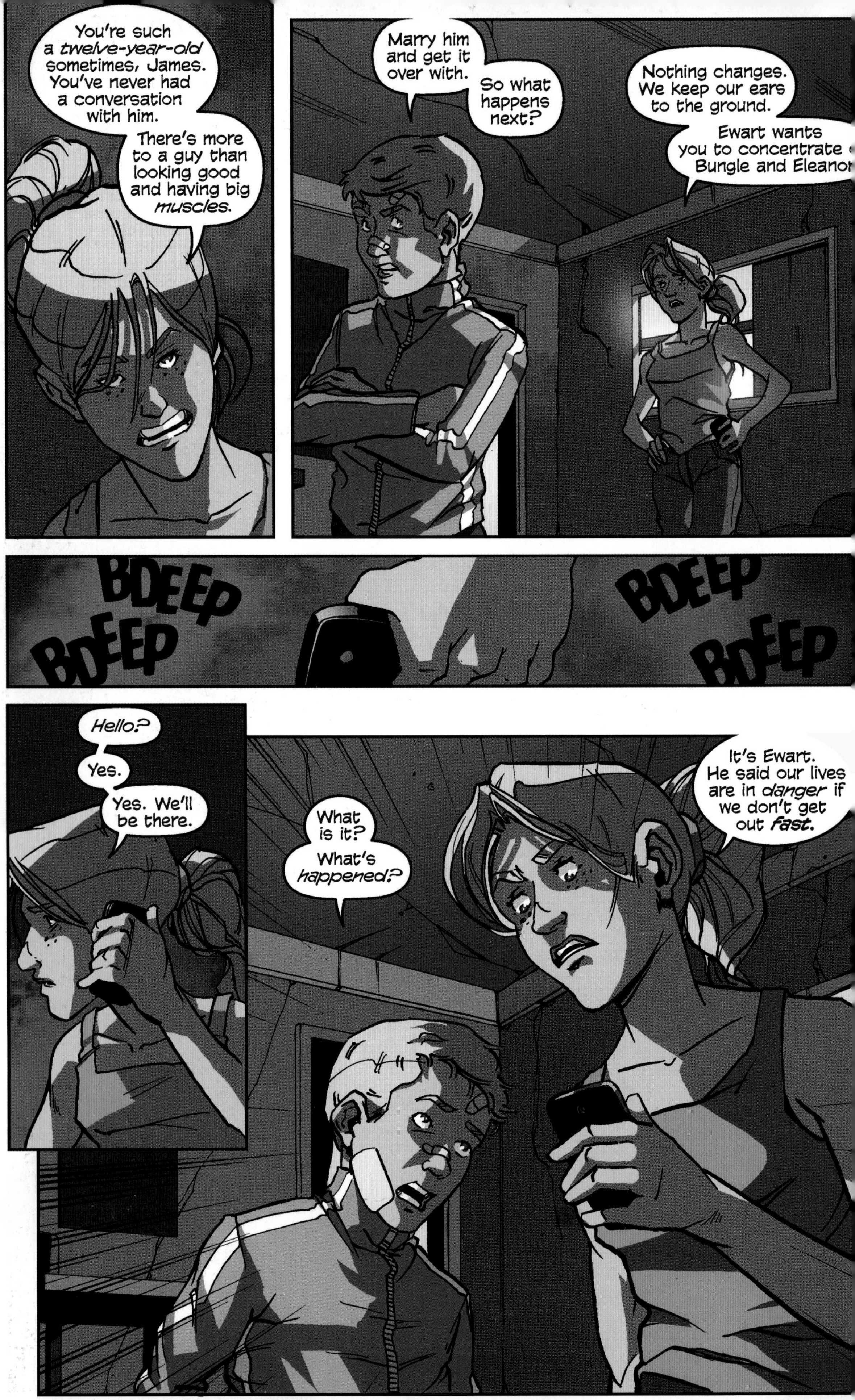
You're such a *twelve-year-old* sometimes, James. You've never had a conversation with him.
There's more to a guy than looking good and having big *muscles*.
Marry him and get it over with.
So what happens next?
Nothing changes. We keep our ears to the ground.
Ewart wants you to concentrate
Bungle and Eleano
BDEEP
BDEEP
BDEEP
BDEEP
Hello?
Yes.
Yes. We'll be there.
What is it?
What's *happened?*
It's Ewart. He said our lives are in *danger* if we don't get out ***fast.***

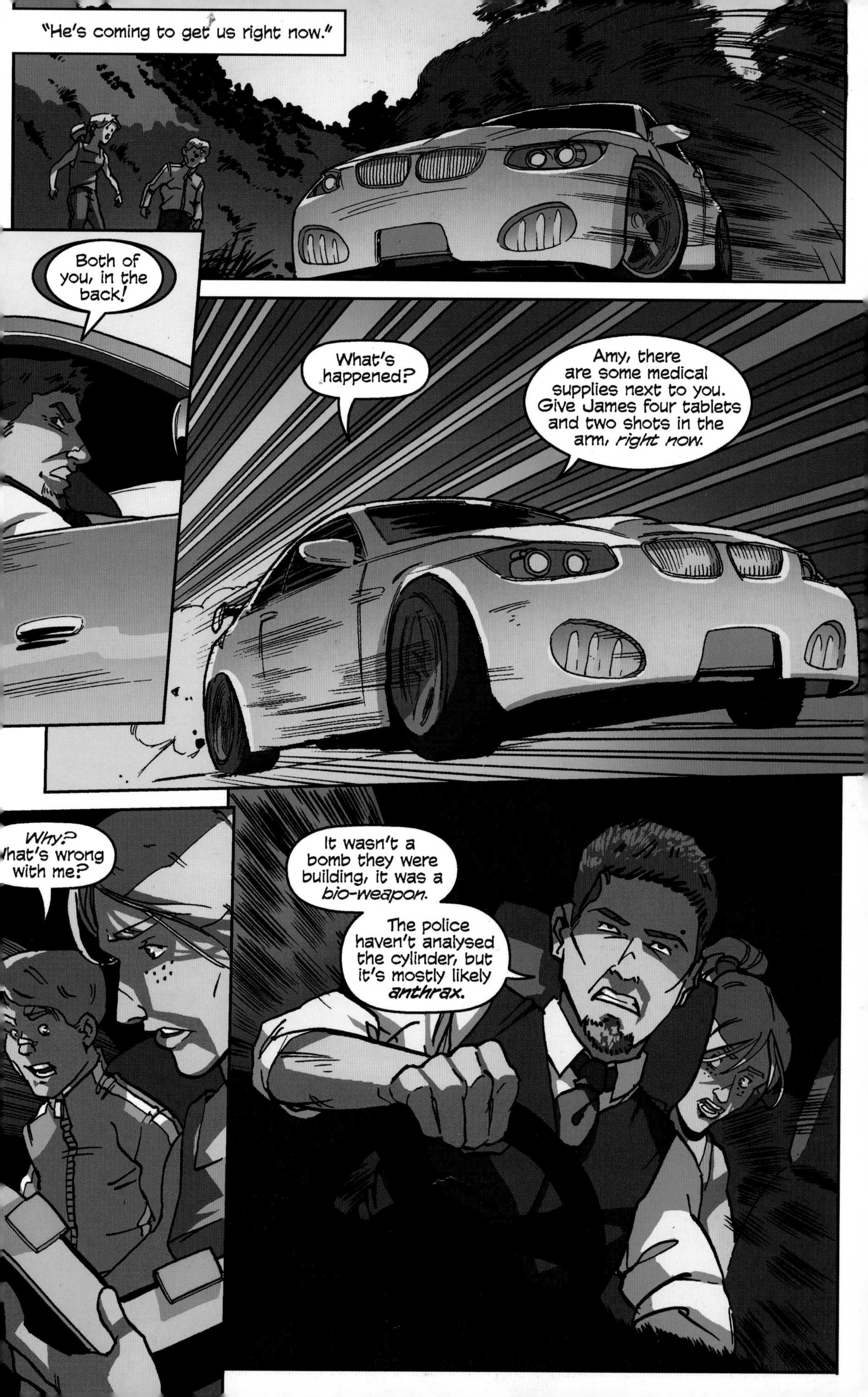
"He's coming to get us right now."
Both of you, in the back!
What's happened?
Amy, there are some medical supplies next to you. Give James four tablets and two shots in the arm, *right now*.
Why? What's wrong with me?
It wasn't a bomb they were building, it was a *bio-weapon*.
The police haven't analysed the cylinder, but it's mostly likely ***anthrax***.

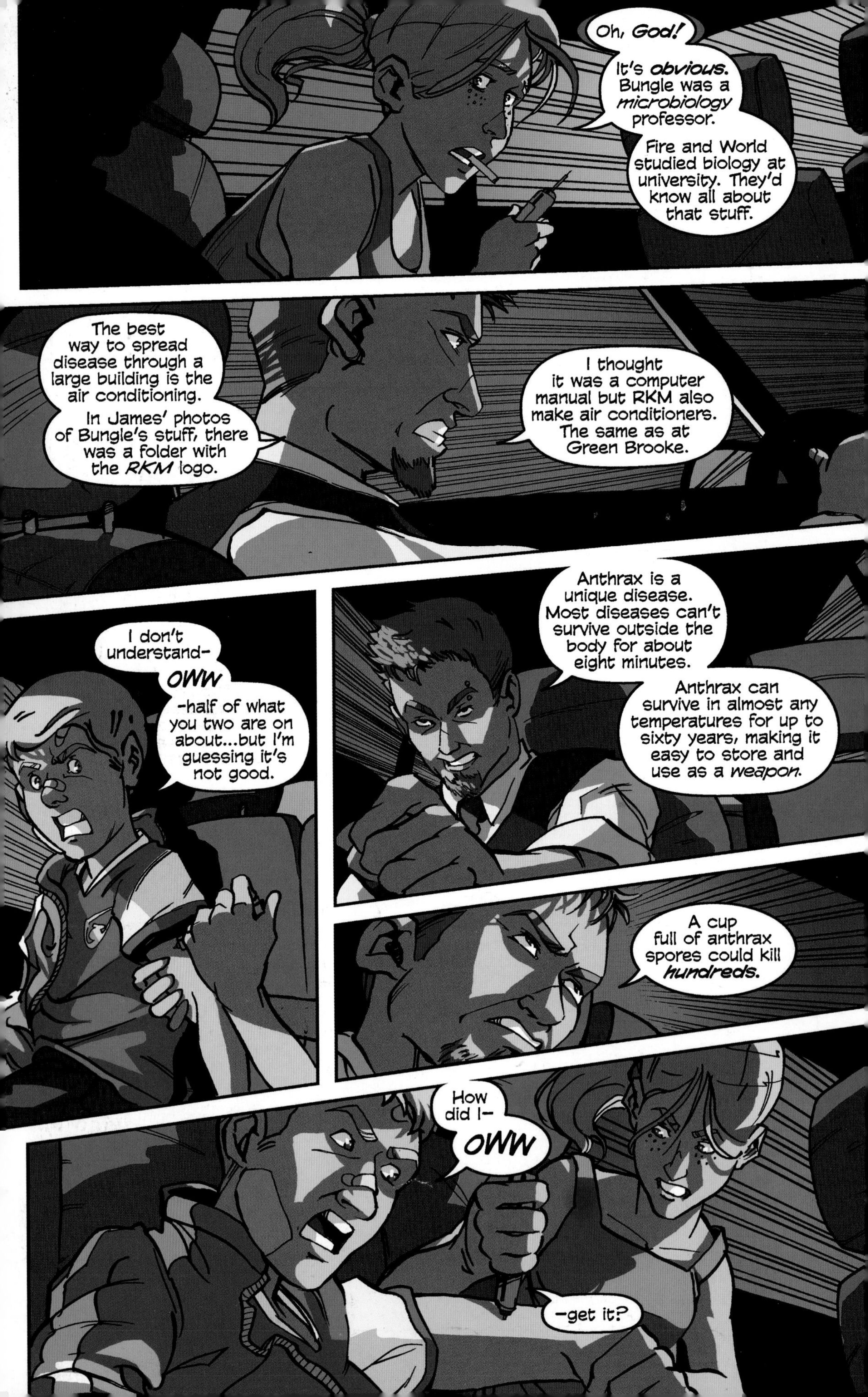
Oh, God!
It's obvious. Bungle was a microbiology professor.
Fire and World studied biology at university. They'd know all about that stuff.
The best way to spread disease through a large building is the air conditioning.
In James' photos of Bungle's stuff, there was a folder with the RKM logo.
I thought it was a computer manual but RKM also make air conditioners. The same as at Green Brooke.
I don't understand-
OWW
-half of what you two are on about...but I'm guessing it's not good.
Anthrax is a unique disease. Most diseases can't survive outside the body for about eight minutes.
Anthrax can survive in almost any temperatures for up to sixty years, making it easy to store and use as a weapon.
A cup full of anthrax spores could kill hundreds.
How did I-
OWW
-get it?

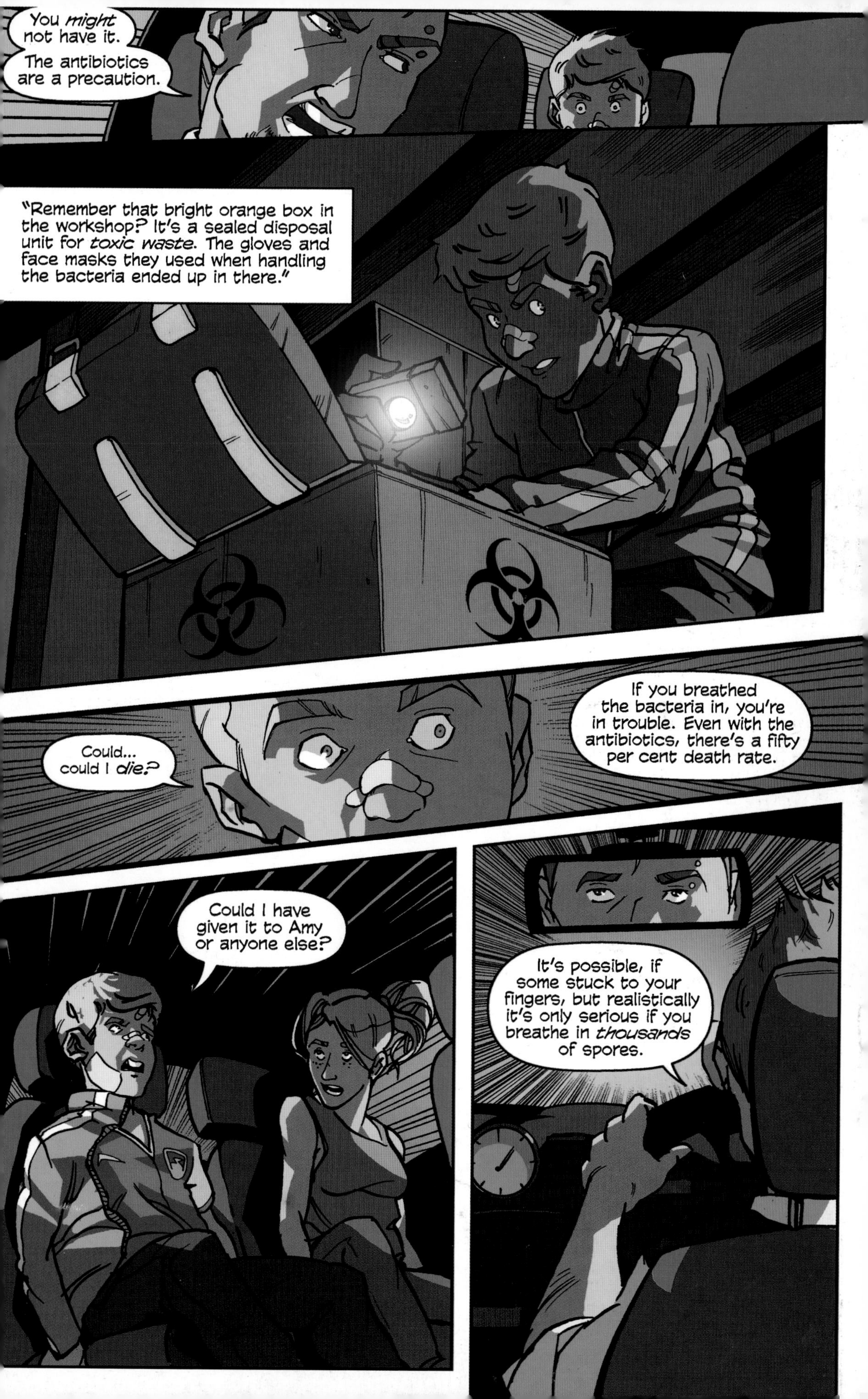
You *might* not have it.
The antibiotics are a precaution.
"Remember that bright orange box in the workshop? It's a sealed disposal unit for *toxic waste*. The gloves and face masks they used when handling the bacteria ended up in there."
Could... could I *die?*
If you breathed the bacteria in, you're in trouble. Even with the antibiotics, there's a fifty per cent death rate.
Could I have given it to Amy or anyone else?
It's possible, if some stuck to your fingers, but realistically it's only serious if you breathe in *thousands* of spores.

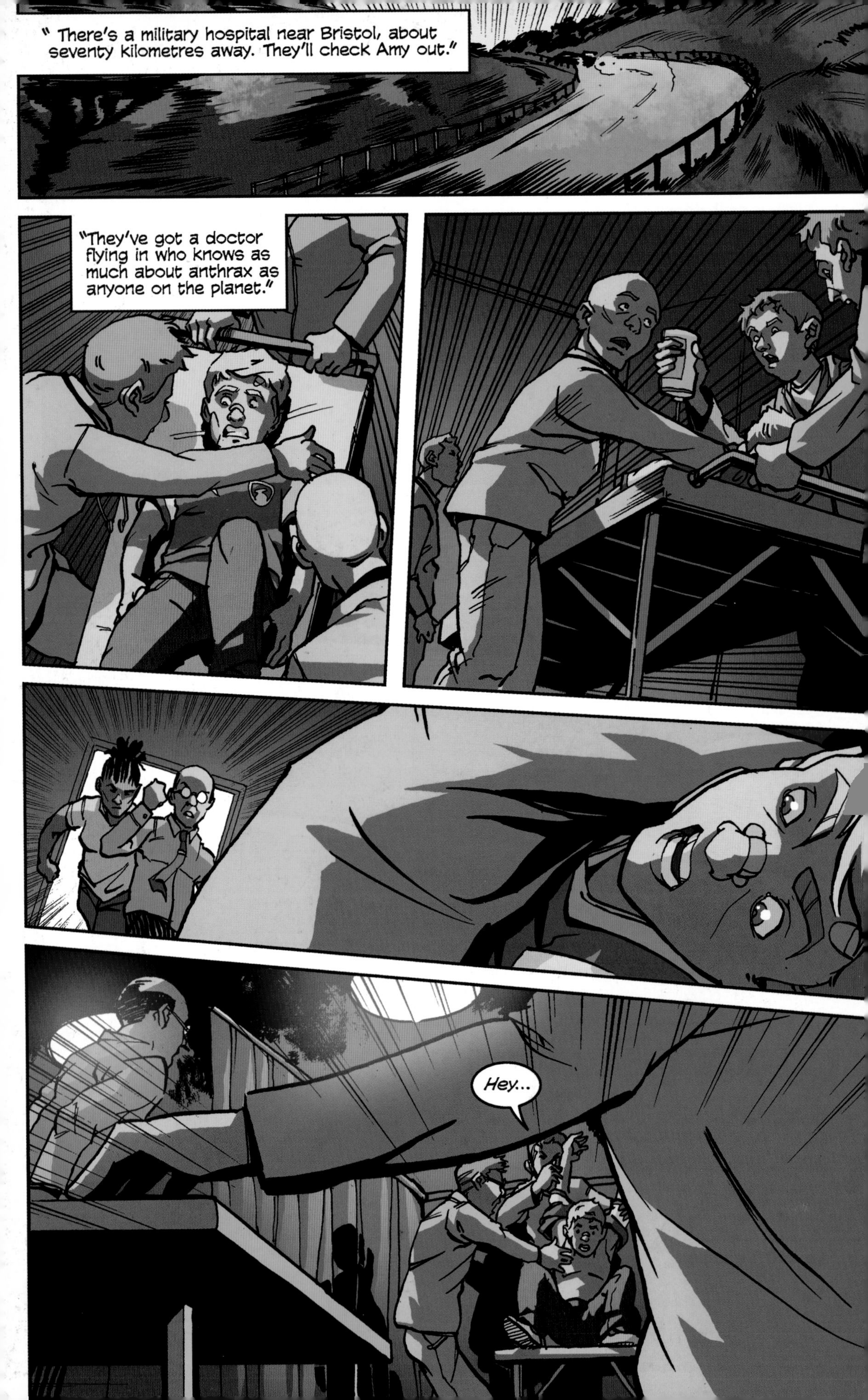
" There's a military hospital near Bristol, about seventy kilometres away. They'll check Amy out."
"They've got a doctor flying in who knows as much about anthrax as anyone on the planet."
Hey...

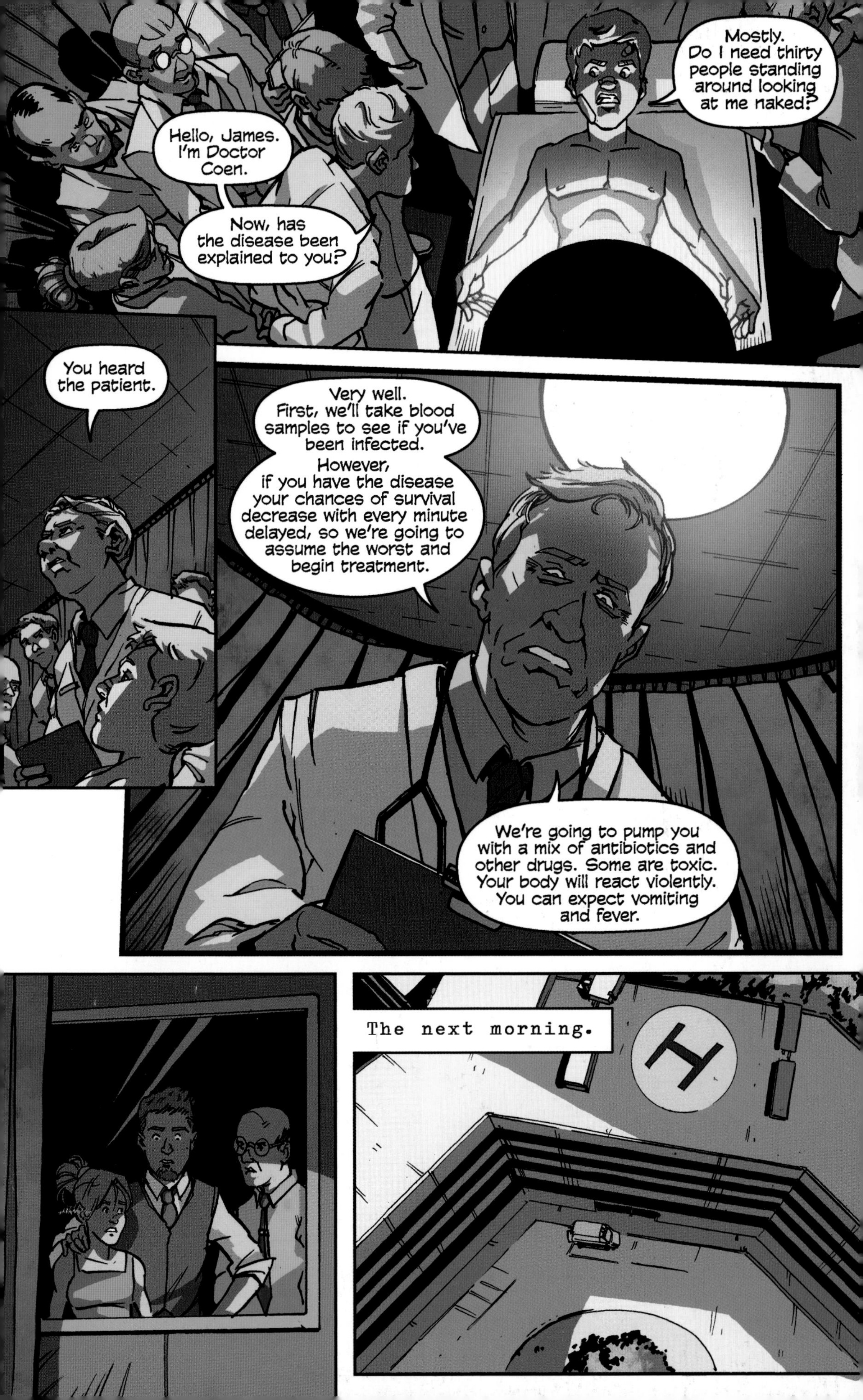
Hello, James. I'm Doctor Coen.
Now, has the disease been explained to you?
Mostly. Do I need thirty people standing around looking at me naked?
You heard the patient.
Very well. First, we'll take blood samples to see if you've been infected.
However, if you have the disease your chances of survival decrease with every minute delayed, so we're going to assume the worst and begin treatment.
We're going to pump you with a mix of antibiotics and other drugs. Some are toxic. Your body will react violently. You can expect vomiting and fever.
The next morning.

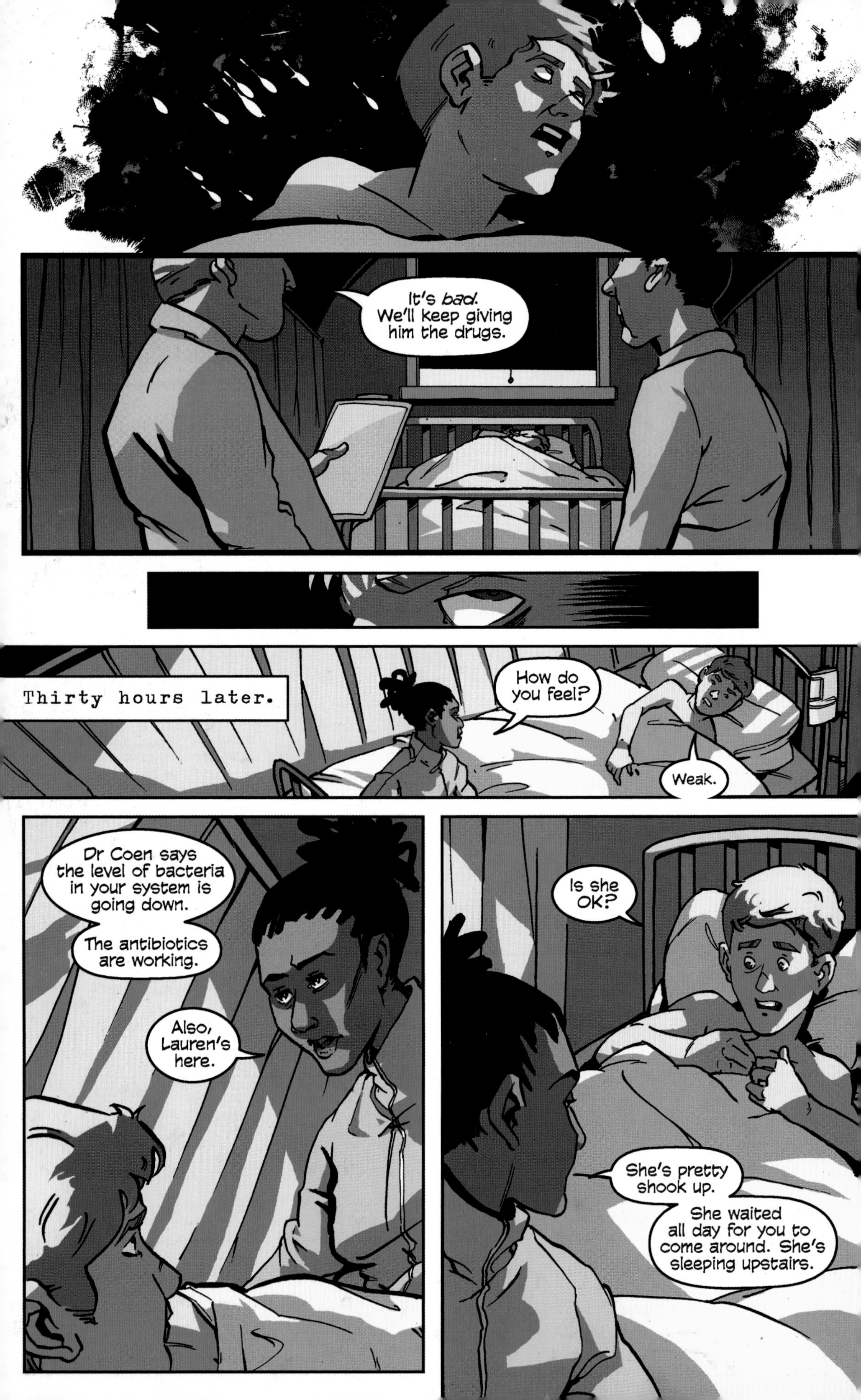
It's *bad*. We'll keep giving him the drugs.
Thirty hours later.
How do you feel?
Weak.
Dr Coen says the level of bacteria in your system is going down.
The antibiotics are working.
Also, Lauren's here.
Is she OK?
She's pretty shook up.
She waited all day for you to come around. She's sleeping upstairs.

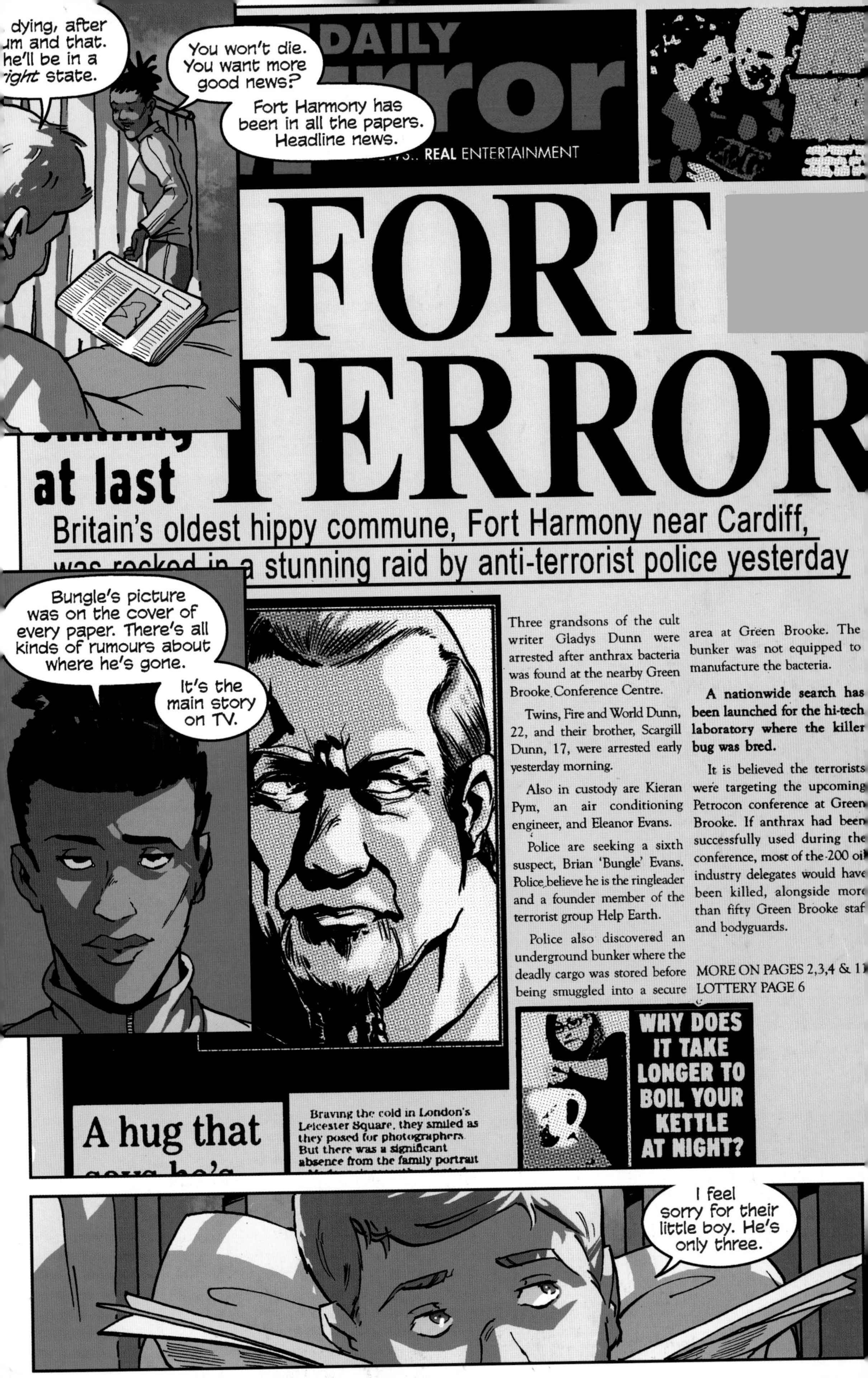
dying, after
um and that.
he'll be in a
ight state.
You won't die. You want more good news?
Fort Harmony has been in all the papers. Headline news.
DAILY
rror
...REAL ENTERTAINMENT
FORT TERROR
at last
Britain's oldest hippy commune, Fort Harmony near Cardiff, was rocked in a stunning raid by anti-terrorist police yesterday
Bungle's picture was on the cover of every paper. There's all kinds of rumours about where he's gone.
It's the main story on TV.
Three grandsons of the cult writer Gladys Dunn were arrested after anthrax bacteria was found at the nearby Green Brooke Conference Centre.
Twins, Fire and World Dunn, 22, and their brother, Scargill Dunn, 17, were arrested early yesterday morning.
Also in custody are Kieran Pym, an air conditioning engineer, and Eleanor Evans.
Police are seeking a sixth suspect, Brian 'Bungle' Evans. Police believe he is the ringleader and a founder member of the terrorist group Help Earth.
Police also discovered an underground bunker where the deadly cargo was stored before being smuggled into a secure area at Green Brooke. The bunker was not equipped to manufacture the bacteria.
A nationwide search has been launched for the hi-tech laboratory where the killer bug was bred.
It is believed the terrorists were targeting the upcoming Petrocon conference at Green Brooke. If anthrax had been successfully used during the conference, most of the 200 oi industry delegates would have been killed, alongside more than fifty Green Brooke staf and bodyguards.
MORE ON PAGES 2,3,4 & 1
LOTTERY PAGE 6
WHY DOES IT TAKE LONGER TO BOIL YOUR KETTLE AT NIGHT?
A hug that
Braving the cold in London's Leicester Square, they smiled as they posed for photographers. But there was a significant absence from the family portrait
I feel sorry for their little boy. He's only three.

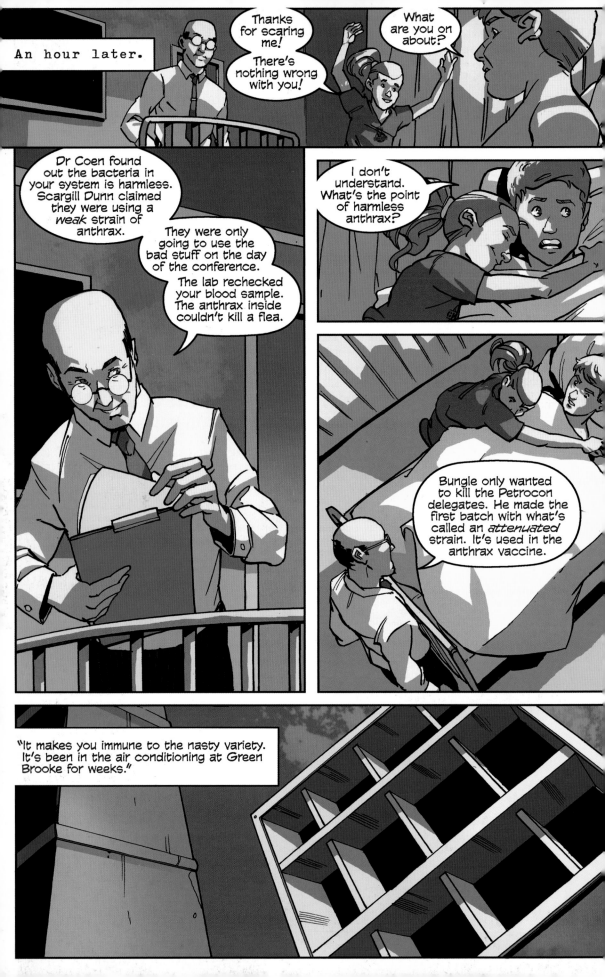

An hour later.

Thanks for scaring me! There's nothing wrong with you!

What are you on about?

Dr Coen found out the bacteria in your system is harmless. Scargill Dunn claimed they were using a *weak* strain of anthrax.

They were only going to use the bad stuff on the day of the conference.

The lab rechecked your blood sample. The anthrax inside couldn't kill a flea.

I don't understand. What's the point of harmless anthrax?

Bungle only wanted to kill the Petrocon delegates. He made the first batch with what's called an *attenuated* strain. It's used in the anthrax vaccine.

"It makes you immune to the nasty variety. It's been in the air conditioning at Green Brooke for weeks."

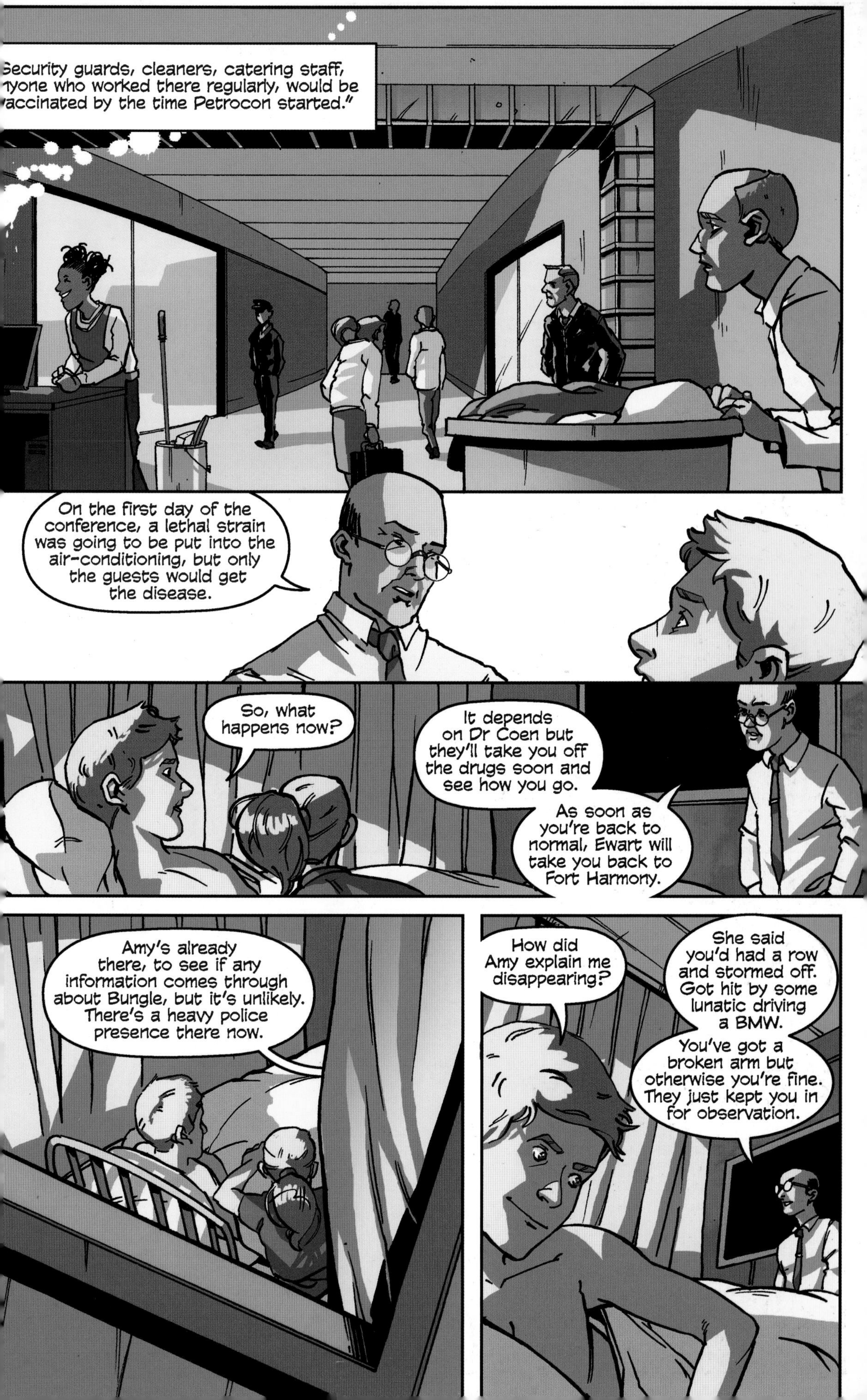
Security guards, cleaners, catering staff, anyone who worked there regularly, would be vaccinated by the time Petrocon started."
On the first day of the conference, a lethal strain was going to be put into the air-conditioning, but only the guests would get the disease.
So, what happens now?
It depends on Dr Coen but they'll take you off the drugs soon and see how you go.
As soon as you're back to normal, Ewart will take you back to Fort Harmony.
Amy's already there, to see if any information comes through about Bungle, but it's unlikely. There's a heavy police presence there now.
How did Amy explain me disappearing?
She said you'd had a row and stormed off. Got hit by some lunatic driving a BMW.
You've got a broken arm but otherwise you're fine. They just kept you in for observation.

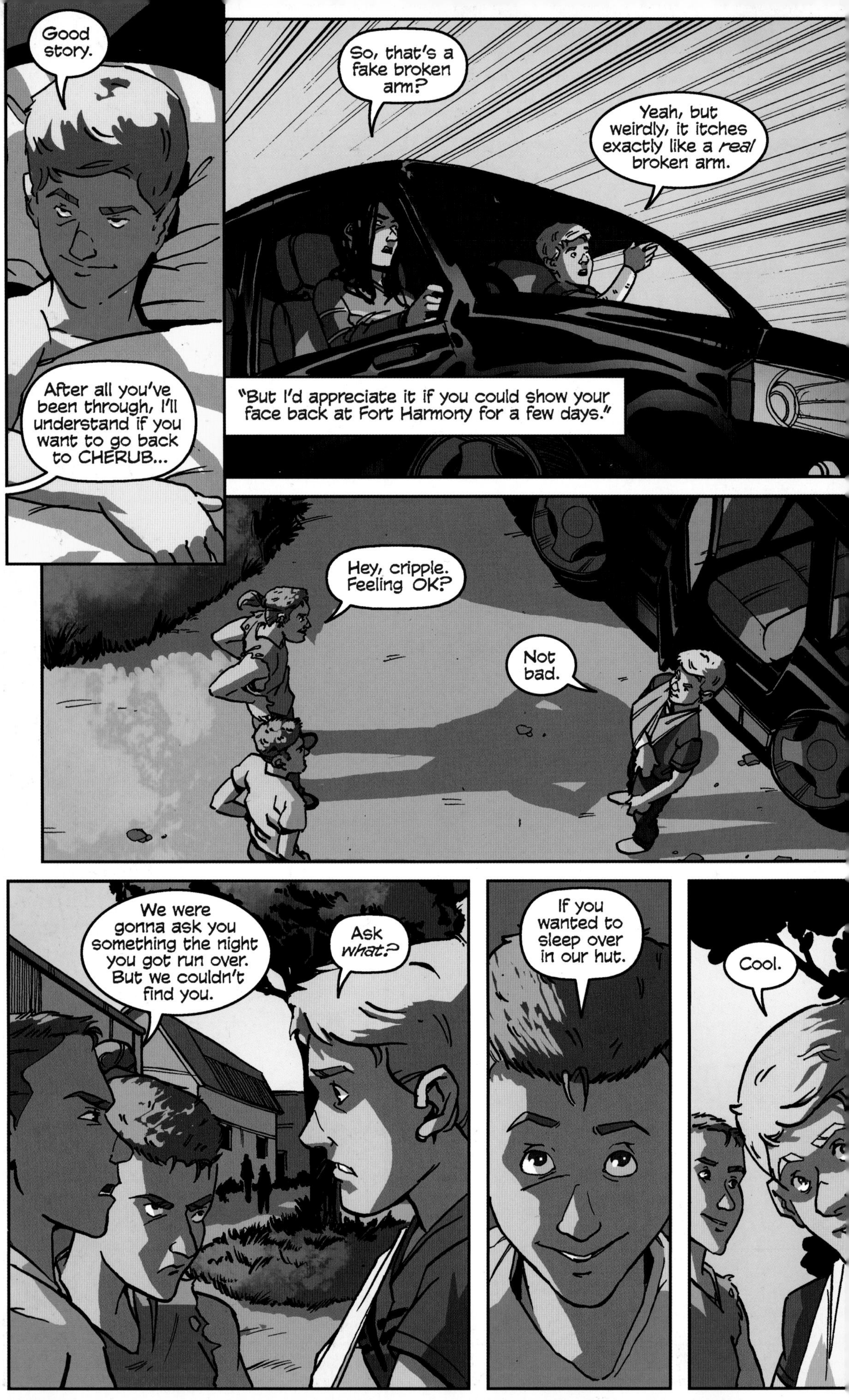
Good story.
So, that's a fake broken arm?
Yeah, but weirdly, it itches exactly like a *real* broken arm.
After all you've been through, I'll understand if you want to go back to CHERUB...
"But I'd appreciate it if you could show your face back at Fort Harmony for a few days."
Hey, cripple. Feeling OK?
Not bad.
We were gonna ask you something the night you got run over. But we couldn't find you.
Ask *what?*
If you wanted to sleep over in our hut.
Cool.

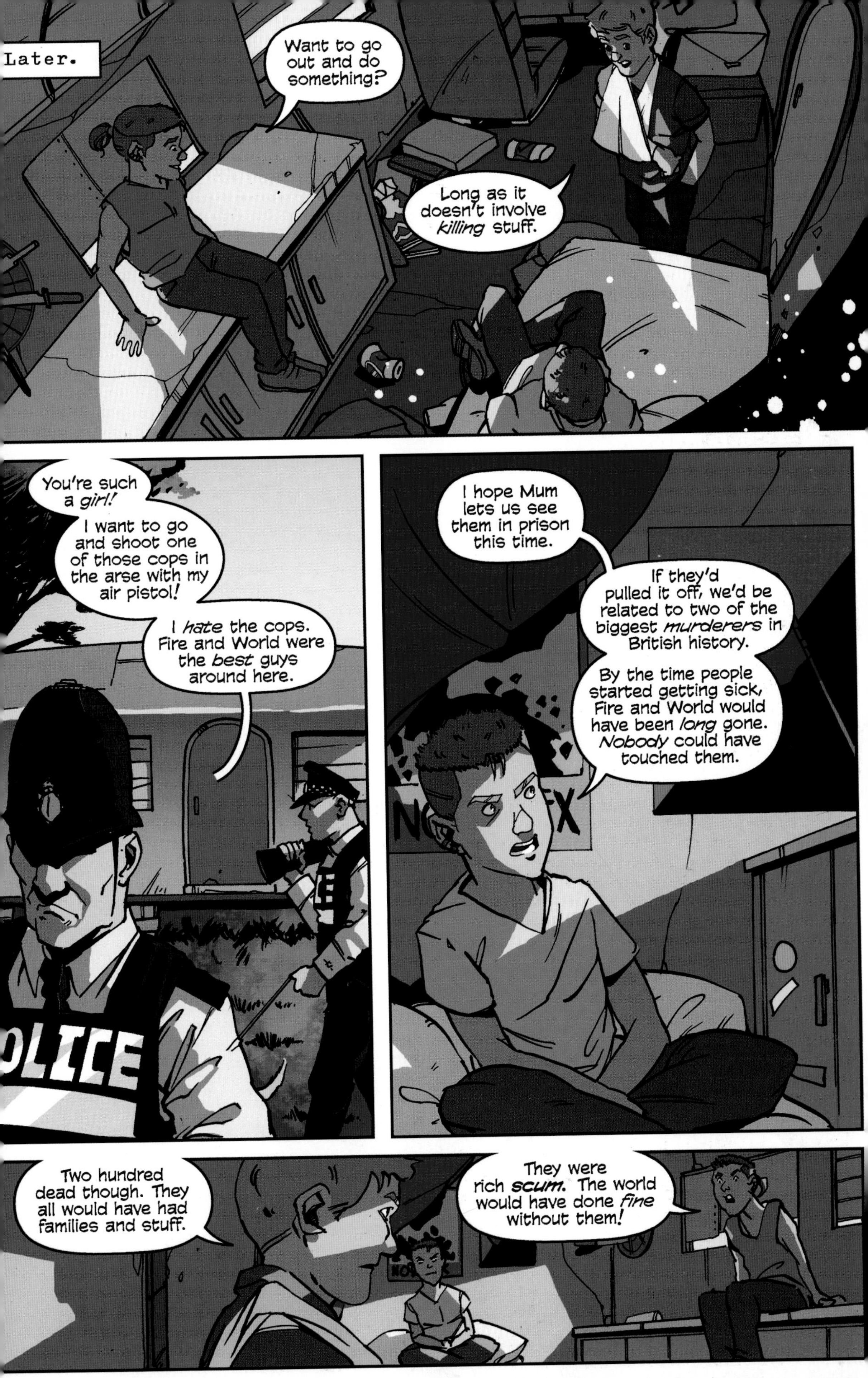
Later.
Want to go out and do something?
Long as it doesn't involve *killing* stuff.
You're such a *girl!*
I want to go and shoot one of those cops in the arse with my air pistol!
I *hate* the cops. Fire and World were the *best* guys around here.
POLICE
I hope Mum lets us see them in prison this time.
If they'd pulled it off, we'd be related to two of the biggest *murderers* in British history.
By the time people started getting sick, Fire and World would have been *long* gone. *Nobody* could have touched them.
Two hundred dead though. They all would have had families and stuff.
They were rich ***scum***. The world would have done *fine* without them!

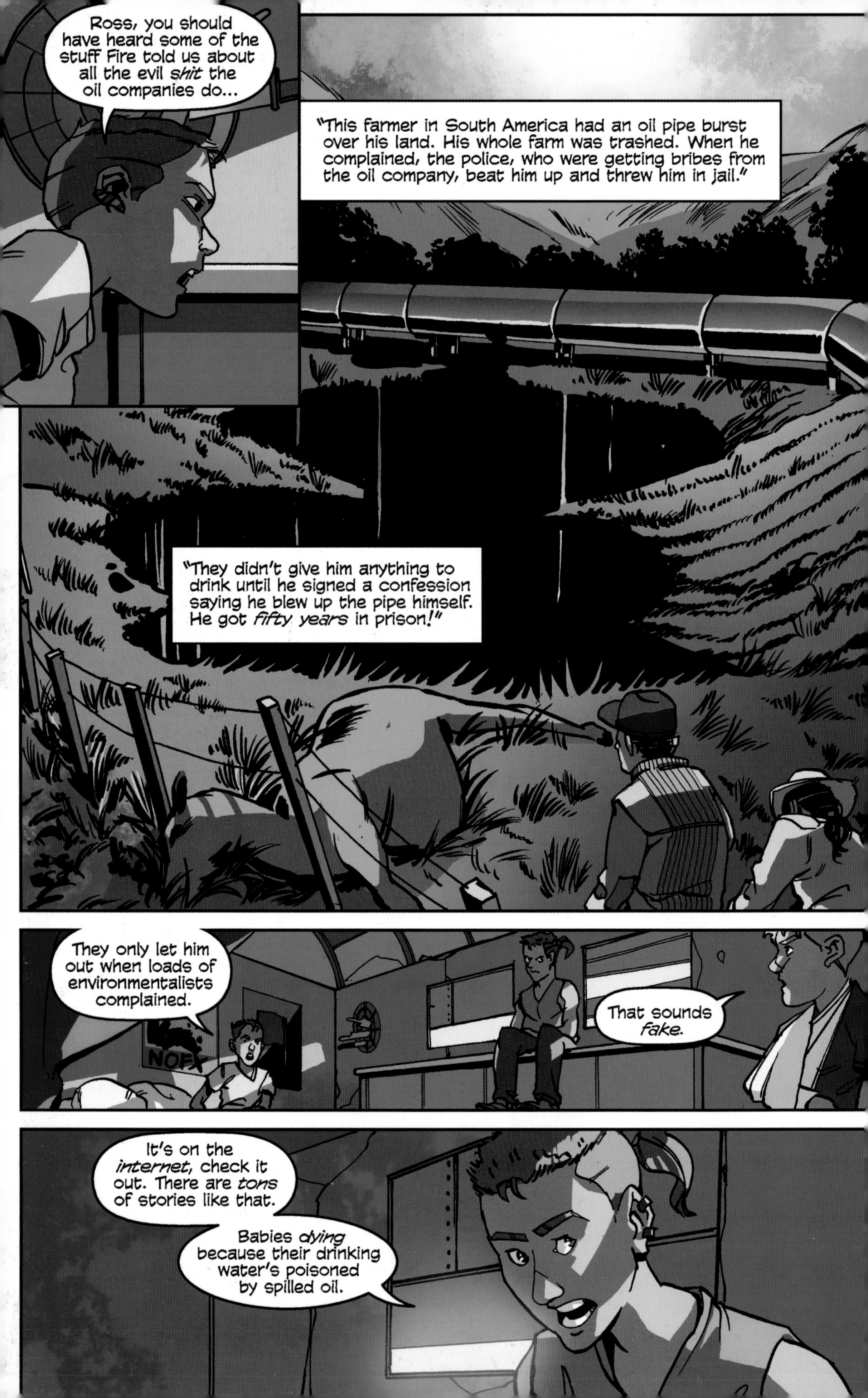

Ross, you should have heard some of the stuff Fire told us about all the evil *shit* the oil companies do...
"This farmer in South America had an oil pipe burst over his land. His whole farm was trashed. When he complained, the police, who were getting bribes from the oil company, beat him up and threw him in jail."
"They didn't give him anything to drink until he signed a confession saying he blew up the pipe himself. He got *fifty years* in prison!"
They only let him out when loads of environmentalists complained.
NOFX
That sounds *fake*.
It's on the *internet*, check it out. There are *tons* of stories like that.
Babies *dying* because their drinking water's poisoned by spilled oil.

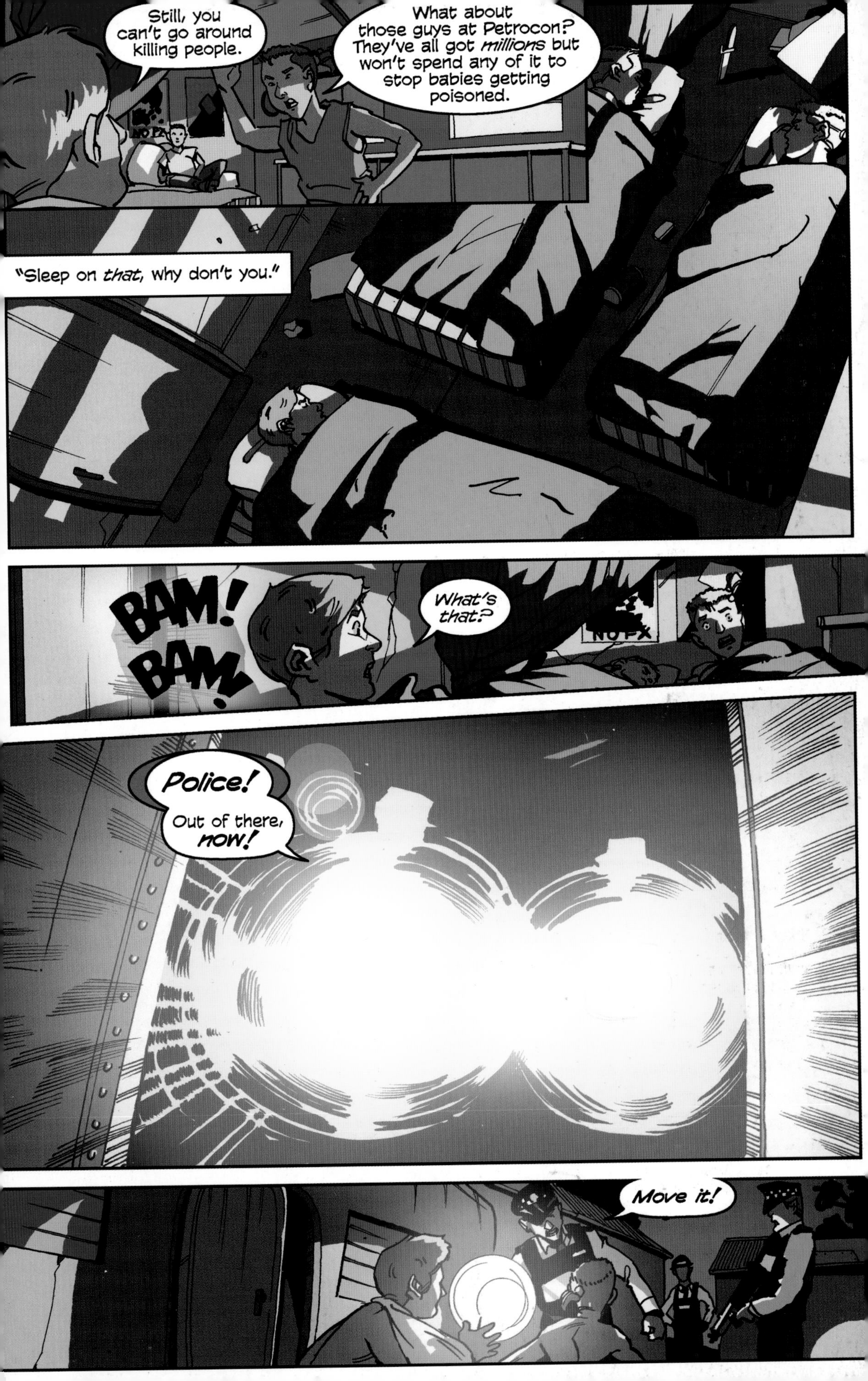
Still, you can't go around killing people.
What about those guys at Petrocon? They've all got *millions* but won't spend any of it to stop babies getting poisoned.
"Sleep on *that*, why don't you."
BAM! BAM!
What's that?
Police!
Out of there, *now!*
Move it!

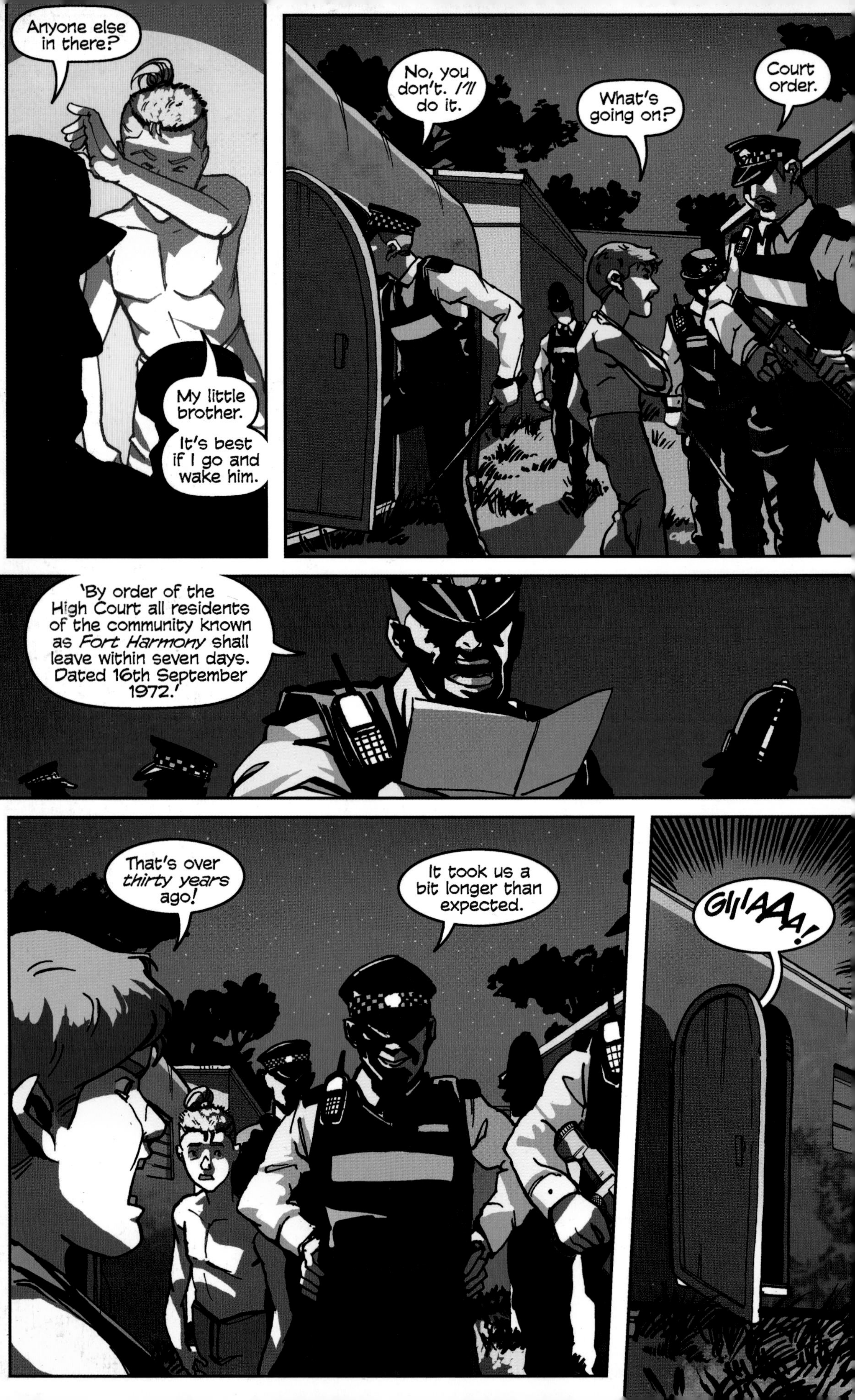
Anyone else in there?
My little brother.
It's best if I go and wake him.
No, you don't. *I'll* do it.
What's going on?
Court order.
'By order of the High Court all residents of the community known as *Fort Harmony* shall leave within seven days. Dated 16th September 1972.'
That's over *thirty years* ago!
It took us a bit longer than expected.
GIIAAAA!

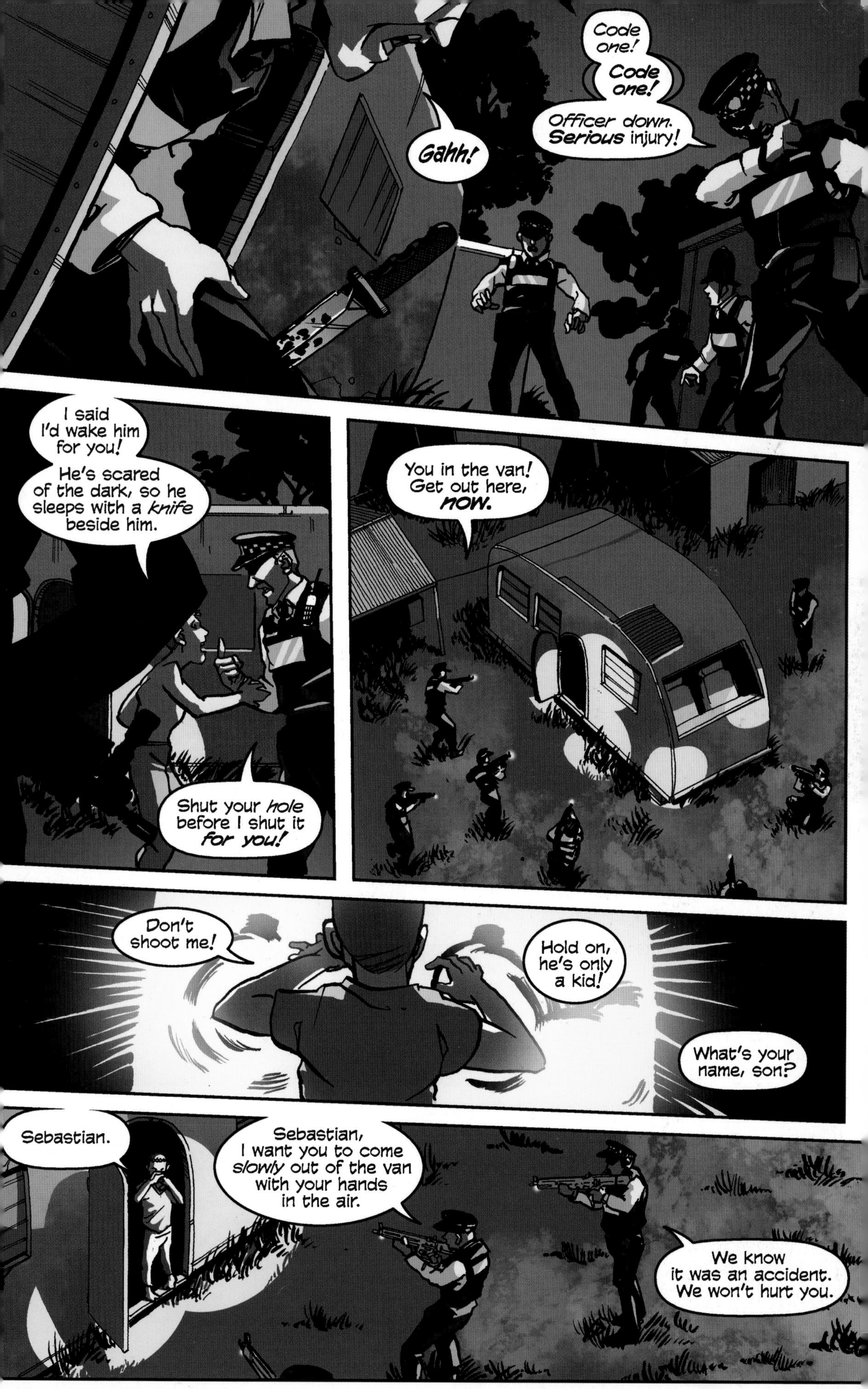

Code one!
Code one!
Officer down. Serious injury!
Gahh!
I said I'd wake him for you!
He's scared of the dark, so he sleeps with a *knife* beside him.
Shut your *hole* before I shut it *for you!*
You in the van! Get out here, **NOW.**
Don't shoot me!
Hold on, he's only a kid!
What's your name, son?
Sebastian.
Sebastian, I want you to come *slowly* out of the van with your hands in the air.
We know it was an accident. We won't hurt you.

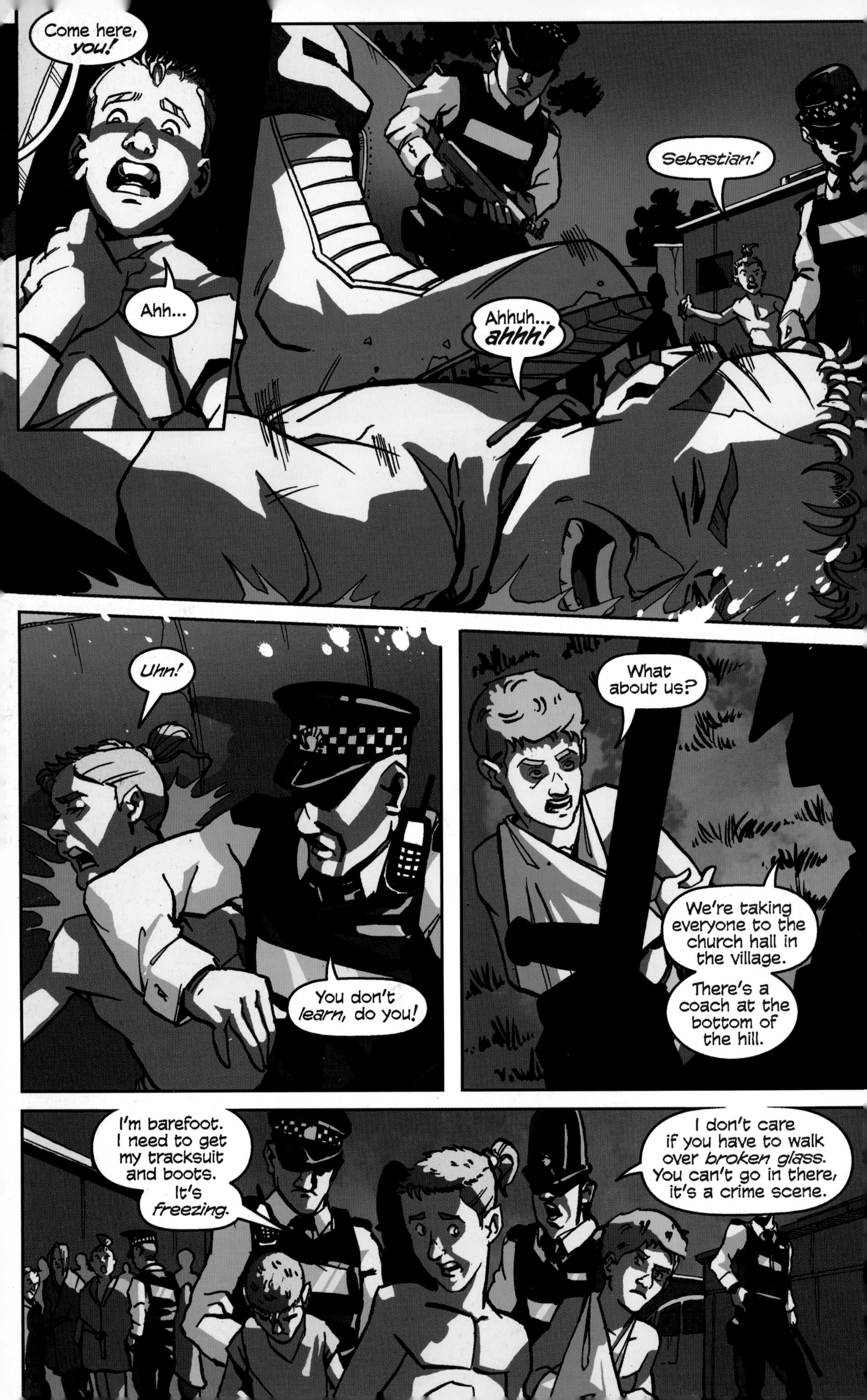
Come here, *you!*
Ahh...
Sebastian!
Ahhuh... ***ahhh!***
Uhn!
You don't *learn,* do you!
What about us?
We're taking everyone to the church hall in the village.
There's a coach at the bottom of the hill.
I'm barefoot. I need to get my tracksuit and boots. It's *freezing.*
I don't care if you have to walk over *broken glass.* You can't go in there, it's a crime scene.

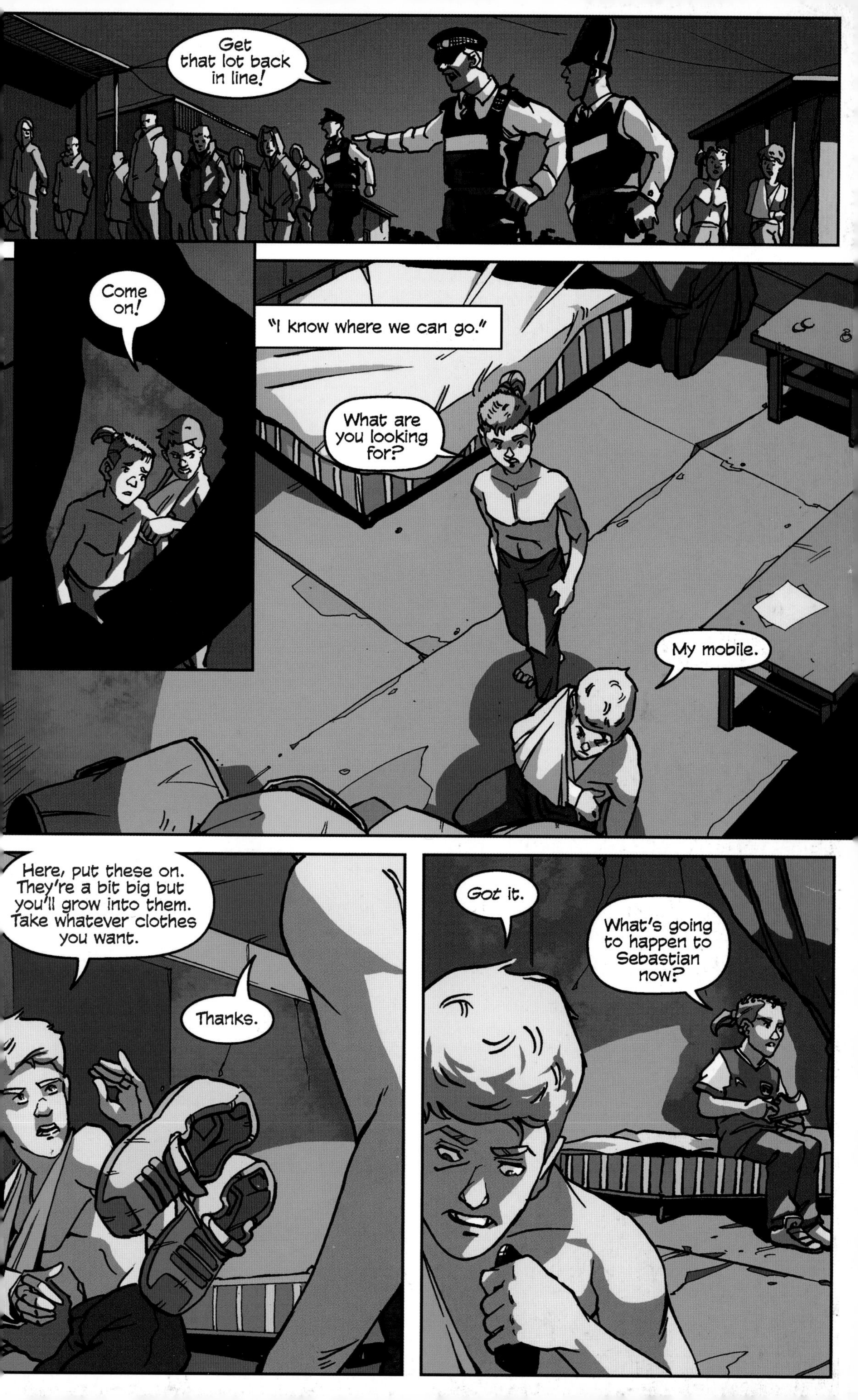
Get that lot back in line!
Come on!
"I know where we can go."
What are you looking for?
My mobile.
Here, put these on. They're a bit big but you'll grow into them. Take whatever clothes you want.
Thanks.
Got it.
What's going to happen to Sebastian now?

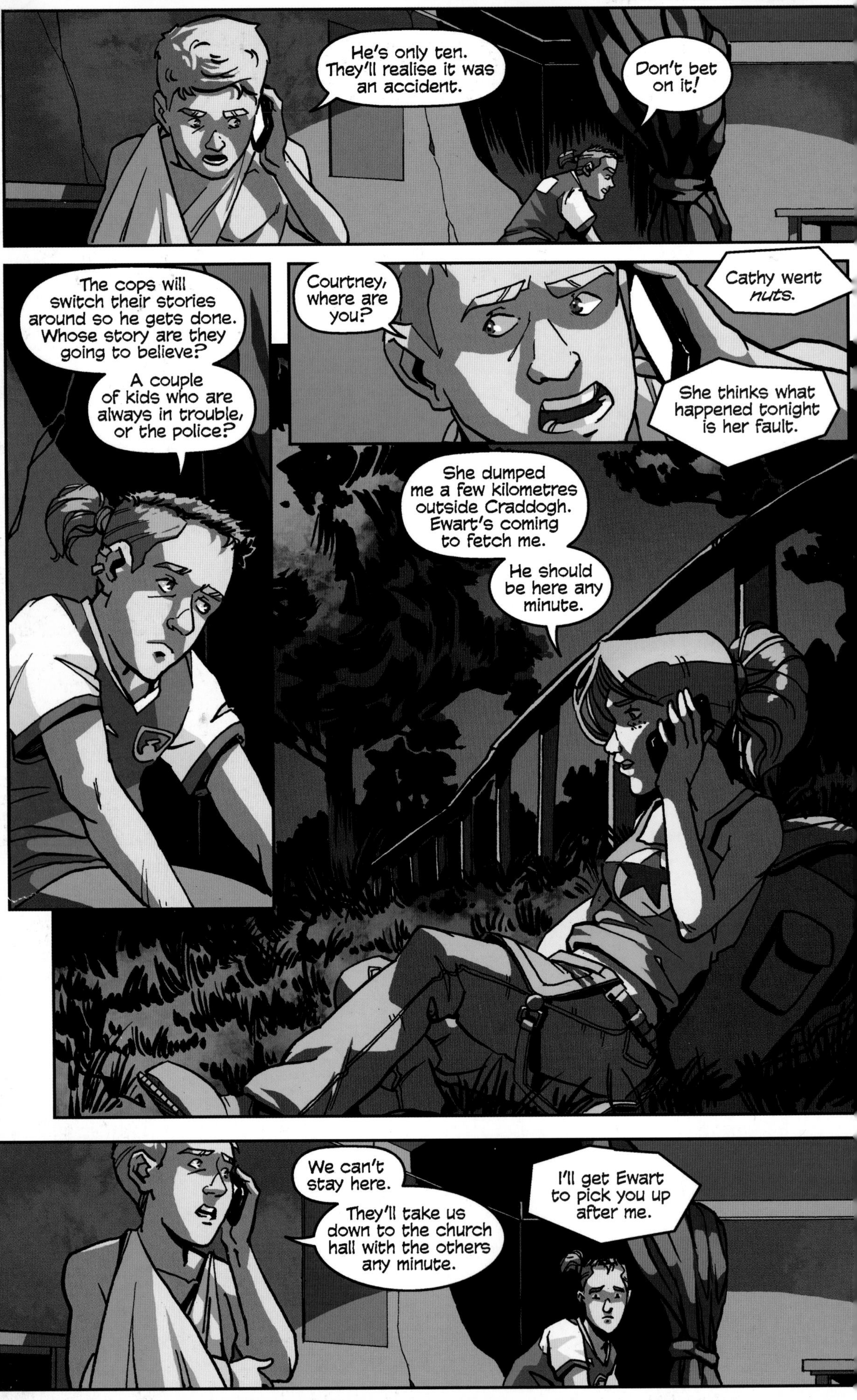
He's only ten. They'll realise it was an accident.
Don't bet on it!
The cops will switch their stories around so he gets done. Whose story are they going to believe?
A couple of kids who are always in trouble, or the police?
Courtney, where are you?
Cathy went *nuts*.
She thinks what happened tonight is her fault.
She dumped me a few kilometres outside Craddogh. Ewart's coming to fetch me.
He should be here any minute.
We can't stay here.
They'll take us down to the church hall with the others any minute.
I'll get Ewart to pick you up after me.

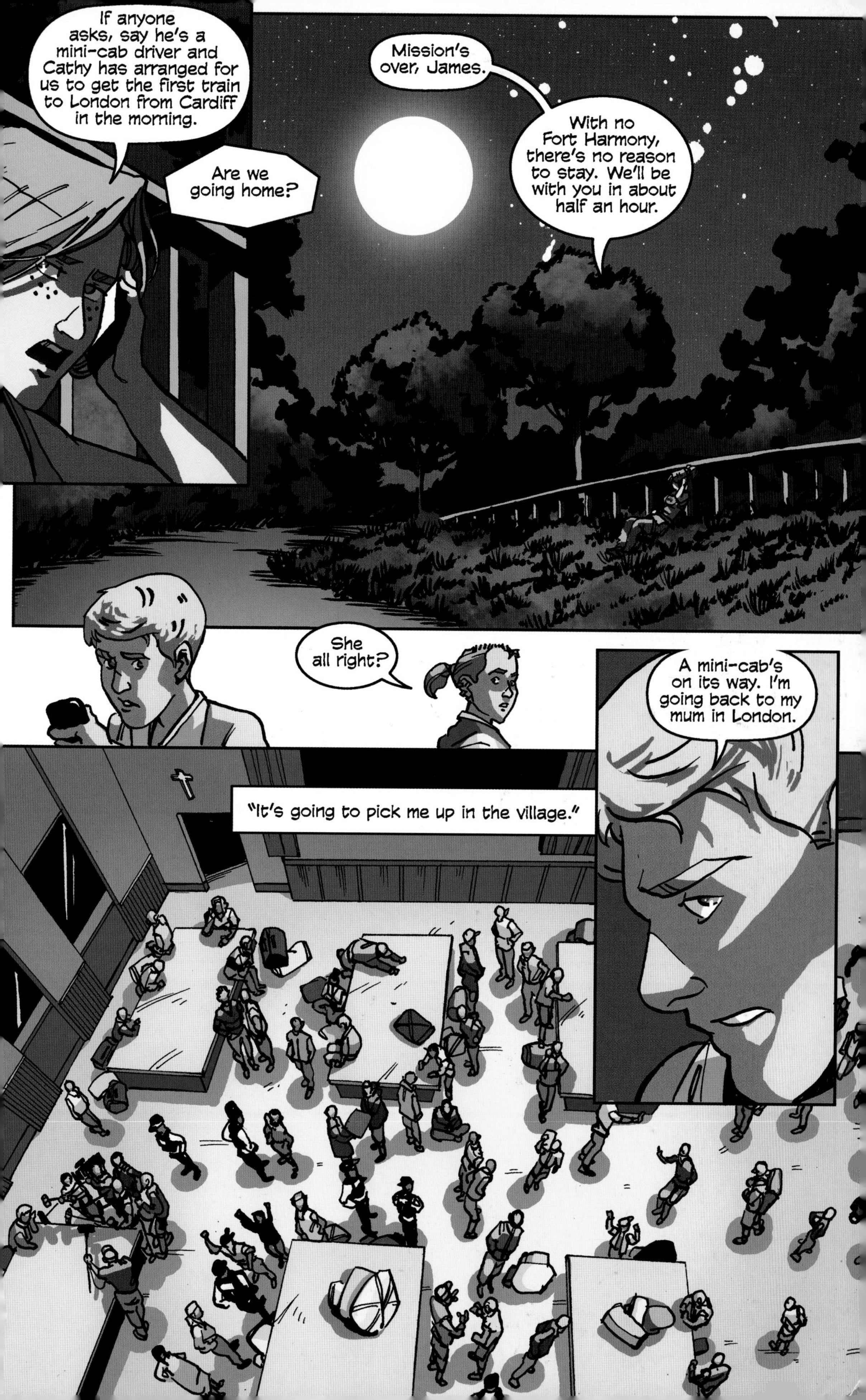

If anyone asks, say he's a mini-cab driver and Cathy has arranged for us to get the first train to London from Cardiff in the morning.
Are we going home?
Mission's over, James.
With no Fort Harmony, there's no reason to stay. We'll be with you in about half an hour.
She all right?
A mini-cab's on its way. I'm going back to my mum in London.
"It's going to pick me up in the village."

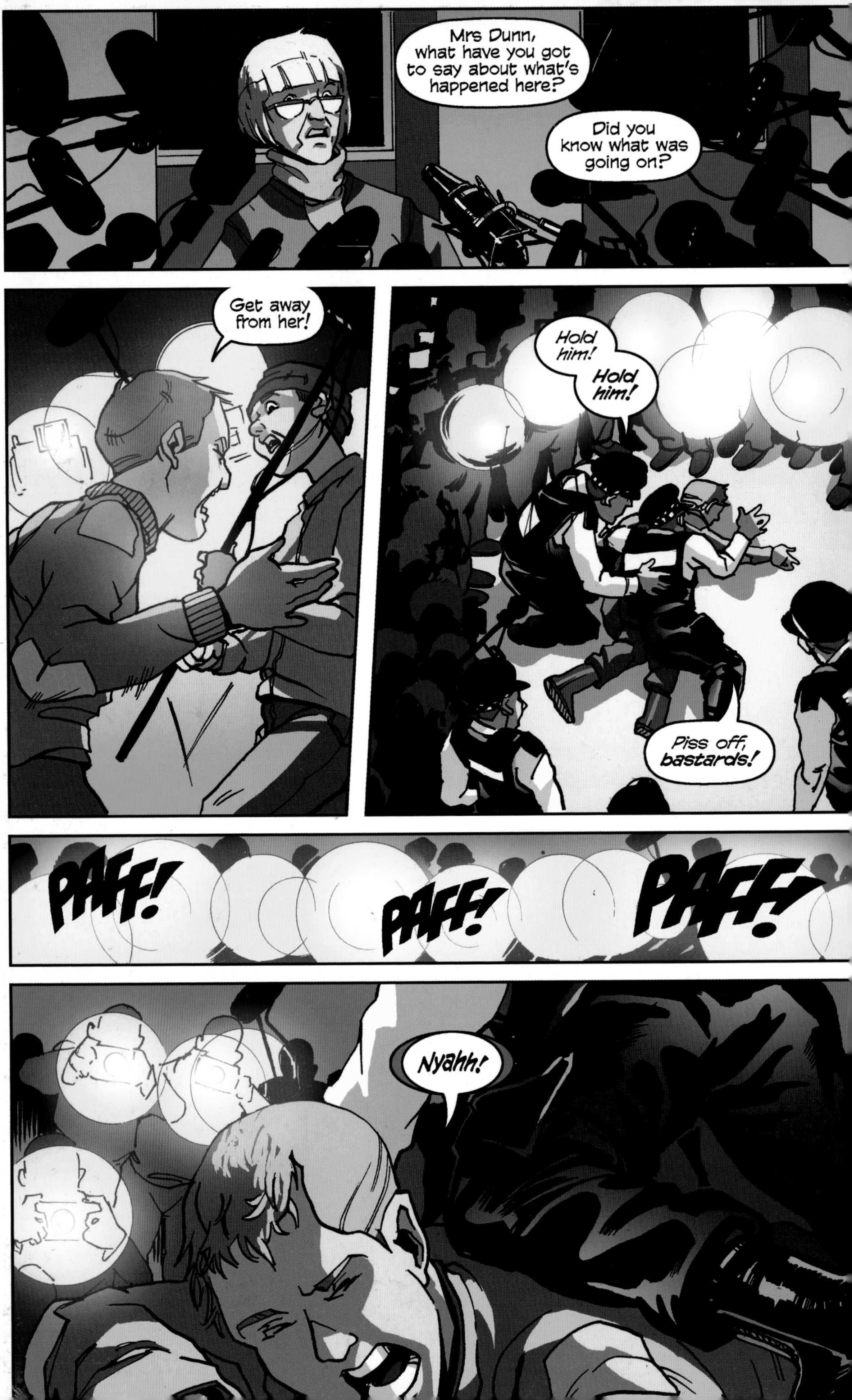
Mrs Dunn, what have you got to say about what's happened here?
Did you know what was going on?
Get away from her!
Hold him!
Hold him!
Piss off, bastards!
PAFF!
PAFF!
PAFF!
Nyahh!

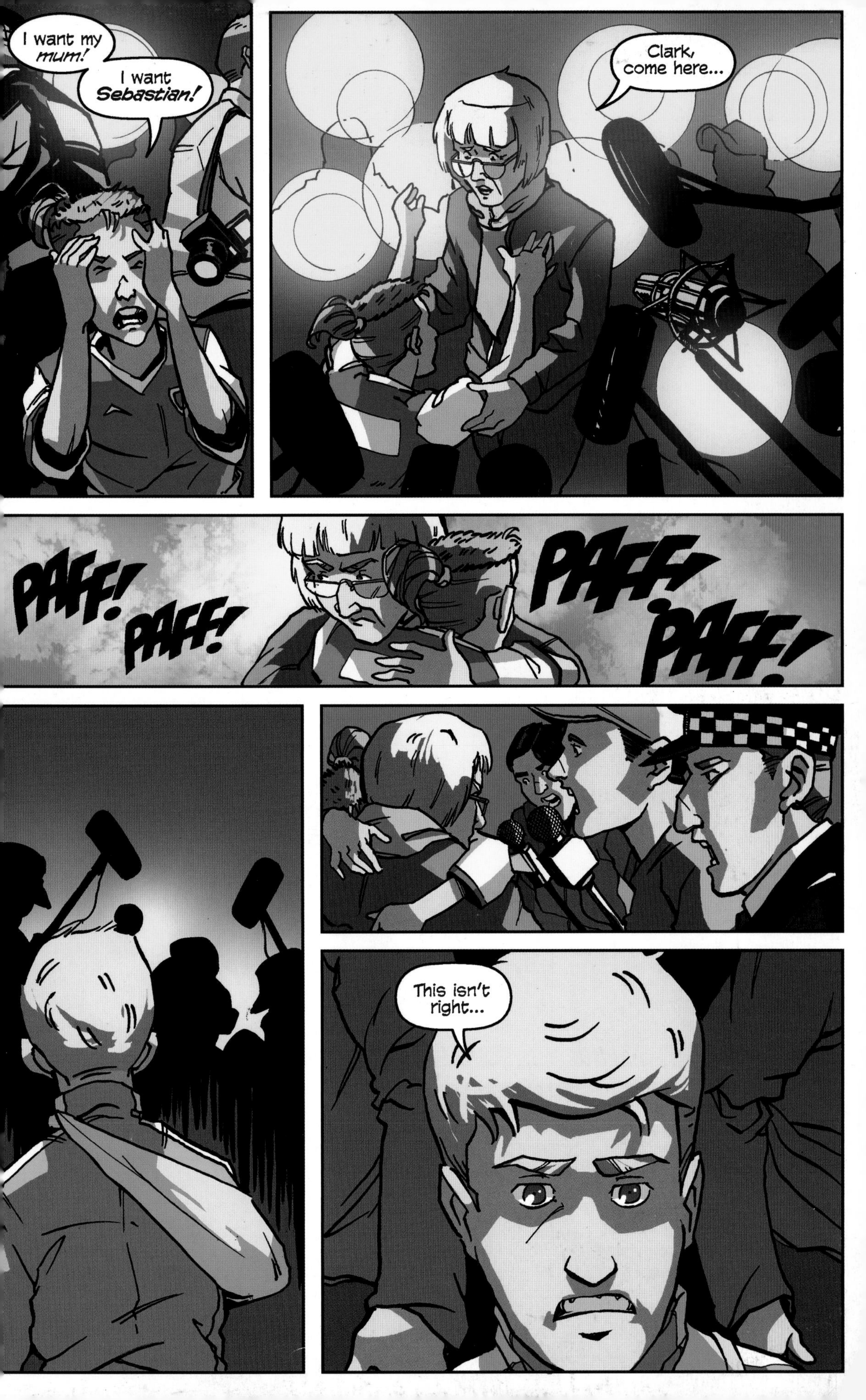
I want my *mum!*
I want *Sebastian!*
Clark, come here...
PAFF! PAFF!
PAFF! PAFF!
This isn't right...

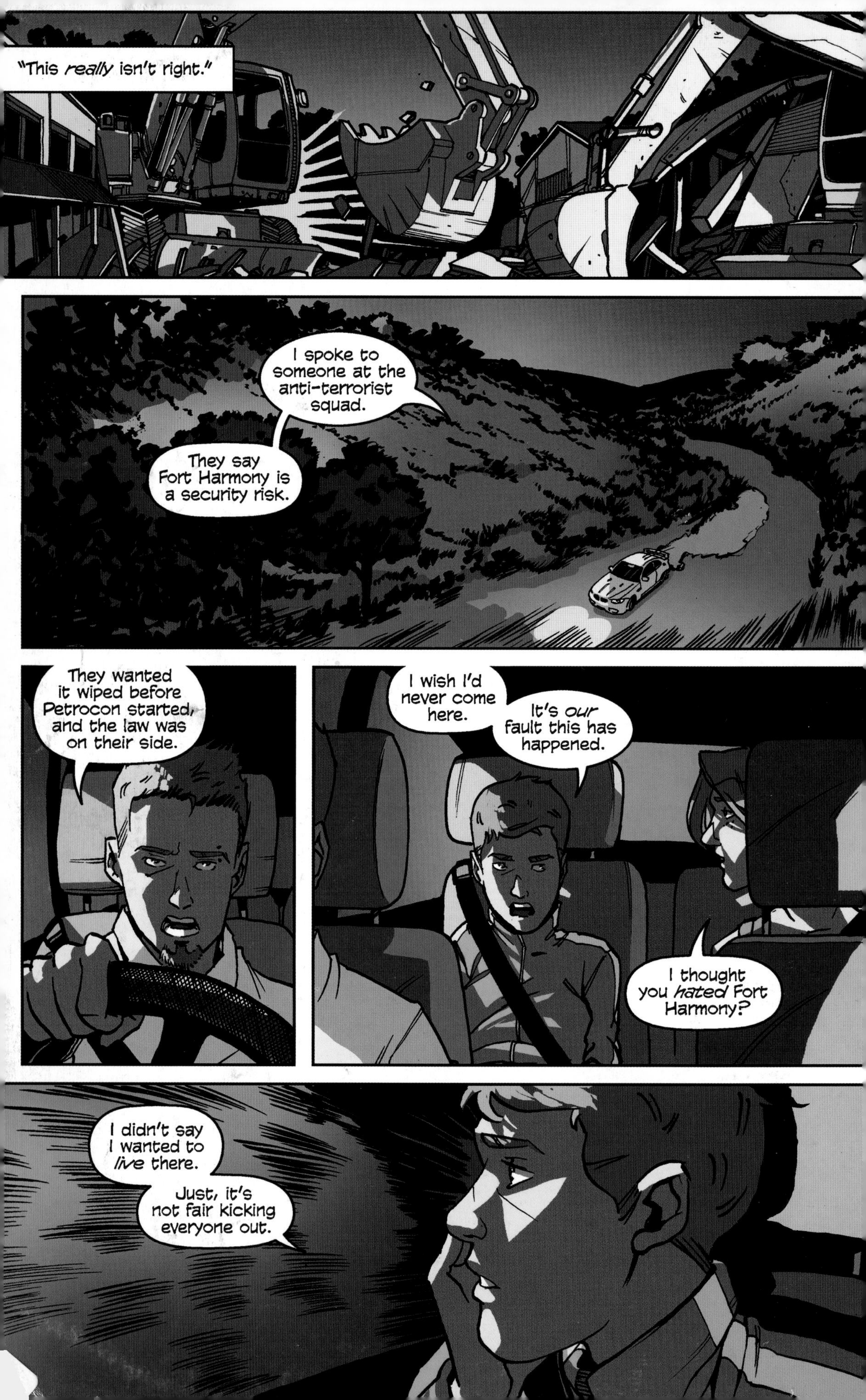
"This *really* isn't right."
I spoke to someone at the anti-terrorist squad.
They say Fort Harmony is a security risk.
They wanted it wiped before Petrocon started, and the law was on their side.
I wish I'd never come here.
It's *our* fault this has happened.
I thought you *hated* Fort Harmony?
I didn't say I wanted to *live* there.
Just, it's not fair kicking everyone out.

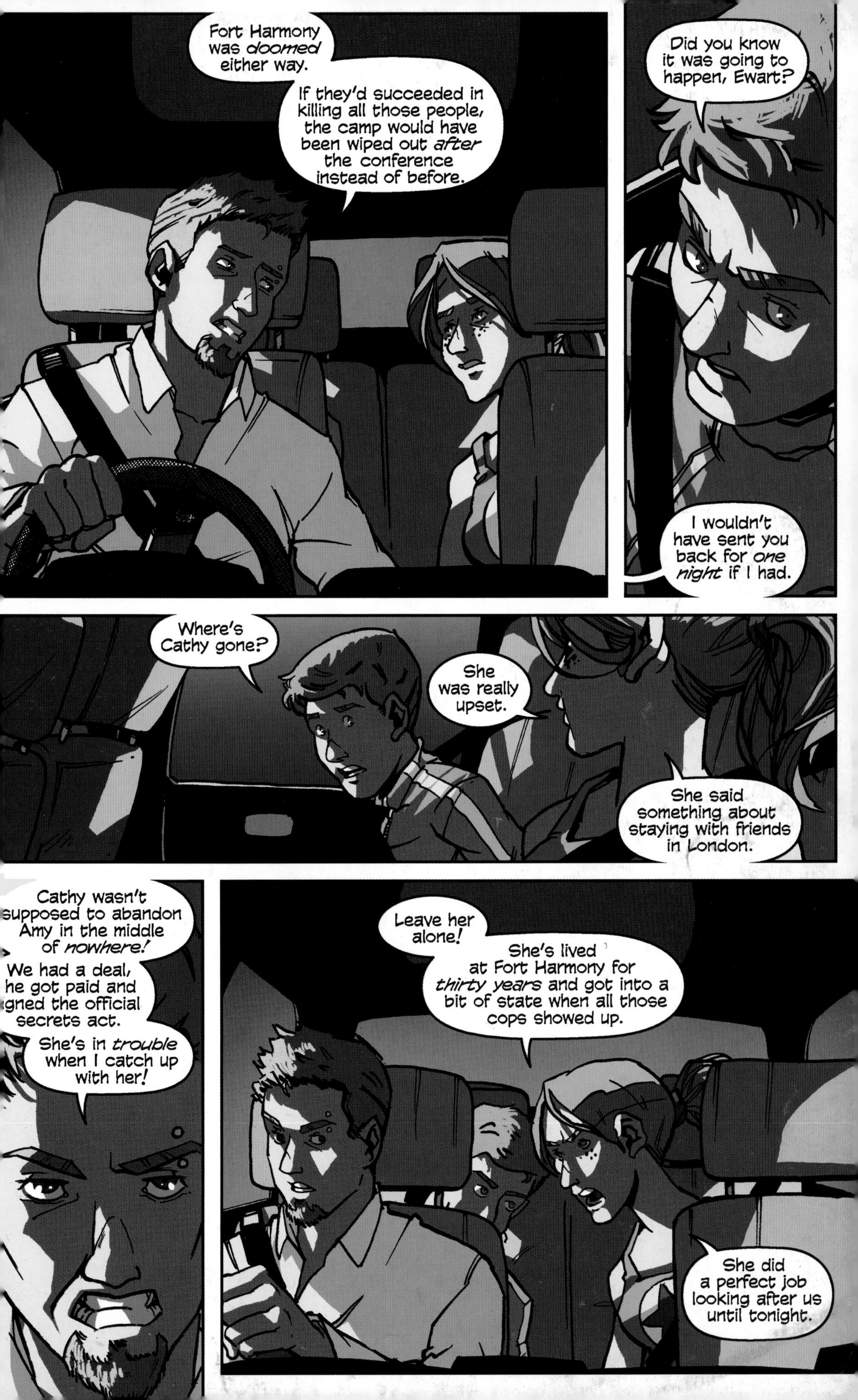
Fort Harmony was *doomed* either way.
If they'd succeeded in killing all those people, the camp would have been wiped out *after* the conference instead of before.
Did you know it was going to happen, Ewart?
I wouldn't have sent you back for *one night* if I had.
Where's Cathy gone?
She was really upset.
She said something about staying with friends in London.
Cathy wasn't supposed to abandon Amy in the middle of *nowhere!*
We had a deal, he got paid and gned the official secrets act.
She's in *trouble* when I catch up with her!
Leave her alone!
She's lived at Fort Harmony for *thirty years* and got into a bit of state when all those cops showed up.
She did a perfect job looking after us until tonight.

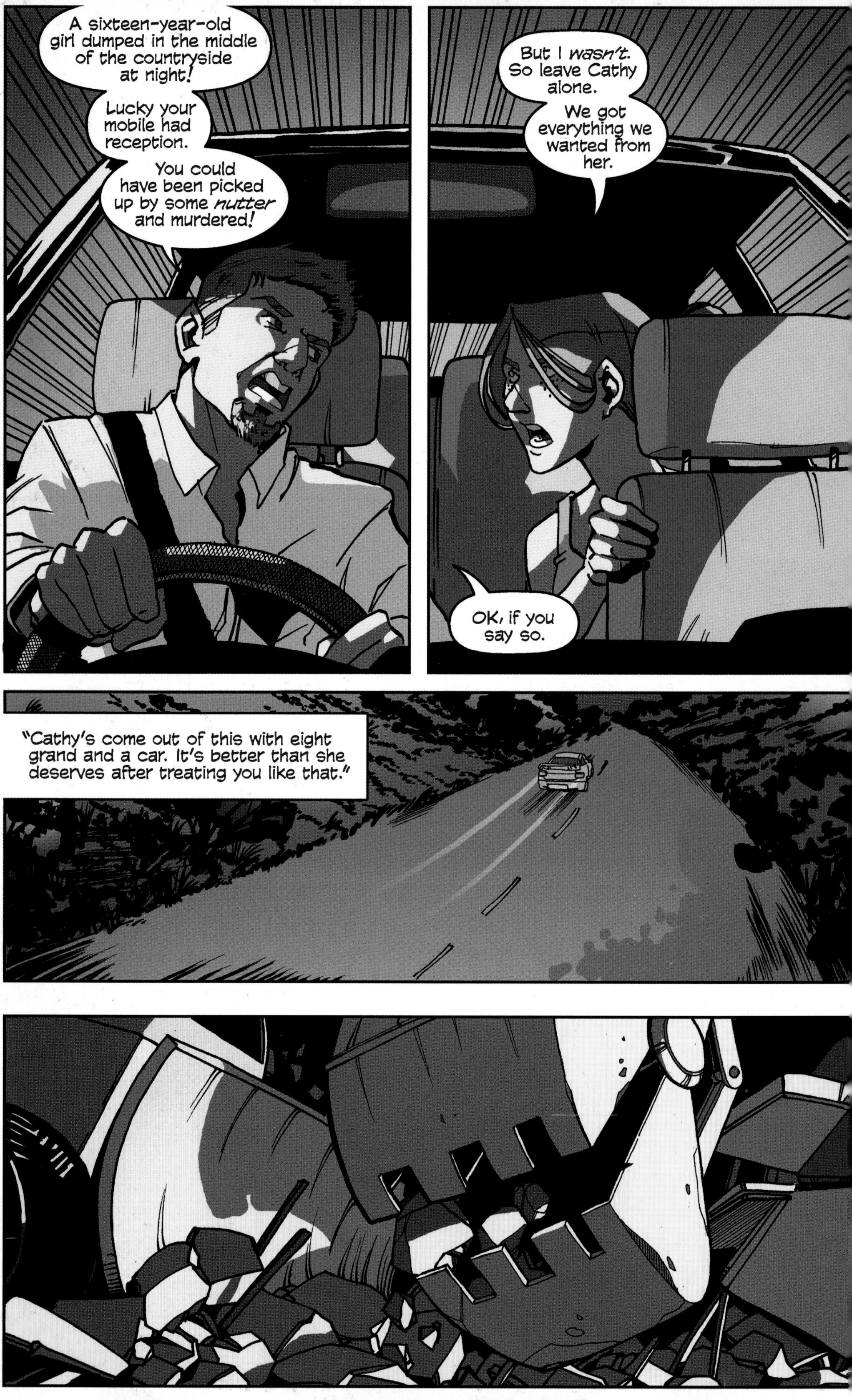
A sixteen-year-old girl dumped in the middle of the countryside at night!
Lucky your mobile had reception.
You could have been picked up by some *nutter* and murdered!
But I *wasn't*. So leave Cathy alone.
We got everything we wanted from her.
OK, if you say so.
"Cathy's come out of this with eight grand and a car. It's better than she deserves after treating you like that."

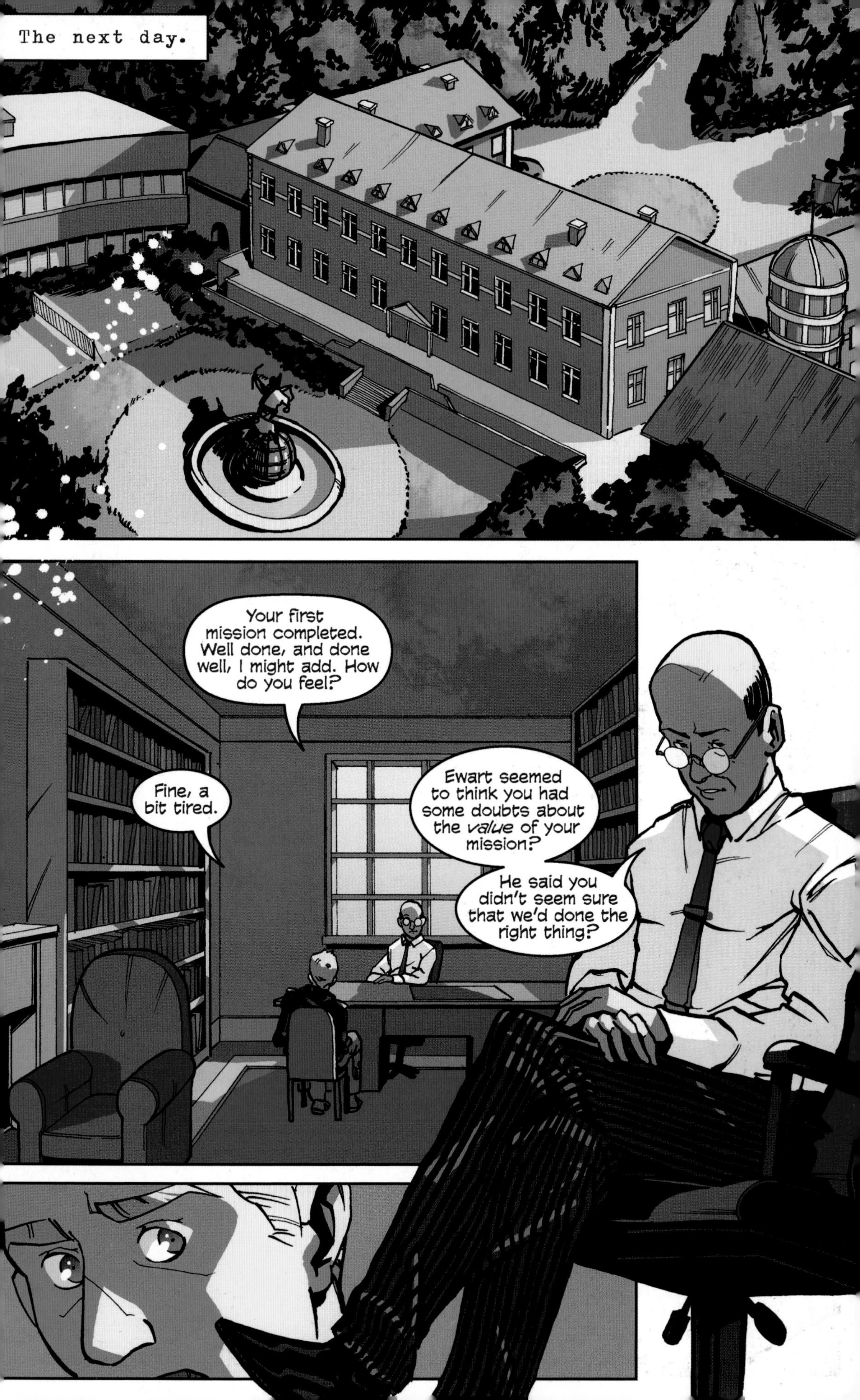

The next day.
Your first mission completed. Well done, and done well, I might add. How do you feel?
Fine, a bit tired.
Ewart seemed to think you had some doubts about the *value* of your mission?
He said you didn't seem sure that we'd done the right thing?

It's... confusing.

I heard some stuff about the people going to Petrocon.

They poison people and beat them up and stuff.

I'm not even sure it's true.

It's mostly true. Oil companies have a terrible environment and human rights record.

Without oil and gas, the world stops working. Because it's so important, companies and governments bend the rules to get it.

Help Earth and a lot of other people, including me, think they go too far.

So you *support* Help Earth?

I want to stop people being exploited and poisoned by oil companies. I don't agree *terrorism* is the way to do it.

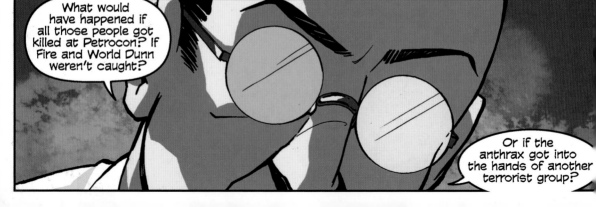

What would have happened if all those people got killed at Petrocon? If Fire and World Dunn weren't caught?

Or if the anthrax got into the hands of another terrorist group?

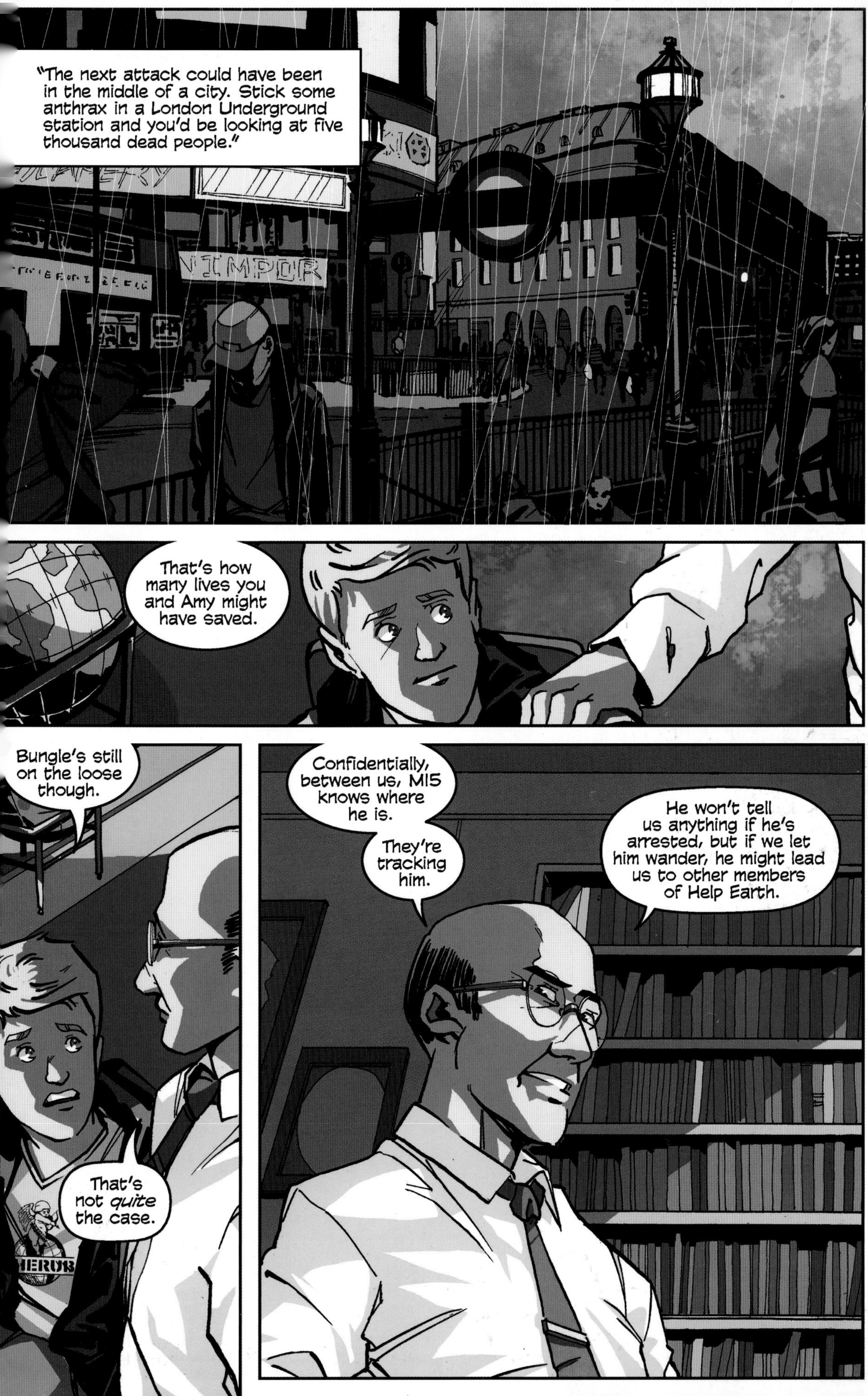
"The next attack could have been in the middle of a city. Stick some anthrax in a London Underground station and you'd be looking at five thousand dead people."
That's how many lives you and Amy might have saved.
Bungle's still on the loose though.
That's not *quite* the case.
Confidentially, between us, MI5 knows where he is.
They're tracking him.
He won't tell us anything if he's arrested, but if we let him wander, he might lead us to other members of Help Earth.

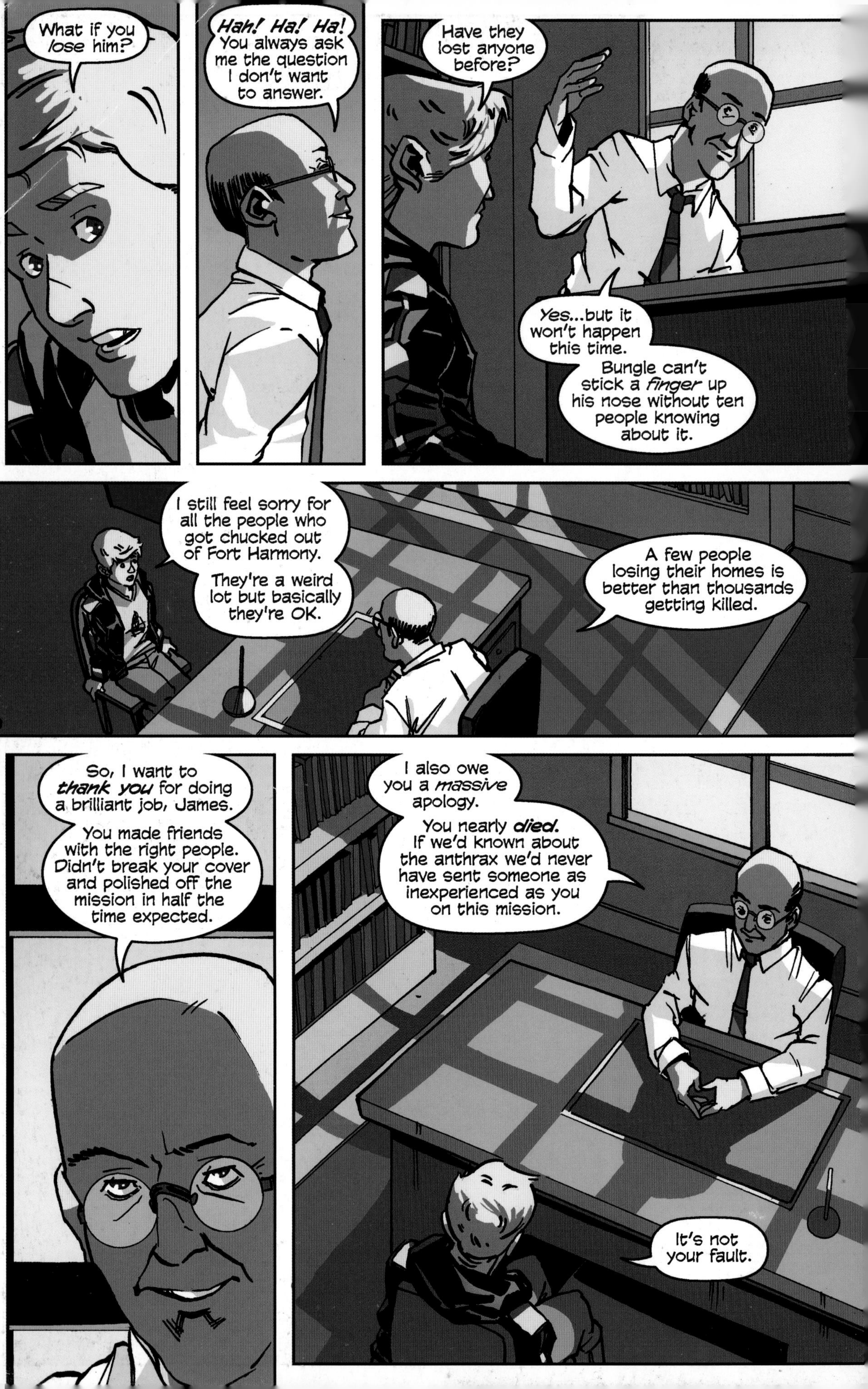
What if you *lose* him?
Hah! Ha! Ha! You always ask me the question I don't want to answer.
Have they lost anyone before?
Yes...but it won't happen this time.
Bungle can't stick a *finger* up his nose without ten people knowing about it.
I still feel sorry for all the people who got chucked out of Fort Harmony.
They're a weird lot but basically they're OK.
A few people losing their homes is better than thousands getting killed.
So, I want to *thank you* for doing a brilliant job, James.
You made friends with the right people. Didn't break your cover and polished off the mission in half the time expected.
I also owe you a *massive* apology.
You nearly *died*. If we'd known about the anthrax we'd never have sent someone as inexperienced as you on this mission.
It's not your fault.

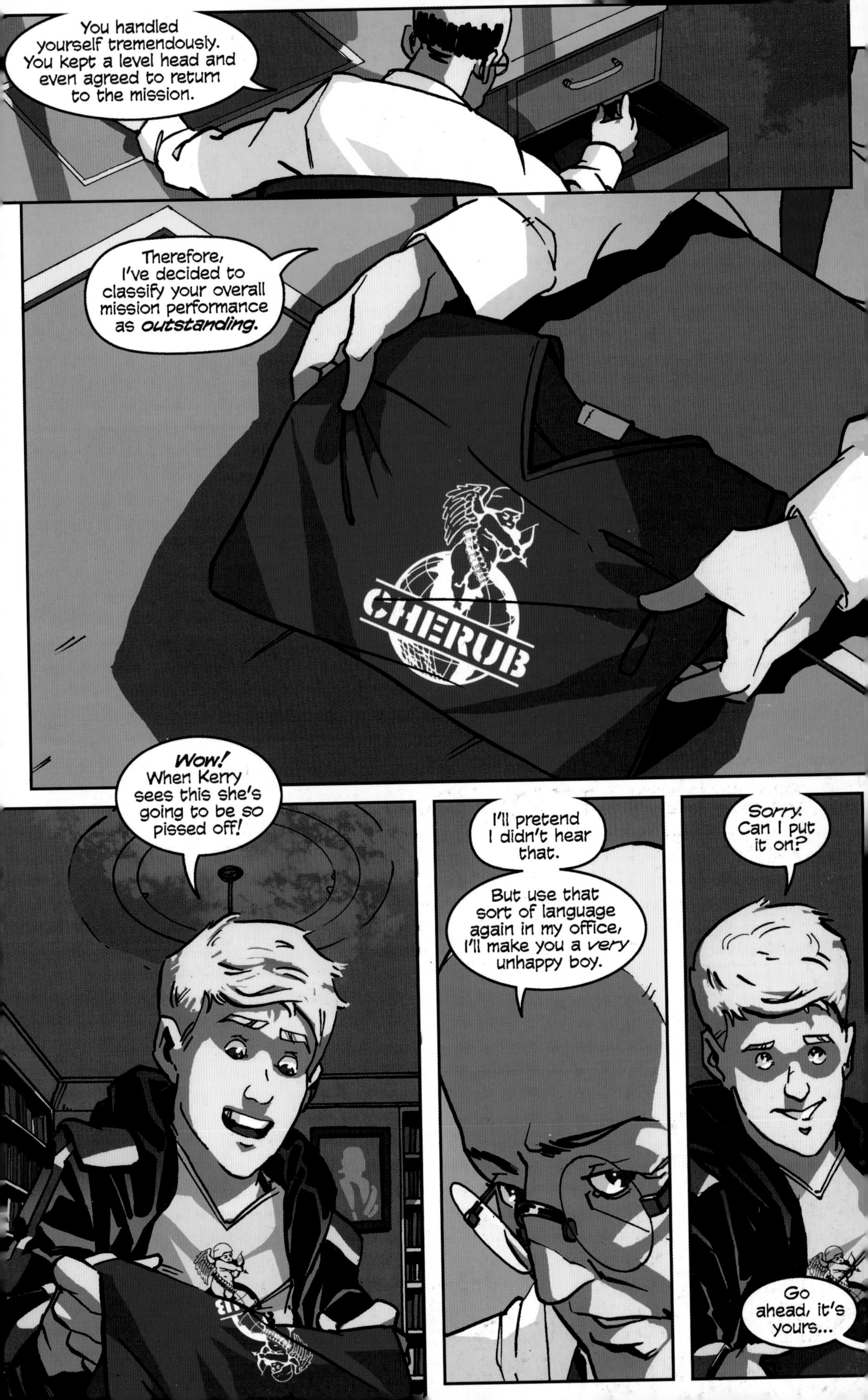
You handled yourself tremendously. You kept a level head and even agreed to return to the mission.
Therefore, I've decided to classify your overall mission performance as *outstanding*.
CHERUB
Wow! When Kerry sees this she's going to be so pissed off!
I'll pretend I didn't hear that.
But use that sort of language again in my office, I'll make you a *very* unhappy boy.
Sorry. Can I put it on?
Go ahead, it's yours...

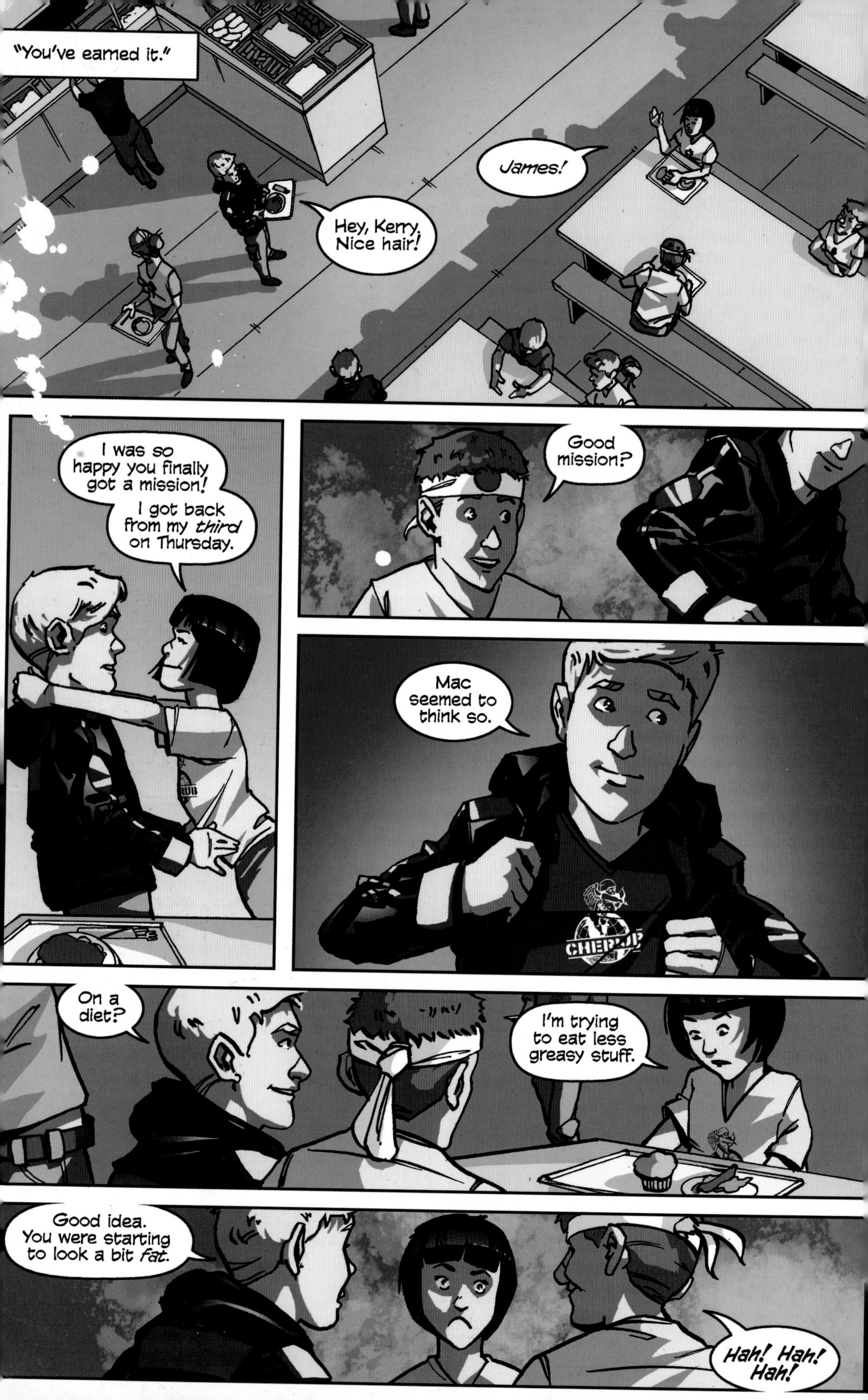
"You've earned it."
James!
Hey, Kerry, Nice hair!
I was so happy you finally got a mission!
I got back from my *third* on Thursday.
Good mission?
Mac seemed to think so.
On a diet?
I'm trying to eat less greasy stuff.
Good idea. You were starting to look a bit *fat*.
Hah! Hah! Hah!

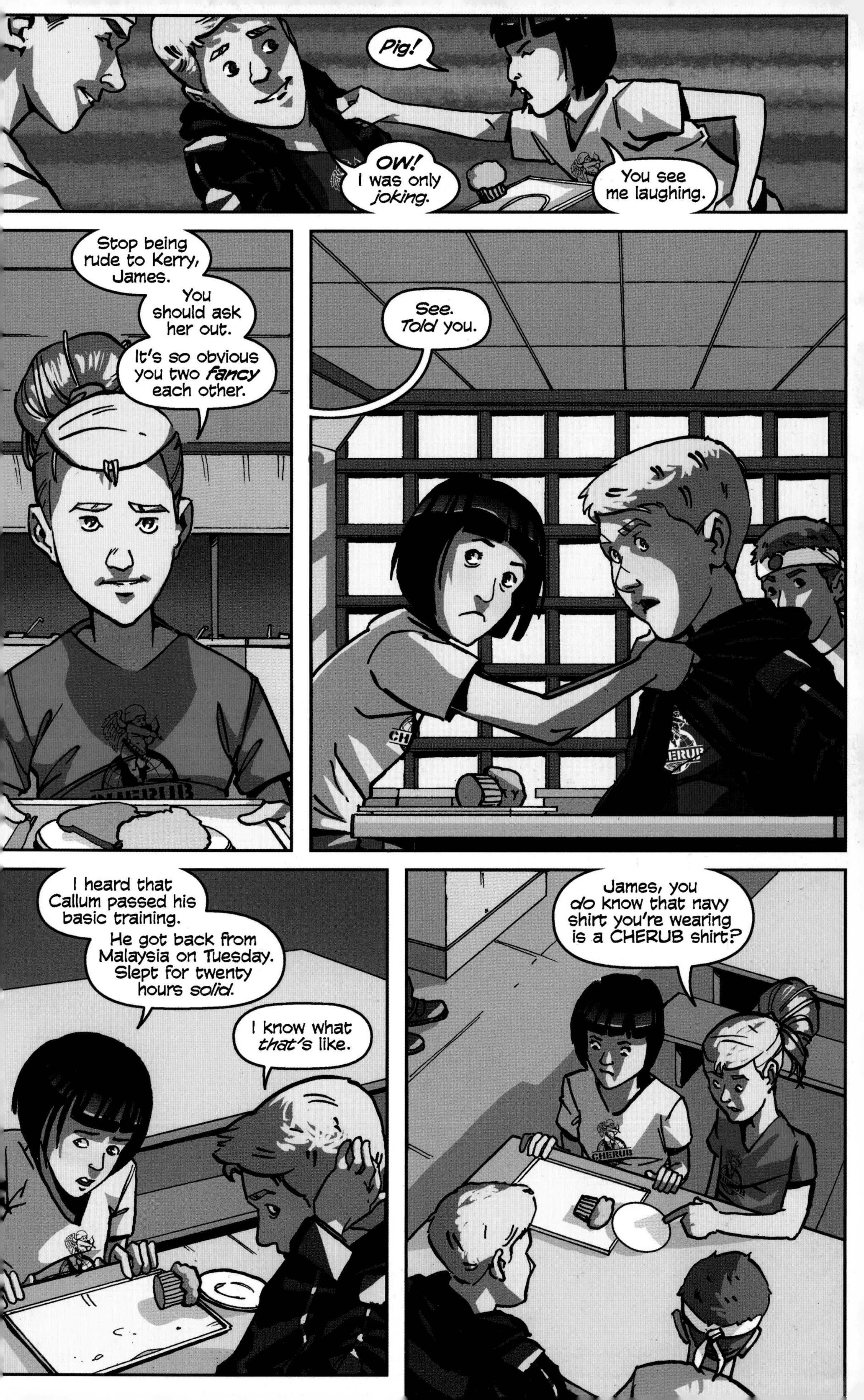
Pig!
OW! I was only *joking*.
You see me laughing.
Stop being rude to Kerry, James.
You should ask her out.
It's so obvious you two *fancy* each other.
See. *Told* you.
I heard that Callum passed his basic training.
He got back from Malaysia on Tuesday. Slept for twenty hours *solid*.
I know what *that's* like.
James, you *do* know that navy shirt you're wearing is a CHERUB shirt?

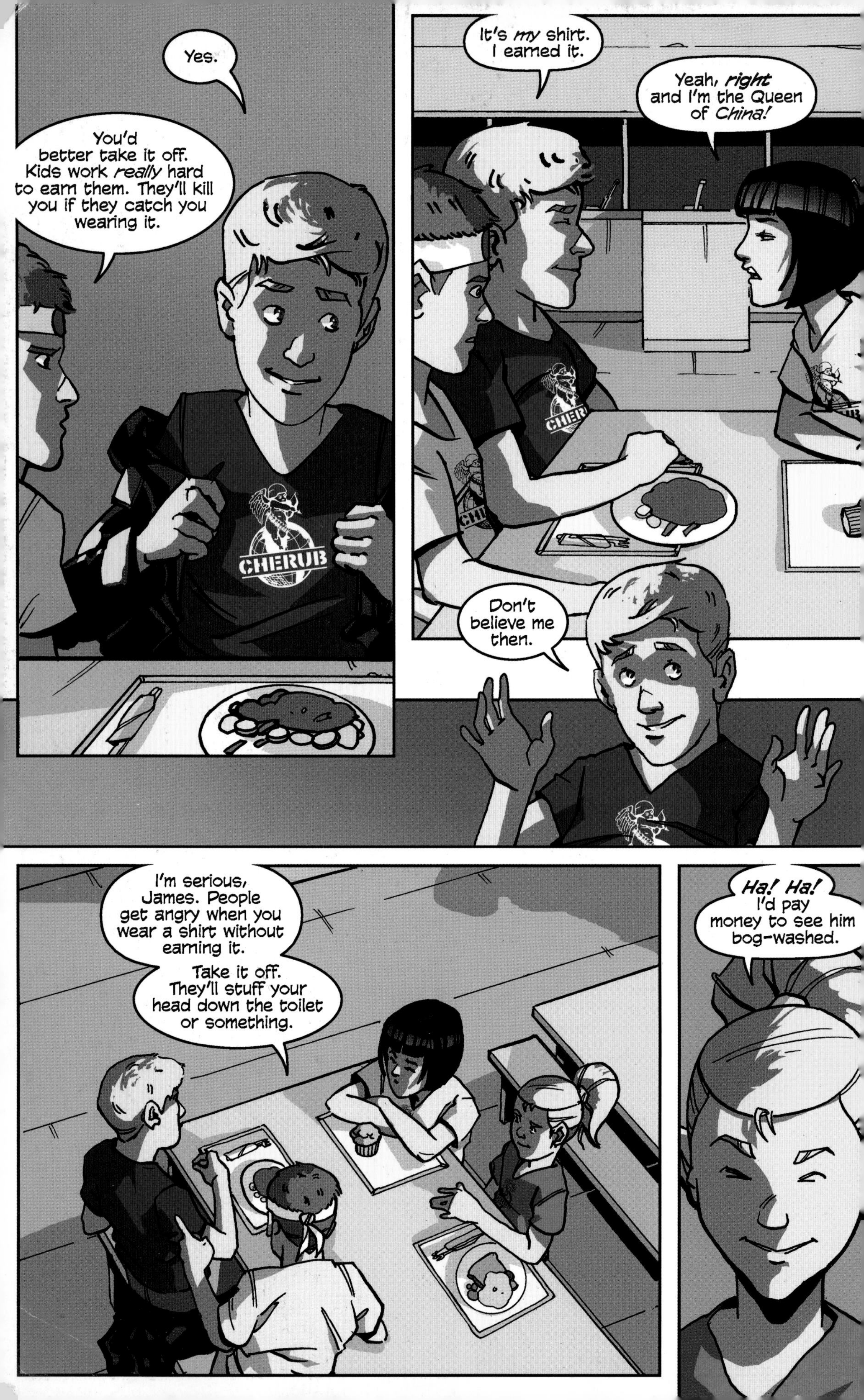
Yes.
You'd better take it off. Kids work *really* hard to earn them. They'll kill you if they catch you wearing it.
CHERUB
It's *my* shirt. I earned it.
Yeah, *right* and I'm the Queen of *China!*
Don't believe me then.
I'm serious, James. People get angry when you wear a shirt without earning it.
Take it off. They'll stuff your head down the toilet or something.
Ha! Ha! I'd pay money to see him bog-washed.

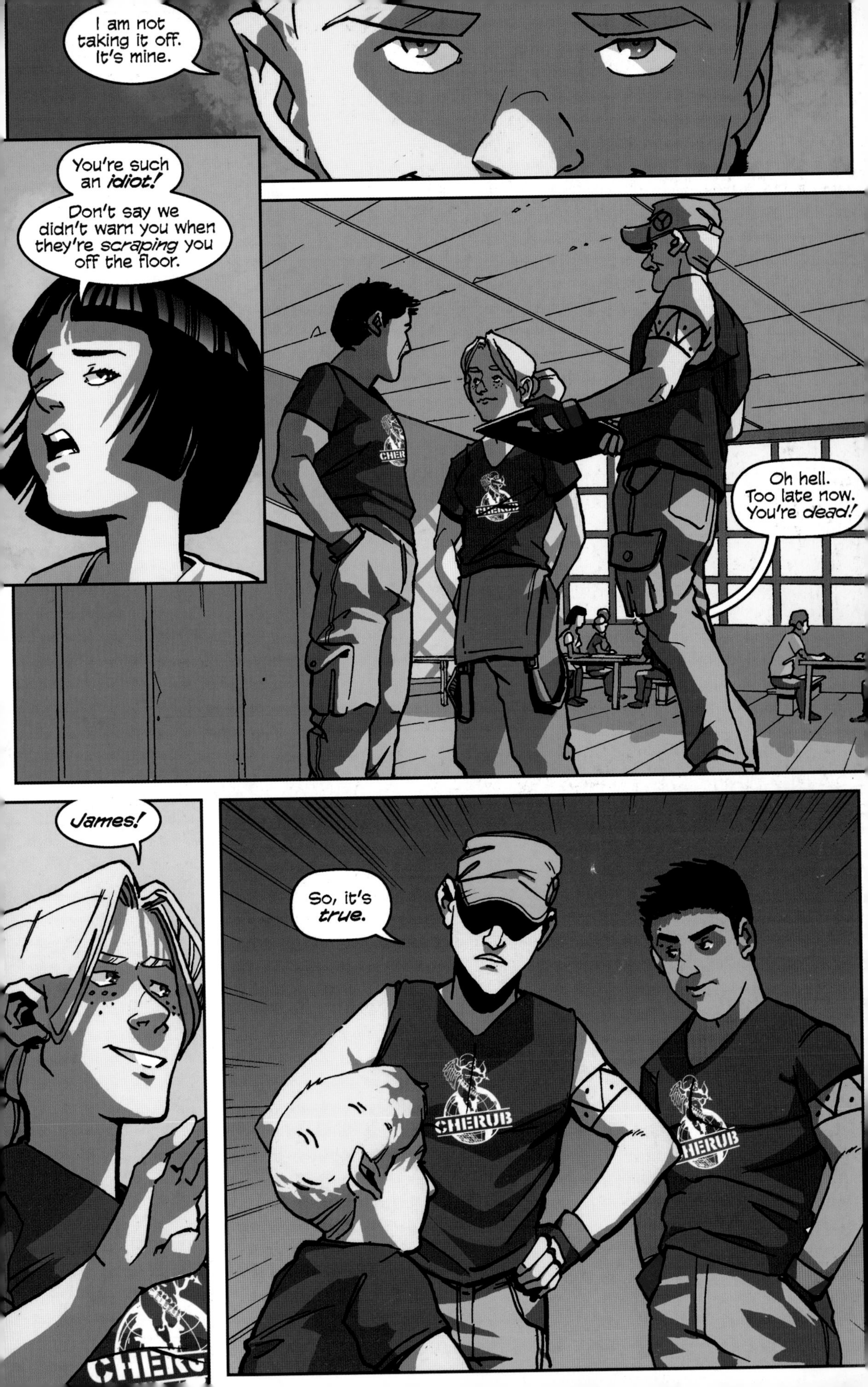
I am not taking it off. It's mine.
You're such an *idiot!*
Don't say we didn't warn you when they're *scraping* you off the floor.
Oh hell. Too late now. You're *dead!*
James!
So, it's *true.*
CHERUB

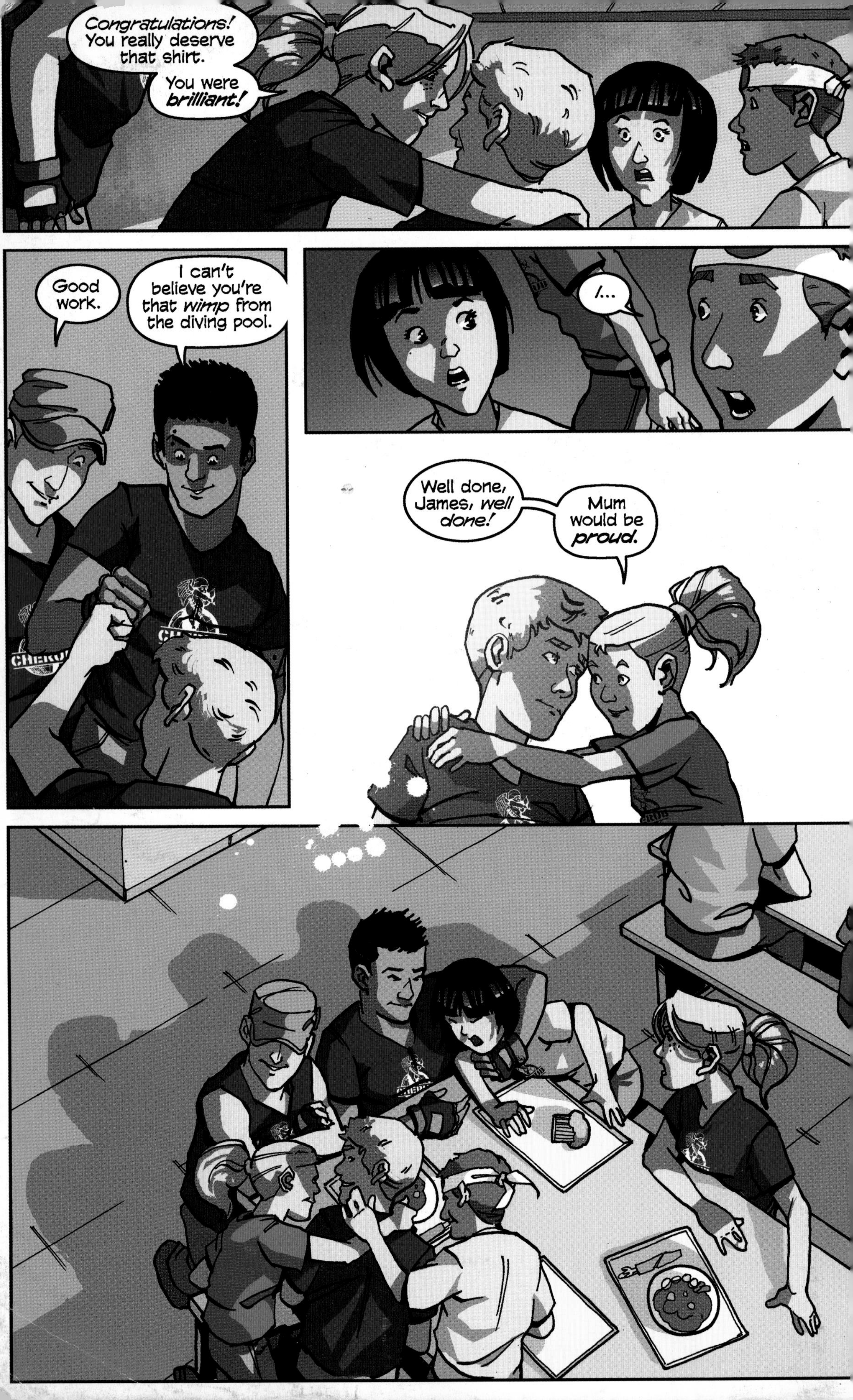
Congratulations! You really deserve that shirt.
You were brilliant!
Good work.
I can't believe you're that wimp from the diving pool.
I...
Well done, James, well done!
Mum would be proud.

Robert Muchamore

worked as a private investigator for many years, giving up when his books became successful. He is now published in over twenty languages, with millions of CHERUB and Henderson's Boys books sold. You can find out more at muchamore.com

Ian Edginton

lives in Birmingham. His work includes Star Wars, Batman, Doctor Who and Sherlock Holmes comics.

John Aggs

studied illustration at University College Falmouth and has since worked with many people including Tokyopop, the Guardian and Philip Pullman. He has worked on webcomics, album covers, film concepts, storyboards, animations and a functioning giant robot suit. He lives and works in a condemned tower block in east London.

For exclusive content including bonus stories, news, games, out-takes and downloads visit the essential destination for all things CHERUB at www.cherubcampus.com